PEACE LILY

BY

Alex Martin

THE SEQUEL TO DAFFODILS

Front cover notes:

Once again, I am indebted to Jane Dixon Smith (*www.jdsmith-design.com*) for helping me with the cover for Peace Lily. Following on from the theme of Daffodils I wanted to keep a plant in the forefront of the picture. I searched for one with the word 'peace' in its name, little realising how its morphology would suit the story. The ship is an ocean liner sailing to America.

Please note that British spelling is used throughout

ACKNOWLEDGEMENTS

In celebration of the Semi-Colons

Copyright Siegfried Sassoon by kind permission
of the Estate of George Sassoon
to use an excerpt of his poem
'Aftermath'

PEACE LILY

CHAPTER ONE

The hall clock chimed the hour at Cheadle Manor, just as it had for generations, as if nothing had happened.

Cassandra Smythe listened to its mellow chant, counting the minutes she had wasted waiting for her fiancé, Douglas Flintock, and watching the pale winter sun filter through the stained glass window. Pockets of crimson and violet light played across the expanse of marble floor.

The hall table bore a simple bowl of white snowdrops. The housekeeper must have placed them there because her mother, Lady Amelia, would surely have demanded something more showy.

Why was Douglas taking so long to get ready? Time was running out to join the hunt. Through the open door she could see several horses and riders trotting up the long manor drive, before turning off towards the stables. She was itching to get out there. She'd been away so long, driving ambulances in France, that it had been years since she'd ridden across her beloved Wiltshire downs.

The view through the front door was unchanged, but she was not. The great war had altered her perspective forever and, looking through its lens, Cassandra noticed that the shrubs edging the drive looked unkempt, even for winter. They had so few grounds-men to keep it in order now, and she was the only one left to make sure they did. How on earth would she bring the manor back into good heart without her brother, Charles?

At last! Douglas appeared at the top of the staircase, where it branched into two wings, before spilling into wide treads at its base. Douglas was hesitating. What was wrong with the man?

"Hi, Cass," Douglas said, his American accent jarring its modernity against the ancient bones of the manor. "You sure we got to wear this fancy dress, just to ride a horse?"

"Darling Douglas, you're in the depths of the country now and you've got to toe the line." Cassandra laughed up at him. "But if you don't get a move on, the rest of the pack will be gone without you."

"That's fine by me," Douglas said. "I feel a complete fraud in your father's scarlet coat and top hat."

He joined her on the bottom step and leaned in for a kiss. His lips were dry and cool; closed. She took his hand in hers. It too felt cold, but also a little clammy.

"Are you nervous, Douglas?" Cassandra asked, tugging him towards the front door, whose two heavy panels stood open to the frosty morning. "You have ridden before, haven't you?"

"Sure I have, honey, but we prefer to use our own two legs to get about in Boston. We live in the twentieth century there, you know, with modern paraphernalia like trams and cars. Give me a motor any day," Douglas said, letting go of her hand and following her through the front door.

Some of Douglas's nervousness connected with her stomach and Cassandra knew a rare moment of apprehension ahead of the ride. Their footsteps scrunched on the frosty gravel, as they crossed the few hundred yards to the stable block, from where a great babble of noise emanated.

"My, my, I never guessed there would be so many people," Douglas said, hesitating again in the stone archway of the stable courtyard.

"Our hunt is a popular one, Douglas. Welcome to the club," Cassandra said, and joined the crowd, nodding hello to people she hadn't seen since 1914. Too many faces were missing. There were more women than men, which was hardly surprising, but it meant that a great many female eyes locked onto Douglas, as he mounted his horse. At least he looked the part in the ancient hunting jacket from her father's younger, slimmer days.

Colonel Musgrove, an old family friend, shook

her hand and smiled warmly at her.

"Glad you survived the fray, my dear, and welcome home," said the old soldier.

"Thank you, sir," Cassandra replied, flattered to be singled out. "I'm glad you're back safe, too."

"Yes, I'm back alright but I left far too many younger men behind. Bad business, Cassandra, but then you'd know all about it. Heard about your ambulance driving from your father. Good show, I say."

Cassandra had always been fond of the Colonel and now her heart warmed to him even more, as he saluted her before turning to greet the other riders.

Cassandra felt a rush of affection for her horse too, when Jack Beagle, the groom, brought her favourite mare to her. It was good to see her old childhood friend and climb on to her back again. She smoothed Blackie's mane and murmured sweet nothings into her flattened ears. It helped to avoid the eyes of the other riders who stared at her, sitting astride her horse, her legs scandalously encased in jodhpurs. She looked at the other women, teetering on their side-saddles, and wondered why she'd put up with riding that way for so long. Ridiculous! Today, she could give Blackie her head and let her soar over any gates the hunt embraced. Already she could feel the mare responding to the squeeze of her thighs, as she guided her into the throng of horses twitching with the jitters, amongst the baying hounds.

Cassandra sneaked a glance at Douglas. He looked far from comfortable on her father's second-best hunter, Leo, whose long russet mane was bound up in neat bundles in honour of the occasion. Leo was a big animal, more than seventeen hands, and used to hunting, but today he was fidgety and pulling at his bit. No horse likes a nervous rider on its back, however broad it might be.

Douglas spoke to her but she couldn't hear his alien accent above the noise of the dogs and their whippers-in. She shook her head and smiled encouragement, watching anxiously as Douglas snatched up the stirrup cup that young Jack handed him, and drank it straight down.

"That's the idea, Douglas, get it down you in one go," said her father, and master of the hunt, Sir Robert. "That'll set the blood roaring in your veins, and if that doesn't do the trick, a good gallop will sort you out."

Typical of her father to encourage someone to drink too much before a ride. He was probably drunk himself. It was a rare day he wasn't since his only son had died on The Somme and his mottled complexion gave livid testimony to his habits. By stark contrast, Douglas looked paler than ever, despite his shot of alcohol, and gave his future father-in-law a wan smile. Cassandra sipped her own draught from the silver cup, closing her eyes as she did so. She opened them smartly when shouts of alarm sounded above the cacophony of the hounds.

Leo had reared up, narrowly missing Jack's black curls and unseating Douglas onto the hard cobbles of the courtyard. Cassandra lunged out and grabbed Leo's bridle, calming the horse with her voice, while pulling him away from Douglas's sprawled body. Sir Robert dismounted swiftly and bent over her fiancé, who scrambled to his feet. Douglas's face flushed as he waved away all attempts to help him.

"I'm alright, really, sir," he said to Sir Robert, and then staggered.

Cassandra looked around at the other riders, some of whom were openly laughing, while others sniggered behind their leather gloves, whispering and nodding to each other. She ground her teeth and bit back the angry words that sprang to her lips. Instead, she dismounted and led both the horses over to Douglas, who was fiddling with his whip and straightening his hat in a confused attempt to regain his dignity. His handsome face was still as red as his hunting jacket.

"Do we have to do this, Cass?" he said in an urgent whisper, as she came up to him.

"I'm sure people will understand if you want to

8

drop out," Cassandra said softly, trying not to let the disappointment show in her voice.

Douglas looked at her with his shrewd blue eyes. He could read her like a book.

"And I'm sure they won't ever let me forget it. Do you think Leo will forgive me if I clamber back on him?"

Cassandra smiled. "Yes, I'm sure he will. It's not just his mane that's like a lion's. Come on, I'll help you."

She walked their two horses over to the mounting block, ignoring the smirks of the other riders. Douglas followed, the smile on his face a perfect lie of confidence.

"If at first you don't succeed, and all that," he said to the crowd and doffed his riding hat to them.

"That's the spirit! Fly the flag for America, Douglas!" they shouted back.

Sir Robert chivvied the main group away from them, and Cassandra nodded her thanks to her father, before turning back to Douglas. "Come on, darling, let's get you mounted up again. Leo's a good old boy really, probably just got spooked by the dogs."

"You told me he was an experienced hunter," Douglas said, as he wearily mounted the stone steps. "Docile, you said."

"He is normally, I promise. Just wants to get going." Cassandra held the horse's head steady.

"He's on his own with that ambition, I can tell you," Douglas said. "This was not a good idea. Give me a sensible vehicle with a motor and nice, round wheels, any day."

"You'll be fine, Doug. I'll stay near you the whole way. You've already impressed everyone by getting back in the saddle."

"And I haven't managed that yet," Douglas said, teetering on the brink of the platform and looking wary.

"Well, you'd better get a move on, or they'll be off without us. Sounds like the hounds have got a scent," Cassandra said.

"Is that why they sound like a pack of deranged

hyenas?" Douglas said, putting one boot in the stirrup nearest him and lunging his tall frame across Leo's back. Leo snorted and pawed the ground.

"Haven't heard a hyena's howl, so couldn't say," Cassandra said. "Right, you're back on board. Straighten up and let's be off!"

"Never, ever, say I don't love you, Miss Smythe," Douglas said. "Rarely have I wanted to do anything less in all my life. I have a bad feeling about this."

Cassandra didn't bother to reply but clicked Blackie into a brisk trot. They rode down the drive of Cheadle Manor just in time to join the tail end of the pack of horses galloping towards the west gate. Cassandra used her leg muscles astride Blackie to nudge her into an easy canter and glanced around at Douglas, who was bobbing ungracefully along to Leo's long-legged trot.

"Push him into a canter, Doug." Cassandra shouted back at him. "It'll be more comfortable."

Douglas lolloped faster.

"That's it! Just sit back in the saddle, loosen your grip on the reins and rest your hands on his withers - the bottom of his neck. Now you're getting there."

She turned to face front again and let herself relax into Blackie's familiar stride. Maybe today she could forget all those wounded, bloodied soldiers who so often moaned through her dreams. She breathed in the cold air, relishing the tang of the winter frost that spangled in the shrubs lining the drive. Douglas drew alongside, propelled by Leo's big strides. Clouds of steam issued from the flared nostrils of both horses. Leo pulled at his bit again, gaining a length on them and easily outstripping Blackie's gallant, but smaller, legs.

"Show him who's boss, Doug. Rein him in a bit. Use your legs too," Cassandra said.

Douglas threw her a look of utter misery. Cassandra's serenity evaporated into the morning mist. The rest of the pack veered off into the woods just before the lodge house. Branches snapped at their faces as they careered through the trees. Cassandra didn't have time to glance back at Douglas. She could hear Leo's hooves thundering behind her and could only trust that he still bore his rider.

A great halloo rose up from a clearing in the copse a few yards ahead of her. The hounds were baying for blood in a frenzied huddle. The horse-riders gathered around them, cheering them on. Her father held a young boy's pony by the bridle next to the pack of hounds. As Douglas and Leo shuddered to a halt next to her, Sir Robert got off his big bay and handed the reins to Colonel Musgrove. She watched him stride into the heaving mass of dogs, brandishing a lethal-looking knife.

"Oh, my God, what is he doing?" Douglas said, his mouth open in horror, as Sir Robert lifted up the bushy tail of the fox. Blood dripped from its end, so recently attached to the rest of its body.

"Brushing the newest recruit's face with the fox blood," Cassandra said, questioning the ritual for the first time.

Douglas looked aghast, as Sir Robert stroked the boy's flushed face with the fox's tail, leaving a vivid streak of fresh blood on each cheek.

"I think I'm going to be sick," Douglas said. He looked at Cassandra with eyes so wide, she could see the whites surrounding each pupil. "No wonder you Brits won the war. It's barbaric."

"I know it looks that way, Douglas, but it's traditional, you see," Cassandra said, hating her own feeble defense.

"Did they do this to you at such a tender age?" Douglas said, his mouth turned down in disgust.

"Of course," Cassandra replied.

Douglas wheeled Leo's head around, away from the group.

"I'm heading back," he said. "I've seen enough blood for one day. In fact, I saw enough blood for a lifetime in France. I don't need any more."

"I'll come with you," Cassandra said, turning Blackie's head to follow.

"Don't bother. I need some solitude," Douglas said, and encouraged his horse into a brisk trot.

Cassandra watched him go with a jumble of feelings. She felt proud of the new assurance with which he rode Leo, as the big horse submitted to Douglas guiding him away from the other mounts. She could tell that Leo trusted him now, as they broke into a harmonious, fluid canter. Douglas learned fast. He'd also been quick to damn them all when he'd seen the visceral ritual of brushing new blood. It was just a part of normal life for her. An initiation ceremony everyone endured, if they wanted to be part of the hunting scene. She wouldn't tell him that it was bad form to wash the red stain off until it faded, days later, and she'd make sure her father never suggested that Douglas might be honoured with the ritual. She shivered at the thought.

The hunt moved off, leaving the torn carcass in a bloody heap. The hounds had stripped it bare of flesh and only the head was left intact. The vixen's eyes still held their terror. Cassandra looked away and dug her heels into Blackie's innocent sides. Her horse leapt forward, as if she too wanted to leave the murderous spot as fast as possible.

The hunt headed up towards the downs spread out behind the manor house in chalky uplands. Here, up amongst the skylarks, Cassandra could release her cares into the wind that whipped across her cheeks. She easily outstripped the other female riders and laughed at her firmer grip in the saddle, jumping every gate they came across with carefree abandon. Never again would she ride in a skirt.

The hounds got another scent and they gave chase across the barren winter fields, scattering sheep in their wake. Even the rain that scuttled across the hill didn't dampen her spirits. Cassandra loosened Blackie's reins and streamed across the high ridge at full pelt. Nothing beat this thrill.

Eventually, Sir Robert called it a day. They never found the second fox and Cassandra was glad. She didn't need to kill anything to feel this liberated. The other horses sauntered back home and she passed them with a brief wave. Blackie still had enough energy to gallop along and Cassandra was in no mood for snide quips about American boyfriends and their lack of equestrian prowess.

Jack greeted her with his usual grin, looking none the worse for the close shave with Leo's hooves, and took Blackie away for a rub down.

Cassandra walked quickly into the house before the other riders appeared on the drive. Raised voices greeted her, coming from the drawing room. Cassandra dropped her gloves and hat on the hall table, noting that the snowdrops had now been replaced by an enormous but flowerless plant in a ridiculously ornate urn. She grimaced and followed the direction of the noise.

Douglas and her mother, Lady Amelia, were sitting on opposite chairs by the huge fireplace, engaged in a heated debate. Douglas had changed out of his hunting gear and back into his normal lounge suit, cut in the American style that suited him best. Her mother looked her usual self, corseted and coiffured in the fashion of the old queen, before a generation of young men had been slaughtered in defence of her son's realm.

So engrossed were they, neither of them noticed Cassandra, hovering in the doorway. She listened to their exchange with increasing dismay.

"So it doesn't strike you as a little anachronistic then, Lady Amelia? Daubing fresh fox blood on to a young boy's face strikes me as positively Neanderthal," Douglas's voice was tight with anger.

"I wouldn't expect you, as an American with no heritage, to understand how people of true aristocratic backgrounds seek to preserve the honourable traditions of their ancestors. After all, do you even know who yours are?" Lady Amelia said, her colour high.

"If my ancestors were crass murderers of innocent wild animals, as yours appear to be, maybe I could understand your precious traditions, but I'll have you know that we Bostonians are a civilised people, who pride ourselves on our culture and education," Douglas said, and uncrossed his legs, planting both his brogue-shod feet firmly on the Persian hearth rug.

"I've never heard of an American yet who was either cultured or educated. All your type know is how to make money. You know nothing of real breeding," Lady Amelia said, sounding shrill.

"And how far do you think you'd get without filthy lucre then, Lady Amelia?" Douglas said, gripping his knees. "I only have to look about the estate here to see you're in dire need of some ready cash."

"How *dare* you criticise Cheadle Manor! I don't suppose you've ever seen so large an estate before and you know nothing about the running of it," Lady Amelia said, tugging at the pearls on her necklace with agitated fingers.

"I know enough to realise when it's not being looked after properly," Douglas said.

"And I suppose you can't wait to get your hands on it, can you?" Lady Amelia said. "Is that why you are marrying my daughter, Mr Flintock?" Her voice caught on a sob and she carried on breathlessly, "With Charles killed defending his country, it leaves the way clear for you, doesn't it? I'm sure it would look very impressive back in Boston to be marrying into English nobility and inheriting the land we have cherished for generations!"

Douglas stood up and towered over her mother. His back was ramrod straight and afforded Cassandra's only view of him. But she could witness this warfare in passive silence no longer.

She stepped into the drawing room and hoped her voice would not betray the speed and irregularity of her heartbeats, as she said, "What on earth has prompted this bitter feud?"

Her attempt at laughter dried up, as she looked at

each hot face, staring with unreserved animosity at the other.

"Cassandra!" Her mother was the first to recover her aplomb. "I thought you were still out hunting. Douglas and I were having a frank discussion about the future."

"Looked more like open combat to me," Cassandra said, still trying to lighten the atmosphere.

"Your mother has displayed her true feelings in a way I cannot ignore, Cassandra," Douglas said, his voice solemn. "Under the circumstances, I do not feel I can remain a guest under her roof. I shall leave today, Lady Amelia, and trespass on your hospitality no longer. I shall return to Boston and leave your precious estate untarnished by my modern opinions."

"Douglas - no!" Cassandra said.

"Oh, let him go, Cassandra," her mother said. "Yes, go back across the Atlantic, Mr Flintock, and see if you can learn a little polish there, as you so fervently claim. Personally, I always doubted an upstart American could fit into our English countryside, let alone own an ancient estate like Cheadle Manor, and run it with any sort of decorum."

"Be quiet, Mother!" Cassandra said, her voice catching in her constricted throat. "Just keep your mouth shut, for once!"

"I see you've picked up some of his vulgar transatlantic expressions already, Cassandra," Lady Amelia said, looking triumphant.

Douglas said, "Then I shall take my coarse manners back to America, your ladyship. I was planning to leave in a week's time anyway, so I've already checked the times and connections. I don't see why I can't bring it forward a week. Goodbye, I'm not sure when, or even if, we shall meet again."

He turned on his heel, and left the room.

Cassandra threw a look of sheer hatred at her mother, who sat rigid and self righteous within her complacent cocoon, and ran after him.

"Douglas, please wait!" she cried, but Douglas was already halfway up the sweeping staircase that dominated the hall. He reached the right-hand branch at the top before she could grab his arm and halt his rapid march.

"Don't take any notice of my wretched mother, Douglas! She's been twisted up with grief ever since Charles died. She doesn't know what she's saying a lot of the time," Cassandra said, her hand gripping his sleeve.

Douglas stopped and turned to face her. He removed her hand and let his drop by his side. "If she meant even half of what she said, Cassandra, it makes it untenable for me to remain here."

"But it doesn't matter what Mother thinks, Douglas!" Cassandra said. "What matters is that we love each other!"

"That's true, Cassandra, but we have to live somewhere and I can't stay here another week. I need to go home to Boston and think things over." Douglas's voice was quiet but firm. "Excuse me, I have to pack. The boat leaves tonight and I need to catch the next train."

He walked into his guest room and shut the door quietly behind him.

He might as well have shut it in her face. All Cassandra's earlier exhilaration deserted her and she felt empty and alone, even though her lover was just a few feet away.

***

A mere half an hour later, they were in the barn, trying to breathe life into the Sunbeam saloon that was stored there. In a daze, Cassandra was helping Douglas to get the beast's engine to fire, even though it was the last thing on earth she wanted to do.

She turned the starting handle round three times in quick succession. Nothing.

"Let me have a go," Douglas said.

"Alright. I'll get in the motor and fiddle with the choke," Cassandra said.

They swopped places. Cassandra pumped the accelerator pedal and pulled the choke button right out to its fullest extent, knowing it wouldn't help and hoping like hell Douglas didn't know it too.

"Ready?" Douglas said.

Cassandra nodded.

"Here goes." Douglas turned the starting handle. The huge engine heaved, belched some smoke and shuddered back into silence. The smoky fumes filled the confines of the barn. Cassandra coughed.

"Again, Doug, do it again," Cassandra said. "She almost fired that time."

It wasn't working. Cassandra willed it to fail.

Douglas turned the handle again, with the same result.

Cassandra's hopes flickered brighter.

"She's not going to go, Cass. My train leaves in just over an hour. I'd better start walking. How far is the station?" Douglas said, his face still stern and tight.

"It's five long miles, Doug. You'll never walk it in time," Cassandra said. "Maybe this is the wrong decision. Stay another few days. Let's talk things over a bit more. Mother will calm down."

"No, Cassandra, my mind is made up. We'll have to ask your groom to hitch one of the horses to the gig; it'll be quicker than trying to get the carriage ready. Come on, let's leg it to the stables."

Cassandra got down from the car and kicked its solid rubber tyre. "Ouch. Damn it."

Douglas put his arm around her, "That won't get it started, honey." His face softened and he kissed her. "God, I'm going to miss you. Can't you come with me? It would do you good to get away from this museum."

"Do you mean it? So, we're not over?"

"Oh, Cass, I don't know. I feel so mixed up. I do love you but we come from such different worlds. I don't know how it *could* work. Come to Boston and see mine; then you'll understand."

"Oh, Doug, I'd love to, I really would, but I simply can't leave now, not after being away so long and with Charles never coming back. Mother needs me here to help with Father. You've seen the state he's in, and the condition of the whole manor. I've got to get things back in working order."

Douglas's face resumed its former mask.

"Very well, and if I were you, I'd start with the car."

Cassandra ignored his frostiness and kissed him back, despite the lump in her throat. She tugged his arm and they ran through the rain that had begun to fall across the yard.

"Bert?" she called, as soon as they got inside the stable block, "Bert?"

Bert Beagle, the head coachman at Cheadle Manor, ambled into view, "Yes, Miss Cassandra? What can I do for you?"

Cassandra hesitated, hoping to drag it out, but Douglas stepped in and filled the void.

"Hi, Bert, I'm sorry to bother you, but I'm in an awful rush. I have to catch the next train or I'll miss my boat to America. Can you hitch up your fastest horse to the gig and gallop us over there?"

"I'll do my best, sir, but Chestnut is lame. I've only got old Larkspur stabled. All the other carriage horses are put out to grass, or never came home from the war."

"She'll have to do. Hurry, Bert."

"Yes, sir."

Bert threw down the bridle he was cleaning and called to Jack, his youngest son. In record time, Larkspur stood hitched to the gig, and Douglas and Cassandra climbed on to its narrow seat, behind the coachman.

"Thanks for doing this so quickly, Bert," Douglas said.

"Just doing my job, Mr Flintock, sir," Bert said, and flicked his long whip down Larkspur's grey dappled spine.

Cassandra looked at Bert's broad back and then at the horse's. Both were generously padded and middle aged. They'd never reach the station in time and maybe, if Douglas missed the train, he'd think twice about leaving. She looked at Larkspur's mouth, champing on the bit. It looked so uncomfortable, and reminded her of the frightened horses at the Front, foaming at the mouth where their bits worried them. She shook her head free of the image and stared instead at Douglas, trying to imprint his profile on to her memory.

Her fiancé sensed her gaze and turned to look at her. "I love you too, honey, even if I can't stand your mother," he said, and held out his arms. "I'll write you, as soon as I reach Boston," he whispered into her ear.

Cassandra loved the smell of him; the scratch of his tweed suit against her cheek; the faint whiff of the American cigarettes he smoked. She lifted her face to be kissed. Bert coughed loudly.

Sooner than she would have liked, Cassandra was standing on the station platform, waving to the disappearing train, with tears running down her face. She never cried. She'd prided herself on never giving way throughout that bloody war she'd survived. No, not even when she was driving her ambulance full of screaming, wounded soldiers, had she shed a tear.

A vestigial drift of steam evaporated in the distance. Douglas had gone.

Gone back to America, to tell his family he'd fallen in love with an English aristocrat, who wore jodhpurs instead of dresses. What would they think? Would he even tell them about her at all, or simply forget she existed?

CHAPTER TWO

Katy held one end of the sheet and her mother, Agnes Beagle, held the other. Between them, they twisted the linen into a long white corkscrew, and squeezed all the rinsing water out, before slinging it in the basket, ready to peg out.

"We'll have to dry the whole lot here, in the barn. Your father has set up a new line for me, away from that dratted automobile, with its smoke and fumes. It's been sat here idle all through the war. Waste of money. Don't know why Sir Robert haven't sold it. It isn't as if Charles will ever drive the damn thing again, though there's no knowing what Miss Cassandra won't do. Women driving cars and you working on 'em. The world's gone mad, that's what. Well, we don't want smuts all over the sheets, but I've no choice but to hang it in here. This drizzle isn't going to give up soon," Agnes said.

"No, I think you're right about the rain, Mum," Katy said, not caring where they hung the sheets and wandering off to the olive green saloon. She ran her hand along its coach lines and added, "But you're wrong about motor cars. They're here to stay. The war's changed a lot of things and motoring is one of them. This Sunbeam is bit old hat now but she's a lovely car. Built in 1913 she was. A 12/16 Tourer, I believe. Six cylinders and very nice lines."

"Nice lines, my foot!" Agnes said, "You concentrate on this washing line, my girl."

Katy turned away from the car and back to the laundry. It was good to be home from the war but she hadn't reckoned on how hard it would be not to have her own home or to leave her old job as a mechanic in the army. Despite the welcome home party that had greeted them on their return, Lady Amelia had been adamant that the workers' cottages, such as the one she used to live in, could only go to those employed on the estate. As usual these days, Sir Robert didn't comment on her decision.

And, truth was, neither she, nor her husband, Jem Phipps, were employed anywhere. What were they to do? He couldn't go back to gardening, with only one arm, and they couldn't stay with her mum and dad forever; she'd go mad if they did, with Daisy, her sister, snooping around them all the time. Daisy was just that age when she wanted to know every intimate detail about young married life. Well, she'd have to find out for herself. Her dad, Bert Beagle, had said they could stay as long as they liked, he was that glad to have them come home safe from the war, unlike his eldest son, Albert, who had died, along with thousands of others, in the deep, greedy mud at Passchendaele.

Albert's cheeky young face flashed across her mind and her vision blurred. She dropped the next wet sheet onto the dusty floor.

"Katherine Beagle! For heaven's sake! What are you playing at, girl?" Agnes said, looking exasperated.

"I'm not Katherine Beagle any more, Mum. I'm Katy Phipps now, don't forget," Katy said, picking up her end of the sheet, which was now covered in bits of straw and motor oil.

"Oh, look at my clean linen! I'll have to damn well wash that sheet all over again," Agnes said, wrenching it out of Katy's loose grasp. "As if I didn't have enough to do."

"With me and Jem living at the lodge too, you mean," Katy said.

"I never said that," Agnes said.

"No, not out loud, you didn't," Katy said

"I don't mind the extra work, Katy," Agnes said in a softer tone, "but I'm not getting any younger. If you did your bit to help, it might make a difference, but you're in a dream half the time."

"I don't like to interfere, Mum. You only have to ask, you know, and I'd be glad to help, but I know you've got your way of doing things and I had mine, when I had a place of my own. Can't you see how I long to have one

21

again? It seems so unfair. Me and Jem did our bit in the war and what are we left with? Living off you and Dad is not my idea of paradise, believe me, but what choice to do we have? What jobs are there for us to start again? I'm sorry I'm causing you extra work, Mum, but believe me, I'd do the work of ten women, if I could call somewhere home again."

Katy didn't like the silence that followed her outburst. When Agnes clammed up and folded her lips tight like that, it was an ominous sign.

The tension was broken by the sound of a horse's hooves on the cobbles outside. Katy poked her head out of the barn and saw her father, drenched with rain, encouraging a very tired looking Larkspur to walk the last few steps into her warm stable. Cassandra Smythe sat next to him on the gig seat, her army coat equally soaked. He got down and touched his whip to his cap, when his wife also came to see who it was and stood, stroking Larkspur's nose. The animal's sides were heaving with the effort of trotting five miles in the drizzling rain.

"Ah, Katy!" said Cassandra, jumping off the gig seat and crossing the shiny wet cobbles to join the two women in the barn. She looked back at Katy's father before joining them, and said, "Thanks, Bert. Take the afternoon off and get yourself dry!"

Bert touched his cap again and chirruped Larkspur to the stables. Both looked thoroughly dejected.

"Doing the laundry then?" asked Cassandra, fishing a damp cigarette out of her trousers pocket.

"Yes, Miss Cassandra. I hope you think it's alright for us to hang it in the barn but there's no way we'll get these sheets dry, if we don't," said Agnes, bobbing a curtsey. "See, they're ours, from the lodge, not the manor ones."

"Can't see you've much choice, Mrs Beagle," said Cassandra. "And you've tucked them away in the corner, so Mother won't see it. She never comes out here anyway, so you should be in the clear."

22

Agnes bobbed another curtsey and nodded to her daughter to return to their chore, but Cassandra said, "Katy, could you wait a minute?"

Katy nodded, "Of course, if you wish it, Miss Cassandra."

"Oh, Lord, Katy, we don't have to go back to all that infernal formality do we? Not after all we've been through together in France."

Agnes sniffed but Katy smiled and said, "I suppose not, but then, it's not up to me."

Cassandra turned to Agnes and said, "Can you spare your daughter for a bit, Mrs. Beagle? I want her to take a look at this motor. Couldn't get the blasted thing to start earlier."

"Of course, Miss, I've only one more sheet to peg. I'm sure I can manage."

Agnes threw the white cotton square over the line, before bundling the soiled one under her arm and glaring at her eldest daughter.

"Right, I'm off, Katy," she said, and, pulling her shawl over her greying hair, before heading off, her back stiff with hostility, to her lodge house at the western gate of the estate.

"Cigarette?" asked Cassandra, offering the packet to Katy.

"Why not?" Katy said.

Cassandra lit Katy's from her own burning embers and passed it over. Katy inhaled the blue smoke and felt her shoulders relax.

"What's the problem with the car then, Cass?" Katy said, wandering over to the enormous Sunbeam saloon.

"Well, I had the choke out and both Doug and I cranked her over a few times, but no joy."

"You probably flooded the engine. Too much petrol drowns the engine and the spark can't light." Katy lifted up the bonnet and held it open with the rod inside. "Yes, I'll have a good look at her and see what might need doing. I doubt she's been fired since you left for the war and the carburettor might need a tune up, if the mixture was too rich. I've told you before about using too much choke. You only need *so* much fuel, you know. "

"I bow to your superior knowledge, Mrs Phipps. The engineering remains a mystery to me. I just like to get in and drive them," Cassandra said, in a tight voice.

"Jack told me you were taking Douglas to the station," Katy said, her head inside the engine, but holding her cigarette well away.

"Yes. He's on his way to Southampton now, to catch his boat to America. I feel totally lost without him."

"I'm sure you do, but why was he off in such a hurry? I thought he was staying for quite a while?" Katy said, replacing the bonnet and turning to look at Cassandra.

Cassandra clenched her jaw, in a way Katy remembered from their army work, when she'd delivered a fresh load of injured soldiers to the hospital after their hopes had risen during a lull. To her surprise, because it had never happened on the Front, Cassandra's eyes welled up.

"What's the matter, Cassandra?" Katy said, stubbing out her cigarette and reaching out to her friend.

Cassandra blinked and dashed her hand across her eyes. "I just don't know if he'll ever come back. To be honest, I deliberately flooded the engine in the hope he'd miss the train but everything conspired against me today, including my blasted mother. She's very pleased to see him go, I can tell you. But it wasn't just her, the hunt didn't help."

"Oh dear, did Douglas come a cropper?" Katy said.

"Yes, but not in a spectacular jump over a five bar gate. It was in the yard, with everyone watching. Poor Douglas, it was so humiliating for him, but he got back on and we had a good ride, until he witnessed the dogs killing a vixen. He couldn't stomach it, especially the brushing of a young lad from over Woodbury way. All he needed was a run-in with my ruddy Mama and he'd had enough," Cassandra said.

Katy had been on the rough end of one of Lady Amelia's dressing downs enough times to know how cutting she could be. And, no doubt, so had her daughter, but she had a hunch that Jem wouldn't have cut and run like Douglas had.

"That doesn't sound like the best of mornings," Katy said, keeping her thoughts private.

"No, it wasn't," Cassandra said.

"So, when will he be back?" Katy said.

"That's just it, Katy," Cassandra said, "I'm not sure he will be."

"Oh, surely not, you both looked so happy while he was here, Cass," Katy said, patting Cassandra's arm.

"Well, I was an hour or two ago. I feel utterly miserable now and I have no idea what Douglas is feeling. How can I? Soon he'll be thousands of miles away, as if he'd never been here at all," Cassandra said, and ground her cigarette stub into the mucky floor.

CHAPTER THREE

Jem walked back down the hill towards the manor. His mood hadn't lifted after his long walk on the chalky uplands. Usually, he could look out over the Wiltshire downs, yes, even through soft rain, and feel his heart swell at the broad expanse of farmland; get a sense of renewal at its unchanging beauty. It would be a treat, snatched from the working week. Somehow, now he had all the time in the world to wander at will, any joy he might glean from the familiar landscape eluded him. At least his ex-army coat kept the weather out. God knows he had little else to show for serving his country in that bloodbath.

What use was he with only one arm? He'd never be a gardener again. Jem loved the soil, just like his father, George Phipps, the head gardener. They'd worked this Wiltshire loam side by side, man and boy, ever since Jem could remember. Once he'd grown up and worked for the estate on a more formal footing, he'd made the poor wages stretch by growing his own vegetables in the little cottage he'd shared with Katy, down in the valley at Lower Cheadle. But that was before the war had clawed him away with its vicious hook.

He was lucky to have returned at all. He *tried* to remember that every time he struggled to do something with one hand. Katy said it made no difference; that she loved him more than ever. His heart skipped a beat when he remembered her telling him so, with a kiss. That was the ember that could still glow. Katy was different too. Her fine cheekbones, once round and rosy, had sharp-edges now. She, like him, was thinner, with angles that cut through to the quick. No room for cosy illusions after what they had both seen. Thank God she knew what war was really like. His mother, Mary, didn't understand his moods; his sudden need to withdraw up to these hills to try and blot the pictures out.

Would it be easier if they lived with *his* parents,

instead of Katy's? No, Katy and Mary would never get on. Mary had never liked her, especially after Katy's flirtation with Cassandra's brother, Charles Smythe, and her losing her job over it. Mary always thought that Katy had trapped Jem into marrying her. She couldn't have been more wrong. Marrying Katy had been Jem's one and only ambition in life and they had been so happy, until Florence died. Sweet baby Florence. How like Katy she had looked, with her pretty face and dark curly hair, until the typhoid snuffed out her little life. No, his mother mightn't like it, but Katy's love was the only thing that kept him going.

Katy didn't find it easy, living with her parents, but it irked him even more. Not having his own roof over his head and feeling so useless. Making love silently in the furtive darkness; snatching moments when they hoped no-one could hear them, as if they weren't man and wife, desperate to be re-united after years apart. And her sister, Daisy - he could swear she had her ears on stalks, all night long.

If only he could sleep. Every time he shut his eyes, all he saw were battlefields strewn with body parts. Or cheeky Davey Pringle stretched out baking in the sun on that gun-wheel when he'd been punished for speaking out of turn. What had been the bloody point of that? Young Davey hadn't lasted another month. Jem's skin prickled and itched, remembering the crawl of the lice that had lurked in the seams of his uniform. Didn't matter how many you squashed with your bayonet blade, they would come crawling back to bite you, just like the ruddy Germans. And that stench - would he ever get it out of his nostrils? And why did his arm ache where it used to be? Phantom pains, the doctor had told him. It was painful alright and shot out of the ends of fingers that no longer existed, worse than anything real. Made him feel sick sometimes.

He knew every inch of that bloody ceiling at the lodge house. He should do. He spent each endless night studying its beams. He was weary to his bones and had nothing to show for it. He couldn't even chop logs to help Agnes out. Yes, useless, just about summed him up. Might as well have copped it in France.

Except for Katy, but what sort of a husband was he now?

Jem kicked a stone and sent it spinning down the lane.

He wandered into the greenhouse, where his father was potting up some house plants.

"Hello, Jem," George said, looking up from the rows of pots on the slatted bench.

"Hello, Dad," Jem said. He'd give anything to be able to help him. "What plant are you splitting there?

"It's a peace lily, of the Spathiphyllum family," George said.

"Blimey, that's a bit of a mouthful," Jem said.

"Hmm, Lady Amelia wants one in each reception room up at the house. She made me take one up to the hall this morning and put it in a very ugly urn. Says it's an emblem for the future."

"Oh, yes, the future."

Through the distorted glass of the greenhouse window, Jem watched a couple of young under-gardeners throw turves of grass between them.

Two hands each.

CHAPTER FOUR

"It's no good, Cass, I'll have to go and change. I can't work on the car in this dress," Katy said, wiping her greasy hands on a piece of hay she'd snatched up from a bale thrown against the wall. "And to be honest, you shouldn't let them store such combustible stuff in here with the drums of petrol for the car. Don't you remember how they blew up during the bomb raid in Étaples?"

"Goodness, Katy, I hadn't thought of that. You're right. We need to get organised." Cassandra sighed and continued, "There's so much that needs organising, I don't know where to start. If only Douglas was here to help me."

"The estate does look a bit run down, if you don't mind me saying so," Katy said. "You know, if I were you, I'd turn this barn into a proper garage for the car and use that old cowshed for the other things. Unless you are intending to set up a new herd?"

"Lord, no. I want to simplify things on the estate, not add to the responsibilities. I must have a meeting with Mr Hayes. All the stuffing's gone out of him since he lost both his sons in France."

"And who can blame him? Jem keeps fretting over his arm but I just keep thinking how lucky he's been to come out of that hellhole alive, even if he's not in one piece."

Cassandra nodded, "I know. It's no wonder Father's drinking himself into oblivion over Charles and letting things go. That's why I didn't go to America with Douglas. It would have been the final straw if I'd run off too, but I don't blame him, after what Mother said." Cassandra looked to Katy for a comment but when none came, she added, "I'd better go in and dress for dinner, though I'm tempted to throw it at her."

Katy raised her eyebrows at this confession but she knew just what Cassandra meant. The mood in the West Lodge wasn't too clever, either.

Cassandra gave a hollow laugh and said, "Isn't it getting a bit dark for mechanics on the car?"

"Perhaps, but I could bring in an oil lamp and get Jem to hold it for me. We've nothing better to do."

Cassandra squeezed her arm on her way to the barn door, that stood permanently open on broken hinges. Katy watched her go back out into the rain. It was pouring down in sheets now and hammering on the slate roof of the barn. She sat back down on the running board of the car and watched the rain falling onto the wet courtyard. Pools collected where the cobbles had been worn down by horse's hooves for so many years. The sky, pregnant with water, dimmed into twilight with not even a nod to a sunset. The gloom matched her mood.

Jem had six months' pay from the army after being demobbed in December but that would dry up in June. The thought of living with her parents for much longer, much as she loved them, was not an inviting prospect. Jem didn't say anything, he was too polite, but she could tell he was hating being shoved in the back bedroom with Daisy and Jack a thin curtain away. And she could tell he wasn't sleeping. He looked more tired in the mornings than he did the night before.

Perhaps, if she got Cassandra's motor running smoothly again, she could drum up the courage to ask her for a cottage on the estate. Except it wasn't up to Cassandra. She'd give her the shirt off her back if Katy asked her, but Lady Amelia was a very different kettle of fish. Funny, she didn't even consider what Sir Robert might think. These days, he just sort of melted into the background or disappeared on his hunter for hours on end. Not that she went up to the house much. How could she, without a proper job there? And could she really go back to being a housemaid?

Katy looked back into the engine of the car. This was what she wanted to do. She loved making an engine throb with life. She'd thoroughly enjoyed learning how to look after them during her time in the Women's Army

Auxiliary Corps. The last thing she wanted was to be under the housekeeper's thumb again. Thumbscrew, more like, as Mrs Andrews kept all her staff to a very strict regime. But there were no jobs in cars. No jobs anywhere but on the estate. A lot of armament factories had shut now and what men were left had returned to the land. Plenty of other women were feeling as lost as her, now the war was over.

She wiped her hands on the hay again and carefully stowed it behind some stacked bricks near the outside wall of the barn. A bit of modern electrical lighting in here would be safer than an oil lamp, if Cassandra really wanted to get organised. Katy ran back to the lodge through the driving rain, holding her coat over her head and wrapped around her thin body.

She unlatched the cottage door and stepped into the warm kitchen. The oil lamps were bright in here and the fire blazed through its grille on the big range. Savoury steam escaped through the oven door. Her mother was cutting bread for the table.

"Shut that door against the rain, Katy," she said, laying the platter of sliced bread in the middle of the table. "You'd better wash those filthy hands before supper, too."

Katy ground her teeth. As a married woman of twenty four, she really didn't need to be told to wash her hands before eating. Folding her lips tight, she went to the scullery sink and poured water from the jug on to her palms before soaping off the black carbon. She left her nails banded with grime to remind her of the sheer joy that awaited her in the barn.

Bert came downstairs, together with her brother and sisters. "Come on, Daisy, get Jack and Emily to sit down tidy, will you?"

Daisy lifted little Emily up and plonked her in the wooden high chair. Emily wailed in protest. Jack clamped his hands over his ears and starting singing tunelessly to drown his baby sister out.

"Where's Jem?" asked Agnes, over the noise,

31

ladling out mutton stew into bowls and handing them round.

"I don't know, Mum," Katy said. "He said he was going up the hill for a walk."

"In this weather?" Bert said. "You wouldn't catch me going out in this. It was bad enough driving the gig to the station and back. I wasn't sure Larkspur would make it in time. These Americans. Always in a hurry."

"Douglas had a train to catch and a boat after that, Dad," Katy said, reaching for a slice of bread to mop up the delicious gravy.

"Mr Flintock, to you," said her mother.

"They'll always be Doug and Cass to me, Mum. We've worked side by side together. Cass said as much today," Katy said.

"Well, it don't seem right to me," Agnes said. "The world's upside down since that damn war." And Agnes pushed her plate away, her food half eaten.

Bert patted his wife's rough hands.

Katy looked at the empty chair, Albert's. She wished Jem had joined them for supper.

"I think Jem must have gone to his mother's for tea. He said he might," Katy said.

"Well, has he or hasn't he? Am I supposed to plate something up for him, or what?" Agnes said.

"Oh, don't bother, Mum. I can fry him up an egg or two, if he turns up."

"I've made plenty, I suppose I can keep some by." Agnes got up and lifted the heavy casserole dish back onto the hob. "Who's for pudding, then?"

Jack and Emily, her two youngest, banged their spoons in reply.

"Yes, please, is the right way to say it!" Agnes said, her cross frown easing into a smile.

Katy smiled back at her siblings. "Mum's puddings are the best, aren't they?"

All three children nodded, as the treacle sponge took pride of place in the middle of the table and Agnes put a jug of custard next to it.

"Aren't you having any, Katy?" Bert said.

"I'm full, thanks, Dad. If you'll excuse me, Mum, I think I'll get changed and go back to the barn to look at the car. Can you tell Jem where I am, if he turns up?"

"Am I supposed to be a signal box like on that noisy railway?" said Agnes.

"Have you got permission to fiddle with that old lump of metal? You could get yourself in trouble if you starts pulling bits out of the engine that you can't put back in the right place," Bert said, shaking his head.

Katy's anger flooded through to her face, making it hot. "Do you really think, Dad, that I didn't learn how to look after a car in the Women's Army? What do you think they paid me for? Sitting idly by while some man did the dirty work for me? I can tell you, I know my way around an engine like the back of my hand. And anyway Cassandra wants me to do it. She knows what I did in the war, even if you've got no bloody idea!"

"Don't you swear at me, young lady!" Bert said, "especially not in front of the little ones. I've a good mind to put you over my knee, grown up or not! And don't you think about *my* future at all? What do you think is going to become of my horses if the Smythes change over to motorised vehicles?"

"You can't stop change happening, Dad. Don't you see? The war's pushed us all on. It's a new age," Katy said, feeling her face getting hotter than ever.

Her father stood up, leaving his pudding untouched. Katy had never seen the like. There was a sudden hush around the table.

"You wants to think on, Katherine, my girl. You wants to think about them that's gone before you, yes, and remember who's kept you fed all these years. And who's going to feed the only brother you've got left and his little sisters, hey, if their Dad's out of a job? No, you'll stay here with us this evening, and mind your manners while you're about it," Bert said, his own face flushed and his eyes bright with anger.

"Your father's right, Katy," Agnes chipped in. "Why can't you stay and finish your supper, and for that matter, you can give me a hand to clear up after."

"Daisy can do it, can't you Daisy?" Katy said, itching to get away before she exploded with fury.

Daisy looked mutinous, her mouth bulging with treacle pudding. She swallowed it down and scooped up another spoonful saying, "I always have to do it. Mum's right - why don't you help for once?"

"Daisy's got a point there, Katy. You might have been a trained mechanic for the British Army, but you're just one of the family here," Bert said.

Katy couldn't beat them all. She looked around the table. Every pair of eyes was on her, brimful of upset emotions. Even little Emily was on the brink of tears. Katy could hear her father's quickened breathing and registered how hurt he must be feeling to speak like that. Her shoulders slumped into resignation and she said, "Yes, I suppose you're right, I should help. It's just that the car's carburettor needs a good clean and tune up."

"Carbur-what? If it's cleaning you're in the mood for, there's plenty plates need washing, my girl," Agnes said, folding her arms across her chest.

Katy sighed.

Plates it was then.

CHAPTER FIVE

"Drink up your soup, Cassandra. Cook tells me this is forced celery, from the greenhouses, and Phipps has excelled himself this year. The Ponsonby's don't eat nearly so well."

"It's delicious, Mother, but I don't have that much of an appetite since Douglas left," Cassandra laid her soup spoon across the dish to signal she'd finished to Andrews, the ever silent, henpecked butler, who came and collected it.

She tried not to notice how her father, Sir Robert, slurped his soup so noisily, or the amount that dribbled down his napkin. Had Andrews seen it too? She watched him but, as usual, the butler stared rigidly at the wall opposite. Cassandra followed his gaze. Those curtains must have been installed when her mother was a bride, they looked so Victorian. She couldn't imagine a time when her mother wasn't part of Cheadle Manor but knew Sir Robert had married his wife for the fortune that she had brought. Lady Amelia had been plain Miss Hepworth until her wedding. Mr Hepworth, her father, though it was never mentioned, had made his money in Bristol and Cassandra had caught whispers that slave trading had coloured his family's past. Her mother had never confirmed these rumours and as both her parents had had the good sense to die within two years of her marriage, their daughter took care never to refer to the source of her income. Sir Robert knew where his bread was buttered, and with the wool trade that had funded Cheadle Manor for generations in decline, he had been happy to invest his wife's dowry in new horses for the hunt, which was where his true passion lay.

Cassandra's eyes travelled around the grand dining room. Shabby. That's how it looked. The paint on the woodwork was chipped and worn and the rug had threadbare patches. Did her mother not notice these things? She'd been quick enough to see the flaws in

Douglas. Cassandra felt like picking up her wine glass and flinging it at her mother's black satin dress.

Instead, she attempted to make conversation. "Any news from the village, mother?"

"No, and quite frankly, I'm enjoying the peace and quiet. Douglas Flintock seemed to think that dinner must be conducted through a constant stream of trivial chit-chat," Lady Amelia said.

"I liked the fellow," Sir Robert said.

"Thank you, father," Cassandra said, seething with anger, "So do I. But after Mother's horrible remarks, I don't know if he'll be back."

"Really?" Lady Amelia's spoon paused in mid-air.

"You needn't sound quite so hopeful, Mother. Don't you want me to be happy?" Cassandra said.

"If Douglas really cares about you, I'm sure he will return to plague us all," Lady Amelia said, releasing her soup plate to Andrews.

The second course arrived. Oh, no. Duck terrine. After the simple stodge the British army served up, all this rich food no longer sat so well on Cassandra's stomach, but Mother would never let her get away with refusing again. She fiddled about with the paté on her plate until her father had finished his generous portion. Andrews refilled his glass yet again. That must be nearly a bottle he'd put away already and they hadn't had the main course yet.

By the time each dish had been served, Cassandra felt sick. Without Douglas's easy chatter, the meal had largely been conducted in the silence her mother cherished, punctuated only by her father's noisy chewing. The cavernous room amplified the sounds. Not for the first time, she questioned the size of the manor house for the three of them; but Douglas had loved its aged stone walls, and how it formed the central core to the community that served it. He'd admired how the weathered grey stone fitted so naturally into the landscape and how its tall gables pierced the sky. The sooner it was back in shape, the sooner she and Douglas could get married, if he still wanted to, and who knows, maybe the beauty of Cheadle Manor would draw him back.

And it wasn't just her own future she'd be securing. She had to remember just how many people depended upon the estate. Yes, she must get cracking with putting it in good heart again and then, if that didn't lure him home, she'd damn well go to America and drag Douglas back, kicking and screaming, if need be.

Before her father retreated to his study for his cigar, she grabbed the opportunity to broach the plans she'd been hatching.

"Father?"

Her father's eyes slewed around to hers. She was shocked at how bloodshot they were. He belched and forgot to apologise.

She'd better include Lady Amelia in her ideas. "Mother, Father? We need to talk about the estate. I wonder, would you mind if I had a meeting with Hayes tomorrow? I thought it might be a good idea to look at the books and get an idea of how things are? What with the war and, and everything..." She decided to leave Charles' death out of it and continued, "Err, things need patching up, don't you think?"

"I'm sure I don't know what you mean, Cassandra." Her mother's face was etched with disdain. "Young women don't speak of financial matters to estate managers! That is a man's role."

"With all due respect, Mother, Father isn't as young as he was and I'm the only one here."

"Do you think I'm not aware of that fact? If Charles was here, everything would be different." Lady Amelia dabbed at the corners of her eyes with her lace-edged handkerchief, as she stifled a thinly-disguised sob.

"Yes, I know, Mother, but he isn't. So, I'll just have to get on with it myself," Cassandra laid down her final spoon of the evening.

"I've never heard of such impertinence. Your

father has always managed perfectly well, haven't you, Sir Robert?" Lady Amelia said, after clearing her throat noisily.

"Humph," was Sir Robert's only contribution.

"Mother, don't you think it's time to let me play my part? I've got lots of ideas on how to improve the estate and, besides, when Douglas and I get married, I want to live here with him and we can run the estate together."

"Do you really think an American could run Cheadle Manor, always supposing he does return?" Lady Amelia's eyes were wide open in horror.

"He's as good a man as any other. His family came from sound stock in Scotland originally and his father is a lawyer in Boston. Did I tell you that I'm going over there in a few months?" Cassandra said, neglecting to add that Douglas knew nothing of her plan. Hardly surprising when she'd only just thought of it.

"To America? All that way?" Lady Amelia's voice lost its strident tone and a discernible quaver diluted its strength.

More gently, Cassandra said, "It takes less than a week on the ocean liners these days. You could come too."

"I? I don't think so!"

"Why not? Wouldn't you like to meet Douglas's family?"

"Don't you remember what happened to the Titanic, Cassandra? The ship that couldn't sink?"

"All the more reason to have faith that another boat won't do the same, I should have thought," Cassandra said. "They're not going to make that mistake twice and it was years ago, before the war."

"There are still icebergs in the Atlantic ocean!"

Cassandra laughed, "Well, you don't have to decide now, Mother. Wouldn't you like to go to America, Father?"

"What?" Her father said.

"America, Father. It's on the other side of the Atlantic. It's where Douglas's family lives, you know, the Flintocks."

"On the other side of the world? No, my dear, I'm happy where I am. Home is where the heart is, you know." And Sir Robert stood up, missed grabbing his chair to support himself, and toppled over. Andrews was there in a flash, helping Cassandra lift him up.

"Oh, take him straight up to bed, Andrews," said Lady Amelia. "He won't want a cigar tonight."

***

When her Mother retreated to the drawing room to eat sweetmeats and drink tea, Cassandra excused herself. She shrugged on her old army overcoat over her silk dress, snatched up her fag packet, and escaped into the night air.

Inhaling deeply on her cigarette, she looked up at the sky. The rain had finally stopped and stars whispered infinities to each twinkling neighbour. Smothering a scream of frustration, Cassandra stubbed out her cigarette on the terrace balcony and, buttoning up her heavy coat, descended the wide steps onto the driveway.

The January night was turning frosty after the rain storm, and her breath left her body in warm clouds. She hugged her arms around her torso. Was it only yesterday that Douglas's arms had done that? Where was he now? All that talk of icebergs had chilled her already queasy stomach. There *was* a risk to that journey, however much she denied it. Oh, Douglas. Why didn't I go with you?

She wandered into the barn. Those door hinges would be the first thing she'd get mended. Hayes might be suffering a double bereavement but it was high time he started earning his keep again. Cassandra instinctively went to the motorcar and slid on to the driver's seat, behind the wheel. She ran her hands around its circumference and closed her eyes, pretending she was careering down the road at a rate of knots, with Douglas grinning at her side.

"What are you smiling about?"

Cassandra opened her eyes.

"Hello, Katy. Couldn't resist either?"

They both laughed.

"It's not easy, is it?" Katy said.

"What?"

"Being home again."

"No, it certainly isn't. Not without Doug."

"No, I can imagine." Katy's eyes misted up.

"At least you have Jem," Cassandra got down from the car and put her arm around her friend.

Katy blew her nose fiercely into her handkerchief. "Sorry, Cass, don't know what came over me. So silly. It was one of those moments when you feel like someone has walked over your grave; do you know what I mean?"

"Yes, Katy, I do, and there are so many graves."

"Too many ghosts disturbing the peace," Katy said. "Now, about this motor."

"Is there something else bothering you, Katy? Is it Jem? Is he well? You're not, um, expecting, are you?"

"No chance of that, living at Mum and Dad's. Not that I want more kids, anyway."

"What do you mean?"

"Come on, Cass, isn't it obvious? There isn't much privacy in a two bedroom lodge house."

"Oh, I see! I hadn't thought," Cassandra said, dropping her arm.

"Cassandra, I know I shouldn't ask you this, but is there an empty cottage on the estate somewhere? We wouldn't mind what state it was in but it would be heaven to have our own roof above us again. I missed Jem so much during the war and I am truly grateful that he's home but..." Katy dried up.

"Of course! I'm sure we can find something. How stupid of me not to think of it before. I've been so wrapped up in my own affairs. I'm having a meeting with

Hayes, the estate manager in the morning, whatever Mother thinks about it. I'll ask him and get back to you," Cassandra said, feeling mortified.

"Would you? Really? That would be wonderful, Cass! The only thing is, I don't know how we'd pay the rent once Jem's pension runs out?" Katy's unusual violet-blue eyes darkened with anxiety.

Cassandra patted her shoulder. "We'll think of something. Leave it with me, Katy. And if you get this motor running, I'd be very happy to pay you for your time."

"Would that be in order? I mean, I'm no longer on the estate payroll. What would Lady Amelia say? She was glad to get rid of me before the war. I can't see her taking kindly to me becoming an employee again," Katy said, shaking her head.

"Leave Mother to me. You sort out the car! But it's too late now. Come back in the morning. I can pay you in cash, out of my allowance. We needn't make it official but you shouldn't work for nothing. Don't worry, Katy, there's always a way around these things. Trust me."

Katy surprised Cassandra with a quick hug and a big grin. Then she turned quickly away and headed back to the lodge. Cassandra lit a final cigarette. Sorting out the estate would present many different challenges but it would also be immensely satisfying, she could see that now. Katy had worked like a Trojan during her time in the WAAC. She deserved a home and so did her crippled husband. If they couldn't house this young couple after all the sacrifices they'd made, it would be a poor thing. And, once she'd explained it carefully, she was sure her parents would agree. Well, almost sure.

***

The next morning, Cassandra lost no time in tackling Hayes. She rose early and headed straight for his office, above the stables. She was shocked at his

41

appearance. Hayes had always been rather dapper, and had received a fair amount of stick for it from the other men working on the estate, but their gentle mockery had always been tempered by a hefty dose of respect. Hayes knew his job, and Cassandra now realised how much they had depended upon his competent running of the house and lands she was due to inherit. Today, Hayes sat hunched over his books. His hair, once carefully oiled and black as a raven's, was coarse and grey, and stuck out in disordered strands. His hands, that used to be so carefully manicured, were grimy and shook so much, his writing wandered off the lines on the page.

Cassandra took a deep breath and crossed the threshold, after knocking softly on the door. Hayes obviously hadn't heard her, because he dropped his fountain pen when he caught sight of her, and a pool of ink stained the page.

"Miss Cassandra, you startled me!" And Hayes ripped up the page he'd been writing on, scrumpled it into a ball, and threw it in the bin.

"Hayes, I'm so sorry. You've wasted all your work. Do forgive me," Cassandra said.

"I wasn't working on estate duties. I was copying out a poem. " Hayes' finger still rested on the line in the book on his cluttered desk.

"Oh? Whose poem is it?" asked Cassandra, not bothering to reprimand him. They were both beyond that.

"It's by Siegfried Sassoon, Miss. It's just come out."

"Which one is it, Hayes?"

"It's called *'Aftermath',*" said Hayes, his eyes wandering back to the slim volume.

"Ah, yes, it's his new one," Cassandra said. "May I read it?"

"You sure you want to?"

"Yes, Hayes, I'm sure," and Cassandra lifted the book from the desk and read the first two verses out loud in a soft voice. When she got to the last verse, she stumbled over the words, and read the rest with a throat choked with emotion:

"Do you remember that hour of din before the attack--
And the anger, the blind compassion that seized and shook you then
As you peered at the doomed and haggard faces of your men?
Do you remember the stretcher-cases lurching back
With dying eyes and lolling heads--those ashen-grey
Masks of the lads who once were keen and kind and gay?
Have you forgotten yet?...
Look up, and swear by the green of the spring that you'll never forget."

Cassandra paused when she had finished, before daring to look up. Hayes didn't brush away the tears that trickled down his lined face.

He stared back at her, unabashed, and said, "You see, I don't know how my boys died. Were they together? Were they in agony, like in this poem? Did they have an officer who cared, like Sassoon, or more likely one of those brutes who didn't give a damn?"

"I don't know the answers to your questions, Mr Hayes. I saw lots of young men dying when I drove my ambulance. All I can say is, everyone looked out for everyone else and, in the end, they were all peaceful. Your sons are at peace now. I hope you can find some for yourself."

"Thank you, Miss Cassandra, but I doubt I shall ever find peace again."

Cassandra could think of nothing to say that wasn't a platitude, so she just nodded and waited.

It took a full ten minutes before Hayes collected himself enough to speak.

"Thank you for your kindness, Miss Cassandra; for not running away, but bearing me company. I appreciate that."

"If there is anything else we can do, Mr Hayes - for you or your wife - just say."

Hayes nodded and waved his hand in the negative. He wiped his eyes and then his reading glasses, looked out of the window at the stable boys grooming Chestnut and Larkspur, and cleared his throat.

"So, Miss Cassandra, you didn't come up here at this early hour to listen to my moanings. What can I do for you?"

Cassandra squeezed his tweedy arm and smiled. "Would being busy help?"

"I reckon it might," Hayes said.

"Good, because we've got a lot to do, Mr Hayes!"

Armed with a good overview of the financial status of the whole estate, Cassandra left Hayes' office with mixed feelings. The war had taken its toll, not just on her estate manager, but also on the income and expenditure of the whole shebang. Her mind was teeming with problems that needed urgent attention. She could see no alternative but to sell off a good deal of estate land, just to keep afloat. She'd start with finding Katy and Jem a home; a smaller problem than most, and the only one she'd had a solid idea for.

A telegram was waiting for her on the hall table. It was from Douglas. It was short and to the point.

"JUST COME TO BOSTON SOON - STOP - LOVE DOUG"

Immensely buoyed up by this one line, she folded the slip of paper into careful quarters and slid it into the pocket of her jodhpurs. She found her parents in the dining room, finishing off their leisurely breakfast. Having skipped her own, Cassandra discovered she was famished, and fell on the scrambled eggs and bacon kept hot in silver dishes on the massive sideboard. She served herself a good plateful and sat down between her parents

44

to demolish it.

"Good gracious, Cassandra. Anyone would think you hadn't eaten for a week. Where are your manners?" Lady Amelia said.

"Left them in the army, I suppose," Cassandra said, between bites. "Ugh, this coffee's cold."

"Shall I ring for fresh?" Lady Amelia said, in a more conciliatory tone.

"No, don't bother the servants," Cassandra said.

"Not bother them? What do you think we pay them for?" said her mother.

"Glad you brought that up, actually, Mother," Cassandra said. No time like the present, after all. "I've just come from seeing Hayes. We went over the books and we need to make some changes."

"What did I say last night, Cassandra? I told you that was men's work!" Lady Amelia got up and rang the bell.

"Mother, you must accept that things are different now. There simply aren't enough men to go around, so you're just going to have to put up with me."

"I've never heard such nonsense," Lady Amelia said, sitting back down with a rustle of silk.

"Hear the girl out," Sir Robert said. He even laid his newspaper down and folded it. "Cassandra's right, Amelia. Time we took stock."

Lady Amelia was struck dumb by this interjection and Cassandra seized on the hiatus.

"Thank you, Father. We are in a new situation, not one any of us would have chosen, but we've got to face the future," she took a deep breath, "without Charles. Hayes has lost two boys of his own, but he's prepared to get down to work, with me giving the instructions, as long as you'll approve."

Cassandra took her mother's silence, despite the pursed lips and watery eyes, as consent.

Again, her father surprised her, "You'll have no objections from me, Cassandra. I've no stomach for estate business these days. Frankly, I'd be glad to hand over the reins to you, my dear."

"Robert!" Lady Amelia's pursed lips burst open with her husband's name.

"No, my dear. Cassandra's only speaking the truth. Time we faced up to it." Sir Robert heaved his bulk upright and laid a hairy palm on Cassandra's slim shoulder. "I'm grateful to you, Cassandra, for taking it on. I'll be in my study, should you want me."

Sir Robert almost bumped into Andrews as they passed each other in the doorway.

"Pardon me, sir," Andrews said.

"You'd better see what her ladyship wants, Andrews," Sir Robert said, before disappearing behind the study door.

"You rang, my lady?" Andrews said, bowing to Lady Amelia.

"Yes, I did, Andrews. We need more coffee. And make sure it's hot!"

"Yes, ma'am," and Andrews followed his master out of the room.

"Now, young lady," Lady Amelia said, turning to Cassandra. "You had better explain yourself with all these plans."

"Yes, Mother," Cassandra replied, trying not to let the triumph she felt seep into her voice. "I've spoken to Hayes and we need to make some difficult decisions. We need to increase our income to cover the taxes that are now due. Quite a few of our tenants have lost fathers and sons and will struggle to pay the rent. I think we'll need to sell off some land to realise some capital."

"Cassandra, you will break up the estate if you do all this!"

"No, Mother, I'm aiming to keep it together. And don't forget Douglas is not a poor man. You might not like me marrying an American, but his income will greatly help our predicament, if you haven't already scared him away."

"We'll be selling our souls to trade," this was said with a sniff and another flurry of the lace handkerchief.

"This is no time for false pride, Mother," Cassandra said, the corners of her mouth twitching involuntarily at her mother's blatant hypocrisy. "I want to keep the estate going but we'll have to make compromises. The price is unusually high for wheat at the moment, due to the Government's subsidies, so Hayes and I plan to plant extra fields of it this year. That will mean more labour, but it should be worth it."

"Cassandra, you sound like a farmer!"

"Needs must. Anyway, I won't bore you with more of the details. Except for one thing, I want to find a home for Katy and Jem. Do you know if there is a cottage going spare on the estate?"

"Who?"

"Katy, and her husband, Jem Phipps. He lost an arm in the war, you know." Her mother still looked blank. "Katy used to be Miss Beagle, the coachman's daughter."

Her mother's brow immediately cleared. "I'll not have that hussy getting above herself again. No, Cassandra, you will be making enough changes around here without promoting her type. I shall never forget finding her with dear Charles, wearing your ballgown and in your bedroom. No, I draw the line at that. Do what you must, grubbing about on the farms with Hayes but I will not give Katherine Beagle a house!"

With that, Lady Amelia swept out of the room and shut the door with a firm slap.

Cassandra's shoulders slumped. She'd lost that skirmish outright but the battle wasn't over yet. This was the beginning of a long campaign but she wasn't looking forward to telling Katy about her failure. She'd have to think of another way to help her old comrade. If she couldn't find her a house, maybe she could think up some sort of job for her. There were so many things to sort out. Cassandra had never felt more alone, as all the problems mounted up in her head, overwhelming her crowded brain.

How she wished she knew what Douglas was planning to do. Every time she thought of him, her stomach flipped over, but at least that telegram lay snug against her thigh.

CHAPTER SIX

Katy sang as she worked on the big engine of the Sunbeam saloon. Today the sun was shining through the open barn doors and she didn't mind the arctic wind that came with it. She needed the bright sunshine to see what she was doing.

Jem lounged against the stone wall, chewing a stalk of hay, and watching her. She enjoyed feeling his gaze on her busy back and hoped he was impressed with her expertise. She looked around to check, and his face lit up with a smile, but not quickly enough to fool her. New, downward lines around his mouth had pulled his face into a frown that spoke of bitter sorrow, not joy. That was how he was really feeling, however much he tried to hide it. She wished he wouldn't try to bear the burden alone. She would do anything to lift it for him.

"How's it going, love?" he asked.

"Really well, actually," she said. "Pass me that rag, will you, Jem?"

He peeled himself away from the bumpy wall and joined her. "This one?"

"No, the flannel one, please, Jem," Katy said, still smiling at him.

"I love to hear you sing," Jem said. "I can't remember the last time you did."

"Do you? That's nice, considering I've a voice like a foghorn," and Katy laughed.

"You sound like a lark to me," and Jem sneaked a quick kiss onto the back of her neck, sending goosepimples rippling down her spine. "Oh, Katy, it's so good to have you to myself for once."

"I know, I know, dearest. Just to talk without Mum interfering or Daisy giggling behind her hands is bliss!"

"Can't you stop for a moment, and give me a proper kiss?" Jem stroked her cheek.

"I'll never get the job finished if you keep

distracting me, Mr Phipps!" Katy said, feeling torn between her twin loves of carburettors and her husband.

"Well, what's the hurry? We've neither of us anything better to do," Jem said, and chucked his straw onto the earth floor.

"Cass said she'd pay me for this work. We both need new shoes and maybe, we could put a bit by, so we could rent somewhere of our own," Katy said.

"Little chance of that. It'll be shillings and pence, not pounds, you'll get for this. Oh, Katy, it should be me bringing in a wage, not you. What are we going to do when my pension runs out?"

Katy put her rag down and put her arms about Jem. "We'll think of something, you'll see," and she kissed him long and hard, relishing the lack of a witness.

Soon their breath came in hungry gasps. Jem drew her towards the ladder at the back of the barn, that lead up to the hayloft.

"Come on, Katy, let's make love without Daisy's sniggers, for once," Jem said, his voice low and urgent.

"Jem, I want to, you know I do, but what if someone sees us?"

"Who's to know? We'll go up behind the hay-bales where no-one will find us. You are my wife, Katy! I want to show you how much I love you. At least that part of me still works."

Katy didn't have the heart to deny him after he'd said that. With her heart thumping so loudly she thought its pump might be overhead, let alone any moans of joy she might let slip, she laid in the soft, fragrant hay and opened her arms to her husband. Her darling Jem, long lost and missed. How could she not love him back?

"This would be a damn sight easier, if you had your skirt on and not these confounded dungarees, Katy," Jem said, fiddling with her buttons.

"How was I to know you would come and ravish me?" Katy laughed softly and undid his flies.

"Can't you take the whole thing off? I want to see

you in all your glory," whispered Jem.

"Here let me help you," Katy said, scared they were taking too long.

Jem was getting good at using his one hand but they had no time to waste.

"I can do it. I'm not completely useless!" Jem said, louder this time.

"Hello? Anyone there?" called a voice from below them.

Katy and Jem both froze. Jem lifted his hand and signalled silence with his forefinger over his mouth. Katy nodded and held her own hand over her thudding heart.

They stared at each other, eyes wide and bodies, so recently aglow, now rigid with the fear of discovery.

"Don't think they's here, Dad," came little Jack's unbroken voice.

"Maybe not, son," Bert Beagle's bass voice sounded unnaturally loud. "You run along and see if you can find Katy and Jem at the lodge. Off you go. I'll be back at the stables, alright?"

"Rightoh, Dad. I'll find them!"

They heard Jack's feet pounding off into the distance. Below them, Bert cleared his throat noisily and stomped off, his steel capped boots ringing out on the cobblestones in the yard.

Katy let out her breath again.

"He knew what we was up to," Jem said. "I feel like a ruddy thief."

"Maybe he did, Jem, but he covered for us. Dad understands what it's like."

"I don't want another man, especially your father, to know about our private times." And Jem hurled himself away from her, fumbled with his buttons until they were fastened again and, with difficulty, climbed back down the ladder.

Katy didn't go to help him. It wasn't her kindly Dad that had disrupted their romantic moment, but Jem's infernal pride. And if the tables were turned, she'd be just

51

the same, or worse. Katy smoothed back her short hair, used her two hands to do up her dungaree clasps and went back down to the car. Thank God this metal hulk was inanimate and silent.

She worked away all morning, cleaning the inside of the car and the rest of the vehicle's bulk, until it shone. But she didn't sing again.

In some ways, she wasn't sorry their clinch had been interrupted. The last thing she needed was another baby right now. She'd found a copy of Marie Stopes' book, *'Married Love'* in the glove compartment of Cassandra's car, while she was cleaning, and had read it from cover to cover between bouts of feverish polishing. Her mind was spinning with the implications of what she'd read. No wonder the newspapers were making such a fuss about it. To talk publicly of such intimate things - to write them down in black and white! Katy was shocked and fascinated in equal measure. To know she wasn't the only woman in the world who didn't want to be constantly breeding babies was a revelation. And, having lost Florence so young, she couldn't bear to lose another and break her heart all over again. From now on, she'd keep a close eye on the calendar and make sure Jem withdrew at the right time at her fertile time of the month. Katy felt emancipated by this knowledge. She longed to discuss it with Cass, after all, she must have read it too. Were Cass and Doug already as close as that?

As if she'd conjured her up, Cassandra strolled into the barn, her long legs reaching Katy's side before she could safely stow the book back in its discreet compartment. She felt as if her hands were burning when Cassandra met her guilty look.

"Don't be embarrassed, Katy. Very good book that. I thought I might as well mug up on the delicate subject before I get wed. The car seemed the best place to hide it from Mother. If you ask me, it's about time we women took charge of the whole reproduction thing."

"Oh, Cass, I didn't mean to steal it or anything,

but the title caught my eye and, to be honest, I've not been able to tear myself away from it since!"

Cassandra laughed. "I was just the same. It's a real eye-opener alright. And, quite frankly, Katy, there's more to both of us than being brood mares, isn't there?"

"Exactly what I was thinking. And, between you and me, I'm racking my brains as to how I can earn a living, with Jem the way he is, and if I was expecting again, it would be impossible. As it is, no-one wants to employ a married woman. His pride is hurt that he can't get back to his old job and I can't help that, but we must find a way somehow."

"Yes, that's why I came to find you. No joy on the house front, I'm afraid. Mother won't hear of it. Hasn't let go of your little fracas with Charles. You'd think it was water under the bridge by now but she hasn't forgotten or, I'm sorry to say, forgiven."

Katy turned away so Cassandra wouldn't see the tears that sprang into her eyes so quickly these days. It was ridiculous and she hated her own weakness. But what a disappointment! Only now did she realise how much hope and confidence she'd placed in Cassandra to come up trumps with a cottage. Katy rubbed the already shiny chassis with more vigour than it warranted, keeping her face averted until she felt more in control of its waywardness. A waft of smoke from Cassandra's familiar Woodbine cigarette made her turn to look at her friend.

"I'm so sorry, about it, Katy. Mother wants everything to stay the same, especially the pecking order. All this change terrifies her but she's going to have to get used to it."

Katy nodded, unsure of her ground.

Cassandra looked thoughtful, puffing away on her fag and lounging against the polished body of her car, one knee bent up like a stork. "I've got an idea, Katy. You won't like it, but you could look on it as a temporary solution, perhaps."

"Oh?"

Cassandra threw her stub on to the earth floor and ground out its glow with the toe of her boot.

"How about you working for me as my personal maid?"

Cassandra held her hand up for silence, when Katy opened her mouth to protest.

"Hear me out, please. I know it's not exactly your vocation in life; I expect you'd rather be my chauffeur! But, I'm afraid, I simply can't think of anything else. You would have a wage again but you'd have to live in the manor house, in the servants quarters, and keep well out of Mother's way."

"But Cassandra, I'd never see Jem then!"

"Oh, come on, Katy. He's not that far away. You'd have time off and no expenses. You could save enough to rent a place of your own quite quickly."

Katy shook her head. So many thoughts were competing for her attention inside it.

Cassandra carried on, "Look, you don't have to decide about it now, but I'll say two more things that might persuade you. One: I can't think of anyone else I'd rather have to help me get ready to be a bride, and two: I'm going to America in a few weeks, and you would be coming with me. Don't you fancy another adventure?"

"America? Me?" Katy said, unknowingly echoing Lady Amelia's response to the same invitation, issued only the night before.

"Yes, America, Katy. Lord knows, it's going to take some skilled artistry to help me look the part for Douglas's family and, to be honest, I'm terrified of meeting them and not being able to come up to snuff."

"You're frightened of them? I can't imagine you being scared of anyone," Katy said.

"Well, I can assure you that I am. They must be horrified that Douglas is marrying some obscure Brit who lives buried in the countryside. From what he's told me, they are sticklers for etiquette in Boston."

If Katy's mind was confused before, it was now

boggling at thoughts of oceans and Bostonian society. All the sentiments she'd just read about married love were receding fast at the heady prospect of travel.

"I, I don't know what to say, Cassandra. I need to speak to Jem about it."

"Of course you do, I quite understand, but don't take too long." And Cassandra strode off, smiling.

America! Going on an ocean liner! Getting a wage again! Hmm, but living up in the garret at the manor house under Lady Amelia's nose wouldn't be so exciting. But it wouldn't be for long. Oh, what would Jem say? Could he go with them? Be a valet for Doug? But Douglas would have his own servants, if they did it that way in Boston. *Boston!* And how could Jem serve anyone one-handed?

Katy climbed in to the car and shoved the illicit book inside the glove compartment, making sure it was covered up with one of Cassandra's long scarves. She shut the little door and let her reeling head rest against the red leather seat. She shut her eyes. Visions of huge boats surrounded by a limitless ocean floated across her mind. She'd crossed the channel in a little ferry on her way to and from France in the war but a whole vast stretch of the Atlantic?

It was everything she'd ever hoped for. At last she'd be escaping the prison her life had become, and the world wouldn't be at loggerheads like the last time she'd left home. This time she'd be travelling for a happy reason, without her having to witness mass murder and clean up after all that human slaughter. She'd be seeing a bit of the world, thousands of miles away from Cheadle, just like she'd always craved.

Jem would come round, wouldn't he?

CHAPTER SEVEN

Bloody car; bloody father-in-law; bloody war; bloody *hell*! Jem strode up the hill in the brilliant, but cold, January sunshine. His wide strides brought him to the summit in record time. Too restless to admire the view, he carried on walking until he found the Great Ridge path, chalk-white and heading north. He marched along its straight line for a couple of hours, as fast as he could, to escape the thoughts that circled fruitlessly around his weary brain. The north wind whipped across the downlands and he relished its icy blast. Any sensation was welcome other than the burning, frustrated desire for his own wife that powered his legs.

How could he have survived that hellfire in the trenches and end up unwanted and redundant like this? What was he to do with his life? He'd always worked the soil, dug it, watered it, sifted it and planted it. Nothing, apart from satisfying his love for Katy, gave him more pleasure than watching a seed grow and flourish and be harvested. Good God, was it so much to ask?

He broke into a run and sprinted until he was out of breath and giddy. Jem ran his hand through his thatch of chestnut hair and screwed his brown eyes up against the glare of the bright winter sun. His heart pounded with the effort of running, making the blood thump through his young body. He closed his eyes, tired from lack of sleep after turning and tossing in the makeshift double bed at the West Lodge, and felt the wind scarring his eyelids with the astringent arctic air.

Snow, he could smell snow.

Jem let out a yell. He shouted into the wind all the swear words he'd learnt from other soldiers. It took a while, he'd learnt a few.

Images of men he'd befriended and lost flashed across his mind. Young cheeky Davey Pringle, the cockney who couldn't obey a rule, even if he'd tried. Tom Anderson, as obedient as Davey was a rebel, meek as a lamb and full of unwritten poetry; shot through the forehead on his first day at the Front. All that waste, all that blood!

What had it been for? Both sets of parents - Bert and Agnes; George and Mary - they still had to scratch about to put enough food on the table for their families. The manor was unchanged. Sir Robert and Lady Amelia were still lording it over the rest of them. What right had they to live in that fucking great mansion when he and Katy - and God knows she'd worked as hard as any man during that Godforsaken war - were bunked up with the Beagles in the tiny lodge house that guarded their posh, locked gate?

His breath steadied, Jem turned back and headed for home, before the end of the short winter's day nibbled at his heels. The sun slipped silently behind heavy clouds and the sky darkened, ready to spew something vile at him. He must have walked miles without thinking about it, he reckoned. Looking about him for the first time, Jem became aware that the landscape was entirely unfamiliar and he'd come further than ever before. He pulled up the collar of his ex-army coat, grateful for its weight and the warmth of the scratchy wool. He shoved the empty sleeve deeper in his left pocket to block off the draught that whistled up to the ever-sensitive stump at his elbow. A thin rumble of thunder rattled in the distance as a flinty snowflake grazed his cheek. He'd better step on it. Spending the night stranded on a snowbound hill, miles from home, wouldn't resolve anything.

Good job he'd stuck to the well-defined Great Ridge that marched northwards in an unbending, easy-to-follow line. Its pale gravel helped him to see ahead, as the twilight arrived with alarming speed. More snowflakes licked his face and he lengthened his stride to his maximum stretch. He supposed he should be grateful for two working legs. He was grateful, he *was*. Hurried on by the north wind pushing him home, Jem pictured Katy waiting for him; getting anxious that he was still out.

Katy. The woman he'd always loved and *she loved him back*. With every pounding step of his boots he felt new energy seeping up his legs. Strong legs, yes, and his heart full of love and pumping him along. He broke into another run, longing to see her sooner, hold her in his arms, tell her how much he loved her. What a fool he'd been! Moping and wasting time. They had their whole lives ahead of them. They'd work something out. He'd get an artificial limb and learn to use it. Why let the bastards win? Time to fight back. Time to fight for their future.

It was hard to see where to turn off the ridge and descend to the lodge. Night had fallen fast and the surrounding fields were now as white as the track, where the snow had fallen on the frozen ground. Jem looked about. He couldn't get his bearings. Had he overshot? Suddenly panicky, he halted his march. The chalky whiteness of the path was no use when everything else was also monochrome and there was neither sun nor moon penetrating the storm clouds. Thunder rippled across the hills again. Louder and closer this time.

Jem was afraid to leave the straight path and plunge into the woods. He'd left it too long, walked too far. How stupid was that? Katy would be frantic. He could make a bivouac and sit it out, he supposed. No, that wouldn't be fair on her and set all sorts of embarrassing alarm bells ringing. He knew the estate like the back of his hand. Come on, think, man!

Right, the estate was bounded by a Cotswold stone wall, wasn't it? Jem picked up a stick and held it out to his left. It wasn't easy without a left hand and holding it across his body shortened it considerably, but the boundary wall would be on that side and the stick might just hit it. He kept on walking, stumbling every now and then in the pitch blackness. He could time it too - of course! If he walked too long, he'd be bound to overshoot but without a watch, how would he know how long he'd been?

A flash of sheet lightning lit up the sky,

reminding Jem of the flash of the cannons he never wanted to see again. Despite the freezing temperature, beads of sweat broke out under his hairline and tickled his brow. Would he ever forget that rumble of artillery? Unwelcome memory though that was, the illumination briefly picked out the line of trees to his left, and beyond them, a stone wall. The estate boundary! Thank God.

Emboldened, Jem strode on, leaving the main path and striking out towards where he'd seen the wall. Amongst the tall oak and ash trees, in the hush of the snow and leaves at his feet, he had only his memory of that one image and his homing instinct to guide him. After a quarter of an hour of heart-thumping suspense, his staff hit stone. He'd made it! He let the stick rattle against the masonry until his arm ached. He bumped along the boundary, ignoring the twigs that clutched at his face and coat and the occasional root that tried to trip him up.

Eventually the bulk of the manor house cast a shadow against the white expanse of the estate lawns he used to trim, and a friendly yellow light glowed from the casement windows. Jem's stomach grumbled, reminding him that he hadn't eaten all day, and food was waiting in the refuge of West Lodge, now so near.

All the adrenaline that had fuelled his descent drained away and he felt exhausted. Tears welled up in his eyes. Tears of gratitude for all that waited for him a few hundred yards away. In that moment, he resolved not to complain anymore but to look forward and love his Katy with a heart now so brimful, he thought it might burst.

He threw away his stick with a light laugh and dashed his hand across his eyes. Jem ran the last hundred yards. He couldn't wait to see Katy. She'd be worried sick.

Jem tumbled in through the lodge door. There they all were. Every big-hearted member of the Beagle family. He'd come to love each one. They'd been so kind to him, taking him in and putting a roof over his head and all he'd done in return was to moan about it. Never again.

"Jem!" Katy cried, and ran to him.

He enfolded her with his arm, crushing her to his chest. Snowflakes tumbled off his shoulders and melted onto the flagstone floor.

"Good God, Jem, where have you been?" Bert said.

"Honestly, Jem, we thought you were stranded in the snow somewhere," Agnes said.

Katy just clung to him. For a moment, Jem was too choked to speak.

Then he released his wife and shook off his coat.

"You're covered in snow!" Agnes said. "Oh, for goodness sake, lad, don't shake it off in here. Come into the scullery and we'll hang your coat over the sink."

Smiling at Katy, Jem followed his mother-in-law to the lean-to at the back of the cottage.

"Give it here, you daft man," she said.

Katy had followed them in. Jem was surprised not to receive a tongue lashing. In fact, now he'd collected himself and the warmth of the little house was unfreezing his brain, he realised she was unnaturally quiet.

"Oh, Jem, we've been that worried about you," Agnes said, then looked at them with an odd, sideways look, and added, "I'll go and serve supper then, now you've finally turned up. She shut the door behind her, leaving them alone.

Jem broke the silence first. "Katy, I'm sorry if I worried you all. I set off up Great Ridge after, after we, you know, in the barn."

Katy nodded, her wonderful eyes never leaving his face but why was he not on the receiving end of a scold? Perhaps she'd been more worried than he thought.

"Katy, I, well, I walked for miles and do you know, it did me good. I got to thinking about things. And when the snow and the thunder came, I didn't know where the hell I was, but, getting scared like that, it made me realise how lucky I am. I was that glad to come home, my dear, and glad of all we've got. And, Katy, I don't know how I'm going to do it, but I've made up my mind to stop

60

complaining about my arm and get on with things. You can get artificial ones now and I'm going to see about it. Then I can get a job, and we'll get a place of our own somewhere - it doesn't have to be on the estate, does it? I'm going to make it work, Katy, my love, I promise. I must have survived for a reason, and I'm not going to waste another second!"

He opened his arm wide again and went to embrace her, longing to kiss those full red lips and feel the aliveness of her.

But, instead of welcoming him, Katy took a step back. A worm of doubt crawled into the pit of his stomach. He'd known something was up, the minute he'd laid eyes on her. And why had Agnes left them alone like this? They'd all been worried about him being out in the winter storm so why wasn't she force-feeding him hot stew, like she normally did?

Jem's arm fell to his side and his heart slid down to his boots.

"What is it, Katy? What's happened?"

Katy had never looked more beautiful. A plump rosebud of a girl she'd been when they'd married but now her fine bone structure set off those violet eyes to perfection. And solemn they looked too. Had someone died?

Katy cleared her throat. Never a good sign.

"Jem, I do have something to tell you," she began.

His heart fluttered upwards again.

"You're not? Are you with child again? Oh, Katy, that would be so wonderful!"

Katy flushed pink and Jem's heart soared. He reached out for her again but she went as stiff as a board.

"No, Jem, I'm not pregnant."

The bald statement deflated him as quickly as his hopes had risen.

"Katy, is someone ill, or, or worse?"

"No, Jem. I'm sorry, I'm not doing this very well. No, no-one has died or anything bad. It's just that, um, oh, dear, I might as well just come out with it."

"I wish you would!"

"Right. Cassandra has offered me a job. As her personal maid."

"But that's lovely! Why are you so serious about it?"

"I'm glad you're pleased, Jem," Katy looked relieved and said, more lightly, "but it does mean I'll have to live at the manor house."

"Oh, I see. That's not so good."

"And that's not all." A little tremor of excitement betrayed Katy, as she continued, in a rush, "And we're going to America. Cassandra has to meet Douglas's family, the Flintocks, you see. They live in Boston and we're to sail there at Eastertime. Cassandra said she'd rather have me than anyone else to help her and I was so flattered, Jem. You know how I've longed to travel all my life and this is my big chance!"

All the warmth of being indoors deserted Jem. He might as well still be in that bitter wind up on the hills.

"How long for?" was all he could say.

"I'm not sure. I didn't think to ask, to be honest. Oh, Jem, say you'll let me go! It'll mean a proper wage again too and I'll save it all up and when I come home, we can rent somewhere of our own. So you see, it'll all be for us, really."

And finally, she kissed him.

CHAPTER EIGHT

Katy surveyed the tiny room she'd been allocated by a disgruntled and extremely taciturn Mrs Andrews on the top floor of Cheadle Manor. It was bare, with not even a rag-rug on the floorboards - and they were rough - she'd have to watch out for splinters in her feet. Dust-motes danced in the feeble sunbeam struggling to find its way in through the small dormer window, even though there were no curtains to impede it. She sat on the metal-framed single bed. A spring broke and the mattress sagged into a defeated sigh. No wardrobe, but there were a few hangers dangling from a hook on the back of the door. A small bedside cabinet, obviously a cast-off from downstairs, bore a candlestick almost completely covered by contorted wax in grotesque shapes.

She crossed the short distance from the door to the chest of drawers and opened it. A moth flew out and tickled her nose. She swatted it away, reminding herself that she wouldn't be here for long, and at least she was a good distance away from Lady Amelia's much grander quarters. It was a comfort too that she'd been appointed directly by the daughter of the house, not the austere housekeeper. Mrs Andrews's reaction to her return to the manor had chilled her to the bone in its frozen disdain. She hadn't been surprised to find no creature comforts to welcome her in her new quarters.

Katy went to the window and opened it. The air that streamed in was cold, but she welcomed the oxygen cutting through the stale air. A basin and pitcher stood on the chest of drawers and there was a thin, but freshly laundered white towel, hanging on a clothes horse beside it. While she had the leisure to do it, she might as well fetch some water and give the whole room a good going over.

Katy let her bundle of clothes drop onto the bed. They were tied up in a sheet, a present from her mother. She could see the West Lodge, if she stood on tiptoe, from the garret window. It was both comforting to see her childhood home but also a reminder that she hadn't come very far. Well, that was about to change. It was a pity that Jem had taken it so badly, but it couldn't be helped. If they were going to make any progress in their lives, they must each take risks and opportunities as they came along, and he'd just have to lump it, like her.

There was a communal bathroom at the end of the long corridor outside and she took the jug and filled it with some water. It was barely tepid. No long baths at the end of a long working day, then. No matter.

She'd brought some rags for the purpose and set to scrubbing out her new bedroom with her enthusiasm undimmed. She started with the dirty glass in the windows. It was surprising how much more cheerful the little room looked with the sun shining through the clean panes. Katy wiped down all the furniture and then knelt down to tackle the floorboards with the rest of the water. She'd got halfway, when there was a knock on the door. Slinging her filthy rag into the basin of grey water, she got up and opened the door, to find Cassandra lounging against the architrave.

"Everything alright, Katy? Have you got all you need?"

"Yes, it's fine, thanks. Come in, won't you?"

"Thanks. I've got you a moving-in present," Cassandra said.

"Really? That's kind; what is it?"

"It's a poster. Thought you might like to pin it on the wall," Cassandra said, holding out a roll of paper tied up with a velvet ribbon in a deep violet shade.

"What's it of?" Katy said, holding out her hand.

"Open it, and see," Cassandra smiled.

Katy pulled at the ribbon, and made a mental note to keep it for her hair, though it was now not long enough to tie up, since she'd cut it during the war. She unrolled the stiff paper and gasped in delight. It was a picture of an ocean liner ploughing through turquoise waters, carving out white surf with its prow. Well-dressed passengers strolled about on deck. Others, equally colourful, were playing croquet or sunning themselves on stripy deckchairs. A calm sea encircled the ship, looking benign and never-ending.

"Oh, Cassandra. How thoughtful. I love it! I shall pin it up opposite my bed, so it's the last thing I see before I go to sleep and the first thing I'll look at in the morning. Thank you," Katy said, smiling.

"No problem. Lord, I hope you'll be comfortable in here. It's a bit Spartan, isn't it?" Cassandra said, as her eyes flitted about the room behind Katy.

"Have you forgotten our quarters at Étaples? You might have had the luxury of a Nissen hut, but me and Ariadne had to rough it in a tent for a couple of years. This is a palace compared to that and, at Mum's, Jem and I only had a bedroom half this size, with a thin curtain between us and Daisy and Jack. I shall be fine, I can assure you."

"Good. Glad you're settled. I'll leave you to it. Do you think you could commence duties before dinner tonight and somehow make me a tad more glamorous? About six o'clock? You know which is my bedroom, don't you?"

"I should do by now, Cassandra. I've been working here since I was thirteen!"

Cassandra laughed, and said, "See you later then. Glad to have you aboard."

She shut the door behind her. Katy smoothed out the poster and, with a couple of drawing pins she found in the bedside cabinet, obviously left behind by some previous servant, she pinned it up opposite her bed, next to the window. It livened up the drab room no end. She scrubbed the remaining bit of floor and hummed *"Pack Up Your Troubles In Your Old Kit Bag"*.

After the exertions of her clean-up operation and putting her few things away, Katy laid out on the bed for a rest. It was probably the last chance she'd get, now she had a job again. She stared at the poster of the ship sailing to America and tried, unsuccessfully, to quell both the excited butterflies in her stomach and the prick of her guilty conscience about deserting Jem. It wasn't an easy balance to strike.

Maisie, the timid housemaid, delivered an unwelcome package at four o'clock. Her new uniform was exactly the same as the one she had worn before she'd been sacked by Lady Amelia, all those years ago, for stealing up to Cassandra's bedroom and borrowing one of her gowns. And, of course, kissing Charles Smythe. Poor sod. He was dead now. Like so many others.

Katy dragged on the hated uniform. It was too big and she drew the waistband of the white pinny tight around the saggy black dress. It gathered in unbecoming bunches at her waist. Too bad. She didn't care what anyone thought. If Jem loved her when she was naked, she didn't give a stuff about anybody else. She was missing him already and wondered how soon she could sneak away to visit him. He'd moved back to his parents' house at East Lodge, next to the manor gardens, down in the valley near Lower Cheadle. Oh, dear, if she was missing him before one day was out and he was only across the way, how on earth was she going to cope for several weeks on the other side of the world? It didn't bear thinking about.

There was a small, spotted mirror above the chest of drawers. Katy stood before it and pinned her unbecoming frilly cap on her head. How stupid it was! All that fiddly ironing. It was nothing but a complete waste of time. Still, if she wanted a wage, she must put up with it. She wondered what the time was. She could do with some sort of timepiece in this room; then she remembered there was a big clock on the wall at the top of the servants' stairs. Of course there was, the Smythes would make sure they got their money's worth from the staff. No timewasters allowed.

Katy walked softly along the corridor and

checked the time. The plain round clock-face said it was a quarter to six. Better go down then. She felt more nervous than she'd expected. What with being a married woman, having been a mother, and an ambulance mechanic in another country, she didn't think she'd be worried about bumping into an old harridan like Lady Amelia. But she was, she was terrified, now it came to it.

She reached the galleried landing on the next floor down and turned left for Cassandra's room, very relieved to escape an awkward collision with the lady of the house. Lady Amelia and Sir Robert's suite of rooms were, fortunately, on the right hand side of the grand staircase.

Katy knocked on Cassandra's door.

"Come!" Cassandra sounded different to her normal friendly, informal self. Imperious was the word that sprang to Katy's mind.

She entered the room. She had forgotten how huge it was and how richly furnished. The furniture, like that in the rest of the house, was heavy and Victorian, and the curtains were overblown and fussy. She dropped her critical gaze and tried to concentrate on her new employer.

Cassandra was frowning. "Hello, Katy. Listen, I'm not sure what to call you in this situation. It's a bit awkward. I mean, whilst we're alone in my bedroom, it's alright but then, if I call you Katy all the time, I might forget when we're in public. Do you get my drift?"

Katy nodded, waiting for instructions.

"Look, I know we're friends really, but I think, in these new circumstances, you'd better call me Miss Cassandra, like the other servants do, and I suppose, I'd better call you Phipps. Would that be too ghastly?"

"No, Miss Cassandra, I quite understand," Katy said, feeling sick to her stomach at the humiliation. "What would you like me to do?"

"Glad we've got that cleared up. War's over, after all. Right, could you fetch me my green dress from the wardrobe - the one with the sequins. Mother seems to think it suits me and we'd better keep her sweet and make an effort. If she sees me looking all spruced up, she might look more kindly on you."

"Does she, excuse me, um, Miss Cassandra, but do you mind me asking if she knows about my appointment?" Katy asked, fishing frantically in the enormous wardrobe for something green and shiny amongst the rainbow of dresses.

"Not yet, no, not just yet," Cassandra said, and turned her back.

CHAPTER NINE

Cassandra took a peek at herself in the ornate mirror in the hall, as she crossed its marble expanse. Katy had pinned her long, flyaway hair in a different style, and she rather liked it. She'd never mastered its brown wiriness. She was glad that they had got through that awkward first session in their new relationship. Glad, too, that Katy had risen to the occasion with grace and skill. Not being one to fuss for long over her appearance, Cassandra could see there were going to be genuine benefits to having her friend as a personal maid.

Squaring her shoulders, she walked into the dining room. Her parents were already there, waiting for dinner. Oh, dear, being late wouldn't help.

"Cassandra! Finally!" Lady Amelia never liked to wait for her food. "Andrews, you may advise Cook that dinner can now be served."

"Yes, ma'am," Andrews said, and Cassandra watched him melt silently away. That butler got creepier over the years but now wasn't the time to share that thought. Cassandra smiled at her mother and said, "Good evening, Mother. Sorry I'm a tad late. It's been a busy day."

"Care to talk about it?" Sir Robert said. "More estate business was it?"

"Yes, Father. I've finally got Hayes to get the barn doors mended. They've been hanging off their hinges forever. And we've drawn up a planting scheme for the arable fields."

She ignored the indrawn hiss from her mother's end of the long table.

"That's early, Cassandra. You are getting organised," said Sir Robert, between glugs of wine.

"Well, Father, the government are handing out generous subsidies for wheat, so we may as well capitalise on it. Imports are restricted because of the war, so they are encouraging farmers to grow enough to feed the hungry nation."

"That's all well and good, Cassandra, but we are not farmers and I do not wish to discuss crops at the dinner table." Lady Amelia had found her voice.

The arrival of the soup did nothing to quell her mother's disapproval. Cassandra sipped hers quietly. The last thing she needed tonight was a disagreement before she let her news out. It was tempting not to tell her mother about her latest appointment, but the chance of Lady Amelia surprising upon Katy without prior warning was a scenario too grim to contemplate.

Cassandra had never been a fan of Vichyssoisse, too much cream, but she drank enough to forestall comment. When Andrews came around with the soup tureen for seconds, she politely but firmly refused.

"No, thank you, Andrews, but tell Cook it was delicious," Cassandra said, and was rewarded with a gracious smile from her mother.

"I'm pleased to see you're enjoying your meal, Cassandra," said Lady Amelia, with an incline of her head. Her tiara caught the candlelight and sparkled softly.

With Andrews absent, fetching the second course, Cassandra seized the moment. "Mother, I know you set great store by a smart appearance and I've been sadly neglectful in that department lately, but I hope you will approve of a new appointment I've made to redress the situation."

"Oh? You never cease to surprise me, Cassandra. I thought you were far too busy wading around in muddy fields to give a thought to your attire," Lady Amelia said, looking interested at last. "And, I must say, I do like the way you've done your hair tonight."

"Yes, I'm pleased with the effect too. You see, I thought, with my American trip coming up and meeting all those Flintocks in Boston, I'd better smarten up a bit. We don't want them thinking we Brits are behind the times and old fashioned, do we?" Cassandra said brightly.

"No, indeed. I'm glad to hear you've given it some

thought. Ah, here comes the fish," and Lady Amelia concentrated on dissecting her trout.

Cassandra loathed the earthy taste of river trout and groaned inwardly. She ate the cucumber slices surrounding her portion before pulling the flesh of the fish apart and strewing it around her plate.

"Can't beat freshwater fish from our own river," Sir Robert said, beckoning to Andrews for more.

"So, I've engaged a personal maid," Cassandra said, hoping that slipping it in between soup and trout might be an advantage. When roast chicken swiftly followed, her mother's favourite, her confidence edged up another notch.

"Now, I do think that's a good idea, Cassandra. I thoroughly approve, and you're correct about making a good impression with your prospective in-laws, if you insist on pursuing your American scheme. May I suggest that you get this maid trained up to your liking before you meet the Flintocks? What's her name, and how did you find her? Is she a local girl?" Lady Amelia was smiling now and not just at the savoury chicken Andrews was serving.

"Yes, from the village," Cassandra said, remembering the heated reaction last time she called her Katherine Beagle and hoping that breaking it gently, in stages, might ease the news and that her mother wouldn't connect Katy to her married name, especially if she didn't mention it.

"Oh, yes? Wouldn't someone from London be more sophisticated and knowledgeable about the latest modes?"

Lady Amelia was tucking in nicely to her roast and Cassandra congratulated herself on her timing.

"I thought the most important thing to look for was her skills in that department and you said yourself that my hair is better arranged like this. She's a genius with that sort of thing," Cassandra forbore to add that Katy's real area of expertise lay under the bonnet of a car.

71

"Oh, well, I suppose she'll be cheap, and you can always engage someone else in time. By the way, I was thinking about your trousseau. If you still plan to embark on this voyage across the Atlantic, and don't think I approve of that idea because I'm saying this, but you should start to prepare your wardrobe for the event. I've heard," Lady Amelia coughed, "I've heard that passengers on these ocean liners dress rather well for dinner."

"Who've you been talking to, Mother?" Cassandra let out her breath with a smile.

"Mrs Ponsonby knows Lady Hatherington and apparently she went to New York on one of these ships before the war and told her all about it."

Three cheers for Mrs P! Cassandra never thought she'd find an ally in their neighbour. Dessert was consumed without a hitch, in a happy discussion about evening gowns, and Cassandra withdrew immediately afterwards to tell Katy the glad news that she was now official.

Katy responded to the bell within minutes, and stood, hesitating, on the threshold of Cassandra's bedroom.

"Come in, come in, Phipps," Cassandra said, relieved that Katy's new name was tripping so easily off her tongue and that her Mother hadn't made the connection to Katy through it. All the more reason to keep things on a formal footing. "Shut the door, please."

Katy shut the door and stood, mute and expectant. That uniform did nothing for her. Strange, how such a pretty girl could look suddenly drab.

"I'm having an early night, Phipps, I'm exhausted, so could you unpin my hair and fetch my nightgown?"

"Yes, Miss Cassandra," Katy said, obeying her command with speed and efficiency.

As the hair pins clattered onto her dressing table, Cassandra looked at Katy in her mirror, standing behind her, and said, "You're in the clear. I've told Mother that you're now my personal maid and it's all official. I'll stick to using your married name and, hopefully, she'll never realise it is you. So we can both breathe more easily."

Katy looked briefly back at Cassandra's reflection. Her new maid still looked a bit pinched and wan.

"I thought you'd be pleased about it, Phipps," Cassandra said, feeling a little irritated that her announcement hadn't been greeted with more enthusiasm. After all, she'd risked a major row to assign her this post.

"I am, Miss Cassandra, thank you. I'll do my best to serve you well," said her new personal maid, without a flicker of a smile.

Cassandra dismissed her, feeling genuinely let down by Katy's lacklustre response and sour face. She must remember that Katy was working class and not have such expectations of her. Perhaps it was unfair to expect a huge thank you for the appointment, when it wasn't the sort of work Katy wanted, but she was disappointed that her friend didn't appreciate the effort she'd gone to. War had levelled the differences out for a while but, now that life was returning to normal, it was just as well to preserve them and there was so much else to occupy her thoughts, she just didn't have enough room in her head to worry about it.

CHAPTER TEN

Katy's first reprieve came on Sunday afternoon. She'd been at the manor house for three days and so far, had avoided coming face to face with Lady Amelia, who'd become pre-occupied with her latest project of building a war memorial next to the church in Lower Cheadle. Katy was relieved that galvanising the local community to commemorate their war dead was keeping Lady Amelia away from the manor every day, because she was having enough trouble getting used to working for her two-faced daughter. Cassandra seemed to have been transformed into her mother overnight, once she'd taken her on as a personal maid, and completely reverted to the snob she'd been when both she and Katy had grown up under the same large roof, but in radically different circumstances. All the camaraderie of their time in France had evaporated the minute she'd donned that disgusting black dress.

The other servants hid behind spiteful smirks at her return to her former station too and whispered to each other when she joined them for meals. Mrs Andrews could barely bring herself to be civil at all and as Mr Andrews never countermanded his wife, there was no-one to protect her. Katy spent the minimum amount of time in their company and kept to her room, which had the added advantage of avoiding Lady Amelia as well.

Only the thought of boarding that ship to America kept her from running back to Jem and chucking the whole idea out. That was a once in a lifetime chance she couldn't bear to lose, so she kept her head down and her lips buttoned every time Cassandra called her 'Phipps'.

But by Sunday she'd had enough. Few things could be more satisfying than hanging up that wretched uniform and donning her own clothes again, if only for one afternoon. Katy didn't want to waste a minute of her precious time off but quickly chose her brightest dress to go and visit her husband. A brief glance in the little mirror told her that her new employment had stolen her bloom and she pinched her cheeks to pink them up, before grabbing her hat and, on silent tip-toe, descending the servants' stairs and into the back hall.

Mrs Biggs, the cook, nodded to her through the kitchen steam as she passed the doorway but, other than that, Katy escaped into the January afternoon unscathed. She wasted no time but walked, almost ran, all the way to the East Lodge down the hill towards Lower Cheadle.

The Phipps's Lodge mirrored West Lodge exactly, except that it was down in the dip of the river valley, whereas Katy's childhood home was windswept and facing west, up on the hill of Upper Cheadle. The cottage she and Jem had shared, before the war, had been even deeper down in the valley along the main road of Lower Cheadle and she'd hated living in the shadows with the hill looming over them, but she'd give anything to have her independent home back now.

She knocked on her in-laws' front door and tried to steady her ragged breathing. Oh, but it had felt good to run away from the big house. Mary Phipps, Jem's mother, opened the door. A waft of raw onion surrounded her and she had a knife in her hand.

"Oh, it's you, I suppose you'd better come in," Mary said.

Katy looked warily at the kitchen knife and followed her mother-in-law into the scullery.

"I'm putting a casserole together for supper," Mary said, scrunching her shoulders into resentful boards.

"Smells lovely," Katy said, and looked about for Jem.

"It's only a couple of rabbits but at least we always have plenty of vegetables from the gardens," Mary said, her back still between them.

"Yes, I'm sure it will be tasty. Your stews always are." Katy hoped the compliment would be welcome.

"It's not a stew, it's a casserole. There is a difference you know," Mary said, chopping carrots with enough force to cut wood.

"Sorry, casserole. I meant to say casserole," Katy said. How many minutes would be wasted on her mother-in-law's petty squabbling when it was her son she needed?

"I suppose you're looking for my Jem?"

Katy felt like saying 'he's not yours anymore, he's mine' but restricted her response to, "Yes, I would like to see him. It's my only afternoon off, you see, Mary."

"Hmm, he told me you had a job. I always thought that maids couldn't be married, being as how they have to live in, without their husbands. He's feeling quite in the lurch, you know. I don't think it's right, a married man having to come back and live with his parents."

Mary chopped the naked rabbit into chunks, splintering bone and cartilage with her sharp knife. Katy shivered involuntarily, thinking how like a human baby rabbits looked, once they'd been skinned.

"It's not for long, Mary. Just so's I can earn some money for a place of our own," Katy said, feeling more impatient with every second.

"No, not for long. I heard. Then you're off to America with Miss Cassandra! And what's our Jem going to do then?"

The rabbit flew from chopping board to pot and landed with a sizzling splat into the melted lard.

"Jem understands that I'm doing it for our future. It's the only work I can get and I'll only be away for a few weeks," Katy said, feeling as scorched as the rabbit.

"Well, it don't seem right to me. Not right at all," Mary said, tipping chopped onions and carrots into the pan and slamming down the cast-iron lid.

"I'm sorry you feel like that Mary, really I am, but I don't see what else I can do. Now, if you don't mind, can you tell me where Jem is?"

Katy could see that they could spar all afternoon with the mood that Mary was in, and she didn't have the patience to join in, or the luxury of time.

"And suppose I do mind? Our Jem's come home from the war, and don't think I'm not grateful for that, but it's no thanks to you. There he is, wounded with only half an arm on one side and what do you do? Stick by him through thick and thin? That's what the marriage vows say, after all. Oh, no! Not Katherine bloody Beagle. She swans off to the other side of the world!"

Mary stood, hands on hips and faced her daughter-in-law.

"I can't be doing with this!" Katy said. "Where's Jem?"

"In the gardens, God love him, with his father, trying to pretend he can do the work of ten men with one arm."

"Thank you!" Katy said, and headed straight out of the door. "I can see myself out."

At last she had the information she needed. What a lot of hot air and no time to waste on it either. Katy ran as fast as she could down the path to the walled gardens. In contrast to the East Lodge that stood forever in shadow in the lee of the hill, the productive gardens hugged the southerly slope of Cheadle Hill above it, and basked in sun whenever it shone, protected by the insulating stone walls. It was a blessed spot and rewarded George Phipps' skilled nurturing with bumper crops ahead of every season.

She should have looked there first, knowing that Jem loved this gentle sanctuary. Why on earth had she expected him to be with his sour mother? And there he was, just like old times, on his knees scratching away at some seed drills with a trowel. Seemed there were some jobs you could do single-handed. Katy stopped, panting after her run, and watched him before he knew she was there. The years rolled back to simpler times, before they were married, before they'd created dear Florence, before they'd witnessed the slaughter of a generation, and before she'd recognised what a treasure she had in him.

Jem sensed her gaze, as she'd known he would, and looked up. In the few seconds before his face broke into a smile, Jem looked old and pale. A lump slithered up into Katy's throat and her eyes pricked with tears. She smiled back through them and walked towards him, arms outstretched.

"Hello, love," she said, lifting her face to be kissed, as he stood up to greet her.

No kiss came. "You found me, then," he said, and wiped his soil-stained hand down his corduroy trousers.

Was she to be chastised by every bloody Phipps she saw, just for getting a job?

"Yes, I should have guessed you'd be here," Katy said.

"Oh? Have you been looking elsewhere then?"

Still he hung back from her body. She longed to press it next to his.

"I, I went to your mum's. She was cooking dinner. Rabbit stew you've got for later."

To hell with casseroles. Only difference was one was cooked on the hob and the other in the oven. Who cared?

"I see. Yes, I've been putting some time in here, with Dad. Just seeing what I can do, like, until I get sorted with an artificial arm," Jem said, not looking at her but at the trowel he was twirling round and round in his hand. It was tempting to hit him with it.

"Right. And how's it going? Are you managing alright? You looked just like your old self when I came through the gate just then," Katy said.

"Not too bad, as a matter of fact. Feels good to work the earth again. Just planting broad bean seeds. Bit late but we thought we'd try them for a late spring crop," Jem said, still not looking at her but longingly at the furrow he'd drawn into a perfect straight line.

"That's just wonderful, Jem, but could you leave it, just for this afternoon? I've only got three hours off and I've wasted nearly one of them already, trying to find you. I thought we might go for a walk, you know, up to the top of the hill, like we used to when we lived here, before the war," Katy said, swallowing down the rage that had replaced the lump in her throat.

Jem threw down the trowel sharp end first so it pierced the soil like a spear, ready and waiting to renew its work.

"If you like," he said, and finally looked at her.

His eyes, as brown as the loam beneath his feet, were sad and bruised, not soft and brimming with the love she normally saw in their depths.

She took his hand in hers, "Come then, my love, let's walk together, just like old times."

"My hand's all dirty Katy, you'll soil your best dress," Jem said.

So he had noticed what she was wearing then.

Wildly encouraged by this, Katy clasped his closer and said, "Nothing wrong with a bit of honest dirt, Jem, love," and tugged him away, through the gate in the wall and into the lane that climbed above the valley floor.

They walked silently together, retracing steps they had taken so many times before in their short married life. Was he too remembering that time with little Florence, on that sunny Sunday, just before she died? How she had gurgled in the river when Jem had dangled her little legs in the water. Water that Katy had wanted to drown in when she thought he was killed. Stop! Stop thinking about the past. Katy looked at Jem's profile and guessed he was struggling with similar memories.

She stopped and pulled him towards her. The scowl on Jem's face broke into a tentative smile. No-one was around; only the trees were watching them through their bare winter branches. Katy put both her arms around her husband's neck and pulled his face down on to hers. They kissed like new lovers; hot urgent kisses of discovery and parched longing.

There was a little dell on the other side of the river. In the spring it was covered in sweet smelling bluebells, followed in June by pungent ramson garlic. They'd used it as a trysting place when they were courting and as children, playing hide and seek. They ran to it now in silent harmony, like a pair of homing pigeons.

When they reached the secret glade, and it enfolded them in privacy, Jem said, "This is the nearest place we've got to a home, Katy. Will you let me love you, here? now?"

"Oh, Jem, yes, please! I've missed you so," Katy said, between kisses.

"Won't you be cold? That wind is still whipping across from the north," Jem said.

"I don't care if it's coming from bloody Siberia, just hold me, Jem, just hold me."

CHAPTER ELEVEN

Somehow winter relented into spring without Lady Amelia denouncing Katy and sacking her a second time. Perhaps it was the care Katy took with Cassandra's hair or the way she co-ordinated her outfits, but, other than fierce stares, Lady Amelia chose to ignore the identity of her daughter's new maid and Katy rarely saw her.

Mrs Andrews more than made up for it and Katy had a hard time in the servant's quarters. The prestigious privileges normally afforded to a lady's maid were rigidly denied and cold looks greeted her over the servants' dining table. Some of the younger staff sneaked embarrassed smiles when Mrs Andrews wasn't looking but they were meagre crumbs of comfort and Katy didn't want to get them into trouble by encouraging them. She took refuge in reading her beloved books and dreaming about America up in her garret room, with the poster of the ocean liner the only ornament to brighten the bare walls. Sunday afternoons flew by and she and Jem had precious little time alone, once she had visited both sets of their parents and had done the necessary errands for her own needs.

With spring came the reward Katy had been longing for. Leaving Jem had been much harder than she'd anticipated and he couldn't hide his hurt resentment when they'd said goodbye. He kissed her passionately on their last afternoon together and she'd half decided to stay if he asked, but he was too generous a husband to make her give up the trip, which just made her love him more.

Her feelings were still mixed when she boarded the train for London but, as the downlands surrounding the two Cheadle villages receded, her mood lightened and excited butterflies fluttered in her stomach once more.

Katy didn't find London nearly so frightening this time around, but she could have done without having to dance attendance on Lady Amelia, as well as her daughter. Removed from Cheadle Manor, Lady Amelia had decided to acknowledge Katy's station as Cassandra's maid but with a cutting aloofness she reserved especially for her. Her own maid was elderly and grumbled a great deal, when not in her ladyship's presence, about the discomforts of travel. Miss Sprockett's dour mood infected them all and Katy found herself called upon to take up more and more of the old crotchet's duties.

Katy found the change of scene a great consolation to the extra work. She'd only passed through the capital before and her memories were a jumble of train stations and wartime formalities when she, and her friend, Ariadne Pennington, had joined the Women's Army Auxiliary Corps. They'd both been turned down by the Red Cross and the whole episode had passed in a blur of interviews, before they'd ended up in Aldershot at the WAAC training centre within twenty four hours of her arrival.

But at least she'd been treated as an equal there. Being bossed around by both ladies of the Smythe family had much the same effect as an old-fashioned corset; it was hard to breath or move easily without feeling crushed. Cassandra continued to be stand-offish in public but confessed, in the privacy of her bedroom, that buying a trousseau with her mother was nothing less than purgatory. At least Katy was spared going with them to the dressmaker's.

The Smythe's London house stood, white and elegant, in a large Georgian terrace, with its long casement windows overlooking Hyde Park, in Kensington. While Cassandra and Lady Amelia were out choosing silks and satins in the latest vogue, Katy escaped their Bayswater residence for as many minutes as she thought she could get away with, and walked amongst the daffodils now blooming in the leafy green space opposite.

The staff didn't appear to know about her background and Katy silently blessed Miss Sprockett for not disclosing it. As a result, they respected her position as Miss Cassandra's personal maid in a way that no-one at Cheadle Manor had done. It softened the blow of leaving Jem behind in Wiltshire and there was no denying her frisson of excitement about the forthcoming trip to Boston. Thank goodness Lady Amelia couldn't be persuaded to board a ship, however much Cassandra read to her about new safety improvements from the brochure. Miss Sprockett and her ladyship were destined to return to Cheadle Manor, whereas Katy and Cassandra would be getting back on the train and heading up to Liverpool to sail directly to Boston in a couple of weeks.

Katy, and she suspected Cassandra felt the same, could only be thankful that Lady Amelia wouldn't be accompanying them on the boat. It had been bad enough on the train from Salisbury to Waterloo. She'd sat a couple of carriages down, in second class with the mountain of baggage and a miserable Miss Sprockett, having settled mother and daughter in first class. It had taken that distance for Lady Amelia's stentorian tones not to be heard by the other travellers. Katy had blushed for shame at her employer's rudeness in addressing the porter and conductor. She could see Cassandra squirming too. Maybe that would be a lesson to her not to copy her mother and treat Katy as her inferior all the time. It still irked Katy that Cassandra continued to pull rank. War had many faces, most of which were hateful, but it had broken down some social barriers. Katy was disappointed Cassandra had retreated behind them again. She'd thought her former colleague and new boss was better than that.

Remembering their war experiences reminded Katy that Ariadne lived within striking distance of London. With time to kill, and no Mrs Andrews to ensure it was filled with unpleasant duties, Katy wrote to her war-time friend, inviting her to meet for tea, for old time's sake. With gratifying speed, Katy received a reply from Ariadne. It was addressed to her personally and when Hewitt, the London manservant, brought it all the way up to her attic room on a silver tray, Katy once more felt like a person in her own right, not just some chattel of the Smythe family.

Thanking Hewitt with, she hoped, a damn sight more grace than their mutual employer, Katy withdrew back into her tiny bedroom and ripped open the envelope. Ariadne wrote with as flowing and delicate a script as Katy would have expected. She said she'd be delighted to meet Katy again, and suggested the same Lyon's teashop as they had visited before. Katy was less delighted to return to the venue of her embarrassing meeting with Lionel White, who had been the vicar of Cheadle and had wanted to marry her, but he was now such a distant memory, she brushed the image of his well-chiselled face away, and dashed off an acceptance letter. Hewitt took her reply with a nod of deference. Katy almost felt like a lady herself and walked in the sunny park that afternoon with real pleasure. If Jem had been by her side, she would have been truly happy, strolling in the balmy spring air.

Katy sat on a bench facing the sun and lifted her face to the first warm rays of the year. The other people in the park looked hungry for sunshine too. The war and the epidemic of influenza over the last winter had left its mark on many of the faces walking past her. She wondered how many families amongst the crowd had been bereaved. Nannies anxiously watched their young charges, as they threw bread to the ducks in the pond. How lovely to see new life beginning again, though she was glad she'd had her monthly evidence that she wasn't carrying a child. Tearing herself away from Jem had made her forget everything in that Marie Stopes's sensible book about married love, and she'd grabbed every scant opportunity to be with him before her departure. Katy bought a postcard on the way home from the park to send to him, so he would feel part of her London adventure.

Katy felt really alarmed when Lady Amelia rang for her in the middle of the afternoon, half an hour after her return to the house. This had never happened before, and Katy had a sudden stab of panic that she might be denied the American trip after all. She wouldn't put it past the old battleaxe. Katy checked her uniform in the mirror, hating its old-fashioned long, gathered skirt and preposterous frilly cap and ran down the several flights of stairs to the drawing room to learn her fate.

Lady Amelia was pouring tea into a fine bone china cup. A tier of delicate sandwiches and little cakes stood to attention at her elbow. Katy's empty stomach growled.

"Ah, Phipps," Lady Amelia said, through lips that could have been sucking a lemon, instead of yet more sugary food. It was a wonder the woman wasn't the size of a house. She wasn't that far off.

"Yes, my lady," Katy curtsied in the way Mrs Andrews had taught her, and tried to smile.

"Miss Cassandra informs me, as she insists on your accompanying her to the United States, that you need a new uniform. Apparently the one you are wearing is out of date. It seems perfectly adequate to me, but I don't want anything out of order for this visit. Do you comprehend?"

Katy ground her teeth. She wasn't as stupid as the question.

"Yes, my lady," Katy said, her smile slipping.

"Good. You must present yourself to the dressmaker, Madame Fleurie, tomorrow morning at ten o'clock, after, of course, you have dressed Miss Cassandra and fulfilled any other duties. You must be prompt, so make sure anything else you have to do is done before you leave. I do not want you to be late. Hewitt will arrange for a hackney carriage to take you there."

"Yes, my lady," Katy said.

"Well, aren't you going to thank me, girl? You'll have a new outfit after all, which is more than you deserve!"

"Thank you, my lady," Katy said and couldn't resist adding, "Will that be all, my lady?"

"Yes, yes. You may go," and Katy heard Lady Amelia adding under her breath, "Goodness knows I don't want you here at all, but no-one listens to me anymore."

Katy went back upstairs, seething with anger. She supposed she should be excited about the prospect of a new uniform, but it felt like another nail in the coffin of servitude.

As it turned out, the material the dressmaker used was really good quality and the little Frenchwoman treated her with professional disinterest. Katy was measured from top to toe and was genuinely pleased when she saw the pattern that was going to be made up for her. A shorter skirt, well above the ankles, straight instead of gathered, and joy of joys, a neat little cap with just a little lace and no frills! She'd also be issued with an outdoors hat and coat to match. It might not be haute couture and it might still be black, but at least she'd look as if she belonged to the twentieth century when she reached Boston.

When she was dressing Cassandra for the theatre that evening, Cassandra asked her what she thought of her new outfit.

"It's really nice, thank you, Miss Cassandra."

"Madame Fleurie is very good. I'm glad you like it. I asked for a really modern style. Did she come up trumps?"

"Yes, it has a short, straight skirt and a small cap."

"That's a bit more like it, then. Bit like the WAAC uniform, hey?" Cassandra said, and smiled warmly at Katy.

Katy, mollified, asked Cassandra if she could have the afternoon off the next day, so that she could meet Ariadne for tea in the Lyon's teashop. If only her time was her own, to spend as she liked!

"What? Dear old Arry? Oh, Katy, I'd love to see her too!" Cassandra said, forgetting all formality.

Katy wished she'd kept her trap shut. She'd been so looking forward to telling Ariadne how betrayed she felt by Cassandra's reinstatement of the old hierarchy.

"Would you?" Katy said in a flat voice, hoping it

wouldn't be taken as encouragement.

"Tell you what! I'll come too! In a Lyon's teashop - on the corner of Oxford Street, did you say? What time?" Cassandra said.

"At three o'clock." Damn! She couldn't even let her have this one treat on her own!

"Oh, I'm lunching at Claridge's with some friends, but I could join you later?" Cassandra said, discarding her silk dressing-gown for Katy to pick up.

Katy could only nod her assent; she didn't trust her voice.

When Katy found her war-time friend in the teashop the next afternoon, she was struck by how differently Ariadne, who was every bit as posh as Cassandra, treated her, but then, she always had.

"Katy, darling," Ariadne said, with tears welling up in her china-blue eyes. "How perfectly divine to see you!"

Katy hugged Ariadne back with equal warmth and eyes just as full. You knew a real friend when you saw one. Ariadne had not regained her English rose looks or cut her hair short in the new style. She was still pale and drawn after nearly losing her life to influenza in Étaples, the previous autumn, before the Armistice.

"I see you haven't lost your love of big hats," laughed Katy.

"No, but they aren't very fashionable anymore. Look at that woman in that strange little cloche hat. You have to have short hair for that. It would suit you with your bob, though, Katy. Ah, my dear, how are you? It's so good to see you again."

"And you, Arry, and you," Katy said.

They ordered their tea and some fruitcake. Katy had promised herself that she'd gorge on the cakes while Lady Amelia wasn't breathing down her neck but, seeing her friend, she forgot it all. She had too many confidences to share to waste time on food.

"Oh, Ariadne, I've so much to tell you! But you

must tell me what you've been up to. Last time I saw you was at the homecoming party at Cheadle Manor and Captain Harry Mountford was with you. Have you seen him since? Oh, and how is your dear brother, Edward? Is he over his shell-shock?"

"One thing at a time, Katy! Yes, I have seen Harry again and we've, well, we've been walking out together, or limping, in his case," Ariadne said, with a smile so sad, it smote Katy's heart.

"Is his leg not mended then?" Katy said, as their tea arrived.

"I don't think it ever will be, Katy," Ariadne said, shaking her head. "He's seen several doctors but it was so badly wounded, one leg is shorter than the other. He's having some built up shoes made to level his posture."

"Is he in pain?" Katy said, sipping her scalding tea and burning her lip.

"If he is, he never complains."

"No, I can imagine that, from what Jem told me about him, and from meeting him before."

Ariadne nodded and smiled at Katy again. "Tell me, how is Jem?"

"Oh, where do I start?" Katy replied. "He's a bit mixed up. He tries not to complain, like Harry, but you can see he minds about his arm and not being able to do things. He's not been able to get a job back on the estate, even though his father is the head gardener. Oh, Ariadne, it makes me so angry that these young men have sacrificed so much and now they're just thrown on the rubbish heap!"

"I know, I know, and the poor wounded men just begging on the street. They're starving. It's outrageous."

"I sometimes think that if only the people who stayed safe at home knew what they'd been through; if they'd seen what we've seen, Arry," Katy shook her head. "And how's Edward?"

"Still suffering terribly. He shakes like a jelly during a thunderstorm. He stayed in a sanatorium for a while, but I don't know if it made any difference. Mother gets quite distressed at times but she's got all sorts of ideas to help him. I'm sure it's just a question of time. Harry says it's early days."

"You're right. So much has happened, I forget the war ended only last November. Seems like yesterday and yet longer, too. Time is a funny thing," Katy said.

"Oh? What's been happening then, Katy? Tell me some good news!" Ariadne said, slicing the fruit cake into little fingers.

"I'm off to America!"

"America! My goodness! How exciting, Katy. Is Jem going with you? You're not emigrating?"

"Sadly, no, although it's not a bad idea. When we went back to Cheadle, neither of us had a job. Cassandra Smythe took pity on me and has employed me as her personal maid. You know she's engaged to Douglas Flintock, an American officer that she met in Nevers, after she left Étaples?"

"Ah yes, I remember him from your welcome home party," Ariadne said, her teacup suspended in midair.

"That's right. He visited her at Cheadle Manor at Christmas, but then had to go home in the new year. They're getting married soon, so she's going over to meet his family in Boston and, as I'm her personal maid, I'm going along too."

"Oh, aren't you excited? That's quite an adventure!" Ariadne gulped her tea down and spluttered.

Katy sipped her own. She didn't want to talk about Cassandra behind her back but she was longing to tell someone sympathetic about her treatment.

"I am excited, yes, Arry, but, to tell the truth, I'd look forward to it more, if Cassandra wasn't being such a, well, such a prig!"

"Cass? A prig? She always struck me as being the opposite, when we worked together."

"Yes, she was then, but now, and I think her

awful mother has a lot to do with it, she's reverted to being a proper madam. She calls me 'Phipps' now, not Katy, and, sometimes, Ariadne, it feels like those years on the Front when we worked side by side, as equals, never happened."

"Oh, what a shame! Talk about one step forward and two back."

"Quite," and Katy sank her teeth into the fruitcake.

The doorbell tinkled and the subject of their conversation hailed them from the door.

"I think her ears must have been burning," Katy said, wishing she'd had longer to ask Ariadne her opinion about her new, awkward situation.

Cassandra strolled up. She was dressed to the nines in her new finery and looked very glamorous, with the flimsiest of chiffon scarves floating around her throat.

"Cass!" Ariadne stood up to kiss her. "My goodness, don't you look wonderful! I love your hair arranged like that! I wouldn't have recognised you without your jodhpurs and that coat is very smart."

"Thanks, Arry! I've been pushed and pummelled into shape ready for packing off to America. Did Katy tell you about our trip?"

Oh, so it's Katy again is it? Which way was the wind going to blow next? Katy stayed sitting down and didn't care if it wasn't good manners. She didn't feel particularly charitable after Cassandra had broken up her tête-a-tête with Ariadne.

"Do you want to order something?" Ariadne asked. "Our tea is quite cold now. Shall we get some fresh?"

"Good idea," Cassandra said, "Couldn't eat a thing after that enormous lunch at Claridge's, but I've talked too much and it's thirsty work," and she and Ariadne sat down.

Katy said, "We'd hardly begun to catch up before you arrived and interrupted us."

Ariadne spoke into the deadly silence, "So, Cass, I hear congratulations are in order?"

Cassandra gave Katy a filthy stare, before turning to Ariadne, with a smile pointed exclusively at her, "Yes, that's right, Arry."

Katy could have kicked her under the table. Her foot itched so much she could barely restrain it.

"And you two are off to America, to meet Douglas's family? How lovely for you *both*," Ariadne said.

Katy could have kissed her.

"I don't suppose Katy will have much to do with the Flintocks," Cassandra began.

Ariadne cut in, "But aren't you lucky, Cassandra, to have her support? You will be so glad to have an old friend with you when you meet your new in-laws. I know I can't think of anyone else I'd rather have if I had to go so far away and meet all those new people."

Cassandra cleared her throat but stayed silent.

Katy'd had enough. "That's just what you said yourself, Cass, when you asked me to work for you."

Still Cassandra stayed mute, but Ariadne was obviously determined to drive the point home. "And quite right too! There's no-one more loyal or clever than dear Katy, is there Cassandra?" And Ariadne looked straight at Cassandra with hot, angry blue eyes.

A slow stain crept up Cassandra's neck that no chiffon scarf could have disguised.

When it reached her cheeks, she said, "No, Ariadne."

Cassandra turned to acknowledge Katy at last and said, "I've been a bit of a twit, haven't I, Katy?"

There was another difficult silence until all Katy's anger erupted into a guffaw of laughter at Cassandra's puce face under her new hat.

Then they were all laughing so hard, they couldn't stop.

CHAPTER TWELVE

Cassandra drew her peacock blue fur-trimmed coat tight around her and watched Liverpool's dockside disappear in a swathe of sea mist. Other first class passengers gathered around her in family groups. Some waved to tiny dots of relatives on the quayside and then, when they could no longer be seen, drifted away from the rail and into the belly of the huge ship. Cassandra stayed looking longer than anyone, deep in thought. She was wrestling with the problem of etiquette for her new maid. She'd felt distinctly uncomfortable in that tatty little teashop when Ariadne's blue eyes had bored into her soul, but the thing was, neither of them knew how overbearing her mother was to her own daughter. Katy thought it was hard being a servant. Hah! She should try being a blood relation; the one and only remaining offspring.

And Cassandra found the new order of things confusing. She didn't really *know* how to treat her old friend. In some ways, life was easier before the war, when class distinctions were sharply divided and clear-cut. She was genuinely fond of Katy and had wanted to help her find independence again. Now all she seemed to have done was offend her old comrade-in-arms.

But that problem paled into insignificance when she thought about what kind of welcome she'd receive in Boston because, although Douglas had promised to write, all she'd had from him was that telegram. That one line, dashed off before he embarked for Boston. Nothing since. She was frantic. She'd written to him to say she was coming for a visit but had only had a reply, a very formal one in large flowing copperplate, from his mother, Selina Flintock. Mrs Flintock had issued a warm invitation, on behalf of her son, and Cassandra had seized upon it with desperation, turning the stiff bonded paper over and over, hunting for some word, any slight hint, from Douglas. But there had been nothing - not a thing but this formal summons from his mother.

Their ocean liner, *"The Lapland",* blasted its foghorn and its massive bulk lifted, as they left the wide river-mouth and hit the open sea. There had been few ships to choose from for their voyage, as most were in dry dock, being reconstructed after their service as troopships in the war. Cassandra wouldn't have cared if it had still been decked out with guns on its hulk, just so long as it crossed that expanse of water between her and Douglas. She welcomed the gust of wind that rippled through her scarf and crossed to the other side of the deck to look out towards the west. America. She caught a whiff of its exciting novelty, still an ocean away. Five short days and she'd see Douglas, and then, please God, her whole world would make sense again.

There were so many new things to adjust to. The one sure thing was her feeling for Douglas, even if she now doubted his for her. She'd never, ever believed in love at first sight and yet, she'd known how she felt the instant she had clapped eyes on him. She had always vowed that the usual strategic pairing, orchestrated by third parties, linking fortune to property, wasn't for her, but she'd never expected romance either. Women in her position got married, delivered heirs and then did what they liked and with whom they liked, as long as they were discreet, but she had never yet found any wife living that way who was happy. Her mother might disapprove of an American, but Cassandra knew she'd found the real thing in Douglas and she still held on to the feeling they'd shared. It had to be true, didn't it?

She'd brought her copy of 'Married Love' with her, just in case. She knew she wouldn't want to stop at kissing, if they had time alone together, and Douglas renewed his love. Why wait? Witnessing countless lives cut short by war made her want to live every minute of her own. She'd never waste another second. Three months at home, sorting out the estate with Hayes, had been penance enough. And she wanted to be sure of Douglas, even if that meant love before marriage. This passion she felt could not be denied for stupid reasons such as worrying what people might say. No, if Douglas still loved her, she'd let nothing come between them again, nothing.

She drew in another gulp of ozone-rich sea air. Soon the seagulls would return to land and just the vast Atlantic ocean would surround them. She wasn't frightened of the sea. To Cassandra, it felt like a watery embrace, whatever doom-laden tales her mother told her about the Titanic, and more importantly, it was an embrace that lifted and carried her to the one person she truly loved in this whole, sorry world. She was much more afraid of people, having witnessed man's inhumanity to man in these early, grisly years of the new century. So, if Douglas still loved her, she vowed to have fun at every opportunity.

Fun, and lots and lots of loving.

When the last seagull had wheeled back to port, and dusk hid the horizon, Cassandra went below deck to her cabin, asking her steward to send Katy to her. She supposed she must dress formally for dinner. It was tiresome. She'd rather hole up in her cabin and hide for the duration of the sea voyage but her mother's nagging voice told her that wouldn't do. Who knows whose tongues might wag? And besides which, she was hungry.

When Katy knocked and entered her cabin, Cassandra didn't like the look of her.

"How are you, Katy?" Cassandra said. She'd decided to drop the Phipps misnomer after Ariadne's disapproval. "Not got your sea legs yet?"

"Err, I was alright at first but now you can feel the swell of the ocean, I'm not feeling too clever," Katy said.

"Oh, dear, you do look a bit green about the gills. Listen, I've got to go down to the first class dining-room and show my face. See who's on board and make myself known. You never know if some sneaky hack from the newspapers is snooping about, ready to print lies about you unless you set the record straight. It's a bit dreary, but it's the done thing, but you don't have to. How about I call room service to bring you up a bit to eat here, in my cabin?"

"I couldn't do that! Could I?" Katy said, her hand to her mouth and looking anxious.

"Oh, my dear, you're really sea-sick, aren't you? Have you got a private bathroom in your quarters?"

Katy shook her head, "No, it's not bad, but we're four to a cabin with a shared bathroom down the corridor. The linen's clean and the bunks are pretty comfortable but you couldn't swing a cat in there."

Katy gave a wan smile.

"The steward told me to keep your eyes on the horizon," Cassandra said. "It's the only real cure for it. Have you got a porthole to look through?"

Again Katy shook her head in the negative.

"That settles it. Look out of my window. See the horizon? I know it's dark, but you can just make it out, now the moon is up. Just stare at it a minute or two and, Katy, dear, do sit down!"

Cassandra was rewarded with the first smile she'd seen on Katy's face for weeks, apart from that hysterical laughing session in Lyon's. She'd missed the warm glow of friendship. To hell with protocol. Ariadne was right. She did have a real friend in this working class country girl.

Cassandra laughed out loud at the way Katy stared fixedly at the distant point where the waves met the sky. Her hand was still clamped over her mouth. Cassandra fetched her bowl from the washstand.

"Here, have this close by, just for
emergencies."

It wasn't a minute too soon. Katy clutched the bowl and spewed into it.

"I'm so sorry," she spluttered.

Cassandra handed her a handkerchief. Katy smiled again, a wobbly one, but it reached her eyes, like it used to.

"Thank you, Cass," she said, and took it, wiping her streaming eyes and dabbing delicately at her mouth, as ladylike as any woman Cassandra had ever met. Daft old world.

She ordered a plate of plain cheese sandwiches and some tea from the steward for Katy, who recovered enough to arrange her hair and help her into one of her new, daringly straight evening dresses.

"How do I look?" Cassandra asked her maid.

"Very good. Green always does suit you," Katy said.

"It might not be the most diplomatic colour, if any of the other diners feel like you just did!" Cassandra said and let herself out into the corridor, feeling very alone.

Dinner was long, predictably fussy and attended by just the sort of vapid conversation she detested. The dining room was ornately furnished with fussy gilt chairs and heavy brocade curtains that swayed with the movement of the ship. The food was welcome, though, and she was relieved she didn't know any other passengers. The chatty old gentleman sitting next to her confirmed, at great and tedious length, that the most prestigious ships were still in dry dock after being used as troopships during the war and the other passengers were mostly emigrants, some of them of mixed race, looking for better times in the States. The latter remark was made far too loudly and Cassandra was aware of her fellow diners glaring at her neighbour, whose monologue continued, serene and unabated.

She was glad when it was over and she could retire to her cabin. A heavy drizzle had set in, so even the stroll on deck she'd promised herself lost its appeal. Katy was already there, waiting to help her undress and looking a little better. A half eaten plate of sandwiches stood silent testimony to her maid's Spartan repast. She dismissed her quickly and wished her a good night. Katy looked very doubtful about that prospect.

Cassandra was thankful to climb into bed and lose

herself in a fitful sleep, while her body adjusted to the constant motion of the boat. When she did succumb to slumber, she dreamt that, on her arrival in Boston, Douglas turned his back on her, and his family shooed her away with flapping hands.

CHAPTER THIRTEEN

Jem ripped open the letter. He hadn't expected to hear from Katy again before she reached America, and had resigned himself to re-reading her London postcards until he knew she was safely back on land on the other side of the Atlantic.

But it wasn't from Katy. It was from Harry Mountford, his wartime captain. Harry wrote that he had found a place where he was having treatment for his leg, some medical outfit in Roehampton, near Wandsworth, in London. Jem sat down with a bump when he read the next sentence. Harry reckoned they could fix him up with an artificial arm. This place was the business, he said. And it would all be free, Harry would make sure of that, courtesy of Jem's war record.

Wouldn't it be grand if he was whole again by the time Katy returned? Not completely whole, he'd never be that again, but mended. Oh, to be useful again! Jem read to the end of the short letter.

"So we could meet up at Waterloo Station, under the arch - you can't miss it - and take another train to Richmond. From there we can walk it - even me - now they've evened me up. Write back quickly and say if you can come, Jem, and we'll soon have you sorted. It would be good to see you again."

A grin spread across Jem's face from ear to ear. He read the letter again to make sure he hadn't dreamt it.

"Letter from Katy, is it?" George, his father, said, coming in from work and finding Jem in the dark little parlour of East Lodge.

"No, Dad," Jem said, and told him what Harry had written.

"Why, Jem, that's marvellous, it really is. You must write straight back and tell him you'll be on that train to London right away."

Jem nodded and rummaged in the cupboard for a pen and paper. His mother popped her head around the door to tell them supper was ready.

"What's all the fuss about?"

"I'm off to London, Mum! Captain Harry knows a place where I can get a new arm - you know a what-do-you-call it? Prosthetic. I must finish this reply and get it in the post. I'll have supper later."

"But, it'll be cold by then," Mary said.

"Leave him to it, Mary," George said. "Can't you see what this means to the lad?"

His parents went back into the kitchen, where the rest of their brood were more than ready to eat, judging by the noise.

"Sarah, John, Elizabeth! That will do! Where are your manners? Now, let's say grace, then we'll begin," George said, above the din.

Jem smiled as he passed them on his way out. His Dad insisted on this ritual every night. Jem wasn't sure he had any faith in God any more but Harry's letter had restored his belief in friendship.

A week later he was walking the five miles to the station, whistling a tune. Jem was glad he'd packed his things in his army knapsack, otherwise climbing on the train would have been tricky with one arm, if he'd had to carry a suitcase instead. He wriggled the knapsack off and slung it on the overhead rack. He never thought he'd be glad to leave Wiltshire again, but he couldn't wait to get away. It felt so good to be doing something; to have a sense of purpose again. He was looking forward to seeing Harry Mountford too. What a pal. He probably could have sorted himself out with getting to this hospital eventually, but it was bloody marvellous that Harry had beaten him to it. The sooner he was fixed up, the sooner he'd have a job again.

Travelling alone, without the army barking orders at him, was a liberation in itself. He looked at the other passengers in Third Class and got chatting to another young man who'd managed to survive the trenches, judging by his injured face. The one subject they didn't discuss was the war. It was enough to acknowledge that each had served time in Flanders without dwelling on the scars.

Waterloo station was the terminus, so he knew where to get off. The station looked huge to him and he felt confused in the large, chaotic building. The platform was crowded, and for a moment, Jem felt overwhelmed by the crush of people and the smell of coal smoke. Instinct drew him to the fresh air through the arch and, as soon as he reached it, he found his good arm being shaken so hard, he thought it might fall off.

"Jem! Good to see you, mate!"

Harry looked well and almost level. "See my boot? Look how they've raised it. Not quite there yet, but getting close. Come on, let's get the underground to Richmond. It's not far."

"Hello, Captain Mountford, sir," Jem said, returning the handshake.

"Oh, to hell with that. I'm Harry to you, Jem, always will be," said Harry, using his stick to point the way.

"Good to see you, Harry. Did you say underground?"

"Yes, of course. Got a problem with it?"

"Can't say as I fancy a train going under the ground, no." Jem said.

"You daft bugger! Oh well, it's just as easy to get a bus. You'll see a bit of London that way too. This way."

Harry seemed to know his way around and Jem was profoundly grateful they weren't going to travel through the bowels of the earth. Harry insisted they went on to the top deck of the double-decker which swayed alarmingly around the corners but afforded a grand view of London.

"What's that patch of green over there?" Jem asked, hungry for plant-filled spaces already, between the press of buildings crowding in on each other, as street after endless street criss-crossed each other in a bewildering matrix of bricks and mortar.

"Battersea Park. We're halfway there," Harry said.

Jem virtually slithered down the steep winding stairs of the bus when they lurched to their stop. He hoped Harry couldn't see how his knees shook as they stepped back on to the nice solid pavement and was astonished at how well Harry managed it with his lop-sided limp.

"Just a short walk down here, Jem, and you'll see Queen Mary's Hospital. It's rather a grand old pile and the chaps who work there - my goodness, they're skilled."

"So, how've you been keeping, then, Harry?" Jem asked, as they strolled along the busy street. He had to concentrate hard to hear Harry's replies against the traffic noise. How *could* people stand all this rushing about?

"Very well, thanks, Jem. I've, um, I've been seeing Katy's friend, Ariadne Pennington."

"Have you? Well, I'm blowed!"

"Yes, if it wasn't for you we'd never have met, but I got to know her at that welcome home party you had at Cheadle Manor, and we've been walking out ever since."

"That's wonderful news! Katy did say something about it, when she wrote to me from London, but it's good to hear the happy news from the horse's mouth," Jem said, and added, "Katy told me what a true friend Ariadne has been to her. You certainly get to know people during a fight."

"Don't you just!" Harry said, and clapped Jem on the back. "Here we are, Queen Mary's abode."

Jem couldn't believe his eyes. The hospital was the grandest place he'd ever seen, much bigger than Cheadle Manor, with a pillared staircase spreading out onto a vast lawn, and a huge Greek portico entrance behind it. If Harry hadn't been with him, he'd have been too intimidated to knock on the door. He needn't have worried. As they approached, other ex-servicemen came around the corner of the building and set up a game of football. White-aproned nurses laughed along with them, as the men used their crutches, as well as their wonky legs, to kick the ball about. Some blokes even used wheelchairs for support and careered about, shouting their heads off.

"They have to teach them how to use their new limbs, you see", Harry said.

A file of men walked past them in a crocodile with varying degrees of limps and wobbles.

"Look, these chaps don't use crutches anymore," and he tapped the leg of a passing man with his walking stick. He was answered with a hollow rap and a smile.

"Want to see it?" said the young man, not appearing to mind in the least.

"Yes, please," Jem said.

The man stepped out of line and lifted up his trouser leg to reveal a shapely, wooden calf strapped to his knee stump.

"Blimey," was all Jem could muster.

"Thanks for showing us," Harry said, and the man wandered off, walking almost normally.

"See what they can do?" Harry said. "You'll see. An arm is a cinch for these clever chaps, but we'd better get you checked in. The Matron is the very devil for signing forms."

Jem was shown to one of the nine hundred beds in the huge hospital. Sleeping in a large ward was very reminiscent of his army days, and he found he slipped back into the male banter as if he'd never been away. Harry had gone to kip at his London club but promised to pop in the next afternoon to see how Jem was getting on.

The hospital had an efficient production line in operation and fitted Jem with a wooden forearm within a week. He was measured and examined more times than he could count, from every angle of his stump. They explained about the phantom pains too - how it was where the nerve endings had been cut but still expected to serve his arm, right down to the fingertips, even though they were no longer there. Other amputees shared their experiences with him and Jem felt less alone than he had since the war ended. He felt nervous when it was his turn to have his false arm fitted and walked down the corridor to the fitting room with a thumping heart and an unreasonable level of expectation. Wood would not replace living flesh and he mustn't hope for a miracle, he told himself, but the night before, he'd fallen asleep picturing his coat sleeve full again, with a hand protruding from the cuff.

Jem waited in line, studying the shirt of the ex-soldier in front of him and averting his eyes from the hundreds of wooden legs and arms standing naked on the shelves next to him, trying not to remember how the originals had been separated from their host bodies. How bloodless these replacements looked, dead and stiff, a graveyard of limbs. His turn came and the fitter was brisk and business-like. He had to be, with a never-ending queue to serve. Jem held out what remained of his upper arm and tried not to wince as the man strapped on the prosthetic with leather straps. It felt too tight and very strange.

"Quite normal to feel odd to start with," the fitter said, with a brief smile. He showed him the ingenious metal claws on the index and middle fingers and how to hook objects with them, and told him it would soon stop chafing, once his stump had hardened.

He spent most of the next week at the rehabilitation centre in the grounds, where the nurses and physiotherapists taught him how to use his new arm. The first time he did the exercises, the part where it joined his skin dug in too much and he had to go back to the workshop and have it adjusted. Jem was fascinated at how skilful these carpenters were and the lengths they would go to in making sure a perfect fit was achieved.

Harry popped in every afternoon, and when he saw the new addition, was full of admiration.

"Now that's what I call clever. Look how they've curled up the two little fingers on steel hooks. Can you carry things with it?"

"Let me show you," Jem said, and picked up Harry's hat in his false hand. "I've been practising with the physios. We even had a tug of war yesterday."

"Bravo!" Harry said.

"The tricky bit is that you have no sensation - you know - the wooden fingers can't feel anything. It'll take some practice to get really good with it but already I can do twice as much as before," Jem said, as he narrowly missed knocking over his glass of water.

"Bloody marvellous," Harry said. "I think you deserve a pint. Do they let you out for good behaviour?"

Jem laughed. "I think I can sneak past Matron's office. No-one will miss us for an hour."

Jem stayed at the hospital in Roehampton for three weeks, until he could prove that he could use his arm without blacking anyone's eye or suffering from an infection where it rubbed his stump. He was sorry to head home again. Being with the other blokes had been a real tonic, and it had been especially heart-warming to see Harry again. It would be good to tell Katy she wasn't the only one seeing a bit of the world but the best bit about coming home would be finding a letter from America from her. If only Harry's letter had turned up a few weeks' earlier, they would have been in London at the same time, but it was no use regretting that now.

The train journey was uneventful going back and he walked the five miles from the station in record time. Sure enough, there was an envelope with his name on it on the parlour table. Much to his mother's annoyance, he read it before he did anything sensible, like wash or eat.

Katy wrote that she'd made it across the Atlantic. Now he could transfer his worries about her boat sinking to fretting that she'd meet some slick and rich American who would sweep her off her feet and keep her there. There was no hint of when they might return either. It was anyone's guess how long their trip would take. Katy sounded very excited about Boston.

Jem resigned himself to a long wait and resolved

to use the time to ensuring he was two-handed by the time she came back, whenever it might be.

Without the support and encouragement of the dedicated nurses at Roehampton, Jem struggled to get his artificial arm to behave itself. It was so frustrating trying to pick things up and then drop them, and his mother couldn't hide her despair when he broke her best teapot one warm April morning.

He took himself off for a walk to avoid another ear-bashing. He'd asked for his old job back, working as a gardener for his Dad, but George had already taken on his brother, John, and couldn't create an extra post without Cassandra's backing, as Sir Robert continued to dodge all decisions and Hayes claimed he didn't have the authority. He'd just have to bide his time.

He wandered into the barn, as he often did, to look at the old Sunbeam car that sat, like him, patiently waiting for Cassandra and Katy to return. There was no-one about, as Bert was busy with the blacksmith, who was paying his monthly visit to the stables. Jem climbed into the big car and sat in the driver's seat. He stroked the steering wheel with his good hand and lifted his wooden arm to rest on the wheel on the left hand side. The muscles in his biceps were getting stronger every day. He pushed the wooden limb down on to the wheel and hooked the steel loops around it. The gear stick and the brake were inside the car on the right-hand side of the driver's door.

An idea and a slow smile dawned in perfect unison.

CHAPTER FOURTEEN

"Oh, Cass, I'm so glad to see solid land at last," Katy said, as they finally approached the coast of America.

The roofs of Boston rose up from the water for some distance beyond the sea, on to a hill that dominated the city. Warehouses and busy dockyards stretched out along the quayside for as far as Cassandra could see at its edge.

Cassandra smiled at her, "Yes, you've had it rough, Katy, but we'll soon be there. I just hope Douglas is waiting for us at the dockside. Boston looks enormous. I'd never dreamt it would be so built up. It's bigger than Liverpool, more like the size of London. We'll never find our way through it without him."

The coastline stretched out in jagged wharves ahead of '*The Lapland*', whose prow reached hungrily for shore. It couldn't get there quickly enough for Cassandra, but Katy looked nothing less than desperate. Her maid looked razor thin under her new black coat and her big, violet eyes much too large for her face. She'd lost so much weight during the voyage, that her loose wedding ring had been lost over the side one day. They'd ventured out on deck to try and ease Katy's nausea but the choppy sea had pitched Katy against the rail, where she'd been sick again and the ring had slipped away into the tossing waves. Katy had been bereft.

Cassandra hoped she presented a more healthy picture, in her fur-edged coat and little feathered hat; one that Douglas would still admire. Now she was to meet him on his home turf, she felt more nervous than at any time in her life. Being presented at court was nothing to passing muster with his parents. After all, taking their son away from them was bound to prejudice them against her, assuming he still wanted to come.

As the big liner drew nearer and nearer the quayside, the butterflies in her stomach heaved up and down, like the waves which had undone Katy in mid-Atlantic. The docking procedure of the ship was laboriously slow but it gave Cassandra the chance to rake the wharf with her eyes.

It was Katy who spotted him first. Her calmer gaze had been drawn to Douglas's cream-coloured open-topped car. She grabbed Cassandra's arm and pointed to the tall young man lounging across its bonnet. Cassandra screwed up her hazel eyes against the glare of the sun glinting on the shiny motorcar and then opened them wide, when she saw Douglas stand to attention and start waving like fury.

Cassandra clutched at Katy in return, "I can see him! There he is!"

And she waved madly back, making the other passengers smile. He must want to see her, because there he was, waiting! Would this great whale ever come alongside?

"Look at the colour of the sea water, Cass. It's brown. I don't like the look of that," Katy said.

A middle-aged American man, wrapped up in a heavy, wool coat and smoking a pungent cigar, turned to them and said, "Haven't you heard about the molasses accident?"

Cassandra shook her head.

"Well, my dear, this whole North End harbour was covered in the stuff in January. Killed a lot of people too," he said.

"How did that happen?" Cassandra said, curious to know more, but annoyed she was distracted from watching Douglas get bigger and nearer.

"Great big tank of molasses syrup exploded, don't you know. Spilled all over the place and poured out in a huge sticky wave, taking everything in its path. Look at those buildings - reduced to match-sticks, some of 'em."

Now they were almost alongside the harbour wall, Cassandra could see the scene of devastation around the wharf's yard, but when the big ship bumped against the dock, she lost interest. She could see Douglas's eyes and they were fixed on her, and her alone. Forgetting all propriety, she blew him frantic kisses.

"I'll go and supervise our trunks with the porters," Katy said, "The sooner my feet touch dry land, the better."

"Wait, I'll come with you, Katy. We don't want to lose each other in the crowd," and Cassandra took one last, lingering look at her fiancé's grin, before joining the throng leaving the boat.

Cass laughed at the relief on Katy's face as her boots touched the concrete dock. Then Douglas was at her side and she forgot everyone else in the world.

"Hey, Cass, darling. You're looking mighty fine!" Douglas said, holding her at arm's length and studying her.

"Douglas! You're here," Cassandra wished she could have thought of a more original greeting but her brain had ceased to function.

"You bet I am. Nothing could have kept me away," Douglas said.

"But why didn't you write to me?" Cassandra couldn't help asking, hating the risk she was taking in harrying him already.

"Tell you later," Douglas said, and then laughed. "What happened to the jodhpurs, honey?"

"I thought I'd better look the part of your fiancée, Doug," Cassandra said.

"You'll outshine us all! Come on, let's get you in the car and I'll show you the sights of Boston, though I think I'm looking at the best one right now."

Cassandra laughed, her heart thudding with relief, and then, to cover her confusion, turned to Katy and introduced her.

"Doug, this is Katy. She's working as my personal maid on this trip but she's also a good friend and the best car mechanic who ever served in the WAAC."

Douglas didn't hesitate but shook Katy's hand warmly and said, "Pleased to meet you, Katy. You sound like quite a girl. Say, didn't I see you back in Wiltshire at that welcome home party at the manor?"

Katy replied with a wide smile, "That's right. Pleased to meet you again, sir. Yes, I live in Upper Cheadle too. At the West Lodge with my parents, since the war."

Cassandra could see that this was too much information for Douglas to digest all at once, so she said, "We'll soon be better acquainted but right now, I think we should get off this quay before I'm crushed to death with all these people."

"Yes, let's get out of here, girls," he said, opening the front passenger door for Cassandra.

Douglas supervised the porter strapping their numerous suitcases on the back of the car and settled Katy on the back seat with several more.

"You sure brought enough clothes for your trip, Cass," Douglas said, "I'm running out of straps to tie it all on."

"I've tried to cover all the options, Doug. I thought I'd bring a variety of outfits until I know how the Boston ladies dress."

Douglas, cranked the engine, then got behind the wheel and sat down next to her. He looked at her with his blue eyes full of laughter. Cassandra's stomach flipped over. It hadn't done that once on the long voyage, no matter how big the Atlantic waves had rolled.

"Don't tell me you haven't brought *any* pants or, as you would call 'em, trousers?" Douglas said, adjusting the choke and the oil pump with a smile.

Cassandra laughed back, "I brought two pairs and I wish I had them on now, I'd be so much more comfortable, but it isn't every day you meet your future mother-in-law. Oh, Doug, I'm so nervous!"

"Nervous of Mother? There's no need; she's dying to meet you," and Douglas revved up the engine as a warning to the other passengers milling about on the wharf. The throaty engine of the car roared into life and

Cassandra clutched at her dainty new hat as they lurched forwards into Boston.

"Have we far to drive, Doug?" Cassandra asked.

"No, it's only five minutes away but it's just as well I brought the motor with all this lumber."

Cassandra was surprised when they drove right into the centre of the city. The buildings were all very tall and the streets organised into straight lines. Most of the houses were built of brown brick and were at least six storeys high. The streets were wide and busy with a mixture of horse-drawn and motorised traffic. A tram shuttled past them; its bell ringing out in warning. The blocks of buildings cast shadows right across the street in the bright sunshine, making strong contrasts of light and shade. There were coloured people too, many more than she'd seen anywhere else and she caught different languages from passers-by on the sidewalk - snatches of Italian near the wharves - and in the city, she heard exchanges of slang in American accents so broad, she couldn't make out what they were saying. She was drinking it all in, thinking they would soon leave the city behind as they got nearer to Douglas's house, when he slowed down in a wide residential street, just like all the others. She'd expected the Flintocks to live out of town, in a house as large as Cheadle Manor. Douglas had been so unfazed by her affluent background when he'd visited at Christmas, she found it hard to hide her reaction, when they drew up outside a tall, brownstone terraced house in the middle of the city.

"Here we are, ladies. This is where I call home. Come in, come in. I'll get Gallagher, the manservant, to come and sort out this baggage. Unless, is there anything of a personal nature, you'd wish to have with you?" Douglas said, as he killed the engine.

Cassandra exchanged looks with Katy who looked as surprised as she felt at the modest appearance of Douglas's house, which was reassuring. Cassandra didn't think she was a snob and she knew Katy definitely wasn't.

At least she'd have her to talk it through with. She'd known that America would present challenges but she really hadn't envisaged Douglas's home being the first one. It might mean that his mother was less intimidating than her own, which wouldn't be hard.

"Come on, Cass! What are you waiting for?"

Cassandra suddenly became aware that Douglas had been holding out his hand to help her down.

"Sorry! Just taking it all in," she said and hopped down on to the pavement.

Katy followed her up the few steps to the big brown door, carrying Cassandra's vanity case. Everything seemed to be very brown. Even the sea in the harbour had been brown.

The hall was narrow, and Douglas showed them into a parlour on the right hand side. It wasn't a big room but was of good, square proportions and over-filled with expensive antique furniture. The wide bay window was curved, heavily dressed with net and framed by velvet curtains. Cassandra found it slightly claustrophobic, and the deep red walls crowded with paintings, added to the effect. She was convinced she'd knock over the spindly side tables at some point.

"Take a seat, Cassandra, Katy. I'll tell Mother you're here," Douglas said, still confident, still smiling.

When the door had closed behind him, Cassandra turned to Katy and said, "I'm surprised there's no butler to run and fetch his Mama. What do you think, Katy?"

"Well, I, suppose it's a bit like your London house, Cass," Katy said, voicing the same doubt as Cassandra felt.

"You're right! Of course it is. A town house, that's it," Cassandra said, and twitched at her immaculate new outfit. There was a mirror over the fireplace and she got up to check her appearance for the hundredth time that morning.

"You look wonderful, Cass. Stop worrying," Katy said.

111

Cassandra looked at Katy through her reflection in the glass and gave a nervous smile, then turned, as the door opened to reveal Mrs Flintock.

She could see immediately from whom Douglas had inherited his tall, slim frame. His mother was the same height as Cassandra and very elegant. Her clothes were beautiful but in the style popular before the war, with a nipped-in waist and a skirt that swept gracefully to the floor. It was a delicate shade of pale blue and Mrs Flintock's eyes were only a shade darker. She seemed to glide rather than walk towards Cassandra who, for a tiny moment, felt like running out of the room for some fresh air.

Mrs Flintock extended a white hand; diamonds sparkled on her wedding finger.

Her voice, when she unfroze the moment with it, was soft yet deep, with a strange vibrato tone that lent her Southern drawl musicality. Her accent was quite different to Douglas's clipped tones.

"How do you do, Cassandra. I'm so pleased to meet you. Please won't you sit down? You must be terribly tired from your journey." Mrs Flintock pronounced *'tired'* as if it had an extra vowel, which Cassandra found rather comical and she had to suffocate a disabling giggle before it surfaced to disgrace her.

Cassandra wondered for a mad minute if she was expected to kiss the palm so regally bestowed but she took it in her larger hand, wishing hers was daintier, and shook it as gently as she could. The fingers she touched were cool, and remained distant, with no welcoming squeeze.

"It's lovely to meet you at last, Mrs Flintock. Thank you," and Cassandra returned to her seat, thankful she'd navigated the little table traps along the way without mishap.

"Douglas, dear. Ask Maureen to fix up the tea tray, would you?"

Mrs Flintock waved her son away and he trotted off dutifully back out into the hall.

112

Cassandra wondered why they had no bell for the servants. Boston life seemed an odd mixture of high manners and a strange informality. She waited for Mrs Flintock's lead, before daring a comment that might betray her jumbled, critical, thoughts.

"And this is?" Mrs Flintock turned to Katy, her eyebrows raised in polite inquiry.

"Oh, forgive me, Mrs Flintock. This is Katherine Phipps, my personal maid," Cassandra said, afraid to add Katy was a good friend, until she was more sure of the etiquette.

"Hello, my dear," Mrs Flintock said, and inclined her sleek blonde head, towards Katy, who, Cassandra was relieved to see, seemed far more in command of herself than she was.

"Pleased to meet you, ma'am," Katy said, in a strong, confident voice, with her charming smile lighting up her pretty face.

Cassandra let her breath out.

"Now you must both have some refreshments after your voyage. We usually dine at midday, but in honour of your visit, we are going to dine this evening, at seven o'clock. So you'll have time to change before dinner and settle your things in your room. I've put you on the third floor, Cassandra - may I call you that?" Mrs Flintock's voice flowed effortlessly around the room, filling every crowded corner with its strange timbre.

"Of course, Mrs Flintock," Cassandra said, nodding too much. She could feel the tallest feather in her new hat quivering.

"Good, and you must call me Selina, for we are to be family, and I so want us to be friends," Mrs Flintock said. Somehow Cassandra could feel no warmth accompanying the kind words and puzzled whether it was her nerves, or something to do with feeling that Mrs Flintock had rehearsed her speech, and was still making up her mind about Cassandra behind it.

"There is a dressing room attached to your

bedroom that I thought would be perfect for Katherine. Do you think that arrangement would suit you both?"

Mrs Flintock's dreamy eyes flitted between her visitors. Cassandra looked at Katy who smiled warm encouragement back at her and nodded.

"That would be lovely, thank you, err, Selina," Cassandra said, sensing her feather was still quivering, even though she didn't nod, and longing to take the blasted thing off, so that it's trembling no longer signalled her nerves in such an obvious flag of betrayal.

The door opened and there was Douglas, carrying the tea things himself!

He put the tea-tray down next to his mother on one of the treacherous tables, where it rattled ominously before settling into a lacy curtsey.

Mrs Flintock poured them each a cup of fine China tea into the beautiful cups. "Milk, sugar? or would you prefer lemon? Now, if we were in the South, where I come from, I'd be offering you mint juleps on the porch."

Katy and Cassandra gave their preferences and Douglas handed them the hot drinks. Delicate fancy cakes were passed around, but both girls refused them. Cassandra guessed that Katy didn't have a clue how to balance hers on the saucer and she was much too nervous to swallow anything, however dainty. They all sipped their fragrant brew.

Douglas broke the skein of silence.

"Cassandra, it's so good to see you sitting here, with Mother. Who would have thought that something as horrific as a world war would bring such a beautiful harvest to Boston?" he said.

His mother smiled at her son and looked at Cassandra for a response.

Cassandra felt stifled in the over-stuffed room and unusually tongue-tied.

"Douglas, dear, Cassandra is tired and no wonder. Has Gallagher got all the luggage in from the car? Maybe Cassandra and Katherine would like to see their room and

114

freshen up a little?"

"Of course, Mother. Have you finished your tea, ladies?" Douglas shepherded them out of the parlour, saying, "Follow me," and ascended the stairs.

He showed them into a bedroom two floors up. It was identical to the parlour directly below it. The big bay window look out over the busy road, where cars and horses jostled up and down in the spring sunshine. More tall brown houses stared back at them from the other side of the broad street.

"Here's the dressing room, Katy. We've put a bed in here for you. I do hope you'll be comfortable," Douglas said.

"I'm sure I will, Mr Flintock, sir," Katy said.

"Hey, Katy, I'm Douglas to you, " Douglas said, and closed the door on Katy, leaving them alone together at last.

He was at Cassandra's side in two swift strides.

"I've been wanting to do this since I set eyes on you this morning, when you were still on that boat."

He took Cassandra in his arms and kissed her until she thought she might never breathe again. Her feathered hat was swiftly dispensed with and he ran his hands through her hair so that hair-pins pinged on to the polished wooden floor in a random staccato. His arms crushed her new blue coat around the waist. All Cassandra's nerves from the exchange in the parlour melted away, as she clutched him back. Who cared where she was or what his house was like? Love, real bone-crushing love like this, was the only thing worth living for.

When they finally released each other, Cassandra's wayward hair was careering off in its natural chaotic manner and Douglas's clean-shaven face was liberally smothered in red lipstick. Cassandra wondered if her eyes were as dark with desire as Douglas's.

"Oh, Douglas. You do love me!" Cassandra said.

"How could you doubt it?" he said.

"How could I not? You've sent me no word since that one-line telegram on your way home months ago! I've been in agony until I heard from your mother. Why didn't you answer my letters?" Cassandra said, gripping his coat sleeves with hard fists.

Douglas dropped his gaze and backed away, into the bay window recess. Cassandra froze to the spot; too scared to follow him, terrified of what he was about to say. She touched her fingertips to her lips, still warm and bruised from his kisses.

When he did speak, it was slowly and with obvious care.

"When I got back to Boston from Wiltshire, I admit, I was troubled, Cass. I was no longer sure I was doing the right thing. I could see you are duty bound to reside there but questioned whether I could live in your world. I tried to write and say so but I didn't want to hurt your feelings. I began plenty of letters, I can assure you, but ended up ripping them into pieces. I went back to my old ways. Saw old friends, went to parties, you know the sort of thing, but nothing could replace you. Every girl I danced with, however pretty she was..."

Cassandra winced at this.

"...all I saw, was your face, swimming in front of me. I like to drive, you know, and Lord, I went on some long ones. Right out to the coast. Mile upon mile I drove, but I couldn't get you out of my head. Mother saw the state I was in. She understands me in a way my father never will. Anyway, she could see how unhappy I was, and suggested that she invite you over here, so I could see how I felt about you on our own turf, so to speak, and so you could see what our life is like, here in Boston. It only took one look at you for my heart to tell me what an idiot I've been."

"Oh, Doug," Cassandra said, "You don't know how relieved I am."

"Me, too, honey, but let me finish. You see, my mother understands what it's like to be a foreigner in a strange place. Oh, I know she's American, like the rest of us and that's probably easier than being a Brit, like you, but to us Yankees, a Southerner is just as foreign" Douglas continued and started pacing up and down in the bay window recess.

"You and I have been fighting the Germans but it's not so long ago that Americans were fighting each other - North against South - about slavery. Both my grandfathers fought on opposite sides to each other. Mother comes from a tobacco plantation in Kentucky. It made her family rich but their wealth was built on the backs of negroes and we Bostonians just hate that. Since, the war, tobacco sales have gone through the roof and Mother's family are richer than ever, despite their wartime losses. I've benefitted from it directly, as Mother pays my very generous allowance out of her own money, so I'm pretty compromised. Father just hates our financial independence. He's a man who loves to be in control.

"So you see, my family isn't a bed of roses either, Cassandra. Looking back on it, I realise what a pompous ass I was, facing out your mother like that. Can you forgive me?"

117

CHAPTER FIFTEEN

Katy didn't know what to make of it. She, like Cassandra, had assumed that Douglas would live in as large an establishment as Cheadle Manor, and have a raft of servants to attend to the household, but there was no garret bedroom here to call her own. Her narrow bed was jammed up against the wall in the tiny box room that adjoined Cassandra's bedroom. Neither was there a private bathroom. Both she and Cassandra had to use the facilities at the end of the landing, and wait their turn accordingly, just like the servants at home, except that there, servants and Smythes were segregated.

Her little dressing room had a small skylight window, too high up to have a view of the noisy street, but it afforded just about enough light in the bright spring sunshine to read and write by, and she was grateful for that. Katy hadn't a clue where she was supposed to fit into the pecking order and had been surprised to have been served tea by the mistress of the house. And for Douglas to have brought the tea tray in himself had been truly astonishing. Although it had been gratifying to be included in the welcoming tea party, she was glad not to have to go down and join them for dinner. For one, thing, she only had her maid's black dress to wear. Mrs Flintock had knocked on the door earlier, to ask if they had all they needed, and told Cassandra that Katy would join the servants for supper in the kitchen, after dinner had been served.

Katy went down the two flights of stairs at the appointed time and followed the corridor to the back of the house, then down another flight of narrower stairs to the basement, where she rightly guessed the kitchen lay.

A large and flustered-looking woman was standing by the back door, which stood open to the evening air, fanning her red face with her apron but there were no other servants, unlike the twenty or so housed at Cheadle Manor.

"If it's supper you're wanting, you'll have to wait," she said with a strong, unmistakably Irish, accent, when she caught sight of Katy, hovering in the doorway.

"That's fine, I can wait," Katy said, not wanting to rock any boats she didn't yet know how to steer.

"I know it's fine, didn't I say so?" The woman took a swig out of a glass bottle, as she came back into the hot kitchen.

Someone tutted behind Katy's back and she turned to see it was Gallagher, the manservant, dressed in a smart black suit and carrying a laden tray of dirty dishes.

"Excuse me, miss," he said, with a politeness sadly lacking in the other member of staff.

"Sorry, I'm in your way," Katy said. "Can I help at all?"

"I just need to put this heavy tray down, if you don't mind," Gallagher said, and staggered towards the sink, where he put the tray down with a crash. The china wobbled, and Katy held her breath, but both steadied before they broke.

"Are they wanting their dessert now?" The woman said.

"Yes, please, Maureen. Is it ready?" Gallagher said, wiping his greasy brow with a teatowel.

Katy felt like a spare part, and an invisible one at that.

"As ready as it'll ever be. Here you are - it's raspberry blancmange with meringue. Mind you don't shake it about, or it'll collapse, and then where will we be? Here, let's unload this tray and we can stack it with the clean dishes instead," Maureen said, clattering the dirty china into the big sink. "It would be Abby's day off, today of all days."

Katy walked into the eye of the storm. "Please, let me help you. I'm sure there must be something I can do?"

Gallagher rolled his eyes and walked past her with the laden tray, with the pink blancmange trembling in the centre. Maureen turned to Katy with a hostile stare

119

and took another swig from her brown bottle. Katy smelt beer mixed with onions on her breath, and tried not to recoil.

"I suppose you're too grand to wash these dishes?" Maureen said, her eyes calculating and dark.

Katy had learned the hard way, with Mrs Andrews, to watch for traps like these.

"I'm not sure it's part of my duties, no," Katy said.

"I see, like that is it? I'll just have to do them *all* myself then, won't I?" And Maureen slammed down her empty beer bottle and crashed about with the china in the full sink.

"Who is Abby?"Katy said.

"Maid of all work, but she's got her day off today, so I've got to do the work of two women and with *visitors* in the house," Maureen sniffed.

"Would you like me to dry these up for you?" Katy said, hedging her bets but not wanting to seem churlish.

"If it isn't beneath you. There's clean cloths in the drawer, there."

They worked in silence, until Gallagher returned and put the percolator on the stove for coffee. He sat at the scrubbed pine table and lit a cigarette.

"If you want to smoke, Sean, you can stand by the door. I don't want you dropping ash all over the place," Maureen said, without even turning around to look at him.

Gallagher got up, scraping his chair loudly on the tiled floor, and went to the back door, which still stood open. He lounged against the door-frame, puffing smoke and staring at Katy, his already pale face still paler in the half-light.

"So, you're from England, then," he said.

"Yes, I am," Katy replied, stacking the clean, dry plates on to the table.

"Big place, is it? Where Miss Smythe's from?"

"Quite big, yes," Katy said.

"Toffs are they, the Smythes?" Maureen chipped

in.

"It depends what you mean by that term," Katy said, surprised she felt so angry on behalf of the Smythes.

"Hoity, bloody, toity!" Maureen said, letting out the plug. Slithers of beans and boiled beef curled in the whirlpool of greasy water, as it gurgled down the plughole.

Katy averted her eyes. The tension in her stomach made her feel as queasy as on that ocean liner, which from here, seemed a very benign vessel.

"Time for us slaves to eat," Maureen said. She looked at Katy, "Looks like you could do with it. We had our mains at lunchtime, so it's cold beef and bread with pickles for supper. That do you?"

Katy nodded. The beef was dry and the rye bread drier. The pickles were strong and briny, full of hot chilli that made her choke and sneeze.

Maureen and Gallagher hooted with laughter at the tears running down Katy's cheeks, as the pepper hit the back of her gullet. Katy got up and picked up one of the glasses she'd dried up. She filled it with water and stood by the sink, glugging down the cool liquid to soothe her outraged throat.

"You know what they say- Phipps - isn't it? If you can't take the heat, stay out of the kitchen!" and Maureen flipped open another bottle of beer with her kitchen knife and swigged it straight down.

"Better make the most of that beer, Maureen," Gallagher said, his fat face smirking. "If the Government gets its way this prohibition is going to lead to a total ban."

"They won't do that. Sure, the ban will be lifted in six months, if they do," Maureen said, taking another swig.

Katy wished she had something more than water to shove the dry bread down. Her throat still felt on fire.

"Well, you'd better not let the missus catch you drinking. You know what they're like and both the young ladies were talking temperance over their dinner, you know," Gallagher said.

"There's plenty more households want Irish to do their dirty work for them, if the Flintocks don't like my ways," Maureen said and hitched up her bosom with her crossed arms.

"Well, don't say I didn't warn you and I'm just as Irish as you," Gallagher said. "I'd better take the coffee in. They'll need something to slick their dry throats!" And he left with the coffee things, chuckling at his own joke.

"Prohibition! Whatever next? They'll start rationing sunshine soon," Maureen said, and helped herself to another sizeable chunk of boiled beef.

"What do you mean by prohibition, Maureen?" Katy said. She'd never heard of such a thing.

"It's only banning all alcohol, that's all! This po-faced family is all for it, except for Mr Douglas. At least he's got a bit of fire in his belly, not like those higher than thou sisters of his," Maureen said.

Katy didn't want to discuss Douglas with this coarse-faced woman but she was curious about the rest of his family, and asked, "So, is Mrs Flintock against alcohol too? What does her husband say about it?"

The beer had had a softening effect on Maureen and she'd mellowed enough to answer Katy with a smile. "Mr and Mrs Flintock only drink for medicinal purposes, so they say, but, and I shouldn't be saying this to a stranger, Mrs F has secret supplies in her dressing room."

"Oh, dear," Katy said.

Maureen needed little encouragement now, and continued, "Yes, I'm sure of it. I'm the only one allowed in there to clean, you see. Cheryl and Rose, her daughters, never go in the inner sanctum. And it's not just booze either, she's got bottles of laudanum stashed away too," Maureen nodded and swigged.

The second bottle was emptied and followed the first into the trash can. Talk about the pot calling the kettle black, but no wonder Mrs Flintock had looked so distant and dreamy.

"So, Maureen, do Cheryl and Rose Flintock live here, at home, with their parents?" Katy said, playing the innocent, which seemed to be working well, now Maureen was two bottles in.

"They do indeed, but Cheryl is never at home. She's a medical student you know, at Boston College, and will give you a lecture about your health at the drop of a hat, if you give her the chance. And she thinks the Irish need educating. Gets right up my nose; mind you, that Gallagher could do with it. Lazy good-for-nothing."

Katy ignored that last remark and asked, "What about Rose?"

"Now she's a different type altogether. More like her mother. Always making up poems and reading books. She's out a lot too, but not at college. Trying to change the world in a different way, with good works. Helps her father a bit in his office. Got a big case on, they have."

"Oh?"

"This molasses accident. Mr Flintock is working every hour God sends on the case," Maureen said, wiping crumbs off the table straight on to the floor.

"Oh, yes, another passenger on the boat was telling us about it. He said that's why the sea in the harbour is brown," Katy said, drinking in all this information about the family, ready to relay it to Cassandra before bedtime.

"That's the way of it. Great big tank of the stuff exploded at North End. Killed and injured no end of people. Mr Flintock's law office is trying to get them compensation. It's a hopeless case, but can't blame him for trying." Maureen heaved her bulk upright. "Well, I'm off. I've had enough for one day. Got to be back at the crack of dawn to do breakfast and I've me own family to sort out at home."

"Don't you live in then, Maureen?"

"No, I don't. I get more money this way, and God knows we need it. Goodnight."

"Goodnight, Maureen. Nice to meet you," Katy said.

"That's as may be. See you tomorrow," and Maureen buttoned up her wool coat, which had seen better days and strained across her chest so much, Katy thought the buttons might fly off. Maureen crammed a purple velvet hat on to her topknot and then she was gone, leaving the door wide open to the Boston night sky.

Katy had no idea where the pallid Gallagher had got to. Her curiosity about this strange American city drew her to the open door. From the basement level, the street loomed high above her, up a flight of stone steps, bordered by ironwork railings. The terraced houses blocked out most of the sky but were separated by a small yard at the back, where the houses narrowed. Washing hung limp and neglected in the Flintocks' yard. Katy decided not to bring it in. She suspected Maureen would not welcome any invasion of her territory.

Beyond the red-brown brick walls, that stretched five floors up, the small square of night sky was clear. Stars winked back at her. Katy leant against the door post and gazed up at them, grateful for a moment's solitude. There wasn't much peace to go with it, as other back doors opened and shut, people chatted as they walked along the pavement and horses clattered among the car engines. Someone hawked and spat on the pavement just above her.

Katy looked up at the stars again. Would Jem be looking up at them too? Back in Wiltshire, back *home,* would the stars have the same formation on the other side of that vast, nausea-inducing ocean? How silly that, now she was really far from home, travelling as she had always longed to do, all she really wanted was Jem's arms about her, his lips on hers and his warm brown eyes reflecting back the love she felt for him at this very moment.

"Bit cold with the door open, isn't it?"

Gallagher had finally returned, with silent footsteps.

Katy looked around at him.

"I usually lock up around this time, before going up to bed," he said, hitching his trousers back up over his round belly.

"I see," Katy said, and closed the door.

"Where are you sleeping, then?" Gallagher said, looking her up and down again.

"In Miss Cassandra's dressing room," Katy said, regretting she couldn't think of a way out of telling him such an intimate detail.

"Not in the servant's quarters, on the top floor?"

"No, I think it's fourth floor up. This house is very tall, isn't it?"

"Yes, it is. Pity we won't be neighbours," and Gallagher gave a snigger.

Katy bolted for the door.

CHAPTER SIXTEEN

Cassandra was grateful that she and Katy had taken such care over her outfit for the evening, when she entered the parlour for the second time that never-ending day. She'd chosen a muted but elegant cream evening dress that dropped in a sheer, fashionably straight line, to just above her ankles, and was gathered around her slim hips with a contrasting coffee-coloured sash. Katy had spent time on her hair, always an awkward customer, and had tamed its wild profusion with a pearl covered comb and discreetly hidden pins. Drop pearl earrings emphasised her long neck and were echoed around her throat.

Douglas seemed to like it anyway, and he kissed her in the hall before they entered the parlour, hand in hand. Cassandra congratulated herself for not wearing rouge. She could feel her cheeks burning where his lips had brushed them.

The Flintock clan had gathered to meet her and sat, squashed into the sofas and chairs in a sea of unknown faces. Her only raft was Douglas and she gripped his hand harder with every introduction.

"Cassandra, darling, let me introduce you to my sisters, Cheryl and Rose," he said.

Cassandra just about refrained from a curtsey and extended her other hand. Both young women stood up to greet her and, unusually, they were all three much the same height. Cassandra was used to being half a head taller than most women and found the sensation of looking into two pairs of enquiring eyes, at the same level, quite challenging.

"Pleased to meet you, I'm sure," Cheryl said, in a clipped Bostonian accent.

Cheryl's angular frame was soberly dressed in a severe navy dress with just a touch of white here and there but Rose wore a soft pink evening gown that flowed in chiffon waves around her generous curves and matched

126

her apple cheeks. She smiled back at Cassandra with real warmth, and pressed her hand with both of her own.

"Welcome, Cassandra. I feel I have been blessed with another sister, and it's so lovely to see Douglas happy," Rose said.

"You've met Mother, Cassandra, and now it's Dad's turn. Sir, allow me to introduce the most beautiful girl in the world," Douglas said, drawing her towards the man who had got up from his chair and now stood in front of the ornate fireplace, watching her with his piercing grey eyes. Mr Flintock was, inevitably, also tall, and had a restless energy about him, despite the fatigue etched into his handsome face. Cheryl had obviously got her angularity from the paternal side. Mr Flintock's stare was unflinching and astute. It was a great relief when his frown broke into a brief smile.

This time, Cassandra did curtsey a little bob. Such an imposing man deserved one.

"Now, now, my dear. We don't stand on formality here!" Mr Flintock boomed. "This is Boston, you know. You're in the New World now, not the old one. We regard everyone as our equal."

Cassandra found this speech of welcome oddly condescending, but ignored the niggling irritation and smiled back. Her transatlantic journey was discussed and sympathised over, before a gong, sounded from below stairs, broke the genteel tedium and they all trooped into the dining room. The long, rectangular room was much smaller than the grand, echoing affair at Cheadle Manor but furnished with lavish attention to detail. Silver cutlery and cut glass twinkled in the gaslight on the walls, and candles further illuminated the beautifully set table.

Douglas sat next to Cassandra, on his father's right-hand side, with his two sisters opposite them, which, to Cassandra, felt a little confrontational at such a narrow table. Then she felt Douglas's foot against hers, soothing her with little taps of affection. The knot in her stomach relaxed and her lips unsealed under the memory of his kiss in the hall.

All were silent as their soup cooled rapidly during Mr Flintock's grave rendition of grace. After a few further seconds of stillness following his sombre prayer, he turned to her and said, "We do not serve wine with our meals, Cassandra. We are all firm believers in the value of temperance but I trust you will find our cordials an acceptable alternative."

Cassandra inclined her head, and said, "I'm sure everything will be delicious, sir."

She could forego the wine, though it would have helped, but how she longed for a cigarette!

The soup was predictably tepid, but palatable, and the rest of the meal much the same, and served up with silent efficiency by the ubiquitous and rather greasy-looking Gallagher.

Mrs Flintock spoke only once, to enquire whether Cassandra liked beans with her beef.

"They're a Boston speciality, you know," she added, her musical voice soft and so low, Cassandra could barely catch what she said.

"They make a delightful change, thank you, " Cassandra lied.

"Beans are very good for the bowels," Cheryl said, nodding sagely. "Bowels need roughage. We all eat far too much fat and refined foods these days. I had a lecture about the gastro-intestinal tract only yesterday."

"Thank you, Cheryl, but I don't think we need to discuss it at the dinner table," Mr Flintock said, without a hint of humour.

Mrs Flintock sipped from her glass of cordial and gave Cassandra the smile her husband lacked.

Douglas filled the breach and said, "So, Father, have you made any progress with the molasses compensation case today?"

"If you came down to the office, you could find out for yourself, Douglas," Mr Flintock said. "But yes, Rose and I have had a long day, interviewing some of the victim's families. Rose has been very useful, taking notes for me. She has a very quick hand," and Mr Flintock smiled at last, at his youngest daughter.

"Oh, Father, I'm glad to help, if it makes your workload lighter, and besides, Douglas is busy with Cassandra. He's got to show her around the sights of Boston, haven't you, Douglas?" Rose's pale blue eyes looked anxiously from father to son.

Cheryl rolled her eyes to heaven and clattered her fork and knife on to her empty plate. "You know I'd help you if I could, Father, but I'm sure you understand that my studies must come first."

"Yes, of course Cheryl, that's perfectly reasonable. You won't qualify as a doctor without a great deal of application," her father said, inclining his high-browed forehead in her direction, before darting a pointed look at Douglas.

"You're all living saints," Douglas said, with one of his lop-sided grins. "If I was wearing my hat, I'd take it off to you all. I might not be a war hero but I have just come back from fighting for our dearly beloved country, might I remind you."

Rose jumped in quickly, "Of course you have, Douglas, dear, and we're all so proud of you! Now, tell me, where are you going to take Cassandra tomorrow? You must show her the Public Gardens, if the weather is nice."

"Capital idea, Rose! Anyone have any idea what the weather has in store for us?" Douglas said, shovelling the last bean into his mouth.

Cassandra could see that the safe topic of the weather had prevented a family squall and suspected that storms like these were often averted by Rose, the peacemaker. The meal eventually petered out with a disgustingly sweet pink blancmange and then they filtered out to the parlour. Both Cheryl and her father pleaded work commitments and to everyone's thinly disguised relief, disappeared elsewhere. Mrs Flintock complained of a headache and retired for the night, which left Cassandra and Douglas with only Rose for company.

Douglas riddled the coal fire in the grate and added more fuel to the blaze. He flopped back onto the largest sofa and patted the cushion next to his.

"Come here, Cass, honey, and tell me I am a hero, despite what my family thinks of my lazy ways."

"Oh, Douglas, dear. Don't take on so! Cheryl and father work twice as hard as normal people, so you mustn't think they don't admire you in lots of other ways," Rose said.

Cassandra was reminded of the saccharine dessert and chided herself for regarding Rose's charity as too sweet to be true. In fact, all these Flintocks seem to have outsize consciences and duty-filled missions in life. Thank God Douglas seemed to have inherited the family's entire humour allowance.

"This molasses case sounds interesting, Rose," Cassandra said. "Do tell me more about it."

Douglas rewarded her with a surreptitious squeeze of his thigh, deliciously warm against her own.

"Oh, yes, it is interesting, but it means Father is working harder than ever. It's the biggest compensation claim there has ever been! You see, the Government was a big purchaser of molasses during the war, because one of its by-products is used in the manufacture of nitro-glycerine - you know - for explosives?"

"I know all about explosives," Cassandra said, as images of mutilated soldiers flashed across her mind.

"Do you? Of course, how silly of me. That's how you met Douglas, wasn't it? Well, the big silo tank at North End built up gases inside it to such an extent that it exploded, sending a huge wave of molasses cascading across the dockside and killing twenty one workers and injuring another one hundred and fifty. Now they are claiming compensation and father is one of the lawyers handling the case - it's the first of its kind. If he wins, he'll be making history."

Rose sat back on her seat, the animation draining from her face, leaving her looking pale and tired.

She smiled politely and said, "What did you do in France, Cassandra? That is, if you don't mind me asking? So many servicemen would rather not discuss their wartime experiences, I find, so I usually stay clear of the subject," Rose said, her gentle face troubled by more anxiety.

"I don't have a problem with talking about it," Cassandra said, "but I don't want to be a bore, either."

"Oh, I don't think it's boring. It's fascinating. You must have been so brave," Rose said.

"Not as brave as the boys in the trenches. I drove ambulances for the wounded. Sadly, I saw the consequences of high explosives more times than I can count," Cassandra said.

"Oh, yes, you must have done. I do admire you, Cassandra, for your courage. I'm sure I wouldn't have stood it for a minute!" Rose said.

Cassandra smiled, "Well, Rose, I'm certain I couldn't write down someone's witness statement with the speed and efficiency that you must have done to win your father's admiration like that."

Rose's kind face broke into a beaming smile, "That's so kind of you! Douglas? I'm so glad you've brought Cassandra into our family. I'm sure we're going to get along very well."

Rose yawned and tried to hide it behind her hand.

"You're tired, Rose," Douglas said. "Why don't you go up to bed? You've worked so hard today. Are you going to the office again tomorrow?"

"Oh, yes, I am a little weary, and you're right, Douglas, I am going in again tomorrow. Poor Father, he's so over-worked with this insurance claim by the workers. He believes in them having the same rights as the owners, you see, Cassandra, so, for him, it's more than work, it's a public duty."

And Rose got up to go. Cassandra and Douglas

131

both stood up and kissed her goodnight. She smelled of Castile soap and ink.

When Rose shut the door softly behind her, Douglas took both Cassandra's hands in his, and stood there, sheepish and apologetic, his eyes as guilty as a puppy's who'd messed on the carpet.

"Oh, Cass. I hope you're not ruing the day you met me! My tribe are a mirthless lot, aren't they?"

"Well, they do seem very hardworking and admirably public spirited," Cassandra replied carefully.

Douglas laughed and dropped her hands. He went to the fireplace, to the same spot his father had stood on earlier.

"Thing is, Cass, I'm a disappointment to dear old Dad. I went to Harvard, like a good boy, but I didn't do so well. Sure, I got some sports medals to prove I was there, but no bits of paper to impress the legal profession."

"Is that what he wanted you to do?" Cassandra asked.

"Yes, follow in his footsteps, you know the sort of thing."

"And what do *you* want to do with your life, Doug?"

"Make love to you and get away from this place," Douglas stared into the fire, as he said this.

"Is that why you wanted to be with me? So you can live in England, far away from your family? That is, until you learned how ghastly mine are?"

Douglas span around and grabbed her hands again, "No! God, no! Cassandra, you have to believe me. I love every gorgeous inch of you, darling. Every strand of your hair, every wonderful curve of your body and your big, generous heart. You see, Cass, you're so much fun! With you, I can laugh at their absurd ambitions. I don't feel a failure, when I'm with you, my dearest darling."

"You're not a failure, Doug!"

"I don't think my father would agree with you there," Douglas said.

132

Cassandra drew him close and pressed her tired body against his lean one; all fatigue from her long journey melting away, as she felt his warm aliveness against her.

"Douglas Flintock, now you just listen to me. My mother has tried to marry me off to all sorts of eligible bachelors for simply years, and, as you know, I met thousands of other men during the war and I never fancied a single one of them. I never believed in love at first sight either; thought it was utter tosh. Then I saw you, standing in your uniform in the mess tent at Nevers, and my stomach turned over, and I just knew that I would love you for the rest of my life. Who cares what parents want? Mine have given up on me, what with my driving and wearing trousers - they probably thought I'd pal up with another woman, if they are aware of Sapphic relationships, which I doubt."

Douglas laughed and put his arms around her.

Snug within them, Cassandra added, "To me, Doug, you are perfect. Let's be happy while we can, if only for all those men and women who died out there and will never know what being in love feels like. Our parents have no idea what we've seen. The deaths, the destruction and the waste. I'm going to make the most of the rest of my life and you're going to help me. Got it?"

Douglas's eyes looked suspiciously moist and he said, his voice husky, "Got it."

CHAPTER SEVENTEEN

The clatter of the street woke Katy the next morning and for a moment she couldn't recall where she was. Neither could she see where the noise was coming from through the skylight, so she just lay on her makeshift bed listening to the sound of the busy traffic outside. Horses clacked their hooves above her, occasionally an engine growled past and mixed up in them both were the chatter, shouts and whistles of passers-by. Then a pressing need for the bathroom interrupted her daydreams, so she got dressed and tiptoed through Cassandra's bedroom, who seemed to be slumbering on under the heap of bedcovers. When she returned, Cassandra was wide awake and sitting up in bed, surrounded by expensive-looking boxes and a tray laden with breakfast.

"Good morning, Katy," Cassandra said, with a broad smile and a piece of toast in her hand. "Come and see what I have got for you!"

"For me?" Katy said.

Cassandra's smile widened. "Yes, these are for you. I can't wait to see your face when you open them. I had an idea last night, before I went to bed, and gave Douglas a secret mission, which he did early this morning, while we were still sleeping our heads off. It's quite late you know, we've both had a bit of a lie-in. Come on, open these up and see what's inside."

Katy undid the dress-box ribbon, lifted the lid and the embossed tissue paper inside it, to find a fashionable shift dress underneath.

"There," Cassandra said, "that lavender colour will draw out your beautiful eyes. Black does nothing for you, Katy."

"It's lovely," Katy said, and held the dress up under her chin, then turned to stare at herself in the long cheval mirror in the dressing room.

"Go on, put it on. I've got to send another missive to Mama, before she convinces herself that we were swept overboard on *'The Lapland.'* Then Douglas has promised to take us out to look at the city. I couldn't bear to go without you, dear Katy, so I guessed your size and Douglas ordered it from Stearn's, the big clothes store, at the crack of dawn, so it would be a surprise. I can't wait to see you in it and with that on, you can come with us."

Katy withdrew into the tiny dressing room and took off her black dress. The new one shimmered over her head and settled in graceful folds. The delicate fabric moved with her when she went to look in the mirror again. Cassandra was right, the colour suited her perfectly. She opened the other big box to find a matching coat and slipped it on. The coat was a deeper shade of mauve and managed to be both warm and light at the same time. Katy guessed it was manufactured from a fine, closely woven wool. There was a hatbox alongside the others. Too excited to be careful, she wrenched off the lid and found a modern clôche hat to match, decorated with just one tasteful appliquéd flower, in contrasting lemon.

Katy opened the door to Cassandra's room, wearing all three new items, and cleared her throat nervously. Cassandra was seated at the big bay window, writing her letter at the desk that caught the light there. She turned around and her frown of concentration disappeared.

"Well, look at you, Katy! Don't you look smart. I knew lavender would be your thing. That hint of yellow in the hat sets it off a treat. Those black boots don't work though. Give me your size and we'll order some from the same store. I'm sure they'll find a good match. And, I think, lemon gloves, don't you?"

Katy said, "But Cassandra, are you sure you can afford all this? And won't people think I'm getting above myself, not wearing my maid's uniform?"

"Rubbish! Why should they? Who's to know in Boston? This is my new idea - from now on, I'm going to call you my travelling companion and you shall be part of all I do. I shall call you Kate. It seems more modern than

Katy, if you'd like that?"

Katy was stunned and silently nodded her assent.

Cassandra continued, "Believe me, after last night's supper, I could use an ally. I just wish I'd thought of it before we got off the boat. It's such a good wheeze - don't you see? And besides, what else are you going to do here all day? How was your meal yesterday, by the way?"

"Hot pickles and dry bread with chunks of boiled beef. The chilli sauce almost blew my head off. Maureen, the Irish cook, thought it was hilarious," Katy said, smoothing down the coat once more, just for the luxurious feel of it.

"Oh, dear. That settles it. You deserve some fun. I'm not sure if I can wangle it for you to join the family for meals, but I'll ask Douglas. If you are my companion, it changes everything. America is very liberating, don't you think?"

Katy laughed and a ripple of freedom shivered through her. She nodded at Cassandra and said, "Cassandra, I can't tell you how ready I am to be liberated."

They both laughed at that and Cassandra said, "Good, we'll say no more about it. Here, give this note to Gallagher and he can deliver it to Stearn's. You should have your shoes before we go out. What size are you?" Cassandra jotted it down on the note.

Katy ran down the stairs to the kitchen, taking their empty breakfast tray and the note with her. She found Gallagher there, reading the morning paper over his coffee and ignoring poor Abby, the downtrodden maid, who was doggedly ploughing through a mountain of washing up.

"Where's Maureen today?" Katy asked.

"Gone to the market at Faneuil's for more supplies," Gallagher said, without looking up. He carried on reading his paper. No doubt it was the only bit of peace he ever got.

"Oh, I see. I've got an errand that needs doing,"

Katy said.

"Oh?" Gallagher couldn't have been less interested. He hadn't even noticed her new outfit.

"Miss Cassandra wants this note sent round to Stearn's. I think it's a department store?"

"I haven't got time to run all the way to Tremont Street!"

Gallagher looked up at last. He must have seen how crestfallen Katy looked. "Well, don't you look nice today? Tell you what, if it's an order, you can telephone the store. Come on, I'll show you where the instrument is."

"Would that be alright, Mr Gallagher? Won't the family mind me using their telephone? I've never used one before," Katy said.

"Call me Sean, and there's nothing to using the telephone. I do it all the time. Look, give me the order and I'll ring it through," Gallagher said, relenting.

"Thank you, um, Sean." Katy smiled at him and he smiled back, and gave her a wink.

"Sure, we're becoming friends already," he said, an even bigger smile cracking across his pale face. "What's your first name?"

"Katherine - Kate for short," Katy said, hoping her new shoes would be worth all this unlooked-for intimacy and slipping into her new nickname without thinking.

"Okay, Kate. Consider it done," Gallagher said, letting his voice linger over her name.

He licked his lips and came towards her, with a smirk across his oily face. Abby looked over her shoulder, frowning a warning.

Katy turned abruptly and climbed the stairs back up to the fourth floor more thoughtfully than she had run down them.

"Gallagher is going to telephone Stearn's and order the shoes for me," she told Cassandra.

"Splendid. Let's root out Douglas and see the

sights." Cassandra said, sealing up her envelope. "First stop, the Post Office, then at least Mother will be out of my hair. Then we can call into the department store and pick up your shoes and gloves before we venture further."

There was a brisk rap on the door, which opened to reveal Douglas.

"Good morning, ladies," he said. "Ready for an expedition? The sun's out."

"We're looking forward to it, aren't we, Kate? Look Douglas! My new travelling companion would pass muster anywhere in her new outfit, wouldn't she?" Cassandra stood back so Douglas could see Katy, who stood in front of the big window, backlit by the bright morning light.

"Say! Look at you. You look real smart, Kate, you really do. I'll be honoured to have you with us," Douglas said.

Katy squared her shoulders at his compliment, "Thank you Douglas, that means a lot to me."

Yellow spring sunshine greeted them when they stepped outside a little later. Katy sniffed appreciatively. Boston had an intoxicating smell. Diesel fumes mixed with horse manure were subdued by the whiff of the salty Atlantic air but there was something else. Something that smelled like fresh laundry off the line, new and clean and invigorating.

Once the letter to England was safely despatched and Katy's black boots swopped for some flattering new shoes, Douglas offered to show them the public library.

Katy worried about scuffing the soft leather on her grey shoes when he beckoned them to climb aboard a passing tram. "Come on," he said, hopping onto the platform, "we'll take the subway."

"The subway?" Cassandra asked, grabbing the rail and joining him.

Katy skipped on before the tram rumbled off and only just made it.

"Yeah, this old tram goes under the road, don't

you, know? First of its kind anywhere. Beats walking!" Douglas said, laughing at the two Englishwomen as the tram lurched around a corner and made them stumble before they could safely sit down. The tram rang its bell in triumph.

"Library first stop, then," Douglas said and added with a twinkle, "May as well start highbrow and work downwards," as they disembarked and made their way to Boston Library.

They stood before the edifice a moment before ascending the wide, shallow steps. "Goodness." Cassandra said, "What an impressive building."

The library was made of white stone and colonnaded along its massive length. Katy counted thirteen big arched windows along its impressive frontage, which seemed an odd number and she wondered if the architect had a hidden meaning for his choice. They walked through the centre of three even bigger archways that each housed impressive double doors underneath more glass.

"Wait till you get inside," Douglas said, leading the way.

There were acres of space under the vaulted ceilings of the interior, and bookcase after bookcase bore silent testimony to the industrious study of Bostonians, but the area that Katy admired the most, despite her own love of reading, was the Italianate cloistered courtyard garden.

"I think I might come here quite often and read a borrowed book in this peaceful place," she said.

"Beats that old library at Cheadle Manor hands down," Cassandra said. "Douglas, I'm getting a little hungry, after all this rushing about. Where are you taking us for lunch?"

"I know just the place," he said. "We'll pop into Faneuil's market - that's a must see and will sharpen your appetite even more, before I take you to my favourite restaurant. We're meeting my friend, Fred Stavely, there.

Won't he be jealous when he sees I have *two* beauties in tow."

They walked back through the hush of the library, past the white alabaster busts that stared back at them with impassive indifference, and out into the noisy, crowded street. The market was even busier, and packed with determined shoppers haggling for chickens and cabbages at the overflowing stalls. Katy's stomach started rumbling at the hot pies wafting their savoury aromas between the stalls. After a quick survey of the market's delights, they made their way along the sun-lit streets, bordered by yet more brown-stoned terraces, before turning the final corner and entering an expensive-looking restaurant.

Douglas made no distinction between her and Cassandra and invited Katy to order whatever she liked, as his guest. Douglas did not share his family's distaste of alcohol and Katy sipped the chilled white wine the waiter poured for her in heady appreciation. If her Mum could see her now! Or Lady Amelia, for that matter. No, it was a bad idea to imagine her disapproving presence here in this breezy town.

"We must start with lobster," Douglas said. "You have to have lobster chowder in Boston. It's the best in the world!"

"*Start* with lobster?" Katy said, wondering how much they were going to eat and what on earth chowder was.

"That's right, and then we'll have some Boston beans, before we despatch a good old American steak."

"Gracious, that's more than I've eaten in a week," Katy said.

"That's probably true, Kate. Douglas, she was as sick as a dog on the boat over," Cassandra said.

"I didn't know that, sorry to hear it, Kate. All the more reason to make up for it now," Douglas said and topped up her glass.

"Hey, Douglas! You can't keep these lovely young ladies all to yourself."

A tawny-haired man, of about twenty five, approached their table and was now smiling appreciatively at them.

"Hi, Fred - you made it! Come and join us, old fellow," and Douglas got up and clapped his friend on the shoulder. He drew up a chair and Fred, after bowing to both Katy and Cassandra, sat down between them.

"Fred, this is Cassandra Smythe, my fiancée," Douglas said, not bothering to disguise the pride in his face.

"Charmed, I'm sure," Cassandra said, and extended her hand. Katy watched Cassandra's etiquette with intense concentration, as she waited for her first greeting as an equal. He might be American, but it was obvious from his dapper appearance that every inch of Fred was upper class. Katy swallowed nervously.

"And this is my travelling companion, Kate Phipps," Cassandra said, before Douglas blundered into reinstating her previous maid's status.

"Pleased to meet you," Katy said, and shook the hand so readily held out to hers.

"Why, you sound like you come from America already," Fred said.

Katy blushed. She'd forgotten how her Wiltshire accent might betray her.

"Kate comes from the same neck of the woods as myself, Fred," Cassandra said. "Just went to a different school, that's all."

Fred's easy manner didn't flicker for a moment and he said warmly, "I think you're going to fit right in here, Kate."

Fred's smile reached right up into his eyes, which crinkled at the corners and rested on Katy's face for longer than she thought they should.

Douglas poured him some wine. Fred looked like he enjoyed his creature comforts, judging by the buttons straining across his waistcoat, and the reddish complexion of his round face. He was also a gifted raconteur, and told them hilarious stories about Douglas's sporting days at Harvard, until Douglas protested enough to make him stop.

When the long lunch was over, Fred didn't seem at all inclined to break up the party and instead, suggested they all went for a walk in the public gardens.

Douglas linked Cassandra's arm in his and they wandered ahead through the dappled sunlight under the tall trees. Katy relaxed in Fred's congenial company and strolled beside him, as if it was the most natural thing in the world. She declined his arm when he offered it, preferring to retain a little independence. She felt transformed in this young country, chatting easily to this stranger, wearing beautiful clothes, with her stomach full of bountiful food and her head swimming slightly from the wine. Somehow it didn't seem important to inform Fred that she was a married woman, and a lowly maid at that. It could have been her, washing up like Abby in Maureen's hot kitchen, instead of ambling in the park, dressed like a lady.

Katy felt as if she was on holiday or living someone else's life, suspended from the normal rules that had always constrained her life into tight, narrow margins.

CHAPTER EIGHTEEN

Right, here goes, Jem said to himself. He was sitting in the Sunbeam inside the barn. He'd been studying the vehicle for days, getting familiar with the layout of the dashboard, judging the distance of the gearstick on his right hand side and testing out the pedals with his feet. At least he had two of those to play with. He'd got a book out of the library in Woodbury on how to drive. If he mastered this, he planned to ask Sir Robert for a post as chauffeur, if only temporarily, until Cassandra came home. Sir Robert might hate cars, but his guests might be glad of being driven around on country weekends. He'd taken Mr Hayes to one side the day before, and explained what he was trying to achieve. Mr Hayes looked at Jem for a such a long moment, Jem thought his ambition was a non-starter.

"Do you really think you can manage one handed, Jem?" Mr Hayes said, sucking on his pipe.

"I can only try, sir," Jem said.

"True enough," Mr Hayes said. "Well, it's nothing to do with me. My eyes aren't what they were. As long as I don't see you, I don't suppose I'll know much about it, will I? And what the eye don't see, the heart don't grieve over. Though there's plenty else to grieve about. Get on with you, lad, but mind you keep safe and remember, I don't know anything about it."

Jem had chosen a day when the manor was quiet. Lady Amelia and Sir Robert were away on a country weekend and had taken several servants with them, including Bert Beagle, who had driven them to the next county in the carriage, with four horses pulling it. Jem sat in the driving seat of the car and listened to the peace. Jack Beagle was at home helping his mother, and the other servants had been given the day off as the Smythes were away. He'd never get another chance like this.

Before he cranked the engine into life, he went through the motions again. A little bit of choke, not too much. He pulled out the stopper on the dashboard a quarter of the way. The manual about driving lay open on the passenger seat and Jem re-read it for the thousandth time. The page was smudged by the finger he still needed to draw along the line to make out the words. He knew it off by heart by now but one more read through wouldn't hurt. Then, taking a deep breath, he got out and went to the newly-mended barn doors, propping them open with the stakes provided for the purpose. Jem peeped out. All he could hear were the birds twittering as they busied about, building their spring nests. Before he'd left, Bert had put out all the horses to grass in the paddocks, now green with new growth. Even Mr and Mrs Andrews had gone out visiting. No, there would never be a better time than this.

Butterflies refused to be quelled in his stomach as he took up the starting handle and inserted it into the engine, through the front grill of the big car. It was hard to grip with his wooden hand, so he had to use twice as much pressure with his good one. But Jem was strong, and the muscles in his good arm had bulged since he lost his left one, and the engine started first time. It sounded deafening in the still morning air. Jem could swear the birds had stopped singing to listen to its thundering roar.

Once he was confident that the engine had settled into a reliable chug, he opened the driver's door and climbed in behind the wheel.

Cassandra made nothing of driving and Douglas made it look easy too. Couldn't be that hard, could it?

He shoved the two wooden fingers of his left hand onto the steering wheel so they wedged onto its circular shape. There were two knobs attached to a smaller brass circle within the steering wheel that he could latch on to if he needed to for extra steerage. Then he forced the gears into reverse with a horrible crunching sound, before remembering he had to depress the clutch pedal first. He released the handbrake and lifted his foot slowly, just the way the book had instructed. The car lurched backwards and then shuddered to a halt. Damn! He'd stalled it.

Out he got and cranked the engine back into life. Sweat beaded his brow and he threw off his tweed cap with an impatient tug. Jem ran his hand through his hair and willed his breath to slow down. He settled himself back on the seat and got comfortable. Then he looked around to check exactly where the open barn doors were, depressed the clutch, pushed the gearstick back into reverse and let off the handbrake before lifting his foot up, much more slowly this time. The car eased backwards, slewing off to the right. Jem grabbed the wheel with his good hand and wrenched it to the centre, overcompensating by a yard, so that the car veered violently to the left. He put the clutch in and the car stopped moving. Aha, so that's how you did it! He eased the clutch up again and using both his wooden and his flesh hands got the wheel plumb centre. The old Sunbeam glided smoothly out of the barn and into the spring sunshine.

Brake! He must stop before he hit the stable block! Jem wrenched on the handbrake with his good hand and found the brake pedal with his foot. The car stopped so abruptly he bumped his chest onto the steering wheel. No matter. He hadn't crashed into the wall. Right, then. A glance at the driving manual told Jem where first gear position was and he pulled it out of reverse and into first. Handbrake off, clutch up, accelerator down. Whoa! The Sunbeam had some power under its bonnet. He grabbed the steering wheel and careered through the gap in the courtyard buildings, missing the corners by inches. The engine was screaming its outrage. That didn't sound right. The book said you only needed first gear to start with. He changed up into second and the engine relaxed. Phew, this was much harder than it looked. He bumped over the cobblestones until he met up with the dust and gravel driveway. Sharp left! Sharp left! Not easy when you couldn't feel any sensation in your left hand. He used his right hand to push the wheel upwards but not quickly enough to prevent the car tyres gouging out a good bit of lawn edge, before regaining the drive.

Oh, my, this drive went downhill much too steeply! The car rolled away, gravity nudging it on and making it gather speed at an alarming rate. The engine started screeching again. It must need to go up another gear. Jem scrunched into third which seemed to stop the protesting noise but it made the car travel even faster. He whizzed past the copse in front of West Lodge and vaguely saw Agnes in the garden, waving her arms like mad. He heard her shouts, but he was going so fast now, they receded before he'd barely registered them. The manor gates raced into view and he slammed on the brakes, stalling the engine again. What was it the book said about changing back down the gears before halting? He picked the book up and squinted at it, whilst trying to ignore how it shook in his trembling hand.

He heard footsteps behind him. It was Agnes. She was running *and* shouting now.

"Oi, Jem! What do you think you are playing at?"

Agnes wasn't the fastest runner. He got out and turned the engine over with the starting handle again and got it going before she caught up with him. She was red in the face and out of breath.

"Jem!" she panted. "Whatever are you doing driving the master's car?"

"I'm learning to drive, Agnes," Jem said, with far more confidence than he felt.

"Have you got permission?"

"Got to go. See you later!" Jem said, and this time, he managed to co-ordinate letting off the handbrake and engaging the gears in one go. He yanked the wheel round to the right as hard as he could and avoided the ditch by the narrowest of margins. Agnes's furious yelling faded as he accelerated away up the road towards London. Thankfully there was a good straight bit on this stretch of road and he managed to get right up to fourth gear. He looked at the speedometer. Thirty miles an hour. Almost as fast as the train!

Jem sped along the road with his heart in his mouth. Adrenaline surged through his bloodstream, making his heart pump as hard as the engine he drove. A right-hand bend, a sharp one, loomed into sight; he lifted his foot off the accelerator too suddenly and the car lumped into a lower speed, making the engine complain with a loud groan. Pressing his wooden hand firmly onto the wheel, he let go with his good hand and shoved the gearstick down into third gear, before whipping it back on the wheel in the nick of time to pull it down to the right hand side and away from the ditch as the road curved round. That had been close, really close.

If he had a bend to the left as sharp as that, he'd struggle to pull the wheel around quickly enough. Jem motored on, switching to fourth gear again and cruising along another straight section. Another car came towards him. He gripped the wheel, his sweat making his good hand slippery. At least his wooden one didn't do that.

The other driver shouted, "Get out of the way, you fool!"

Jem lurched to the nearside, bumping along the grass verge, before slewing back onto the road. He bumped his head on the ceiling of the car as he careered off the higher verge and back on to the tarmac. Oh, no! Here came the big left hand bend he'd been dreading. Change down, change down. Good, he was in third gear, that's right, ease that accelerator, now for the turn. He just couldn't feel the wheel with his left hand. He pulled at it, tried to bring it down but it wouldn't respond, it just kept slipping. He gripped the wheel with his right hand and took the wheel rim right over towards the left in an awkward manoeuvre across his body. His perspiration acted as a lubricant and his right hand slipped. He stabbed at the wheel with his wooden claw and just caught the inner circle knob on the wheel, pushing it downwards. Finally, the car responded and, with a screech of burning tyres, the car dragged across the road to the left, narrowly missing a tree on the right hand side of the road before going too far to the left and running into the hedge on the nearside.

There was a horrible scraping noise as hawthorns scarred the burnished paint on the side of the Sunbeam, drawing uneven parallel lines in the coachwork. The car shuddered to a halt in the soft ground, throwing Jem forward, so his chest hit the steering wheel and the small levers at its centre jabbed into his chest, knocking the air out of his lungs. His head was thrust over the rim of the wheel and he caught his lip on its edge but the rest of his face just stopped short of the windscreen.

He leant back against the seat, panting for breath and felt his chin where a large lump was rising like one of Agnes's scones and a thin drizzle of blood ran out of the corner of his torn mouth. His ribs ached, making it hard to catch his breath. Jem sat in the driver's seat until the shaking stopped. When his vision cleared, and he'd stopped the flow of blood from his lip, he felt his ribs. They were tender but only bruised. He'd live.

He got out and inspected the external damage. Nothing broken on the car, at any rate. Not even the head light. Even the scratches in the paintwork weren't deep. Right, all he had to do was reverse the damn thing on to the road and off he'd go. No harm done beyond a split lip.

Jem got back in the car, having cranked it up again. She started first time with a warm engine. Well done, Katy, my girl, for getting the Sunbeam into such great condition. He felt a thrill of adrenaline, as he pictured her face when she saw him driving the very car she'd serviced so well. Who cared about a few bruises? Jem smiled as he gently eased the clutch up, with the car in reverse. Nothing. The solid wheels spun round alright but all that achieved was a deeper sinking into the earth. Luckily there was no ditch, so the car was square with all wheels level, but the ground was very soft.

Jem got back out, leaving the engine running. He

broke off lots of twigs from the hedge and shoved them behind the front wheels. Never mind the hawthorns; nothing could puncture those solid tyres. Just as well, with all the horse tacks littering the road. It took a while, one handed. When he was satisfied he had some leverage, he got back in and tried again. Eureka! Very slowly, the car got some traction and, once it reached the gravelled surface of the road, latched on to it eagerly. Jem took it out of gear and sat there, stationary, for a moment, thrilled with his success.

An indignant hoot of another car's horn reminded him that he was blocking the road. Dr Benson's black model T Ford zoomed past at a rate of knots. Some poor soul must be in trouble somewhere, the speed he was going.

There was a crossroads a mile up the road. If he took a right, he would come full circle back to the manor. As he approached the crossroads, he realised he would have to stick his right hand out to signal. That would mean he'd have to grip the wheel with his false left hand. Jem looked about and checked the rear view mirror. A gaggle of geese were wandering nonchalantly across the junction. He held the steering wheel in his wooden hand and pumped the hooter. The goose boy looked up in alarm and shooed the birds out of the way just in time, before the Sunbeam scattered them asunder in a cloud of feathers, and a chorus of indignant cackles and hisses.

Sharp right turn, pull that wheel down and he'd done it! On the home strait. Jem enjoyed the last part of his drive. The road here was narrower and much quieter, if rutted. Soon he could see the lodge gates again. He changed down almost smoothly through the gears and took the turning very carefully in second gear. He was a natural. Nothing to it. Going up the drive was much less terrifying than descending it. He pulled up in front of the courtyard and stopped before putting it into first gear to negotiate the courtyard corners. One more turn, through the barn doors, and he was home.

Jem let out a whoop as he parked the car in its resting place and cut the engine. He could master this, no problem!

He sat in the car, letting his heart settle back to its normal rhythm and going over the procedures methodically in his mind, making them stick in his memory, ready for next time. He was concentrating so hard, he didn't see his mother-in-law enter the barn. Agnes was flushed with her long walk up the drive spurred on by a good deal of righteous wrath.

Agnes stood next to the driver's door and banged on the window, making Jem jump. He opened the door.

"Hello, Agnes," he said, feeling a bit sheepish.

"What the hell do you think you are doing, Jeremy Phipps?" Agnes scolded. "If you gets found out, they'll skin you alive!" she told him.

"I've got to find something to do Agnes, or I'll go mad."

"You can't just go stealing cars and driving off who knows where in it and what's that bruise on your face?" Agnes said.

Jem decided to ignore the question, "I haven't stolen it, just took it for a drive. I'm aiming to ask Sir Robert if I can be their chauffeur."

"With one hand? I'm sorry, Jem, I know you can't help that but really, it's not safe, for a start," Agnes said, hands still on her hips and outrage still written large on her face.

"It's fine, Agnes. See, I can hold the wheel with my artificial hand just as well as a real one. I've never driven before but I managed it without any trouble. I'll soon have it off to a tee," Jem said, almost convincing himself.

"I don't hold with it, Jem. You must get some permission. Bert'll be back later tonight. You'd better come round to ours and talk to him about it. Promise me now, lad?"

Jem knew she was talking sense as the madness

of what he'd done, and got away with, dawned.

Later that evening, he walked down the hill to West Lodge. Bert looked tired and a bit grumpy. He was sitting in his favourite chair by the fire with his gaitered legs stretched out to the fender.

"Evening, Bert," Jem said to his father-in-law, who nodded his hello without getting up.

Bert said, "I'm not covering for you lad, if they finds out you've been taking their car out."

"Yes, I've had a think. Now I know I can do it, I'll write to Katy and tell her to ask Miss Cassandra for her permission."

"You'd damn well better, Jem. It's so unlike you to do something as reckless as this. What the hell came over you?" Bert said.

"I can't just sit around, waiting for Katy to come home, waiting for life to begin again. My pension from the army is going to run out soon. I've got to find another way to make a living. Cars are the future, Bert. I'm sorry to say it, with you working with horses, but it's true."

Bert got up, tapped his pipe out into the fire and went off in a huff, grumbling, "This generation thinks they know it all. Flaming cars. Give me horses any day of the week."

Jem posted the letter to Katy the next day. It was a long wait to get her reply but she'd obviously explained things well to Cassandra who'd instantly sent her approval and encouragement with Katy's next letter, ten days after he'd sent his.

Jem thought he'd better come clean with Sir Robert sooner rather than later. He found him in the stables chatting with Bert one morning and broached the subject with some trepidation. After all, if Sir Robert countermanded his daughter's orders, Jem wouldn't have a leg to stand on. Thank goodness Katy had made Miss Cassandra put it in writing. He took the letter out of his breast pocket and cleared his throat.

"Excuse me, Sir Robert, I wondered if I might

have a word?" Jem said.

Sir Robert looked around and Bert's scowl deepened.

"What is it, young Phipps?"

"Sorry to interrupt you, Sir Robert, but I wanted to make a proposal?"

"A proposal? What sort of question is that?" Sir Robert rolled his eyes at Bert, who nodded in sympathy.

"I have a letter here, from Miss Cassandra, sir. She's authorised me to have a go at driving the car, with a view to becoming your chauffeur, if you'll have me. At the moment, with Miss Cassandra away, there's no-one who can drive on the estate and I wondered, um, she wondered, if you could do with a driver?"

"A driver? What would I want one of those for? Confounded machines, cars. Horses have always sufficed for me and Beagle here drives her ladyship anywhere she wishes in the carriage. Always has. Can't see her wanting to travel in a blasted car." Sir Robert looked bemused at the whole idea.

"Yes, sir, I understand that but wouldn't you like to keep up with the times? After all, Dr Benson swears by his car and he's always driving around the place to see his patients. It's much quicker."

"Speed is all very well for a doctor but I'm a gentleman of leisure. I've no need to travel any quicker than a horse can gallop, thank you," Sir Robert didn't appear to want to shift.

Jem shoved the letter under his red-veined nose. "But sir, Miss Cassandra specifically asks me to learn to drive. She thinks your weekend guests might be glad of a lift from the station. See, you can read it for yourself."

"Oh, confound it, man, I don't need to see the wretched letter. Drive the damn car if you must but don't crash the thing and don't expect me to be your passenger. If Cassandra wants you to be her chauffeur, you can go ahead but, if I were you, I'd practise out of earshot of her ladyship, if you get my meaning?"

"Yes, Sir Robert," Jem said. "Thank you, sir. I won't let you down."

"Hmm. I suppose we'd better pay you a wage. Tell Hayes to sort it out. Tell him I said so," and Sir Robert turned away.

Jem couldn't believe his good fortune at Sir Robert offering to pay him. He wasn't going to hang around and give him the opportunity to change his mind.

He went straight to Hayes and arranged the details of his pay. Hayes shook his head at the proposal but was kind enough to remind him, "Oh, and don't forget to get a driving licence from the county offices - I think they're five shillings," and gave him the amount from his wages in advance. Jem hastened into Woodbury and bought the license the same day, in the happy knowledge he had some money coming in again. The doddery old clerk in Woodbury town hall reassured him he wouldn't need to pass a driving test but was most insistent that the speed limit was twenty miles per hour. Jem was startled at this information, knowing he had already exceeded it several times and vowed, silently, to adhere to it in future. He clutched the precious bit of paper as he left the county offices and slipped it into his inside jacket pocket. The official permission made him feel different as it lay against his heart. A driver. Somebody.

After that, he didn't miss an opportunity to practice his driving, but took care only to get in the car when Lady Amelia was out, which she always seemed to be these days.

That war memorial was a godsend in more ways than one.

CHAPTER NINETEEN

Katy had never had so much fun in her life, as she had those first few weeks in Boston. It wasn't *exactly* the same as being happy, but it felt pretty good. Happy was something she only really felt when she was with Jem, but she was glad he was learning to drive. They'd have so much to tell each other when she got home. Her one regret was that he wasn't with her, sharing in the novelty of these lovely, carefree days. Now she knew the way, Katy often stole into the public library for a quiet hour of solitude, while Cassandra was busy with Douglas. She found the atmosphere soothing and conducive to writing long letters home. Then she'd treat herself to a new novel to read for when she had to play gooseberry again. She hopped on and off the subway trams like a native, and could rarely resist reading her new treasure on the way home as she revelled in her first taste of real freedom.

Since Cassandra had hit on the idea of Katy's new role as her travelling companion, she was getting completely carried away, and insisted on buying her new clothes at every opportunity. When Katy protested about all the new outfits, Cassandra refused to stop buying them, saying she was enjoying it far too much and what was money for anyway?

Katy was seeing an altogether new side of Cassandra, who bubbled into laughter at the drop of a hat, unless she was dining at the Flintocks. Katy had been drawn into the family meals and sat quietly throughout the dreary procession of Maureen's offerings. She answered politely when spoken to, but initiated no conversations. As Mrs Flintock was even more reticent whenever her husband was present, it was accepted without question by the rest of Douglas's family, and Katy quickly became accustomed to their solemn ways and earnest discussions about Cheryl's latest medical lesson, or the big molasses insurance claim. Knowing little about either, she never ventured an opinion, but Katy absorbed all this information like a thirsty sponge in a pool of knowledge.

Sometimes Fred Stavely joined them for dinner, and Katy hid a smile whenever she saw Cheryl's stern face light up at the sight of his rotund features. There were no medical monologues at those lunches and Katy was convinced she couldn't be the only one who was relieved about *that*.

Fred appeared unmoved by Cheryl's fluttering eyelashes and uncharacteristic smiles, and Douglas told them that, although Cheryl had always had an eye for Fred's charms, Fred couldn't stand her strident feminism. Katy suspected that Fred's well-bred manners blinded Cheryl to his dislike and, however irritating she might be, hoped Cheryl wasn't in so deep that she would get hurt. If Katy was any judge of character, she would expect Fred might have a number of girls after his money and jovial nature but she doubted he was serious about anyone, or anything. Fred didn't appear to be tied down to any job but to be eternally at leisure, but unlike poor Douglas, no-one chided him about it.

After one tedious lunchtime, while waiting for the others in the hall, Katy saw him lose his temper with Gallagher over something quite trivial, showing a quite different facet to his personality, and she knew a shiver of dislike.

Whenever Fred helped her to vegetables, or topped up her glass of insipid sweet cordial, Katy could feel Cheryl's sharp blue eyes scorch into her. She thought nothing of his attentiveness herself, sensing that Fred's easy graces were bestowed on everyone who came his way, unless they crossed him, but she suspected Cheryl begrudged every little gesture he aimed in her direction.

Just as well Cheryl's studies made her too busy to come to the tea dance they went to at Stearn's one afternoon. Katy was wearing another new dress, made of creamy white cotton, and knew it suited her. Fred obviously thought so too and she didn't know how to refuse politely, when he kept asking her to dance. Fred was an enthusiastic, rather than gifted, dancer and led her round with more confidence than skill. His blithe disregard for the rules was a relief to Katy, as she didn't know any of the steps, unless it was a waltz. All she had to do was follow Fred and keep time.

It took her back to those far away days in Cheadle library when Charles Smythe had taught her to waltz. What a different world that had been and what a different man Fred Stavely was. His hand felt fat and sweaty on her spine, and he had none of Charles Smythe's elegant footwork, but he was very forgiving of her wayward toes.

Katy swirled around the dance floor and the crowded tea tables surrounding her swirled back. She looked up at the sparkling chandeliers and down at their reflection on the polished wood at her feet. Another pair of new shoes, cream this time, followed Fred's big brogues in a dainty mimicry. No-one here knew she was a maid. She didn't look like one anymore, so why would they guess? It was intoxicating. She had dreamed of this since she was a girl. Pity she couldn't change her partner but then, you can't have everything.

"Happy?" Fred said, smiling at her, his face pink and shiny with the effort of dancing.

"Yes, thank you, Fred," Katy said, as the band twiddled to a brief halt between tunes.

"Fancy an ice?" Fred said, steering her back to their table, his hand still clammy on the small of her back.

Katy disentangled herself and walked back out of arm's reach.

"I'd love one, thanks," Katy said.

"Warm work, dancing!" Fred said, and clicked his fingers at the waiter, and giving him instructions in a curt manner that jarred with his usual joviality. Katy noticed the waiter scowl at Fred's rudeness and smiled an apology to make up for it.

"Are you having fun, Kate?" Cassandra said.

She and Douglas had sat the last dance out at the laden table, their hands interlocked across the white linen, amongst the bone china and petit fours.

"Yes, Cass, I'm having a wonderful time, thank you!" Katy said.

Fred beamed at her.

Katy was glad when her ice-cream came in a tall glass, topped with maraschino cherries. She was beginning to feel a little hot under the collar herself. The glacial treat slipped down her throat, cool and sweet. She gave it her full attention, glad of the excuse not to talk, just savouring the moment in the glittering ballroom, letting the shock of the slithering ice in her gullet remind her that this was really happening; that she was really here in America, sitting amongst the élite of Boston.

Cassandra seemed to think it was perfectly natural for Katy to be joining in with all her activities and so Katy stopped talking about her astonishment at being included. She kept her thoughts and sense of wonderment private and only shared them in her gossipy letters back home to Jem, knowing how much he would enjoy her trip, if only second-hand, and wishing he was here to share in all the excitement.

Cassandra's one obsession was her fiancé and she seemed to have an almost desperate urgency to spend every waking minute with Douglas.

Katy worried for her, she seemed so different, almost feverishly happy, and tried to be tolerant.

One especially sunny day, they drove over the river to Cambridge, Boston's twin sister town, for a picnic in the grounds of Douglas's old college at Harvard. The bright weather matched their mood and Maureen had surpassed herself with some rare beef sandwiches, liberally smothered with horseradish sauce. Douglas had added some bottles of lemonade after raiding Maureen's larder when her wide back was turned. Katy watched it pop and fizz in her glass before setting it down on the cropped grass and leaning back against the enormous oak tree that shaded them.

Her eyelids were drooping into a lazy slide when

Douglas said, "Well, ladies, I can think of no more sights to show you in my home city. We've now picnicked in the grounds of Harvard, done our duty by all the museums and churches, walked along numerous waterfronts and visited every park and store I can think of. How about I take you out of town - to the coast?"

"Oh, Douglas, that sounds like a splendid idea," Cassandra said, kissing his cheek.

"Fancy it, do you? We have a summerhouse out at Falmouth," Douglas said, waving in the direction of the harbour.

"Falmouth? Isn't that in Cornwall?" laughed Cassandra.

"That's what it was named after - way back - when the first colonists landed. Must have been some Cornish dreamer who named and claimed it," Douglas said. "It's out on Cape Cod and we go there every summer. It's very beautiful."

"It sounds really lovely, I'd love to go. What about you, Kate? Wouldn't you like to see the sea again, or is that a silly question?" Cassandra said.

Katy smiled at the lovers. "I have no objection to the sea, just so long as I don't have to travel on its wobbly surface."

Douglas said, "We won't take you sailing then, Kate."

"Oh, have you got a boat there, too?" asked Cassandra.

"You bet! There's nothing I love more than sailing across Nantucket Sound. The light is marvellous out on the Cape, you know. It's a bit windy sometimes but all the better for that, when you have a sail up. Have you ever been out sailing, Cass?"

"No, never, but I've always wanted to, and luckily for me, I have a stronger stomach than Katy here."

Katy butted in, "Sounds like we'll have the ideal arrangement. I'll stay on shore and wave you off and you can sail into the breeze without a gooseberry between you."

The other two laughed and Cassandra said, "But, Kate, wouldn't you be lonely?"

"Not at all. I shall go to the wonderful public library and borrow some more books to read. You might love sailing, Douglas, but I'm happiest wrapped up in a good story," Katy said.

"Or under the bonnet of a car," added Cassandra.

"That too," Katy said.

"I still can't imagine you with a spanner in your hand, Kate, but I can assure you, you won't be lonely out at the Cape Cod house," Douglas said. "I'll ask Fred to come along and look after you. Never a dull moment with him around. He's never been a fan of sailing either, but he'll be glad to escort you, I'm sure."

Katy felt a bit doubtful about that idea, but didn't have the nerve to say so.

"Douglas, darling," Cassandra said, "we have the perfect plan. Kate, you have to allow that Fred is good company, don't you? Will your parents mind us being away, Doug, and using their house without them being there?"

"Not a bit of it," Douglas said. "I doubt they'll even notice. We'll go tomorrow and I'll drive us all the way."

They went home for tea and Douglas told his mother their plans. None of the others was present and since Mrs Flintock never objected to anything, the plan proceeded unchecked.

Mrs Flintock said, "Cassandra, dear, I hope you will like our summerhouse. We usually go there when the weather gets hot, so I hope you won't be cold, there isn't a lot of heating. I'd come with you, but Mr Flintock likes me to be at home when he returns from work."

"Thank you, Selina, I'm sure Doug will take good care of us," Cassandra said, smiling at Douglas.

"I do love it out there, on the coast. It reminds me of my home in Kentucky, especially sitting out on the back porch on the swing seat," Mrs Flintock said, her lovely voice throaty with wistfulness. "It's the light, you see. I wish I could paint it, and capture the blueness of the sky reflected in the sea and the white, white surf."

Douglas coughed and said, "We must buy you some brushes and paints for Christmas, Mother."

Mrs Flintock's pale eyes blinked and flickered towards Douglas but didn't quite focus on him.

"Oh, Douglas, dear, that would be lovely," was all she said.

Katy and Cassandra rushed off to Stearn's after lunch and Cassandra spent far more than Katy thought she should on a bathing costume for each of them. Katy couldn't imagine having enough brass neck to wear it, unlike the last time she wore one in the sea at Étaples, when the British Army had been on standby. They spent the rest of the day packing their cases and trying not to take more than they needed.

"Thing is, we've no idea what the weather will be like," Cassandra said, "Do you think I need both pairs of trousers?"

"No, don't be silly," Katy said. "Just take a change of things in case you get soaked, your new bathing costume, one pair of trousers and wear a good all round outfit on the journey. Oh, and something warm. Here, sit down and write another letter to your mother, and I'll pack for both of us. After all, it's what you pay me so generously for!"

Cassandra laughed and conceded, "Yes, you're right. I'd better tell Mother we're heading off, so she'll understand if the post gets delayed or anything. Honestly, I feel she's still sitting on my shoulders half the time."

Supper was a snatched affair that evening, as the family all came home at different times and ate separately. Katy was glad no-one was around to censure their adventure, and especially that Cheryl didn't find out that Fred Stavely was coming with them. She couldn't wait to get out of the city and breathe some fresh air again.

She bumped into Maureen in the hallway when she was carrying the suitcases downstairs to the car the next morning.

"So, off to the coast, is it? And nobody to chaperone the young couple? No-one that counts, that is. Hmm, no good will come of it, you mark my words," Maureen said.

Katy bit her lip and tried to turn away but Maureen was having none of it. She put her hands on her hips and carried on, "Well, I'll have less work to do, with you lot gallivanting off, so that's one good thing, but seeing as you've been elevated to the status of Family, I doubt I'll miss *you*, at any rate. Servants eating with their betters. For shame."

And Maureen stomped back down the kitchen stairs. Katy watched her go without regret. She wouldn't be in poor Abby's shoes for anything, knowing how much Maureen exploited the little servant girl.

She wished she'd never gone down to the kitchen on that first evening and started relations off all wrong. And she regretted giving Gallagher permission to call her Kate. He had a habit of turning up at odd moments and was as silent as a cat, slinking about and brushing up against her in corridors that weren't nearly as narrow as he pretended. Neither was she comfortable around the family table, not that she'd tell Maureen that. She never knew where she fitted in, inside this stuffy house.

She and Cassandra sat in the back of Douglas's car, when they set off, with the two men in the front. Douglas was a good driver, if rather fast, and soon they were cruising along the coast road. They had the top down and Katy thrilled to the feel of the salty sea air whipping about her head. She and Cassandra had tied headscarves tightly around their chins, but Katy wasn't chilled and was tempted to take hers off and let the wind tousle her hair. June had brought warmth in its wake and Mrs Flintock had been right about the light. The nearer they drew to the coast, the brighter the sun shone in welcome.

The noise of the motor, combined with the stiff wind, made conversation impossible and anyway, Cassandra seemed content to gaze at the back of Douglas's head. Katy was happy just to watch the changing scenery and relaxed into the leather seat, feeling all the tension leaving her and staying where it belonged in that narrow, claustrophobic brown house in Back Bay. She had no inclination to look at the back of Fred's tawny locks flapping under his sporting cap, and the thought of entertaining him on her own daunted her. She hoped he would find something to do while Douglas and Cassandra were out sailing and leave her in peace to read her books. She longed for some quiet solitude and looked forward to writing some really long letters to Jem and her mother.

"Hey, girls, fancy a soda?" Douglas said, steering the car into a garage forecourt off the main road. The garage was no more than a jumble of wooden buildings, one of which sported a makeshift sign with 'CAFÉ' written in blue paint which had dripped at the bottom of each wonky letter. "This old girl is thirsty too and I got to fill her up with some gasoline."

He pulled up next to the petrol pump on the side of the road and they all clambered out. Katy's legs felt stiff and she wandered over to look at the pump when a spotty young man came to top up the roadster's tank. Katy was fascinated by the pressure gauge on the pump and stayed behind to study it, when the others went into order their drinks inside the wooden café.

"So, you don't use cans for petrol?" she asked the adolescent, as he inserted the pump handle into the nozzle of the fuel tank.

The boy just shook his hand and said, "Nah, we ain't used them for over a year now."

Katy was intrigued as the fuel glugged straight into the car, and stayed to watch.

Fred called to her from the door of the cafe, "Say, Kate, don't you want a soda?"

Katy called back, "I'll be there in a minute."

"What flavour do you want?" Fred shouted.

"Coca Cola, please," Katy called back.

The young lad finished filling the car and screwed the petrol cap back on. Katy stayed and watched carefully as he replaced the nozzle back into the pump and calculated the quantity to charge.

She followed him back into the garage workshop, a ramshackle barn by the side of the café. A much older man stood there, with his back bent over the engine of a Model T Ford, the parts of which lay scattered about the oily floor.

Drawn by the lure of diesel fumes, Katy went up to the car.

When she peered under the bonnet, the man jumped back in alarm and said, "Hey, lady, whaddya want? Ain't no soda's gonna come out of the gas tank, you know."

"Oh, sorry!" Katy said, "I didn't mean to be nosy. I just like working on engines."

"Oh you do, do you? Well, if you don't mind, I'm kind of busy," the mechanic said, looking like he didn't believe a word of it.

Fred peered around the door and squinted into the darker light of the workshop. Spotting her, he came over, holding a bottle of Coca Cola, with a straw in it.

He held it out to her and said, "Hey, Kate, I didn't know you were interested in the innards of cars."

"Oh, she knows all about 'em, apparently," the mechanic said, tipping his cap back.

"It's just that I was a mechanic in the WAAC, in the war," Katy said.

"The WAAC? What's that? Some kind of baseball team?" the mechanic guffawed.

But Fred's eyes widened. "You don't say! Did you serve in the army? I had no idea someone as pretty as you could wield a wrench," Fred said, and looked at Katy with renewed interest.

"The Women's Army Auxiliary Corps, yes, I did,"

163

Katy said, and stared at the mechanic, who had the grace to shut up. "Cass and I worked alongside each other in France. She drove ambulances and I mended them."

"Well, heavens to Betsy, I didn't mean to cause offence," the mechanic said, and held out a greasy palm.

Katy shook it. She didn't mind a bit of engine grease and smiled at him.

"Pleased to meet you, ma'am," he said.

"You too," Katy said. "By the way, I think your radiator is leaking. See that puddle underneath - it's just got a lot bigger."

"Well, I'll be damned!" said the mechanic and stooped to look under the chassis.

"You probably will be if you don't fix it!" Fred said, laughing too loudly.

The man stood up, glared at Fred and picked up a large spanner. Fred stopped laughing and squared up to him, his face wiped clean of any smile. Suddenly, the mood was quite menacing and Katy didn't like it. She grabbed Fred's hand and ran back out into the sunshine. She took a swig of Coca Cola through the waxed paper straw and it fizzed up her nose. Fred laughed again at that, as if nothing had happened, and swabbed her down with his handkerchief. Katy was glad when the others joined them by the car.

To her annoyance, Cassandra chose to sit beside Douglas and study his profile for a change. Fred jumped into the rear of the car, with an alacrity that alarmed her. He threw his arm across the back of the seat, behind her head, and all the tension she thought she'd left behind in Boston returned, making her spine rigid. She clutched the handle on the side of the door and concentrated fiercely on the surf breaking on the shoreline she glimpsed between the clapperboard houses dotted here and there along the road.

It was a relief when they drew up outside their destination, a large gabled house made of weathered wood. Douglas didn't get out immediately, but said,

"There she is. My favourite place in all the world. What do you think, Cass?"

He cut the engine, put his arm around Cass and whispered something privately in her ear. Cass took off her scarf, leaned her head into his and they sat there together, spellbound and silent.

Katy could only watch and wait, acutely aware that Fred's arm was now lying across her shoulders, and no longer innocently along the back of the seat. She was itching to get out of the car but didn't want to spoil Cassandra and Douglas's special moment.

When Fred leaned in towards her, however, she decided that, just sometimes, her own needs must come before her employer's, and she opened the door and jumped out.

Douglas had parked at right angles to the wooden building, so she walked around the side to look at the front. Katy stood before the house and drank in the scene. It's angular gables were made of clapperboard, like the others they had passed along the way here, its wood silvered by the salty winds that buffeted it. The house seemed to smile at her.

Katy didn't wait to be invited by its owner, because the house had already said it for him. She felt drawn into its welcome and walked up the veranda steps, stroking the banisters' smooth wood before turning to look at the view. Its wide veranda looked out over the water.

Katy gasped with delight. Before her lay a silky stretch of estuary and, in the distance, a sailing boat, sleek and lithe, was moored next to a wooden jetty that carved into the clear, still river. Reeds on the strip of rough grass beside the creek waved hello and then, beyond that, the magnificent ocean pounded its breakers on to a beach of golden sand.

It must have been a trick of the light, but the sea looked higher than the thin spit of land, and the sparkling diamonds of the breaking waves danced above it, leaving the skirt of blue sea stretching wide to the eastern horizon, where Katy's home and all those she loved, waited for her.

CHAPTER TWENTY

"Cass, darling, I can't tell you how happy it makes me to have you here. I love this place almost as much as I love you, and that's as big as that ocean out there," Douglas whispered in her ear.

Cassandra wished Fred would get lost, as Katy had done. She tingled all over and longed to turn into Douglas's embrace and kiss him. Douglas withdrew from her and she felt like he was stretching glue between them; that they were still somehow entwined and would never be really separate again.

Douglas turned to Fred, still sitting in the back of the car. "Um, Fred, would you mind taking some of the luggage into the house? Here's the key to the front door."

"Sure thing, Doug. I'd be glad to," Fred said, winking at his friend and getting out at last.

Cassandra didn't bother to watch Fred fiddling with the front door lock. She couldn't see Katy, who must have wandered off into the garden. Cassandra turned to Douglas and gave him the kiss that had hovered on her lips for so long.

A while later, Douglas said, his voice hoarse with longing, "Cassandra, you know that we can't count on Fred as a chaperone, while we're here. No-one will know what we get up to. Fred won't tell, that's why I asked him, and Kate's in no position to spill the beans, if we, if we..."

Cassandra touched his lips with the tips of her fingers, and said simply, "Good, I'm glad. You know how much I want to make love to you, Doug, don't you?"

Douglas nodded, his eyes dark and serious, though his mouth still smiled where she had touched it. "Let's pretend we're already married then, shall we?" he said, "And share a bedroom?"

"Do you have help in the house?" Cassandra said, still smiling.

"Mrs Silva, a very reliable Portuguese lady, and one of her many daughters, I can never remember which one, usually oblige," Douglas said.

"In that case, we'd better preserve the status quo, darling. I'll have my own room but visit you secretly at night and you can visit me," Cassandra said, giving him another deep kiss.

Douglas's smile faded with a heavy sigh and he said, "You're probably right, honey. Word does have a habit of spreading around, doesn't it? But, I was thinking, I don't know why we don't just get on with getting married anyway. How about getting hitched in Boston?"

"I'd never get my parents to sail across the Atlantic, Doug!" Cassandra said.

"Do they need to attend?" Douglas said, his blue eyes dancing with mischief.

"I can't imagine getting married without them. Mother would never forgive me," Cassandra said.

"Oh, well, I guess I'll just have to wait, but I honestly don't want to, Cass. I want you to be my wife now and for us to be together properly, in every way, and for the world to see how much I love you."

"I know, darling," Cassandra said. "Let me think about it, but for now, let's enjoy this wonderful place. I can't wait to see inside your beautiful house."

They got out of the car and walked around the side of the house, to the back veranda. Cassandra looked out over the creek to the bay and clapped her hands in delight when she saw the spectacular view.

"Douglas, this is fabulous! No wonder you love it so."

"Come on, then, and I don't care what you say, I'm carrying you over the threshold. This is going to be our private honeymoon. We can get the bits of paper later. I make a solemn promise to you now, Cassandra Smythe, to be a loving, faithful husband to you and only you, for the rest of my days."

"Oh, Doug, that's so lovely, and I feel just the same, and I make you the same promise - to love you until I die," Cassandra said, and then shrieked with laughter as

Douglas scooped her up and carried her up the veranda steps and through the open front door.

They kissed again, on the doorstep, until Fred's throat clearing drew an embarrassed halt. Cassandra pulled her dress straight and reluctantly separated herself from the magnet of Douglas's vibrant body.

"Sorry to interrupt you lovebirds," Fred said, grinning, "but there's not a bite of food in the kitchen."

"Oh, lord!" Douglas said, "I meant to send a message to the grocer's store from Boston and I clean forgot in the rush to get away."

"I can't imagine why you were in such a hurry," Fred said, with a leer that Cassandra found distinctly unnecessary.

She decided she'd better take charge, which meant delegation. "Douglas - is the shop far away? And where's Kate when I need her? Fred, could you go and find where she's got to? And Doug, you'd better fetch the help too. I'll take the suitcases upstairs and allocate the bedrooms."

"Aye, aye Captain!" Fred saluted her, winked again at Douglas and ran down the veranda steps to the garden.

"Douglas, is there a telephone here?" Cassandra said, frowning.

"No, honey, we don't even have any electricity out here on the coast. Don't worry, I'll go and fetch Mrs Silva, and at least two daughters, and get some supplies at the same time. By the way, I usually have the bedroom at the back, overlooking the bend in the creek. You'll know which one when you get up there because there's a model sailing boat on the windowsill. I'll be as quick as I can."

"Right. I'll see you later. We'll soon have things ship-shape. It certainly needs a good clean," Cassandra said, drawing her finger through the dust on the table.

She went to the door and watched Douglas as he drove off, holding one arm aloft in a cheery wave. As soon as he had gone, she shouted for Katy, who appeared, with Fred in tow, clutching an armful of wildflowers.

"There you are, Kate. You've been ages! Oh, what beautiful flowers," Cassandra said, relieved that help was at hand. "Come in, do. There's a lot to get organised. We'll need to twitch a duster around, just for starters."

"Oh, leave it to Mrs Silva," Fred said. "I've been here many a time and she's a proper tornado. She's as silent as the grave - saves all her energy for cleaning. She'll soon have the place spruced up. We'll need some heat tonight though. I'll get some wood in from the store, out back."

"Thanks, Fred," Cassandra said, and added, "Do you have any preference for a bedroom?"

"No, I can sleep anywhere!" Fred said, and took off back outside.

"Come on, then, Kate. Let's sort out the sleeping arrangements," Cassandra said, neglecting to add that the strategic positioning of the bedrooms was her highest priority.

"I'll follow you up in a moment, Cassandra. I just need to put these flowers in water," Katy said. "Isn't this place heavenly?"

"Yes, it's gorgeous," Cassandra said, one foot on the stairs and her eyes firmly fixed on the number of doors off the landing. "See you in a minute."

She counted six bedrooms in all. Two rather grand ones at the front of the house, two smallish ones at the side, one of which had recently been converted into a bathroom, and two bigger ones at the back, centred around a generous landing. All were flooded with natural light and afforded different, but equally beautiful outlooks, either over the creek, the woods that lined the road leading to the house, or over the sea.

Cassandra wasn't bothered about a view. She knew she wasn't going to spend time looking out, but in, at her lover. If Douglas had the room at the back, she would take the other one, adjacent to his, and let Katy and Fred enjoy the ocean. *They* would have nothing else to do.

Katy found her unpacking in one of the back

rooms, and knocked before she entered. "Don't you want one of the bedrooms overlooking the sea?"

"No, you have it, Kate. I rather like the look of the river there," Cassandra said, turning her pink face away from her friend.

"Really?" Katy said.

"Yes, really, I'm quite sure about it. I think the sound of the waves might keep me awake," Cassandra fibbed, hoping the surf pounding along the shore might drown out any noises that she and Douglas might make while they were busy *not* sleeping.

"Well, if you're sure, I would love a room looking out across the bay," Katy said.

"Take it, take it, my dear, and make the most of it," Cassandra said, stuffing her underwear into a chest of drawers with her back still to Katy.

She heard Katy clatter back down the wooden staircase and then puff back up with some cases and disappear into one of the bedrooms at the front.

Cassandra took out the new nightdress she'd ordered and had sent round to the Boston house, while Katy was at the library. It was made of lace so fine, you could see right through it, which was the whole idea. Cassandra folded it with a caress and slipped it in the drawer, with her fragrant soap, and smiled.

Fred called up the stairs, "Hey, ladies, here's Doug, coming back with reinforcements!"

They all congregated in the big living room, that also served as the hall.

There was a picture window overlooking the creek and the sea beyond it, and a large dining table stood next to it, bathed in light. The rest of the room was also generously lit by big windows. Some squashy sofas were gathered in a friendly fashion around the fireplace, where Fred was busy stacking logs.

"These should burn well, they're beautifully seasoned. I reckon they must be at least three years cut and stacked," he said. He'd already discarded his jacket and was working in his shirtsleeves.

Katy went into the kitchen and began to sluice down the sink. Cassandra opened the front door and Douglas tumbled in, laden with bags of food and accompanied by a middle-aged woman and two younger ones, who all bore a strong family resemblance, with their colourful headscarves and strong, stocky bodies.

"Cass, I've bought everything I could think of at the grocer's store and brought Mrs Silva and, um, her daughters to give us a hand. Mrs Silva is a tower of strength and she'll soon have the place as spick and span as you would like, won't you, Mrs Silva?"

"Yessir," said Mrs Silva, obviously a woman of action rather than words.

"Splendid!" Cassandra said. "Mrs Silva, would you mind getting your girls to make up the beds and then could you give Kate a hand in the kitchen?"

Mrs Silva nodded, still silent, and followed her upstairs, where she showed Cassandra a capacious linen cupboard stacked with neat piles of sheets and blankets. They left the two daughters, still unnamed, to make up the beds, and descended into the kitchen, where Douglas was unloading numerous brown paper bags.

"Why don't you leave us to it," Katy said, "and explore the garden - Cassandra, Doug?"

Cassandra took the hint and, clasping Douglas's eager hand, seized her escape route.

"Seems we're not needed, after all," Cassandra said.

"I need you," Douglas answered, pulling her towards the river. "I've got something to show you."

They ran to the water's edge at Douglas's insistence. Cassandra was quite out of breath by the time they reached the creek.

"Look! Isn't she a beauty?" Douglas said, pointing to the yacht that lay, moored against the bank, her fine lines pointing to where the estuary met the sea.

"See, Cass. Here's the sailing boat. Oh, it's a fine

sight alright when that sail's up and billowing in the wind. You can feel her lift under you when you speed across the bay. There's nothing like it. We'll go tomorrow, shall we? I bought stuff for a picnic. The others won't want to come. It'll just be us two, alone on the ocean and completely private. I know some tiny coves off the islands and we'll be like Adam and Eve and let the world go hang. What do you say?"

"I say it sounds idyllic," Cassandra said.

They wandered around the garden, which surrounded the house, holding hands and kissing when the fancy took them.

"Wouldn't it be wonderful, if this was our home, and we were moving in for good?" Douglas said, as they stood looking out to sea.

"If only life were that simple, Doug," Cassandra said.

By the time they returned to the house, Katy had set out a cold lunch on the newly polished table.

"Where's Mrs Silva and her daughters?" Cassandra asked. "I can see they've been busy, the place looks spotless now."

"They're in the kitchen. Mrs Silva wanted to mop the floor in there. Douglas, I think they need paying and a lift home. They've worked like slaves!" Katy said, as she counted out four plates.

"Of course, I'll find them and take them home. These Portuguese are famous for their hard work. Hopefully they'll be glad of a bit of extra cash, out of season. Won't be long," Douglas said and disappeared into the back of the house.

When he returned, they all sat down to their cold collation. Katy had made a salad and there was fresh bread, cheeses and a ham. After lunch, they all strolled together down to the beach, which stretched as far as they could see in an unbroken line. A breeze rippled Cassandra's skirt and she opened her arms to catch its briny breath. A bubble of happiness expanded in her chest, as she watched Douglas race Fred to the breakers.

"What a huge stretch of sand," Katy said, stopping to gaze.

"I'm going to paddle," Cassandra said, kicking off her shoes and stripping off her stockings. She tucked her skirts up into her waistband and ran towards the sea's edge, where she plunged into the white surf, gasping as the cold seawater slapped her feet.

Soon all four of them were splashing about in the water. Cassandra stopped to stare at her feet, fascinated by the tide sucking the sand from between her toes and then whooshing it back over them. Then she ran barefoot along the beach and whooped for sheer joy.

Douglas and Fred got chatting to a fisherman, and helped him haul his boat out of the water, leaving Cassandra and Katy to explore the beach. Cassandra noticed some tiny pink shells lining the strand. She and Katy picked them over, looking for the prettiest ones to take back to the house. Cassandra was attracted to their exquisite markings and collected them slowly, hoping that, if she kept them, she would always remember how she felt on this glorious day. When her shadowed silhouette made it hard to see the pastel colours, Cassandra looked up from her absorption to see the sun slinking behind the house to the west.

"It's getting late," Douglas said, "and I'm getting hungry."

"Race you back!" Fred said.

"Hey, you've got a head start!" Douglas called back, and sprinted after him.

Cassandra and Katy stayed behind to put their stockings and shoes back on. They sat above the strand line trying not to shiver without the sun's warmth, with their wet dresses clinging to their goose-pimpled legs. A gull screeched goodnight overhead but other than that, the only sound was the rhythm of the sea, as it tumbled the millions of shells they'd left behind.

"Kate?" Cassandra said, looking out to sea, rather

than at her friend.

"Hmm?"

"I've decided to sleep with Douglas tonight," Cassandra said, keeping her voice low, although there wasn't another soul to be seen.

"I thought you wouldn't be able to wait," smiled Katy.

"Is it so obvious?"

"Frankly? Yes!" Katy laughed and rubbed her arm affectionately.

"Should I know anything beforehand, Kate? You being a married woman and everything?"

"Just enjoy what comes naturally, but Cassandra, don't forget there are consequences and you're only engaged, not married."

"I know, but I don't think I can wait. Douglas is keen to get married as soon as possible, over here in America. What do you think? I can't see my parents making it across this ocean but I'm scared to leave it too much longer. He had such doubts back in England."

"Why should you wait? Do what makes you happy, but I think Lady Amelia, and in fact the whole village, might feel a little cheated of a wedding at the manor." Katy shook her head and added, "But you could always throw a party to celebrate when you got home - then you could invite everyone from both villages, because it would be less formal, you know, less bound by tradition."

"Brilliant idea! And we could just have a simple ceremony here. Oh, Kate, would you be my bridesmaid?"

"Of course! I'd be delighted but, Cassandra, wouldn't it be more proper to have Cheryl and Rose?"

The thought of her future sisters-in-law checked Cassandra's enthusiasm. "Oh, yes, you're right. Well, you must be my maid of honour then, and look after me, just like always. Will you? Please?"

Katy smiled, "I'd be honoured, Cass."

"That's settled then. I'm going to treasure these

175

days here in this fabulous place, away from the elders, for the rest of my life and be a heathen to my heart's content. Things will never be as simple again, they never are," Cassandra said, suddenly knowing her prophesy to be true. The red sunset staining across the western sky backlit the silvery house, now dark with twilight. Momentarily, Cassandra felt sad. The day had passed so quickly, as all the days in this hidden sanctuary inevitably would, before duty once more drew them back into the real world. She shivered.

"Another ghost passing over?" Katy said, reading her mood with uncanny accuracy.

"It's gone now. Come on, let's get back and see what the night brings," Cassandra said, and ran to the house.

Fred had got the old ironwork range alight in the kitchen and it was now belching smoke. Katy took charge immediately and banished both men into the sitting room. Ever a dab hand with large metal machines, she soon had the fire burning brightly, but Cassandra giggled when Katy quailed at the sight of the lobster Douglas had bought for dinner.

"I'm not touching that monster!" Katy said, laughing.

"I'll call Douglas, he can deal with it!" Cassandra said.

Douglas came in, clutching a bottle of champagne. "Can I offer you a glass of bubbly, ladies?" and he popped the cork.

Fred caught the froth in the glasses. "A toast! To Cassandra and Douglas!"

Cassandra drank hers straight down, "Oh, alcohol, how I have missed you! Hey, Doug, want to join me for a cigarette on the porch? I've missed tobacco too. Oh, we've been so *good!*"

Fred said, "Go on then, you two. I'll help Kate with this lobster - you only have to boil it anyway!"

Lubricated by the wine, supper was an uproarious

affair as they crunched the lobster shells by candlelight, and drank a lot more champagne. Katy offered to wash up afterwards and Fred seemed keen to help, so Cassandra grabbed Douglas's hand and made a dash for upstairs, while the other two were busy.

"Goodnight!" she called out, but didn't wait for replies.

Cassandra's lacy nightgown never got a look-in either, as Douglas bundled her quickly into his room and locked the door behind him.

"I've got you now!" he said, grinning like a Cheshire cat. "You're all mine at last. Come here, Cass."

Cassandra needed no encouragement and melted into his arms. She slipped off his shirt and ran her hand across his chest. He smelled of the sea. She licked his salty neck, as he unbuttoned her dress and let it fall to the floor. Soon they were skin on skin, lying on the bed, limbs and hearts entwined.

Douglas hesitated only once, "Are you sure you want this, Cass?" he whispered.

"I've never been more sure of anything in my life," Cassandra said. "Please take me, Doug. Make me truly yours."

Cassandra couldn't believe the exquisite pleasure when they became one. There was a little transient pain, after all, it was her first time, but then sheer ecstasy. Wave after wave of sensation consumed her, as her body rocked against Douglas's and she clung to him until they were spent. They lay together, gasping for breath and laughing softly. Tears sprang to Cassandra's eyes and she turned her face to Douglas.

He licked them away and kissed her eyelids, before they yielded into a blissful sleep.

CHAPTER TWENTY ONE

All through that halcyon week at Falmouth, Katy wondered how she could be homesick at the same time as loving a new, foreign place so much. For love this weather-beaten, salt-rimed house, she certainly did.

Cassandra was so wrapped up in Douglas, literally, that she had plenty of time to herself while they were out sailing or upstairs canoodling, as long as she managed to avoid the increasingly attentive Fred. Katy became adept at finding chores away from him and, to be fair, he spent the greater part of each day out fishing for their supper. Katy kept the house running and loved the freedom of managing her own time. She was no stranger to hard work, preferring it to the dull hours she'd spent in Boston, listening to the Flintock family droning on and dodging encounters with their grumpy staff. So she cleaned and dusted and made up fires in the mornings, grabbed a sandwich for lunch and walked along the beach in the afternoons. If it rained, she read her library books or wrote letters home, and took pleasure in walking to the local store to post them and top up supplies with the housekeeping money Cassandra slipped her.

In the evenings, the four of them would prepare a meal from the fish Fred had caught that day. Katy had never tasted proper seafood before coming to America, and couldn't believe the variety of fish she had to fathom out how to cook. Cassandra was hopeless in the kitchen and took over setting the table, making it inviting with soft lamplight and flowers from the garden. Douglas lubricated their evening feasts with improvised cocktails, while Fred kept them entertained with an endless supply of jokes. Katy doubted she'd ever laughed so much, or felt so carefree.

One night they made a clam bake on the beach. They drank beer and ate cornbread, while Fred and Douglas made a bonfire out of driftwood they'd collected over the week, and heated a great mound of beach pebbles in the fire-pit. Then the two men went off to dig for clams, with a special shovel they'd found in the house, while Katy and Cassandra gathered seaweed. When the stones were heated right through, they used sticks to hollow out the centre. Then they covered it with half the seaweed, threw on the washed clams and the rest of the seaweed and topped the lot with the leftover hot stones. They sat and chatted until the fragrant steam told them the clams were ready. Katy had never tasted anything quite so fresh and delicious.

Their bellies full, they sat around the fire after the sun had set, instead of going back up the house to get warm. Cassandra and Douglas snuggled up close, warming their backs to the fire and gazing out to sea. They talked to each other in low, private tones. Fred threw some more logs on the fire and the flames leapt higher, lighting his round, suntanned face in erratic wisps. Katy wished he would stop staring at her in sly moments.

"So, Kate, tell me about what you actually did in the war. I'd love to know more about it," Fred said.

Kate stared at the bright flames and cast her mind back to that time devoid of colour. Right now, she didn't want to remember that bleak chapter of her life, when she'd believed Jem was dead. Her longing for him increased daily. Maybe it was seeing how happy Cassandra was with Douglas, now they were lovers. She and Jem had never enjoyed that sort of freedom. She doubted they ever would. If only it was Jem sitting next to her now, instead of nosy Fred, but it would be very churlish to ignore him. It wasn't his fault he wasn't the man she hungered for.

So she smiled back at him and said, "What do you want to know, Fred?"

"I can't forget the way you knew about that radiator leak at the gas station. Did you really work on ambulances?" Fred said, poking the fire with a long stick.

"Yes, I did. Cassandra got me the job. I had tried to get into the Red Cross, but I didn't have the right training, so I got shoved into the Women's Army Auxiliary Corps. I was just peeling spuds in the mess until I bumped into Cass. She was driving ambulances and they were very short staffed in the maintenance section. I volunteered for the work, because I've always loved fixing things and, to be honest, I was like a duck to water. Never looked back after that," Katy said, watching as Fred's stick jiggled sparks into the night sky.

"So, did the army train you up then?" Fred said.

"Yes, I learned so much. I'd love to do that sort of work again," Katy said.

"Really? I'm keen on motor-cars myself, so I know how fascinating they can be, but wouldn't you rather do something a little more ladylike? Because you are such a ladylike kind of girl, Kate," Fred said, his voice sinking to a pitch too low for the others to hear.

Katy laughed, "You wouldn't think I was so ladylike if you saw me in my dungarees!"

"Dungarees - do you mean - pants? Oh, I'll bet you looked pretty neat in those, alright," Fred said and threw the stick on to the fire, where it bloomed into flames.

"Shouldn't we be getting back?" Katy said, as Fred turned towards her and shuffled his body closer.

"Why hurry? The fire's warm enough. I brought plenty logs from the house to add to the driftwood. Dragged them all the way here in that sail cloth you're sitting on. We could stay all night, if we wanted to. You know, we could even sleep out here on the beach, under the stars," Fred said.

Katy stood up quickly, and her swift movement sprayed sand into Fred's eyes.

"Hey! Ouch! You just covered me in sand!"

Fred looked very angry all of a sudden. Even in the flickering firelight, Katy could see how his face looked quite different to its normal smiley plumpness. All his usual joviality had stripped away, leaving him looking ugly and mulish.

180

Douglas looked up from his deep conversation with Cassandra. Katy could see he'd sensed the change of mood. "Come on, Fred, don't get that look on your face, now. It always spells trouble. Did I tell you girls about the way that Fred got mad at our school baseball matches? Hell, he'd get so steamed up he'd blast his way around the pitch. Won loads of cups fuelled by that rage, didn't you, Fred?"

Fred scowled at his friend. Katy backed away from him, distrusting his black mood. She'd better watch her step even more carefully from now on and she wondered how much longer Cassandra intended to stay out here on the coast. Suddenly it didn't seem quite so perfect. Oh, if only Jem were here!

Fred kicked sand over the fire and extinguished it. In the sudden darkness, Katy found it hard to adjust her vision. She felt Fred lunge out and try and clutch her hand but she skipped away smartly. The waxing moon picked out the pale froth of the breakers and enabled her to see the glow of the stones around the steaming sand. Their heat was dissipating as fast as her feeling of tranquillity.

"Come on," Cassandra said, looking from Katy to Fred. "Time for bed, children. We'll clear up tomorrow. Anyone got a light?"

There was no fire left to light a stick, so Douglas used his cigarette lighter to show up the tricky bits on the short walk back to the house.

They all knew it well enough by now but somehow its familiarity did not reassure Katy as she stumbled back up the dunes.

The sand felt cold and heavy through the soles of her thin summer shoes and its coarse grains chafed between her toes. She would be glad to be safely back in bed. In fact, she would be glad to be home in Cheadle, if she was really honest.

Fred's mood remained as black as the short summer night and he stomped off to bed as soon as they reached the veranda.

"Night, Fred," Cassandra called to his retreating back.

"Oh, let him go, Cass," Douglas said. "You can't reason with him when he gets like this."

Katy shivered, "I'm a little chilled. I think I'll go up too. Goodnight to you both."

She banged the sand from her feet before entering the house and wished Fred had done the same, as she crunched up the trail he'd left on the stairs. She made use of the bathroom in record time and scurried back to the sanctuary of her bedroom. Katy looked out across the water. The beauty of the scene was tarnished now. She pictured the green of a Wiltshire summer. Beaches were all very well, but they could look very barren. She climbed into bed and drew the covers over her, glad of their warmth and wondering again how much longer they'd stay here.

Cassandra and Douglas gave no hint of their plans the next morning, which was Saturday. They'd been in Falmouth a whole week.

Katy longed for the opportunity to ask them if they were going to stay longer, but Douglas was determined to sail across to Martha's Vineyard with Cassandra, and said the weather was just perfect and they mustn't waste a minute of it.

He flurried around, making preparations. Katy helped him pack a picnic to stow in the boat and smiled when he tucked a bottle of champagne into the wicker basket. Never had she seen a man so in love as Douglas. No wonder Cassandra was glowing - who wouldn't with all that adoration lavished on her. Cassandra confessed, as she descended the veranda steps, that she did want to stay by the sea for a bit longer. Katy supposed they would continue as they had the previous week - either out sailing all the time, though Katy had doubts about how much sailing actually went on, or up in their bedroom - all pretence of sleeping apart having long gone - as they shamelessly made the bedsprings squeak.

Katy had no choice but to accept it, but wished she didn't have to fend off Fred's clumsy compliments. The atmosphere in the house was dominated by Douglas and Cassandra's sexual passion. You could smell it seeping through the bedroom floorboards. Katy was afraid that Fred was finding it contagious.

She followed them out and stood on the veranda to wave them off up the creek. Fred had already gone off somewhere with his net and fishing rod and his own packed lunch. She was deliciously free for the day. After a stroll along the beach, Katy returned to her bedroom and settled down to write a long letter to Jem. She sat down in front of the big bay window that looked out over the sea, and pictured Jem reading her words on the other side of that vast stretch of water.

"Dear Jem,

I wish I could bottle this sunlight and send it with this letter. Better still, I wish I wasn't writing a letter at all, but sitting here, gazing out at the sea, with you by my side. I have never seen such a blue sky. There isn't a cloud in it. A much deeper blue than we get at home, nearer the colour of cornflowers when they first open. The sea mirrors it, and you should see how it sparkles, Jem, better than Lady Amelia's diamond tiara.

There is a freshness here that I can't capture in words. Maybe because everything is so big. When it rains, it's not like the grey drizzle at home. It comes with a roar across the ocean, making the waves crash against the shoreline, leaving a strand of debris washed up like a tidemark in the sink.

I can hear the waves from my lovely bedroom. That's where I'm sitting now, looking out over the bay towards England, but the sea is calm today. Just as well, as Cassandra and Douglas are sailing out to an island called 'Martha's Vineyard'. I don't know if they grow vines there but Douglas packed a bottle of champagne for their picnic. They are so in love, Jem! They can't leave each other alone, like honeymooners. If only we could have that sort of privacy and time.

I don't draw the curtains at night, but fall asleep looking at the stars winking at me in the huge sky, because I know the same stars shine on you, even if you can't see them through the English rain. And there is so much space! You should see the beach - it's miles long - much bigger than at Étaples. I feel free here, Jem. This place makes me feel so alive - sort of newly made and full of energy. Maybe because the war never scarred it. I'm learning to forget that drab sea of khaki with red blood the only splash of colour.

America makes me feel that anything is possible. It doesn't matter so much where you are from, everyone treats you as an equal, instead of making you sit in third class on the train or only speak when spoken to, like a child. Americans call it 'The Land of the Free' and I can see why.

It reminds me of one of Mum's washdays. You know, when the sun bleaches the white sheets and makes them smell of pure air, as if the linen caught all the oxygen and trapped it in its woven net, so we can bring the outdoors into the house and smell it again. That's what Cape Cod smells like, Jem. I feel washed clean of that filthy war and ready to make a new start. I'm not sure how yet, but we'll do it, just like you said. We'll find somewhere to live, somehow, my love.

I wish we were rich and could travel all over the world together, Jem. Crossing the Atlantic in just five days makes the world seem much smaller. There's just got to be a little corner in it somewhere we can call our own. Wouldn't that be fine? Oh, I sound like an American! They are always saying things are fine. Well it won't be fine if I don't catch the post. It's Saturday today but I think there's one post in the morning.

Write back soon, Jem. I won't get your letters until we get back to Boston, but I look forward to them so much. I've no idea when that will be. The way Cass and

184

Doug are carrying on, they'll have to get married soon, or they'll be starting a family. Cass was saying they were thinking of having the wedding here anyway and coming home to Wiltshire as man and wife. I think she wants to make sure of Douglas before he changes his mind. She's written to ask her parents to come over but I can't see them making the trip. If you hear anything about that, be sure to write and let me know. I can't wait to see you again but I do love this house on the coast. If you were here, it would be quite perfect.

> *Your ever loving wife, Katy.*
> *PS. I kiss the paper and wish it was you."*

She made no mention of Fred. What was the point? It would only worry Jem, and there was nothing he could do about him from the other side of the Atlantic. She'd just have to keep the pest at arm's length. She made up her mind to ask Cassandra if they could go back to Boston soon, when they returned from their sailing trip later that day. She might even give a hint that she was finding Fred's attentions too uncomfortable to bear much longer. Cassandra would surely understand, wouldn't she?

Katy folded up the letter and sealed the envelope. Goodness only knew how much it would cost, being two pages long, but if she didn't get to the Post Office soon, it would be shut and she'd miss the Saturday post. They needed more butter and milk for supper too. The day was so warm, Katy didn't bother with a jacket but grabbed her straw sun hat and shopping basket and skipped down the veranda steps. She hummed a tune, as she walked along the dusty road, between the other wooden beach houses. By the time she returned to the house, she was hot and sweaty.

No one was around, so she went upstairs and took off all her underwear except her drawers, relishing the solitude, and covered herself with her thinnest dress. It was too warm to be very hungry so she ate a peanut butter sandwich in the kitchen, then peeled some potatoes for supper, ready for when the others returned. The windows spilled sunshine onto the floor, making dust motes jig in its beams, but the sun was too strong today, even for Katy. She drew the curtains on the west side of the clapperboard house, facing the road, to shade the sitting room. It was too hot to light the stove for the coffee she'd come to love, so Katy took a jug of barley water out onto the porch. She sat on the swing-seat, enjoying the satisfaction of knowing her chores were done, and her letter sent, and let the sea breeze cool her, until she fell into a drowsy doze.

A heavy tread on the wooden steps roused her a while later. Fred wandered in from the beach, laden as usual with fishing gear. His broad face looked hot and sulky but lit up with a wide smile, when he saw her sitting there. He slung his jacket in the kitchen, after propping his gear against the veranda wall, then came and sat next to her on the swing bench.

"Couldn't catch a damn thing today. I swear all the fish have gone to the bottom of the creek to cool off. Never known a day like it. Usually you can catch anything here but I didn't even get a crab," Fred said.

The seat was snug for two people and Katy had no room to budge up.

"Now don't back off, Kate. I swear you've been avoiding me all week," Fred said, too close for comfort and smelling of stale sweat. "As soon as I walk into a room, you walk straight out of it."

"I don't know what you mean, Fred," Katy began. "But as it happens, I must go and see about supper."

"Oh, no, you don't, young lady," Fred said, grabbing her hand. "Stay and talk to me awhile. Those lovebirds are so busy honeymooning, I'm lonely. Doug said they were sailing right out to Martha's Vineyard today, so they won't be back for hours."

Katy smiled but felt trapped, her head still muzzy from her nap. Unless she shunted forward on the seat, her feet didn't touch the ground.

"Tell me about your life back in England, Kate,"

Fred said. "I'm curious about you. It's hard to know where you fit in. Are you part of Cassandra's family or did you meet at school, or what ?"

Fred had started to swing the seat in a wider arc than Katy liked.

"Neither," she said, and tried to touch her toe to the floor.

"Hey, don't look so alarmed!" Fred said, "I'm just interested in you, that's all. I've never met a girl quite like you before. You look so pretty and delicate, but you work as hard as any man I know, and have all this knowledge about cars. It's quite a combination."

Fred laid his meaty hand on Katy's thigh. Its heat scorched through the thin cotton of her dress.

"Don't do that, Fred," Katy said.

"I'm sorry, I thought you liked me. Plenty girls in Boston do, you know. I'm considered quite a prize, but I've never yet met anyone who's tickled my interest the way you do. I've been thinking about you a lot, Kate, while I've been out trying to catch fish. I think I'd like to catch one more, right here and now," Fred said, and leaned his head in towards Katy's face, his lips puckered up ready for a peck.

Katy shot forward and hit the deck with both feet in an ungainly leap. She clutched the banisters to stop herself tumbling down the veranda steps.

"I'm sorry, Fred, but I'm not interested. Now, if you'll excuse me, I really must see to the stove," and Katy marched into the house.

To her annoyance, Fred followed her in, still smiling his confidence.

"Oh, Kate, now don't take on so, I didn't mean to cause offence. I just really like you, that's all," he said. "I thought you realised how I was feeling. Don't tell me you didn't know I was falling in love with you?"

"What did you say?"

"I said," Fred's voice went husky, "I'm falling in love with you. Is that such an alarming prospect?"

"Yes, no, I, I..." Katy was genuinely shocked at Fred's announcement.

"You're not spoken for back home, are you?"

Dismayed at his outburst, Katy looked at him directly, and said, "Yes, Fred. Actually, I'm married. I thought you knew. Didn't Douglas tell you?"

Fred's face was a picture and Katy had a job not to laugh at the way the complacent smile had been wiped off his plump features, as if she'd scrubbed it with her dishcloth.

"Married? Why, I had no idea! You're not wearing a ring! And I've been harbouring such hopes, Kate. Why didn't you tell me before?"

Fred's large hands clenched into angry fists.

Katy felt suddenly frightened and backed away from him.

"I lost my ring on the boat over and I had no idea you felt that way, Fred. I didn't mean to give you any encouragement. I'm only here because Cassandra is my employer. I'm just a housemaid at home and not even that these days, since the war," Katy said, as her back hit the wall.

"You're a *what*? A housemaid? A *servant*? I thought you were Cassandra's friend, just along for the ride, to keep her company?"

"No, well, I am her friend but, but well, it's sort of awkward," Katy said, wishing she'd made her situation clearer from the outset, and eyeing up the exits.

"Well, I'll be damned!" Fred said, and his face darkened as he added, "And did you say that you are *married*?"

"Yes, yes I am. I'm married to Jeremy Phipps."

"Do you love him?"

"Do I love him? Of course, I love him! I love him with all my heart and soul," Katy said, horrified that Fred hadn't realised this.

Fred's face flushed an ugly brick red, and he said, "Well, if you're married, you'll know what Cassandra and

Douglas are up to, won't you? And you're a long way from home, Mrs Phipps, the housemaid. And I thought you were a lady all this time! That husband of yours ain't here to protect you, is he?"

Before she realised what was happening, Fred had got hold of her, and was bundling her upstairs to his room.

"Stop! Stop!" Katy cried, but there was no-one to hear her.

Fred had her arms pinioned around her back and his other hand over her mouth. When he let go to open the bedroom door Katy screamed as loud as she could. She tried desperately to hit him but he still had hold of her hands and obviously had no intention of letting them go.

"Shut up, just shut up, will you?" said Fred and pushed her on to the bed, using his knee against her stomach to hold her there, while he unbuttoned his flies.

Katy pummelled his chest with her fists and kept yelling. She tried to kick him away but he laughed at her attempts to stop him, saying, "So, with you being married and all, I guess you know all about what's coming next," he said, his round face puce from running up the stairs, carrying her weight.

Katy was wearing nothing but her light cotton dress and Fred pushed it upwards over her head in one swift movement, covering her face. Katy tried to grab her dress and pull it back down to cover her body, but Fred was tearing off her equally lightweight drawers, while she was blinded by her dress. She was still pinned against the bed, as he'd placed one of his big hands on both of hers, above her head. He seemed to have twice as many hands as she did, as, however much she struggled to break free of his grip, he always managed to trap her and soon he had got rid of her dress too.

Katy tossed her head from side to side and tried to wriggle from under him, but Fred was strong and muscular. She attempted to knee him in the groin but he'd already laid his weight on top of her, squashing out her breath, so her lungs felt like they'd never inflate again.

That plump look disguised his strong frame, and she was powerless to stop him. He thrust into her and silenced her mouth with his, smothering what little breath she had left.

A door banged downstairs, startling Fred, who looked up at the noise and let go of her hands for a moment. Katy drew a ragged breath, her open mouth gasping for air. The oxygen hit her brain, giving her the energy to jab her elbow into Fred's cheek. As bone met bone, he yelled in pain and clutched at his face. Katy sprang away and collapsed on to the floor, with one ankle caught awkwardly under her. Before she could get up and run to the door, Fred grabbed her by the leg, and shouted, "You can't get away that easily. I ain't done with you yet," and he started to haul her back towards him.

"Help, help! Please God, will no-one save me?" Katy cried, flailing her arms out to the side, trying to hit Fred, but he now had her tight around the waist, and his frenzied movements, as he dodged her blows, made him shout out too.

Suddenly, the door burst open. "What's all the noise about? Oh, my God!"

Katy looked across at the door, relief surging into her and then evaporating in the same instant.

Cheryl Flintock stood there, all dressed in white for the beach, her purple face an ugly contrast.

"Fred!" her voice trailed out in a whisper.

Katy stared at Cheryl standing, frozen to the spot, with her mouth open.

"Cheryl!" Fred said, "What the hell are you doing here? We weren't expecting you."

Tears tracked down Cheryl's flushed cheeks, and she sobbed, "I came to see you on my day off, Fred, but I've seen too much."

She clapped her hand over her mouth, turned, and clattered down the wooden staircase. Fred looked at Katy, who had squirmed as far away from him as she could, and sat on the disordered bed, quivering, with the sheets drawn up over her bareness.

190

"You bitch!" Fred said, and slapped her. Then he wrenched on his trousers and threw on his shirt, and left, buttoning them up as he followed Cheryl down the stairs, calling her name.

Katy grabbed Fred's washing basin and vomited into it. She wiped her acid mouth with the back of her shaking hand and stared at the stained sheets that twisted around her. She couldn't stop trembling. A thin streak of blood ran out of her body and down her legs in a warm, sticky syrup.

Silently, she got up and took the dirty basin into the bathroom, tipping its contents down the lavatory. Then, just as quietly, she, took off her crumpled dress, ran a bath and climbed in. The water was cool, as they hadn't lit the boiler that day, but she didn't care. She swooshed the clean water in and out of her a hundred times, before she got out and dried herself.

Her dress was ruined and she walked, wrapped up tightly in her towel, into her bedroom to find another. The sun was setting and the lovely room was gilded by its amber light. Katy put on another dress, stood at the window and looked east, to where her loved ones still waited for her.

Only then did she cry.

CHAPTER TWENTY TWO

Jem was really pleased with his progress. He'd carved his false hand into the perfect shape to grip the wheel now and his last foray down the drive and out on the Woodbury Road had been much easier. Just wait till Katy saw him meeting her in the car when she finally came home! Now he had Sir Robert and Lady Amelia's approval to drive, there was nothing to stop him meeting her from the station in his new chauffeur's uniform. If only he knew when she *was* coming home. Her last letter, received yesterday, had been full of sunshine, now she was at Cape Cod. It did sound a marvellous place. He could picture the light on the sea so well from her descriptions and almost smell those lobsters she said tasted so nice. Seven weeks and three days now she'd been away, and no hint of a return.

Jem shut the car door and gave it a final polish. He was hungry, and had promised Agnes he'd drop by for one of her lovely pies this lunchtime. He whistled a tune, as he walked towards West Lodge and speculated on what filling the pie might have. He hoped it was ham and leek. No-one had as dab a hand as his mother-in-law, when it came to pastry, but he'd never, ever tell his own mother that.

Halfway down the long drive, Jem bumped into Billy Threadwell, from the Post Office in Lower Cheadle.

"Hello there, Billy! I swear you get an inch taller every time I see you," Jem said, restraining himself from ruffling Billy's carrotty head, like he always used to. Billy must be at least fourteen now. How time flew.

"Morning, Mr Phipps. I got a letter for Lady Amelia from America today, not you, for once."

"Oh? Can I see?"

Billy held it out and Jem read the address, disappointed to see it wasn't Katy's handwriting and that the envelope was made of much better quality paper than she could afford. It had the same postmark, of Cape Cod, as Katy's last letter but the handwriting was all over the place. It looked like it had been written in great haste. Perhaps Cassandra had finally got around to writing to her parents again and had scribbled it off in a rush. His sister, Sarah, who worked up at the house, had said only last night that Mr Andrews had to ring Mrs Threadwell every single day, to double-check there weren't any letters from Cassandra.

Jem felt a glow of pride that Katy kept him better informed but was disappointed there was nothing for him today, even though he knew it wasn't fair to expect another letter so soon. He waved Billy goodbye and marched on towards his dinner.

Agnes had surpassed herself. There was a great pile of mashed potato with the pie, and fresh broad beans to go with it. Jem sniffed the pie. Aha! It *was* ham and leek. She was just cutting into the golden flakes of pastry when Bert, her husband, came crashing through the door, looking extremely upset.

"You're late, Bert," Agnes said, as incisive as her knife. "Pie can't wait, so I've started serving without you, seeing as I made it specially for Jem, here."

"Never mind your bloody pie!" Bert said.

Jem had never heard Bert swear before. His mouth, so recently salivating in anticipation, went suddenly dry.

"What on earth is the matter, Bert?" Agnes said. "Can't you even shut the door behind you?" And she went and slammed it shut.

"I'm glad you've done that, Agnes," Bert said. "I don't want anyone else to hear what I've got to tell you. Sit down. Where are the children?"

"At school, and Emily's having a nap. Tell me what's up, Bert. You've got me really worried," Agnes said, sitting down in front of her pie that was now slit open, with all its fragrant steam escaping.

"Jem, I'm glad you are here too. Now I shan't have to say it twice," Bert began. He stayed standing, leaning his hands on the back of the wooden chair and looked from one to the other.

Something cold crawled into the pit of Jem's stomach and he said, "Is it Katy?"

Bert nodded, his mouth drawn into a grim line, "It is."

Agnes's hand flew to her mouth, "Oh, Bert, she's not been in an accident, has she?"

"Not in a manner of speaking, no," Bert said. "But something awful has happened. I've just come from a private interview with Lady Amelia, up at the house." He looked at Jem and said, "It's difficult to say this, Jem. I can't believe it myself, but Lady Amelia has had a letter from one of Douglas's family. His sister, I believe, I think Cheryl Flintock is her name." Bert cleared his throat, "Thing is, this Cheryl is accusing our Katy of carrying on with a friend of Mr Douglas."

"What?" Jem said, flying up out of his chair. "That's not possible! Katy would never do a thing like that!"

"What do you mean, carrying on?" Agnes asked.

Bert's leathered skin flushed beetroot. "This woman claims Katy was found with him, you know. Oh, how can I put it?" Bert looked around the kitchen for inspiration. "Going all the way," he said, finally.

"No! I don't believe it!" Agnes said, "Not our Katy!"

"I don't believe it, either," Jem said. "Someone's taken advantage of her. I'd kill him if I could lay my hands on him!"

There was a sharp rap on the door from someone's cane.

Bert ran his hands over his wet eyes and looked at his wife. "I can't answer it right now, Agnes."

Agnes nodded and got up to open the door. Lady Amelia stood there, leaning on her cane, and looking exceedingly angry.

She swept into the lodge kitchen without

194

invitation, almost knocking the flowers off her large hat in the cottage doorframe.

"I can see by your shocked faces that you have heard the news," she said, looking at each one in turn. "This has brought a terrible scandal upon the Smythe family. Your Katherine tried to seduce my son, Charles, and now she's shamed us in America. Cassandra must be in a terrible position with the Flintock family, and I don't know if her engagement will now continue, and all because of your daughter, Mr and Mrs Beagle, and your wife, Mr Phipps. I have no choice but to dismiss you all from my employment. You will quit this house within the month. I don't care where you go, as long as none of you remain on my land. I hope I make myself quite clear?"

"But, Lady Amelia," Agnes began.

Lady Amelia held up her hand. "I will brook no argument. I'm sorry for you, but there it is. You have given good service, Albert Beagle, and for many years, but this, this terrible event, overshadows everything else. I cannot bear to see anyone connected to that girl ever again. Please make sure that my instructions are carried out to the letter. Mr Hayes will instruct you further, for I have no wish to set eyes upon any of you, for the rest of my life."

Lady Amelia looked at each of them again, and then nodded as if to emphasise her decision, before departing through the door, which still hung wide open.

No-one spoke after she left. They stood in stunned silence, as the pie congealed between them.

CHAPTER TWENTY THREE

"Take everything, Katy," Cassandra said, "I want you to have every single thing I bought you. You're going to need it."

Katy nodded her submission in silence. Cassandra didn't think she'd heard her speak once, since she and Douglas had come home from their wonderful day's sailing to find Cheryl Flintock in the living room of the coast house at Falmouth, crying her eyes out. Cheryl had come down on the train to see them all and had screamed at Douglas, the minute he'd walked in, some ludicrous story about Katy seducing Fred. She'd shouted that Katy was no better than a prostitute and asked them how could Fred be expected not to resist her sluttish charms, before becoming completely incoherent. Douglas had looked at Cassandra in bewilderment and then tried, unsuccessfully, to calm his sister down.

Cassandra knew her friend better than that, and had left them to it, while she went to investigate. She had found Katy in her bedroom, staring out at the sea, as still and white as a marble statue. She hadn't spoken then, or since. Fred had already disappeared. They put Cheryl to bed in Cassandra's room. The bed had never been slept in anyway and Cassandra gave her a dose of a sleeping draught they found in the bathroom cabinet.

The four of them had returned to the town house in Boston, in Douglas's car, the next day. Cassandra hated it now and felt its narrowness mirrored the views of its occupants all too well.

If only Katy would talk! Neither she nor Douglas had seen hide nor hair of Fred Stavely, to ask him what had really happened. Apparently he had run out of the house, very upset, Cheryl had informed them, and got straight on the train back to Boston and then gone who knows where. She'd followed him to the station at Falmouth but he wouldn't let her board the train with him. No-one had heard a word from him since. All that they had to go on was Cheryl's garbled and hysterical account of what she'd witnessed. Cassandra had always known those happy days at the summerhouse would be both perfect and short-lived but she could never have anticipated how they would end.

Mr Flintock, always a stern man, had looked like God himself in his righteous wrath. She would never forget, or forgive, his outraged condemnation of poor Katy, who had stood, head bowed, while his tirade cascaded over her in wave after wave of character assassination. Cassandra couldn't stand to witness it and knew it would have crushed her spirit, had he directed it at her. Cheryl had sat watching the humiliation, like a witch, while her father roared his verbal whipping at Katy. Cassandra could have sworn she saw Cheryl's mouth curl in a sneering smile at one point.

Mr Flintock meticulously sidestepped Cassandra and instead vented the rest of his spleen unremittingly on Douglas. Douglas was told to book Katy on the next boat out of Boston and he hurried off to the dockside to purchase her ticket. Cassandra envied him a task that took him out of the house. She was left to escort Katy back up to their room, and here they were now, packing suitcases for her journey home.

"Kate, before you go, please, won't you tell me what happened? We are completely alone at last. Come, sit down on the bed with me."

Cassandra took Katy's hand, and was shocked at its coldness.

All the fight had gone from her friend and she sat on the satin coverlet, meek as a newborn lamb and looking just as vulnerable. Cassandra was worried that she wouldn't cope with the long sea voyage, seeing Katy looking so fragile, and recalled how seasick Katy had been on the way over.

"Kate? Please, talk to me, dearest? I know you hadn't encouraged that dreadful Fred Stavely. I feel responsible too, Doug and I should never have left you alone with him for so long. We've been horribly selfish, wrapped up in each other and never giving you a single thought. I'm so sorry, Kate. Will you ever forgive me?"

Tears welled up in Cassandra's eyes as she gazed into Katy's troubled ones but then, she saw compassion steal into those unusual violet irises as Katy reached out her other hand and patted Cassandra on the shoulder. *She* was comforting Cassandra! It made her feel more guilty and wretched than ever. She had been cocooned in her personal new heaven of love-making, and now here was Katy looking like a broken doll.

Katy's voice cracked to start with. Cassandra supposed it was because she hadn't used it for twenty four hours.

"It's not your fault, Cass. Don't think that."

Katy's soft Wiltshire accent broke Cassandra's heart. She wished they'd never left home.

"Oh, Kate, that's so generous of you! How typical of you too, but it was my fault. Doug feels awful too. I hate that bastard, Fred Stavely. Please, dearest, tell me what happened?"

"I don't like to remember it, but I suppose you ought to know. Douglas ought to know what his friend is really like, if only to protect other girls," Katy said, her eyes devoid of emotion.

Terrified she would stop the confession, Cassandra just nodded and pressed encouragement into Katy's hands, now both lying still and cold in her warm ones. She didn't seem able to transmit any blood-heat into them.

"I was sitting on the porch, enjoying the view, and I must have dozed off. Fred came back from fishing and sat next to me. He tried to kiss me and I jumped off the bench to get away from him. He told me he was falling in love with me. I told him I was married. He seemed very shocked to hear that. He asked me if I loved my husband and I said I do, with all my heart and soul. That was when he got really angry and..." Katy's narrative dried up.

"Go on," Cassandra said, "You're doing really well."

"He carried me upstairs and ...um, he forced me to have sex with him, in the most horrible way. I can't, Cassandra, I can't tell you all of it."

"There, there, Kate, I understand. Is there anything else?"

Katy shook her head. Misery seeped out of her and stole into Cassandra's hands.

"Just that, when he was nearly, you know, finished, I got away from him but he was pulling me back. Then, the door opened, and there was Miss Flintock. I was shouting for help and he was yelling too, I don't know why. He was like an animal. In a frenzy. Beside himself. And that's how she found us. She looked so shocked. I've never been so ashamed. She ran away. He slapped me then," Katy paused, as Cassandra gasped out her dismay.

Katy continued, "Then he ran after her, down the stairs, shouting her name. I was sick. I had a bath. Threw my dress away. I just wanted to go home. I just kept looking out, over the sea, to where home is. Oh, God, will Jem ever love me again! Oh, Cassandra, I feel so dirty! I'm so shamed."

Katy's slim body wracked with sobs that seemed to dredge up from her very soul.

She looked at Cassandra. Those lovely purple irises had now receded and only wide black pupils stared at her. She looked like she was in torment. Cassandra gathered her up into her arms and let her sob until she was exhausted. Her own tears trickled down Katy's thin back, unheeded by either of them.

When Katy's crying ebbed, Cassandra said, "Thank you for telling me, Kate. That must have been very hard, but I appreciate knowing the truth."

She pulled back from her friend and held her by the shoulders. She wanted Katy to listen very carefully to what she was about to say.

"Kate, Katy, hear this, my dear. You have done

nothing wrong. Nothing whatsoever. I never once saw you flirt with Fred, not once. We should have told him you were married and unavailable and I am responsible for that, not you. If this is anyone's fault, it's mine and Doug's. Fred is a very deceiving person. Always so jolly and telling jokes and stories. He certainly fooled me and that's never happened to me before, so how could you have known what he was truly feeling? He gave no hint of his being in love with you because he flirted with every woman he came across, it seemed to me. Douglas has known him all his life, grew up with the bastard, and he never guessed he was such a brute. He said although Fred was always a bit wild, and had a fearsome temper, he'd never known him to be vicious."

Katy just stared back at Cassandra, with unblinking eyes, as silent tears welled up, one by one, and flowed down her pale cheeks, past the red weal standing testament to her ordeal.

Cassandra carried on, "Douglas is as shocked as I am, and so sorry that this has happened to you. We both know you are completely innocent. As for the Flintocks, there's nothing I can do about them banishing you in this horrid way. I shall tell them the whole truth when you are gone, but I feel it's best that you *do* go while we'll have to remain a little longer, I think. They would make your life hell if you stayed. They're all snobs, that's what. As soon as things are smoothed over, I shall come home too and see you there. Mother and Father need never know anything about this sordid episode. You can rely on me not to breathe a word about it and I shall make sure the Flintocks never tell them either. I can't see why they would anyway, it doesn't reflect well on their care of you. Do you understand? And do you agree that this is the right thing to do? Kate?"

Katy was still crying, but quietly now, and she nodded and squeezed Cassandra's hands.

"I shall have to tell my Jem," she said. "That's what I'm dreading. What if I lose him, Cass? I couldn't

200

bear to lose him!"

"Now, don't start upsetting yourself all over again. Jem will understand, I'm sure. Real love is big enough to swallow this rubbish up and spit it out. You'll see."

Katy shook her head, "I hope you're right, Cass. I hope to God you are right."

CHAPTER TWENTY FOUR

"Come on, honey, let's go home," Douglas said to Cassandra, putting his arm around her shoulders and pulling her away from the edge of the wharf.

The big ship had cast off anchor and was lumbering up the estuary on its way back to England. There was no point waving Katy off, for she was nowhere to be seen on deck. Cassandra guessed that she had gone immediately to her cabin - Douglas had insisted on paying for a private one - like a fox to its lair, and would now be licking her wounds and bracing herself for the Atlantic crossing. At least the weather was set fair, now it was nearly July.

"Do we have to go to your house, Doug? I'm not sure I can face it, just yet," Cassandra said, pulling her eyes away from the strange, brown water and up to his.

"No, we don't have to go straight back, darling. How about some lunch?"

"I'm not hungry, Doug. Could we get out of town? Go for a drive, maybe?"

"Sure, we can, but I guess, not to the summerhouse?" Douglas said, as they walked back to the car.

"That is not funny," Cassandra said.

"I know, I'm sorry," Douglas opened the car door for her and she climbed in, weary to her bones.

Cassandra didn't speak while Douglas negotiated the chaotic traffic through the city. She was too busy thinking. He drove inland, past Harvard College and into open countryside. They stopped at a roadside cafe and gas station for lunch and to refill the car's petrol tank. Flies buzzed around the porch of the wooden shack and they nipped inside through the flyscreen door, smartish. They ordered their lunch and a couple of drinks from the sulky girl behind the bar. Inside, the café was grubby and too hot. A couple of old boys in greasy dungarees eyed them from the bar and chewed tobacco.

Cassandra toyed with her salad. She still had no appetite. Ignoring the baleful stares from the men, she said, "Douglas, I'm going to have to talk to your parents about Kate. Tell them what really happened."

"Do you think that's wise, Cass? They'll never see her again but they will see Fred, when he dares to show his face again."

"Then all the more reason they know how he behaved. Kate isn't a servant to me anymore, Douglas. She's my friend, and one I hope to have all my life. I owe it to her, no, we *both* owe it to her, to restore her reputation."

"I see that, Cass, and I admire you for it, but it won't reflect well on us. They're bound to wonder what we were up to, leaving Kate alone all day with Fred," Douglas said, swigging straight from his beer bottle.

"We'll just say we were out sailing, that's all," Cassandra replied, wondering how Douglas could be worrying about his reputation when Katy's was in shreds and the jury was still out on Fred's. For the first time in their relationship, she felt out of tune with Douglas.

"Are you saying that you won't back me up?" She laid her fork across her plate, her food half-eaten.

"No! Of course not, it's just that I'm not sure what it would achieve," Douglas said.

"It'll put the record straight, Douglas. You never know, it might protect other girls in the future."

"Oh, for heaven's sake! Fred doesn't go around raping women all over the place!"

One of the men hawked his cud of tobacco into a spittoon in the corner. Cassandra felt sick but carried on, "Isn't one enough? From what Kate told me, it was done in the most brutal manner."

"You only have her word for that," Douglas said, and called for another beer.

"And if I had to trust anyone's word in this Godforsaken world, it would be Katherine Phipps'!"

Cassandra got up and walked out of the stifling

café into the warm sunshine. She sat on the bench outside the wooden shack and watched cars zoom past on the long straight road at infrequent intervals. My God, America was vast. She could see across so many miles to the horizon and hadn't a clue where they were. She would have to rely on Douglas to get her back to Boston, but right now, she needed this moment alone to quell her temper.

He quickly joined her, saying, "Cooled off yet? Want to get back to town, now?"

Cassandra nodded and climbed back in the car. Douglas didn't interrupt her thoughts and they drove back in silence until Cassandra broke it.

"I thought you would understand, Douglas. Kate, as my employee, was my responsibility, and I feel I have let her down. I have to put her side of the story to your family. I shan't tell my own parents, or hers, there's no point. Let her rebuild her life in Wiltshire without the shame of this to stain it. She's been through enough already, but I will need your support when I speak to yours. If we can't do this together, Douglas, and see it the same way, I'm not sure we should get married at all."

Douglas pulled over into the dirt on the side of the wide road and halted the car with a screech of brakes. He turned to her and said, "*What* did you say?"

"You heard me, Doug," Cassandra's stomach tightened into knots. There would be no going back from this conversation, but she could not marry a man who was a coward. "We have to make the truth known. It's a matter of principle, and if we don't share the same principles, then we are not going to be good partners in life."

Douglas's face paled in the sunshine under his new tan; a legacy of those halcyon days when they had sailed his beautiful little yacht across Nantucket Sound. On that last fateful day, the weather had been like this, with a blue sky that stretched forever, as if it would never again be sullied by a cloud. With the soft top down on the car, Cassandra welcomed the warm sun on her skin, wondering how her stomach could still have cold lead lining it, while the rest of her was bathed in such benign sunshine.

Douglas looked out at the road, stretching ahead. He swallowed, frowned and then nodded. "Alright, Cassandra, I take your point. God, I wish I'd told Fred she was married. It never occurred to me that I'd need to. We'll tell the family the whole sorry tale, but you have no idea what you are taking on. We'd better leave it until Sunday, when the whole clan will be gathered for lunch, after church, and do it then. Father and Rose are keeping such odd hours on weekdays with that damn molasses case and Cheryl needs to calm down a bit before we release Kate's side of things. Do you agree that would be best?"

"Very well, yes. Today is Tuesday, so how the hell are we going to get through the rest of the week, with this hanging over us?"

"You leave that to me, darling. Just so long as we are together; that's what's important to me," and Douglas leaned over and kissed her, long and deep.

The week dragged by, despite Douglas's efforts to entertain her. They did the usual round of going to the library - for the sad errand of returning Katy's books - and walks in the park and trips to museums. It all felt empty and hollow without Katy's intelligent curiosity sparking lively conversations and providing the companionship Cassandra had come to treasure.

And yet, when Sunday dawned, she would have given anything to be traipsing aimlessly around the streets of Boston again. They all trooped off to church, as normal. And, as normal, the piety spouted by the preacher left Cassandra unmoved. There never seemed to be any compassion in the sermons, only judgement. It didn't help her nerves.

Maureen's best meal of the week was Sunday roast. She couldn't easily ruin that. It was a tired family joke, but this time no-one repeated it, and the meal was conducted with a minimum of chat. Even Cheryl was silent in the awkward aftermath of Katy's dismissal and Rose looked too exhausted to make her usual sweet efforts. Or had they all intuited that a confrontation was in the offing, Cassandra wondered?

After dessert, another safe offering of rice pudding that stuck to the rib-cage, Douglas cleared his throat and said, "Mother, Father, Cheryl and Rose, Cassandra and I would like to talk about what happened at the summerhouse last week."

"I think quite enough has been spoken on that subject, Douglas. Please respect the sensibilities of the female members of our family," Mr Flintock said, and glared at his only son. He turned to Gallagher and said, "Thank you, Gallagher, you may go now. We'll clear away later."

When Gallagher had slunk out of the room, Douglas carried on the conversation.

"I do respect them, Father, but I also respect Mrs Phipps, and although she isn't here to speak for herself, both Cassandra and I feel that her side of the story has not been told."

Cassandra spoke then, while gripping Douglas's hand under the table. "Sir, if I might put Kate's version of events before you?"

Mrs Flintock stirred in her seat but, as usual, remained silent. Cassandra wondered how much she already knew. Cheryl sat very still, almost rigid, but Rose leant across the width of the table and patted Cassandra's other hand.

"I think you should speak up for your friend, Cassandra, dear," Rose said.

"Thank you, Rose," Cassandra said, and squeezed a thank you into Rose's ink-stained hand.

"According to Kate, Fred approached her when she was alone. Douglas and I had gone out sailing for the day," Cassandra began.

"For the whole day?" Mr Flintock interjected, his

206

whiskery eyebrows raised.

Douglas chipped in then. "I took Cassandra to see Martha's Vineyard, Father. The weather was perfect, so we took a picnic and made a day of it. Kate wasn't a good sailor, so she decided to stay home. She was terrific at keeping the place in order for us."

"And what of Fred?" asked his father.

"Fred said he was going out fishing for the day, so we thought it would be fine," Douglas said.

Cassandra hated glossing over the truth but it was as near as they dared get. She continued, "That's right, sir. When we came back, we found Cheryl had arrived by train and the place was in uproar. Fred wasn't there and Kate seemed to be in a state of profound shock and couldn't speak. It wasn't until she was packing to go home, that I heard her story."

"Which is?" Mr Flintock said, looking more irritated than ever.

"That Fred came back from fishing before we returned. He told her he was falling in love with her and tried to kiss her. Kate told him she was married and not interested. At that point, Fred became very angry, took her upstairs and, there is no other way to say this, brutally raped her. Sorry, Mrs Flintock, I can't think how else to put it. That's when Cheryl found them and Fred ran away and got on the train. Kate was terribly shaken up." Cassandra stopped her narrative, unable to ignore the bristling silence emanating from Cheryl, seated opposite her.

Neither, it seemed, could Cheryl's father. "Cheryl? Have you something to add to this sordid tale?"

"Yes, Father, I have!" Cheryl's face went bright pink. "It was the most disgusting thing I've ever seen when I caught them together! Katy was naked and yelling her head off. She couldn't have undressed without helping him. She wanted it. It was plain to see. And now Fred's gone and I don't know if I'll ever see him again!"

"There, there, Cheryl, I'm sure Fred will return,"

Rose said, in her soothing voice that didn't disguise the doubt in it.

"I'm not!" Cheryl turned to looked straight at Cassandra. "You English women, coming over here and stealing our men-folk. Douglas will leave home and go to England to live and I doubt we'll ever see him again and your miserable servant has ruined Fred's good name." Cheryl's voice grew louder as she carried on.

"Oh, yes, Cassandra, you can look daggers at me all you like, but she was nothing but a servant. And a devious one at that. Why wasn't she called Mrs Phipps all the time? Why, if that had happened, if she'd been kept in her place, where she belonged, Fred would be round this table having Sunday lunch with us, as he has done for *years!* You've broken everything we hold dear. Well, I tell you this, Miss Snobby Smythe, I've written a letter to your mother about it. Oh, yes, she knows what really happened. We'll see what becomes of Mrs Phipps when she gets home!" and Cheryl stopped talking, as if she'd run out of breath, and folded her arms across her heaving chest.

"You did *what*?" Douglas stood up, and stared at his eldest sister.

Rose dissolved into tears and held her hands over her ears to block out the argument. Mrs Flintock went quite white.

"When did you send the letter?" Cassandra asked, dreading the answer.

"Oh, I sent it that day. Fred wouldn't let me get on the train with him, even though I pleaded with him. I told him I didn't care what he'd done. I told him I loved him. He wouldn't listen," Cheryl started to sob, then steadied herself and continued with a strange little smile, "so I went to the Post Office after the train had left and bought some paper and wrote it right then and there. I just guessed the address, after all there can't be many Lady Amelia Smythes living at Cheadle Manor in Wiltshire, can there?"

"Do you know what you have done?" Cassandra

said, almost whispering. "Kate will go home, having gone through this terrible trauma, to find her life in tatters and never being able to work again. How could you be so mean-spirited, you little bitch?"

"Cassandra! You may be a guest in my house and affianced to my son, but I will not tolerate this sort of language! You forget yourself, madam!" Mr Flintock said, his own voice getting loud.

"It is not Cassandra you should be lecturing, Father! but Cheryl here! She has done the most foul act of sabotage on an innocent woman's life. That is sheer spite, Cheryl. Just because Fred didn't admire you! How could you defend his actions?" Douglas was almost shouting.

"I don't care what he did, she probably deserved it. Jumped up little thing from the gutter!" Cheryl shouted back.

"And I thought you were all for women's rights and female equality!" Douglas yelled.

"There are some women who can never be equal!" Cheryl retorted.

She was also standing now and had her face in Douglas's. If it wasn't for the table between them Cassandra thought they'd hit each other.

Mrs Flintock put out a shaking hand, "Stop! Oh, please stop! I can't bear to see you fighting like this!"

Rose ran to her mother's side and put her arm around her. They both held handkerchiefs over their mouths and their eyes, so similar in their pale blue surprise, were open too wide, so that their pupils were surrounded by white.

Gallagher crept back into the room. Cassandra realised the door hadn't been shut when he'd left. He'd probably been listening all through the family row from the hallway.

"Is anything the matter?" he asked, "Only, if it's Kate Phipps you're all talking about, I can tell you, she made eyes at me too, while she was here. Maureen always said she was too big for her boots."

Douglas swivelled around to face Gallagher and swung his fist back ready to lunge at him. Cassandra tried to catch his arm and missed by half an inch.

Gallagher took the blow high up on his cheekbone. There was a sickening crash, as his head hit the flock wallpaper. He slid down to the floor and lay there, unconscious.

Mrs Flintock screamed and fainted. Rose stood over her mother, flapping her handkerchief across her still, white face. Mr Flintock grabbed Douglas by the collar and wrenched him out of the way, making Douglas choke. Cassandra flew to Douglas's side and loosened his tie. Cheryl calmly took command of the situation and knelt down next to Gallagher's inert body and felt his jugular pulse.

"It's just concussion. Father, pour some water, no, make it brandy, into a glass and pass it to me," Cheryl said, and undid Gallagher's collar and tie, while her father unlocked the corner cabinet with a key from his pocket and extracted a bottle of brandy.

Cheryl took the glass her father offered her and measured the pulse on Gallagher's wrist, before tipping some brandy into his mouth. Gallagher coughed and spluttered the liquid across Cheryl's white blouse, spraying it with blood.

Cheryl looked in her element and completely in command of the situation, just like the doctor she aspired to become. Cassandra wished she could wipe that smug satisfaction from Cheryl's bony face.

Gallagher opened his eyes and winced.

"You'll be alright, Gallagher. You'll have a black eye for a week, but you'll live," Cheryl said.

Mr Flintock knelt down and patted Gallagher on the shoulder, "I'm so sorry my son attacked you, Gallagher. Please accept my apologies."

Gallagher lifted the other side of his mouth in a lopsided acknowledgement. "It's alright, sir. Maybe I spoke out of turn."

"No, Gallagher, I think you have confirmed our suspicions. I appreciate your coming forward. Please, if you can make it, go to your room and rest for the remainder of the day. I will inform Maureen."

Gallagher scrambled upright and Cheryl helped him to stand.

"Douglas! Take Gallagher up to his room and apologise to him on the way, please," Mr Flintock said.

"But, sir," Douglas said.

"I'm not asking you, Douglas, I'm telling you. Now, go!"

Douglas nodded and gripped Gallagher's forearm and marched him out of the room. Cheryl immediately went to her mother with another glass of brandy and forced some between her mother's alarmingly blue lips. Mrs Flintock didn't spit her spirits out. A sip of the liquid seemed to have a remarkably restorative effect and she sat back on her chair and nursed the glass, smiling in a dazed way at the rest of her family. Rose stood behind Mrs Flintock, her hands resting lightly on her mother's shoulders.

"Selina?" Mr Flintock said to his wife. "I think you should go up and rest now, dear. Rose? Take your mother to her bedroom."

They both nodded and Mrs Flintock went quietly out of the room, gripping Rose's arm and her glass with equal desperation.

Cassandra stood between Cheryl and Mr Flintock. How similar they were, now she came to look at them together. Their strong, uncompromising profiles, dominated by their prominent noses, clearly indicating the strength of their convictions. Was there any point trying to vindicate Katy now? Cassandra doubted it, after Gallagher had put his pennyworth in. Her heart swelled with pride at how Douglas had swung for him. How could Douglas be so different from the rest of his obnoxious family?

But she couldn't remain silent. "Well, Cheryl, I hope you are satisfied now? Not only is Kate's life ruined but Gallagher will never look the same again."

"Oh, don't you go blaming me, you hypocrite!" Cheryl almost spat out her words. "You're the one who brought that harlot here, into our self-respecting home! She was obviously making a play for Gallagher too. More her level, I should think, than my poor Fred."

"He wasn't yours, though, was he, Cheryl? If he had been interested in you, you wouldn't now be so bloody spiteful! And that Gallagher is just a sneak. Kate told me he'd been trying to get fresh with her."

"Enough!" Mr Flintock roared at them both. "I want to hear no more of this subject from either of you. The whole house is in chaos. Cheryl - you should not have sent that letter to Lady Amelia. It will not increase her respect for us, and Cassandra - should I assume you still wish to marry my son?"

Cheryl cut in, "Or, maybe, Douglas doesn't want to marry *her* now?"

Cassandra went completely cold. Something very lovely died inside her. "Douglas and I love each other very much. I also love Kate Phipps. She has been completely maligned and mistreated. I feel I have got to know your family all too well, Mr Flintock, but it doesn't change how I feel about Douglas."

Douglas returned to the room at this point and strode quickly over to Cassandra, while she was still speaking, and took her hand in his bruised one.

Cassandra smiled at him, wondering how she could love him even more than before.

"We shall be married at once, Father," Douglas said, looking Mr Flintock squarely in the eyes and completely ignoring his sister's. "And then I shall return to England with Cassandra. I doubt we shall visit Boston in the future. Come on, Cass, darling, let's get some fresh air, away from this rotten place."

CHAPTER TWENTY FIVE

The sea was kind to Katy on the way home. The gentle swell in mid-ocean soothed her as she lay in the sanctuary of her private cabin, trying not to think, not to remember, what had happened at the summerhouse. She had to lay down to stop the sea-sickness welling up again but that left her nothing to do but re-live the experience that refused to fade, and the reason she was sailing home alone. She tried to concentrate instead on how kind Douglas and Cassandra had been to her, with all these new clothes and the bliss of her solitary cabin. They would make a good pair of landlords, back in Cheadle. How she longed to be home and yet dreaded it too. She would tell no-one but Jem about Fred's vicious attack, but tell him she must, however hard it would be.

It took three whole days for the trembling to stop. Sleep eluded her because, if she shut her eyes, she only saw that bastard's face, livid with animal lust, and engorged with rage, looming above hers. When she did succumb to slumber, she would wake, gasping for breath, as if he still lay across her chest, flattening the very life out of her.

After she managed four hours unbroken sleep on the third night, she woke naturally with her heart beating at its normal rhythm again, instead of racing out of control and threatening to choke her. She even managed some breakfast, now she had got used to the rhythmic motion of the boat and her constant, but mild nausea. As her strength seeped back, Katy felt furious about his attack. She paced up and down the tiny cage of her cabin, fuelled by a hot anger that slowly dissolved the chill of her shock, only stopping when it threatened to consume her to look through the porthole at the rolling grey horizon. Where did she fit in this world now? The vast churning sea gave no answer.

Cassandra was right, she had given him no encouragement but had rebuffed him every time he leered at her. It had never occurred to her that Fred Stavely, spoiled, self-indulgent and rich, might see himself as a suitor for someone in her situation, however free American society claimed to be, or that he would take advantage of her lowly status, once she'd disclosed it. How naive she had been. And what a nasty, violent man he'd turned out to be, underneath that jovial mask. It just went to show, you can never tell what people were really thinking, underneath.

How typical of Mr Flintock, Douglas's father, to vent his self righteous wrath on her before even trying to uncover the truth. He called himself a lawyer and yet had shown her no justice. He'd simply jumped to the wrong, negative conclusion about her because she was a low class foreigner. She despised him and all he stood for. None of his harsh, vicious words had had any effect on her. She'd stood there and let them pour over her head, knowing they were all false, all prejudiced, all invalid; but it left her with a simmering resentment against all religious hypocrites. Now the shock of the violent assault was slowly dissipating, she could think of a hundred retorts to throw back at that pompous, arrogant man.

The gift of hindsight was ever a marvellous thing. If she'd known what Fred was capable of she would have run a mile at the first signs and begged Cassandra to return to Boston, instead of wrapping herself up in Douglas and being blind to everything else, while here she was, the only person to be punished for the crime - and yet she was its victim! The injustice kept washing over her in shockwaves making her alternately hot and cold until she set to pacing again.

She would be content to stay at Cheadle from now on. This sorry episode had quenched all her wanderlust. She longed to be enfolded in Jem's safe, gentle embrace, always supposing he would have her back. What if he couldn't forgive her? What if he didn't believe her? Oh, it was tempting not to tell him anything about it, but that would mean she'd have to live with the inner shame of it for the rest of her life. Why should she live with that lie souring their marriage? And yet, what a risk she would be taking, confessing it to dear Jem. The thought of his reaction made her blood run cold again. And why should he have to deal with this, either? He'd fought for his country, lost his arm, both more brave things than that bloody Fred had done, and here was his wife, soiled forever, coming home in bits and pieces. Life was so unfair. Thank God Lady Amelia and her parents would never, ever know why she was home early and on her own. She must think up some excuse, one that wasn't too lame, to explain it.

Katy took full advantage of the steward's service and ate in her cabin, not wishing to encounter any more stray males who might get the wrong idea or make the sea-sickness worse by wandering about. The steward, Andrew, a spry, wiry Scotsman, took her under his wing. Katy wasn't sure how she would have coped without him. He'd got her measure from the moment she boarded. Andrew told her he'd seen it all on these ships, as they criss-crossed the Atlantic.

She felt, surprisingly considering recent events, that she could trust the humour at the back of Andrew's deep set eyes. His cauliflower nose and pockmarked cheeks spoke of a rounded personal history and she was grateful for his kind wisdom in just letting her be. It meant more work for him, bringing her trays of food three times a day, but he bore it all with cheerful indifference. As each watery mile brought England nearer, Katy began to fret about the journey home on land. They would be arriving in Liverpool the next day and she needed to make arrangements. She could calculate the time the journey would take and roughly how often the trains ran, from the last time she'd travelled that route, but how could she get a message to Jem, to say she was on her way? Andrew, as usual, came to her rescue.

"Och, you can send a telegram from the boat, don't you know?"

"While we're still at sea, Andrew?"

"It's possible, aye, but it'll cost you," he said.

"Well, I never knew that."

"No, people don't realise how easy it is, if you can afford it," Andrew said, with a friendly wink.

"Oh dear," Katy said. "How much?"

"Twelve shillings and sixpence for the first ten words and nine-pence for each word thereafter," Andrew said, shaking his head, and adding, "I wish I could earn that much for writing a couple of words."

"So much! Well, there's nothing else for it and at least that's one problem solved, even if it's expensive," Katy said. "And Andrew, is it far to the train station from the dockside?"

"No, you can easily walk it, Mrs Phipps. And I'll get a porter to carry your things for you, if you'll tip him when you get there?"

"And how much will that cost me?"

"A tanner will do," Andrew said.

"I can manage that," Katy said, and smiled at Andrew.

He winked his conspiracy and left, carrying her dirty dishes. He was the nearest thing she'd ever had to having a servant of her own. She would miss him. Despite the butterflies that lurked in her stomach every time she remembered what she had to confess to Jem, Katy had never been so rested. She even got used to the sway of the big boat as it trundled its way back home over a blissfully calm sea.

She checked her purse for the thousandth time. Cassandra had given her all her wages in a lump sum, in sterling, before she'd embarked for home. She had plenty for the train fares to Wiltshire, especially if she went third class, and would have a good bit leftover to share with Jem. Oh, Jem, not long now, my love!

On the final day of the voyage Katy stood on the deck, leaning on the railings with most of the other passengers, scanning the horizon for a glimpse of land.

When the shout came up, she felt a thrill run through her, a mixture of fear and excitement that was hard to control. The journey had been an oasis of calm but she knew she was damaged forever by Fred's attack. She hated him for his trespass but now, with her physical bruises healed, she was damned if she'd let him ruin the rest of her life. How dare he destroy her happiness? If Jem could still love her, as she prayed and trusted he would, no-one in the whole wide world was ever going to come between them again. No, and she would never leave his side either. All that restless energy, that had itched and scratched her, she would now plough into their future and not waste a minute of whatever time they had left.

Andrew stopped to say hello as he passed her, his tray of tea things held high with expert ease, "We'll be there in a wee while now, Mrs Phipps. Your telegram went off this morning. Now don't forget about the porter. I'll send him to your room when we dock, so make sure you wait there for him now, won't you, lassie?"

"Thank you, Andrew. Your mother was right to name you after a saint!" Katy said.

"Och, just doing my job," he said, with another friendly wink, before he went off to serve a portly middle-aged lady, wearing a feathered hat so large, Katy wondered how she would even see where her teacup was. The woman didn't even smile at him, when Andrew placed her tea service delicately at her elbow. She was as rude as Lady Amelia. War hadn't knocked off the corners of that sort of snob nearly enough.

A boy, of about three or four years of age, nudged Katy away from the salty rail of the boat and peered through the railings, shouting, "I can see it, Mum! Look! Liverpool!"

His mother, looking harassed and with a baby in her arms, grabbed the little boy's hand and said, "Sorry, Miss. Tommy's always pushing in where he's not wanted."

"Oh, please don't apologise, it's exciting to be nearly there, isn't it, Tommy?" Katy said, suddenly

217

wishing she still had a baby to protect. For a moment, she was transported back in time, remembering the smell of Florence's baby hair against her face and the clutch of her little fingers. She'd be around this little boy's age now. Tears stung her eyes.

Tommy smiled up at her, and slid his hand into Katy's. He leaned against the railings, pulling her with him. He couldn't reach the wooden rail at the top but peered through the metal bars, leaving a red mark on his forehead. Katy squeezed his hand and smiled back at him. They looked out at the land looming towards them. Soon, Liverpool's chimneys belched smoke into the clear air and a pall of it hung over the dockside. A great sprawl of buildings and warehouses spread inland from the river Mersey in an ugly collection of bricks and slate.

Three large buildings dominated the dockside as they drew nearer. Tommy's father came up and joined them and told his little family that they were called the 'Three Graces'. One of them was the Cunard Building and rose white amongst the smoke, boasting of its success in ocean liners. Soon theirs was bumping against the wharf and the passengers jostled to the exits in the scramble to step on solid ground again. Katy, said a fond goodbye to Tommy and his family, wishing she'd got to know them better and weaved her way down to her cabin for the last time. Inside, she checked every inch to make sure she hadn't left anything behind. She'd done it ten times already but once more wouldn't hurt. Through the porthole she could see the bustling dock getting ready to receive another surge of eager landlubbers. Katy felt a pang of regret leaving her private cocoon and paused to say goodbye. She could no longer put off facing Jem and finding out if he'd still have her back. Then, there was an urgent knock at the door and the porter was there, testing the weight of her two suitcases and nodding her out of the room.

She passed Andrew in the corridor and slipped him half a crown. She knew he'd get bigger tips from other passengers but doubted they'd be as sincere as hers.

"Good luck to you, Mrs Phipps. Safe journey home, now!" Andrew's face blurred into the others crowded around it, and then it was gone.

Katy turned away and followed the beefy young porter through the passport office and out into the noisy streets of Liverpool. It was less than a mile to Lime Street Station but she was glad not to be carrying those heavy cases. She duly gave the boy a sixpence when they got to the ticket office.

When it was her turn, she bought a third class ticket and went to the waiting room, dismayed at the weight of her luggage when she lifted it herself. The train arrived on time and another porter helped her heave it on. The wooden seat was unforgiving but all these tips were mounting up and a bumpy ride was a worthwhile sacrifice. Those pennies saved would go a long way in Wiltshire.

It was lunchtime when they reached Euston Station and Katy grabbed a pie from a street seller before grappling with the Underground. Enquiries at the station informed her she'd need two trains to get to Waterloo. The first, which took her most of the way, was on the Hampstead line. Changing at Charing Cross was tricky with her two heavy cases but she just about managed it and the last little stretch on the Bakerloo line passed by in a flash. She felt a flood of relief when she saw the familiar names of the stations for the West Country line and only when she climbed aboard that last train did she allow herself to let the well of homesickness consume her. Blinking away tears, Katy stared out at the countryside, as the landmarks became more and more familiar. Would her Dad meet her with the gig? Or would it be Jem walking her home that last five miles? The nearer they got to Woodbury, the harder her heart pounded. Would anyone be there at all?

CHAPTER TWENTY SIX

Cassandra turned to stare at her fiancé, as they sat down on a bench in the Public Gardens. They had walked there in stunned silence after that fateful Sunday lunch but she had now collected her wits enough to question his stark declaration to his father.

"Doug, you cannot cut yourself off from your family over this," Cassandra said.

"After the way they behaved, I feel completely justified. I don't want to see them again."

"That's just your immediate reaction, but you'll regret it, if you do," she said, scanning his face. His mouth was set in a new, thinner line and his jaw clenched tight, making it form a sharp right angle.

"I don't think so, Cass, darling. I was always their black sheep, never coming up to their exalted heights and expectations. Father wouldn't forgive me for not sticking with the law and following him in his career. He should let Rose study properly, she has the right mindset, tidy and steady. I've never settled to anything. It still amazes me that you want to take me on," and Douglas shook his head in disbelief.

"Take you on? You daft old thing. It's the other way around. I can't imagine my life without you by my side, my love." Cassandra's voice had softened as she spoke.

Cassandra leaned in and kissed him on the lips. She knew every contour of Douglas's mouth and pressed hers gently against it, making his lips yield their anger. When they broke apart, a hint of his habitual smile played on the imprint of her kiss.

"Let's get married soon, Doug. Do we need a special licence or something?"

"Let's find out as quickly as we can. We'll go tomorrow, first thing."

They strolled around the park until dusk drew them home. Ignoring the gathered family in the parlour, they went upstairs to their separate bedrooms and kissed goodnight on the landing. Cassandra felt like a thief stealing inside the house in the glooming twilight, instead of a bride on the potential eve of her wedding. She shut the bedroom door and lay down on the bed to think. Despite knowing Douglas was just across the landing, she felt lonely without Katy to confide in. She undressed quickly, letting her clothes drape over the bedroom chair. Katy would have hung them up or folded them in tissue paper. Cassandra washed herself perfunctorily at the washstand and turned back the quilt. She lay back against the pillow, wondering if this was her last night as a spinster; her last night alone in bed. She closed her tired eyes but sleep came only fitfully and, it being midsummer, the dawn broke early. She wasn't sorry to see the short night end, and got up to look out of the window. For once, the street was quiet, and only birdsong disturbed the silence. She might have been at home, in the English countryside. If only she was.

They walked briskly, hand in hand, to the Registry Office the next morning.

"Should we be married in your family's church, do you think?" Cassandra whispered to Douglas, as the clerk wrote out their details.

"What's the point?" Douglas said, and turned to the clerk to ask, "How soon can we be married? And we can do it here, is that right?" He laughed and added, "You see, I've never done this before!"

"And I'll make sure he never does it again!" Cassandra said.

The clerk, looked up at them with world-weary eyes, over his horn-rimmed glasses. "I'm sure you're right, Miss," and he carried on writing at a snail's pace. "You can be married in three day's time. I'll need your passports and social security numbers. You both have to fill in these forms and sign at the bottom, here and here."

"But I'm not a resident of Boston, so I don't have a security number," Cassandra said.

"Then you'll need a letter from the embassy, Miss. It's a couple of blocks away. I'll need it this afternoon if you want to get married in three days."

They filled in the forms and hurried off to the embassy, where they had to queue for an hour before being seen by a helpful young clerk who thought their haste romantic. It made a pleasant change.

They raced back to the Registry Office, before it shut. The man with the horn-rimmed glasses looked as if he hadn't moved all afternoon and didn't even blink when they shoved the embassy letter under his nose.

He squinted at the typed words through his glasses and said, "Right, you can be married on Thursday afternoon. Down the corridor. Door marked 'Ceremonies.' Third on the left. There's a space at three o'clock. Here's your registration certificate. You'll need it with you, and some identification."

Douglas snatched up the paper and kissed Cassandra in front of the disinterested clerk as if they'd already gone through the formalities.

Not looking up, the clerk said, in the same flat monotone, "And you'll need two witnesses. Don't turn up without them."

Douglas and Cassandra skipped down the stone steps outside.

"Who are we going to ask, with Fred and Kate gone?" Douglas said, carefully sliding the precious paper into his inside jacket pocket.

"Not your sisters, please!" Cassandra said.

"No, not them. It doesn't have to be anyone we know, does it?"

"I suppose not," Cassandra said, looking around the street, trying to pick out a face at random who could witness their union.

"We don't have time to waste," Douglas said.

"No, oh, I wish Kate was here. She'd do it at the drop of a hat. She was always so loyal. Oh, Doug, I wish I could warn her about that letter that Cheryl's sent to

Mother. She's walking into a storm. The letter must have arrived by now. Can we go home soon, once we are married? I don't want her to deal with it alone but I don't think I can explain the whole disaster in a letter to Mother, without making things worse. This will need sorting out face to face."

"No, I understand, honey, I remember only too well what it feels like to be on the receiving end of your Mother's fury, but how can we when she's halfway across the Atlantic? Let's concentrate on finding these witnesses, shall we? Come on, I've had an idea."

Douglas grabbed her hand and marched off down the busy street.

"We'll try in my favourite restaurant. They have loads of staff, I'm sure they can spare two for half an hour, once lunch is over."

Encouraged by discreet rolls of dollars, the washing up boy and a novice waitress agreed to witness their marriage and the manager, who got very misty eyed at the proposal, agreed to let them off duty for a hour on Thursday afternoon.

They passed the next three days in a bubble of anticipation, whiling away the hours out of the house as much as possible. When Thursday dawned Cassandra felt ridiculously nervous, but she needn't have worried. The ritual was conducted in solemnity, without the joy, the white lace and the well wishes Cassandra had always thought would attend the event, but she had never been happier than when she kissed her husband for the first time.

Their young witnesses were both too shy and awkward to do more than shake their hands afterwards before scurrying back to the restaurant. Cassandra and Douglas turned to leave, when they saw the registrar was already smiling a welcome to the next pair of hopefuls who hesitated on the threshold, as soon as he had uttered "I now pronounce you, man and wife."

The whole thing had taken less than fifteen

minutes.

And yet Cassandra did feel different.
Bound.
Secure.
Happy.
Pregnant.

CHAPTER TWENTY SEVEN

Mary Phipps came running out into her kitchen garden, waving a piece of paper. Jem looked up from his weeding to see his mother's serious face searching for him. He'd been experimenting with the latest refinement of his clawed hand. It was working well. He'd needed to keep busy ever since Lady Amelia had announced the Beagles' imminent eviction a few days before.

"What is it, Mum?" Jem said, wiping his hand down his old corduroys.

"Only a telegram, that's what!" his mother said, shoving the thin envelope under his nose.

Jem said, "You'll have to open it, Mum. My hand's dirty and you need two for that operation."

His mother slipped her index finger into the edge of the envelope and slit it open with an ease Jem could only envy. She passed it to him without looking at it but stayed, her face agog with curiosity, to watch him read it.

It was very short. He read,

"HOME SATURDAY 12 JULY - STOP - PLEASE MEET TRAIN 6ISH - STOP - KATY"

"Well, what does it say? Don't just stand there like a statue, Jem! Who's it from?" his mother demanded.

"It's from Katy," he said, staring at the paper in disbelief.

"Oh, is it?" Mary did not attempt to hide the disappointment in her voice.

"She's coming home. Saturday - that's today!"

"Today? That don't give you much notice! Do she know about the eviction?"

"I don't know. I must get ready. Where's the train timetable?"

"In the kitchen, on the dresser, same as always," Mary followed her son's rapid footsteps as he pounded along the narrow garden path into her kitchen and snatched up the little book.

Jem shook the timetable open with his hand and used his claw to hold it open at the right page. What was the nearest train to six o'clock? There, the London train stopped at Woodbury at twenty-one minutes past six.

"I'll have to shave, have a wash. The train's in just after six. What's the time now, Mum?"

"It's only eleven o'clock in the morning. You've got plenty of time. What I want to know is, where's she going to sleep?"

"If by 'she', you mean my wife, we can always stay at the West Lodge, if you don't want to make her welcome."

"I never said that," his mother said, shuffling in her outdoor clogs.

"You've said plenty else since the eviction notice, though, haven't you, Mum? And none of it has been kind. Doesn't it occur to you that Katy might be innocent? That she's been taken advantage of?" Jem felt the heat behind his collar and it had less to do with the warm summer's day, and more to do with the secret doubts that surfaced in the semi-privacy of his room, every restless night since Cheryl Flintock's letter had shattered his peace.

"That's as may be, but lightning don't usually strike twice in the same spot," Mary said, slipping her clogs off and replacing them with her tatty slippers.

"Why won't anyone let Katy forget about that bloody Charles Smythe? For God's sake! She was just a kid then. She's been married to me ever since and did her bit in the war as much as any man. Oh, it's no use!" Jem said, when he looked up at his mother's pursed mouth. "Forget it! We'll stay at West Lodge until they throw us all out!"

Jem clomped upstairs in his muddy boots, not caring about the mess he trailed behind him. His heart was racing with excitement at the thought of seeing Katy again, even if it was under a cloud of gut churning suspicions. Would she be upset, injured, even? What *had* happened to her? Her last letter to him had been tranquil and happy. Whatever had occurred must have been after she wrote it. And he supposed he'd heard nothing since because she'd been travelling home this last week or so. At least, if he met the train, he'd have her to himself while he heard the truth from her own lips. He refused to believe what Lady Amelia had said. Katy had never mentioned any bloke being interested in her, in *that* way. This Fred Stavely, whom she had said in her letters was just a friend of Doug's, must have attacked her out of the blue. Unless, oh God, unless she'd been keeping it secret, all along. Jem thought he'd go mad every time that thought crossed his unwilling mind. There was a grain of truth in what his mum had said about Katy only marrying him because of that flirtation with Charles Smythe. He wondered, for the millionth time, if she would have married him for himself. Whenever he'd asked her, she'd always fervently said she would and she loved him with all her heart but then, whilst he'd been stuck in that grim prisoner-of-war camp in Germany, she'd had the vicar after her. He'd wanted to marry her when they thought Jem was a gonner. Could he really trust this wife of his? Was she really so innocent? What if she'd been carrying on with this mate of Douglas's all the time she was in America and those letters were just covering up what she'd really been up to?

Jem stared at himself in the little shaving mirror in the bedroom he shared with his brother, John, who had taken over his old job in the manor gardens. His face looked flushed and angry, as well it might. Katy might have had these blokes after her but she'd always convinced him of her innocence. He must hold on to that conviction. He must quell these snakes coiling inside his brain, whispering infidelity and guilt. He must *not* listen to their insistent voices. No. He'd go and get her from the station, on his own, and try and keep an open mind whilst she told him what had happened. He'd know the truth, just by looking at her, wouldn't he?

227

Oh, but she'd need a lift in the gig, or the car, but he didn't want Bert there as a gooseberry. That left the Sunbeam. Could he take it? Did he dare? What had he to lose? Sir Robert didn't know what day it was and Lady Amelia would be indoors getting ready for dinner at that hour. He doubted they remembered he existed, half the time. They would never notice the car going down their drive and, even if they did, how could they stop him? Mr Hayes hadn't officially terminated his employment as their chauffeur yet. The estate manager clocked off to have his tea at half past five, like most of the outdoor staff, and the indoor servants would be busy getting the high and mighties their evening meal. It would be the hush of early evening. The motor would make a noise but he could let it roll down the drive, once he'd got it out of the barn, and switch the engine off again.

And if they sacked him? Well, it was only a matter of time anyway. What the hell!

He threw some clothes into his army knapsack and splashed some water from the jug into the china basin on the washstand. The spotted shaving mirror told him his ablutions weren't before time and his six o'clock shadow was more like three day's worth of beard. Six o'clock and she'd be home! After so many weeks, months, without her, it was almost unbelievable that he would see his Katy this very day! His hand shook as he scraped his facial hair away with the razor blade. Wouldn't do to cut his throat, today of all days.

He chucked the shaving water out of the window and refilled the basin from the jug, then washed himself thoroughly with a flannel and dried his body so vigorously, it tingled all over. Then he got out his Sunday best suit, the one he had got married in. It hung loose on his frame these days but better that, than too tight. And now he had a wooden arm, instead of an empty sleeve, he looked much more presentable. Jem combed his thick chestnut hair. Its waves obeyed him, for once, with a touch of Brilliantine. He couldn't see all of himself in the small mirror but he felt clean and spruce and hoped it would be enough. Daft, he felt as nervous as a green lad going courting for the first time and yet sick in his stomach at the thought of what might have happened to his wife.

He went downstairs, clutching his tie and his knapsack.

"Will you do my tie for me, Mum?" he said, hoping to restore peace.

His mother put down the loaf of bread she was cutting for sandwiches and washed her hands, saying, "I hope she appreciates her smart husband, when she sees him and that she deserves him, after what she's been up to."

Despite the doubts worming through his own mind, Mary's instant belief in Katy's guilt only served to make her son defend his wife. "Let's wait and hear Katy's side of the story before we condemn her, shall we Mum?"

Mary scowled but was silent.

When the tie was fastened to their mutual satisfaction, Jem said, "Well, I'm off now, Mum. I'll pop in tomorrow, shall I?"

"You do that, son. Here, take this sandwich. Take good care of yourself, now, won't you?" Mary's sharp eyes swam with sudden moisture.

Jem kissed her thin cheek. "Don't worry, Mum. It'll all come right somehow. You wait and see." He only wished he could feel the conviction of his own words.

Jem ate his sandwich in the little glade, where he and Katy had made love that last time. If someone had stolen her trust, had ruined their intimacy, God help him, he'd kill him. The ramson garlic and the bluebells were just over, and dog roses had broken bud in the hedge. The grass had grown long, and he lay back against its welcoming mattress in the dappled shade of the elder bush, whose white frothy flowers provided the perfect parasol against the strong sunshine. He tried to relax, but it was hopeless.

229

He couldn't stop speculating on what disaster had struck Katy. He'd spent every waking minute doing just that since Lady Amelia's announcement and it had been torture, picturing her with another man. Who was this bastard? Had she been tempted into forgetting she was married? And what had Douglas been thinking to allow it to happen? Why had neither Cassandra nor Douglas protected her?

He shook his head free of the doubts that clouded his every waking moment, including the ones in the middle of the night, when his belief in her innocence slid out of the open window, to be replaced by demons that whispered about flirtatious violet eyes, and another man's hands on the curves of her body that he loved so well. Those images tortured him until he wanted to bang his head against the wall. His stump would tingle with pain and shoot sensations into the thin air where his hand should have been.

If he did sleep, he dreamed he still had two hands and they were clamped around the throat of that fucking Fred Stavely. The sound of his choking, as he squeezed the last breath out of the bastard, would wake him in a sticky sweat of twisted sheets. Now she was nearly home, he must suspend his imagination somehow and hold her tight and let her tell him the truth. While separated by geographical distance, they had become closer than ever through their letters. Something in him held faith their bond wasn't broken but would she be able to love again? No, she might be wounded and shaken up, but their love would hold strong and nothing must shake his belief in that while his fists ached to knock seven bells out of the bloke who'd attacked her.

With his sandwich safely dispatched to his stomach, Jem closed his eyes, remembering that last time when the north wind had whipped about their bare skin but their feverish hunger for each other had chased the chill away. Today their secret hide-away hummed with bees drinking elderflower nectar and dipping into long trumpets of honeysuckle. The air drooped with the scent of summer flowers without the slightest breeze to lift it. Having slept little since Cheryl Flintock's letter had blown his world apart, he grew drowsy and dozed off for a few minutes. When he awoke, he reckoned, judging by the shadows, it was well past midday.

With a pang of guilt, Jem remembered he hadn't yet told Agnes that her daughter was coming home. Shame hurried his heels, as he picked up his bag and walked swiftly down the hill to the west lodge.

The July heat had exhausted even his mother-in-law. He found her sitting by her back step in the shade of her porch.

"Now that's a rare and wonderful sight," Jem said, with a determined cheerfulness he was far from feeling. "No, don't get up. It's good to see you taking a rest, for once."

Agnes looked as if she didn't know whether to smile or frown. In fact, she looked downright sleepy and her face was shadowed, not just by the house, but by a new melancholy.

"Hello, Jem. It's this heat. It's so humid, I reckon we're in for a thunderstorm before nightfall," Agnes said, and patted the step of her kitchen door in invitation.

Jem sat down on the cool stone.

"I've got some news for you, Agnes," Jem said, smiling through his fears.

"Oh, yes? I could do with some good news. I'm that sad, our Jem, I've lived here all my married life and I thought I'd end my days in this house."

An uncharacteristic sob escaped her. Jem patted her shoulder with his hand.

"This might cheer you up, or it might not, considering the circumstances."

"What on earth do you mean, lad?" Agnes said, wiping her eyes with her apron.

It was no use prevaricating. Jem could not predict which way this was going to go, so he thought he'd better come straight out with it.

"Katy's coming home. Today. On the twenty past six train."

"What? Today? Why didn't you say so straight away? Oh, my goodness! Our Katy, home at last. Oh, dear, this should be such a happy day but I don't know what to think after what Lady Amelia said. What's to become of us all? I don't know what's happened to Katy or what she's been up to, or even if she knows we're being thrown out of our home at the end of the month!"

Tears welled up in Agnes' eyes again. She turned to Jem and laid her head on his chest and said into his best shirt, "I've never been in such a muddle, Jem. Everything's upside down. Poor Bert, this has broken him."

Agnes sobbed until her strong back shook. Jem didn't know what to do except keep holding her. His mother-in-law had been a rock to him through all his troubles since he married her daughter. A stern, hard rock with edges so sharp they'd cut you, but one that never faltered; never gave way like this. Gradually Agnes's sobs abated. She pulled back from Jem, shook her head and blew her nose. She sat up straight and smoothed her skirts, took a deep breath and gave him a wobbly smile.

"At least we'll hear the truth, Agnes," Jem said. "I know Katy's innocent. She loves me, you see, and I love her. Whatever's happened to her, I'll stick by her, you know."

"Will you? What if Katy meant for it to happen? What if she liked this man? How can you be so sure? I keep hoping there will be another side to the story than the one we've heard from Lady Amelia but, whatever the truth is, I can't see her changing her mind about our eviction. All those years my Bert has worked for that family, day and night, with never a thought for anything but those horses. He lost so many to the war, I thought it would break his heart, and then losing our young Albert, too."

Agnes's bottom lip trembled again but she folded

her lips tight and swallowed the lump in her throat. Jem could see it bobbing as it went down, and his heart went out to her, even as she sowed more doubts into it. If Katy's mother didn't believe in her innocence, should he?

"There's got to be another explanation, I'm sure of it," Jem said, as much to convince himself as his mother-in-law. "We've only got that one letter from that Miss Flintock to go on and she may have spoken out of turn. Until we hear Katy's version, we just don't know, but we haven't long to wait. I'm going to meet the train this afternoon and bring her home. I'll use the car because, if you don't mind, I'd rather meet her alone. I'll bring her straight round here but I think, Agnes, as her husband, I need to hear what she's got to say, privately like."

Agnes patted his hand. "Of course you have, Jem. It's only natural. But what's all this about taking the car; have you got permission? I mean, I know you was going to be the chauffeur of that damn contraption but haven't you lost your post, like Bert?"

"Not yet, Hayes hasn't sacked me officially, so I'm bloody taking it. They're going to get rid of me soon, so what have I got to lose, hey, Agnes?"

Those words rang through his head that long hot afternoon. His jacket and tie soon came off once he started polishing the Sunbeam. It didn't need polishing but he had to pass those slow minutes somehow. Bert wasn't around. He'd gone off to Home Farm with one of the shire horses. They were clearing a gulley that had flooded in the spring. Jem called young Jack from the stables, who came gladly, having been set to cleaning tack for the afternoon, it being a Saturday with no school.

"Hello, young Jackanapes," Jem said. "Listen, your sister Katy's coming home from America this afternoon and I think your Dad should know about it, don't you?"

Jack nodded, his eyes wide at the news. "Yes, Jem, I do," he said.

"Right, then. You run over to Home Farm and tell

your Dad she'll be home about seven o'clock tonight. I'll bring her to West Lodge myself, from the station. No need for him to pick her up, tell him. I want to meet her on my own. You got that?"

"Yes, Jem," Jack said.

"Good. Get off now then."

"I will!" and Jack sped off into the sunshine.

At half past five, after he'd watched Mr Hayes bunk off home, Jem slipped behind the wheel, tested the brakes, adjusted the mirrors for the umpteenth time and twitched his tie straight. He smoothed down his wavy hair and pulled his cap on. Not his new chauffeur's cap that Cassandra had sent in the post. He didn't want to have to explain all that lost hope. His Sunday best would have to do. He didn't feel like adopting any show of allegiance to the Smythe's either. This meeting was between Katy and him. Man and wife - and he wanted nothing to come between them.

The engine roared into life much too loudly. Jem looked about nervously but when no-one appeared, he put the car into reverse gear and kangarooed out of the barn, missing the door post by a whisker. The tricky three point turn sounded deafening to his ears within the enclosed yard. He didn't wait to find out if anyone had overheard it but gunned the car out on to the drive and down the hill to the gates, past West Lodge and out on to the Woodbury road, abandoning all attempts at stealth.

Just as well he had one wooden hand because his real one was shaking like a leaf, as he drove along the main road under the arch of oaks that lined it. The sun blinked in and out of the leaves, blinding him with its brightness. When an oncoming car tooted him for being in the middle of the road, Jem slowed down and hugged the nearside verge.

Better late than never.

CHAPTER TWENTY EIGHT

Katy could see the spire of Woodbury from the train window. How English. How welcome.

Home.

Was there really anywhere better? She'd never doubt it again. She heaved her suitcases to the carriage door and waited for the train to stop. As it slowed into the station, she scanned the platform for Jem's dear face. There were quite a few people waiting to board the train, nothing like the crowds she'd witnessed in Boston, but enough to blur together through watery eyes.

But there he was. He looked smart, as if he was still in uniform in the British Army, standing to attention, and looking solemn. Katy blinked her eyes free of her grateful tears and gripped her suitcases. The train ground to a halt in slow motion; its metal wheels scraping lazily along the rail, reluctant to cease their onward travel.

Another young woman, in black mourning clothes, opened the door for her and helped her heave the heavy luggage onto the platform. Before she could properly thank her, Jem was there, hefting the suitcases away from the edge of the platform, one at a time. Somehow the two cases ended up between them, making their first embrace awkward and clumsy.

Jem was smiling, but then, he didn't know why she was home.

"Hello, love," he said, his voice dry and cracked. "I can't tell you how good it is to see you again."

"Hello, Jem, darling," Katy said, and wondered how long she could continue with endearments once she'd told him her sorry story.

"I'm afraid I can only carry one suitcase," Jem said, "but I do have two arms now. Look!"

"So you do! How wonderful, Jem," Katy said, lifting the other case, which seemed so much lighter now.

"Your carriage awaits, my lady," Jem said, pointing through the railway arch, to the yard at the back.

Katy attempted a laugh but it turned into a silent gulp. Jem looked well, if a little tired, but much better than before she left, with a summer tan and golden lights in his chestnut hair. He'd stuffed his cap into his pocket. A concession to the heat perhaps.

They walked through to the station yard and to her surprise, Jem marched straight up to the Sunbeam and put her case on to the back seat.

"But where's the driver?" Katy asked, forgetting he had news of his own.

"Here, at your service, ma'am," Jem said, throwing her other case inside with the first. "Care to get in?"

"You're driving? Are you allowed?" Katy said, astonished.

"I am, sort of," Jem laughed. "You know I taught myself, while you've been gallivanting on the other side of the world. You're not the only one to have had a few adventures, I can tell you," Jem said, nodding to the station porter, who stood nearby staring at them with his ears twitching, as if he knew her guilty secret - but how could he?

Katy winced at Jem's words but took comfort in believing that the word hadn't spread. She mustn't think of herself as some sort of criminal when she was completely innocent. Well, at least they would be alone when she told him. She just wanted it over with. She wanted to test his reaction to her news. Know her fate. But she wouldn't spoil his moment of triumph. And it *was* a surprise to see Jem behind the wheel, using his clawed wooden hand to grasp it while he changed gear, a little gratingly, with his good right hand. Katy refrained from grabbing the wheel when a stray dog ran across the road and Jem had to swerve. She needn't have worried, he was managing well, but he seemed to need to concentrate in silence. When would she get her chance to confide in him?

"Jem, you are a good driver. You'd never know you had an artificial arm. I'm so impressed. Um, are they expecting me at home, do you know? Only, I wondered if we could stop somewhere, on the way, and have a bit of a chat?" Katy said, knowing her words weren't conveying the warning he would need, but not wanting to distract him.

"Good idea," Jem said, smiling with a new, tight smile. It smote her heart, which had begun to pound.

"You must be tired, after your long journey," Jem said, as they slowed down behind a pony and cart. He changed gear with a clunk.

"A bit, but not too much. It's so lovely to be home," Katy said. "I had a good rest on the boat. Doug paid for a private cabin and I lazed about most of the time. It wasn't stormy like on the journey out, either, and the steward, Andrew, looked after me very well."

How could they be chatting like strangers over such trivialities?

"Oh, I see," Jem said. "I think I'll have to overtake this cart or we'll never get there."

Katy schooled herself not to comment, as Jem pulled out with a jerk onto the other side of the road and accelerated past the pony, who reared up in fright.

"Oops, I think I was a bit close then," Jem said, crunching up another gear and guiding the big car back into the nearside lane.

Katy peered back behind them with her head out of the open window. The cart driver was waving his stick at them and swearing with the ripe English words she remembered only too well. She gave him what she hoped was an apologetic wave and his shouts faded into the dusty heat.

"He's alright, just a bit cross," she said. "My word, it's hot."

Katy took off her hat and placed it on the back seat. Jem's silence, after their initial greeting, no longer felt right. Katy's stomach gave a sickening lurch.

"Let's pull over soon, Jem," Katy said.

"Good idea," Jem said. His smile had slipped

237

right away now. He looked serious, almost grim-faced. As if he knew. She batted the thought away again. No-one knew but he soon would, God help her.

The big car growled up the steep hill to Upper Cheadle. No conversation interrupted the noise of the straining engine. Katy was consumed with dread and yet longing to share her trauma with her husband. She knew she was the victim, not the perpetrator, but it would be hard for Jem to bear witness to her trespass. Their trespass really - against their joint intimacy. Much as she loved him, could she ever *make* love to him again?

A little frown cleft a new line in Jem's forehead as he drove. She looked at his clawed wooden hand clutching at the wheel in an alien grip. She mustn't be critical. He'd been brave to even try to drive, and bumpy though the ride was, it beat lugging those heavy cases five miles home.

Jem pulled into the verge where the road widened at the summit of the hill, affording a view across the downs, away to the west. It reminded Katy of the view from her childhood home at West Lodge. When the engine spluttered into silence, she sat back in her seat and tried to control her breathing, which threatened to gallop out of her control.

They both stared at the view, quietly denying the tension that fizzled between them. Katy broke it first.

"I love this view, Jem. Reminds me of home."

"Yes, I know you do," he said.

She couldn't put off the moment any longer, and yet she dreaded his response. Their whole future depended on the next few minutes.

"Jem, there's something I must tell you. I want to explain why I'm home early, without Cassandra or Douglas," she began, her voice betraying her with its tremor.

Jem's answer shocked her to her core, when he said, "I know why you are here, Katy. Lady Amelia had a letter. It was from Miss Flintock and it was about you."

Katy's chaotic breathing slowed, almost to a stop.

"A letter from Miss Flintock to, did you say, to Lady Amelia? Was it from Rose, or Cheryl?"

"Cheryl, I believe," Jem said, still looking at the downs, as if afraid to meet her eye.

"Then - you know - about?" Katy said, not able to finish the question because she could see the answer in his face.

"Yes," Jem said, nodding. He turned to look at her. His eyes were steady and clear. "Tell me exactly what happened, Katy. Everything."

Katy swallowed. Her breath was still unreliably patchy. She clasped her hands together. They were wet with sweat.

"That's what I want to do, Jem," she said, looking into his hazel eyes and then flitting hers back to gaze out on the downlands she remembered so well.

"I'm listening," Jem said.

"You had my letter, didn't you, from Cape Cod?"

"Yes, everything seemed fine, then."

"It was! Apart from missing you, I felt really happy there. The sea was so invigorating and I loved the wooden house. I had time to myself, because Cass and Doug were always out sailing, and so wrapped up in each other. Literally, if you get my meaning."

"I get your drift, yes."

"I think that played a part in it. You know Fred was there, from my letters. Well, that last day - oh, Jem, it was all so sudden! I had no idea he felt so strongly about me. I feel such a fool."

"Go on."

"Alright. Cass and Doug had gone out sailing for the whole day, to an island called Martha's Vineyard, across Nantucket Sound - that's the name of the bay. They'd taken a picnic and weren't expected back. Fred went out fishing, same as usual, and I wrote that last letter to you. It was very warm weather, like today, and I just had a thin cotton dress on."

Jem flushed at this detail but she could not insult him by holding anything back.

Katy stumbled on. "I got things ready for supper and took a drink out to the back porch. There's a wooden veranda that looks out to the beach. I sat in the swing-seat and dozed off with the heat. Fred woke me, coming back from fishing. He hadn't caught anything and looked frustrated and hot. He sat next to me, on the swing-seat, before I could get away, and told me he liked me. I shook him off, Jem, and tried to leave, but he followed me into the kitchen and told me he was falling in love with me. I told him I was married. He asked me, did I love you?"

Jem's face swivelled round and his eyes never left hers after that.

Katy continued, looking straight at him, "I told him I loved you with all my heart and soul. And I do, Jem, I do."

Jem said, "I know, Katy. Tell me the rest." His good hand gripped the steering wheel. She could see the white knuckle bones.

She could not stop her tears now. "He got really angry, angrier than anyone I've ever seen. It was so quick. He told me that I'd know what was coming next, if I was married, and, if I was just a servant, it was all I deserved - or something like that. I can't remember because by then he had me around the waist and was carting me upstairs. Oh, Jem, dare I tell you the rest?"

"You must," Jem said, tears tracking down his hot face.

"I hit him and screamed but he was like an animal - possessed by his anger. He threw me on the bed, stripped me and raped me. It hurt so much. It was so violent. I was screaming my head off and managed to get away by elbowing him in the face. I fell on the floor and he was trying to haul me back and then, at that awful moment, Cheryl Flintock opened the door. I thought I was saved, but she ran away and Fred followed her, but not before he slapped me, calling me a bitch. As if it was my fault!"

She broke then.

Jem didn't hold her. It was over. Their marriage was ruined. He knew everything and was disgusted.

Katy flung out of the car and ran to the fence, gripping its wooden rails, trying to still her crying, and failing, as the injustice of what had happened choked her. She couldn't breathe. Her throat had closed over in a spasm of crying and wouldn't open to let in the humid evening air. She heard a rasping noise and knew she'd created it but her head span. She needed oxygen. The downs blurred and she hit every rail as she slumped to the ground.

She never knew how long it was before she felt Jem's arm lift her into a sitting position. She leaned back against the fence and drew her breath in shuddering gasps. She didn't dare to touch her husband. He wouldn't want contact now.

"Katy, look at me," Jem said, his voice low and compromised by emotion. "Answer me, Katy. I will only ask you this once. Did you give Fred Stavely any encouragement? Did you have no inkling of his feelings?"

She shook her head and looked into his eyes, trying to focus her own blurry ones, "None, well I could see he fancied me but he seemed to be a gentleman. I thought he knew I was married. I kept avoiding him as much as I could. I honestly never flirted with him, Jem," she said, still staring straight at him, though she thought her head might split open and wanted to shut her eyes and blot the spinning world out.

The car behind Jem caught the sun and stabbed shards of reflected light into her pounding brain but she would not succumb to the pain. She *must* do this fully and openly, even if he never wanted to see her again; she must be able to take her integrity away with her to wherever her aloneness took her, if he rejected her, as he surely would.

"That's what I thought."

Had she heard that right? She clasped her hands

tight.

"Tell me what happened next, Katy. All of it."

"Nothing, really," Katy said, in ragged gasps. "He and Cheryl ran out of the house and left me alone. I had a bath, threw my dress in the refuse, put on another. I went to my bedroom and just looked out over the sea to the east, where I knew *you* were. I just wanted to go home. Then, I don't know what time it was, Douglas and Cassandra came back. There was noise downstairs, shouting, but I felt disconnected from it all. Cassandra put me to bed, and we drove back to Boston the next day, where Mr Flintock, Doug's father, ranted at me as if I was the whore of Babylon. I thought America was free, Jem. It's not, it's as stuck in snobbery as here. Then, a couple of days later, I was packed off on the boat home by Cassandra and Douglas. No-one in the family ever spoke to me again. I felt dirty. I still do."

Jem's silence suffocated her. Her chest pressed in on her, lead-lined like a coffin and she shut her eyes so she could concentrate on breathing.

Then, an eternity later, Jem spoke. "I don't know how I'm going to do it but, one day, I'm going to go to fucking Boston and kill that bastard."

Katy dared to look at Jem. His face was set into granite, the lips taut and pointing downwards, his eyes staring into the distance, unfocussed, glinting with unshed water.

"He has taken what's mine. You are mine, Katy Phipps, mine forever, never forget that."

Jem seized her arms and shook her, until her teeth clattered together.

"You're mine!" Jem shouted, in a strangled voice, and pulled her tight into him. His good arm supported the back of her neck and his wooden one cut into her side, as if she cared.

She was home.

***

242

It was much later than seven o'clock by the time they drove back through the twilight to West Lodge. Katy knew Agnes and Bert would be beside themselves with worry, when they finally drew up outside the stone cottage.

"Do you want me to tell them, or do it yourself?" Jem asked, as they got out of the car.

"I'll try, but I don't know if I'll manage it, Jem," Katy said, and decided to leave her luggage in the car, until she knew her parents wanted her back.

Jem had told her about the eviction. How could so much shame be showered on someone who was without blame? And to punish her whole family! Katy was stricken with remorse over the wanderlust that had brought this about. If only she'd been content to stay home; less ambitious; less hungry for life.

The door flew open, before they could knock on it. Katy was shocked when she saw how much Agnes and Bert had aged in her absence. The children were playing outside in the last whisper of dusk and, late though it was, Agnes shooed them even further away to play, with Daisy minding them. The children looked scared, not excited as they should have been at this licence, and Daisy looked daggers at her older sister, before herding the younger ones away.

"Come in," Bert said. "You're much later than you said, Jem. Was the train late?"

"No, we needed to talk, that's all," Jem said, shepherding Katy into the house within his good arm.

She needed his strength to enter.

"A bit of straight talking is what we all need," Agnes said.

They sat around the scrubbed kitchen table. It was bare and clean, without the flowers that normally graced its worn surface.

Agnes never offered her daughter even a glass of water but sat, mute and expectant, staring at her.

Katy gathered herself for another confession but, before she could begin, Jem spoke up.

"Katy has told me everything. She's done nothing wrong except been the victim of a sexual assault. Everyone has jumped to the wrong conclusion as a result of Cheryl Flintock's letter. As far as I'm concerned, we're back together, as man and wife, and together we shall stay."

"Thank you for that, Jem," Bert said. "Katy? What have you to say? Has Jem told you how this has affected your mother and me?"

"Yes, Dad. I'm so sorry, but I did nothing wrong. This man, a friend of Douglas's, he said he loved me and when I said I was married, he got very angry and, and" she trailed off.

She couldn't speak of such things to her parents.

"The bastard raped her and that's a fact. Katy's not to blame - you're not to blame her," Jem said.

Agnes put her head in her hands and Bert ran his hands through his thinning hair.

Agnes looked up at Katy and said, "Where's your wedding ring?"

"I lost it, on the boat over. I was seasick and had lost weight and it fell off my finger and into the sea. Oh, Mum, if I'd known what trouble it would bring, believe me, I'd have dived in and found it. Right now, I wish I was at the bottom of the ocean but you've got to believe me, I never, ever made him think I liked him! He's fat and ugly and anyway, I love Jem!" And Katy's resolve broke.

Sobs rose up from her in a torrent of mixed emotions, impossible to control.

"Oh, my little love," Agnes said, and got up, scraping her chair on the flagstones, and wrapping her arms around Katy.

"Grim business, this," Bert said to Jem, as he watched the two women embrace.

"She isn't dead, with all respect, Bert," Jem said. "And I'm not letting her out of my sight again. What Katy

244

needs now is looking after; she's been through enough."

Agnes released Katy and turned back to the men around the table.

"You're right, Jem, of course you are, but where the hell are we all going to live?"

CHAPTER TWENTY NINE

Katy lay in the double bed, right on the edge, terrified she might touch her husband's bare body. Every window in the lodge house stood open wide and still not a breath of air stirred the thin curtain that shielded their privacy from her brother and sisters. She wanted to rip off her nightdress, she was so hot, but that would mean skin touching skin. She couldn't face the thought of stirring a desire in Jem she could not satisfy. Maybe she could never satisfy it again. That brute Fred had stolen their ease with each other. All those months after Florence died when she didn't want Jem. What a waste! She didn't want to deny him now. She longed for him but could feel her flesh recoil when he touched her. He'd kissed her only once, by the fence when they'd sat on the ground, next to the car on the way home from the station, and her lips had retreated from his of their own volition.

Jem's face had fallen into a dull, set look then and it hadn't left him. Katy shut her eyes but she couldn't sleep, she was too hot, too remorseful. That Cheryl Flintock was a witch. How spiteful to write to Lady Amelia. She must have done it that same day, before she'd even thought it through. What would happen to her Mum and Dad now? Bert had no pension. Her Mum loved this house. She was woven into its fabric. Where could they go?

All night Katy lay there, still as a corpse, with her eyes wide open, and her skin, trapped in its white shroud, glistening with perspiration. Jem's breathing slowed into sleep after a while and that comforted her. Her father's snores reverberated around the whole house, like a heartbeat, uniting his family under its roof. How could they ever leave this place?

Sunday passed in a daze. Katy refused to attend church, pleading fatigue from her journey, but really, she couldn't face the likes of Mrs Threadwell or Mrs Hoskins goggling their eyes at her solo return. She and Jem had

246

lunch with his parents, after Jem had a quiet word telling them about her ghastly experience. George was surprisingly kind, kinder than he'd ever been, but Mary's sealed lips spoke volumes. An uneasy truce made the meal strangely formal.

Katy assumed that Mary's earlier dislike of her daughter-in-law must now be full-blown hate. She didn't blame her. The rest of the village probably thought the same. She must wish she'd never married her son. They excused themselves as soon as decently possible and went for a walk, carefully avoiding their secret glade in a tacit agreement of sexual abstinence. What a good, kind husband she had and how miserable he looked. She hadn't even needed to explain her distance. His sensitivity humbled her and helped her to relax a little, until she started worrying that he might find her repugnant now. And she *was* tired, more than she'd realised. They sat in the West Lodge garden all evening until sunset, like two old duffers past passion.

"The storm never broke after," Bert said, over breakfast, the next morning.

"It would be more comfortable if it had," Jem said, running his finger around his collar, even though it was open.

"Bacon and eggs anyone?" Agnes said, standing before the stove, hands on hips.

"It's too hot, Mum," Daisy said.

There was a murmur of agreement. Agnes plonked a jar of jam on the table and cut some bread. A blue-bottle homed straight in on it.

"The milk will be sour, and all," she said, swatting the noisy fly away.

Bert went off to work, with Daisy and Jack in tow, now that school was shut for the summer.

"They all walk as if they had lead in their boots," Agnes said, as she waved them off at the door.

"Is it any wonder?" Katy said. "And it's all my fault."

"It don't sound like it was anyone's fault but that ruddy awful friend of Mr Flintock's," her mother said.

"That's right," Jem said, undoing a second button on his shirt.

"I ought to be stripping the beds and washing the sheets but I can't see the point, no more," Agnes said, sitting back down at the table and pouring another cup of tea. Little Emily played on the floor with the wooden doll Jem had carved her and lisped a nursery rhyme.

"Isn't there anywhere you can rent, Mum?" Katy said.

"And how would we pay the rent, when your father won't have a job?" Agnes said, spooning sugar into her cup and stirring it far longer than it needed.

"Daisy's earning now with her Saturday kitchen work at the manor and Jack brings in a few coins, doesn't he?" Katy said.

"That won't go far. Lady Amelia said she didn't want to see any of us ever again. For all I know, she could sack the children too."

"Surely not?" Jem said.

"She's that spiteful, I wouldn't put it past her," Agnes said, shaking her head.

"I'll get a job, then," Katy said. "I don't care what I do, but I'll find something."

"With no reference?"

"I'll get a reference from Cassandra or I could ask the WAAC or Ariadne Pennington. Jem and I could go to London and get work and send the money back home."

"That's a thought, Katy," Jem said, nodding.

"Do you want to live in London?" asked her mother.

"No, but there's jobs there," Katy said.

There was a rap on the door. Jem got up to answer it.

"Hello, Billy," he said, taking a letter from the gangly youth who delivered the mail.

"Telegram for Kate Phipps," Billy Threadwell

said, handing it to him.

"Thanks, Billy," Jem said and shut the door.

"It's for you," he said, and gave the envelope to Katy, who slit it open with the bread knife.

Katy read it quickly, then looked up with shining eyes and said, "It's from Cassandra. I'll read it out to you.

"HEARD ABOUT AWFUL EVICTION FROM MATER - STOP - HOLD FIRE TILL WE GET HOME V SOON - STOP - MARRIED DOUG TODAY - STOP - CASS"

"What does it mean?" Agnes looked blank.

"It means she'll talk to her mother and she's coming home soon, as Mrs Douglas Flintock," Katy let out her breath. "Thank God."

The storm never did break in the end. The air hung heavy with a lassitude that infected them all with a deep lethargy, as they waited for Cassandra and Douglas to come home for two everlasting weeks.

"It's all very well," Agnes said, one afternoon when she was shelling peas in the garden, "but all we've got to go on is that short telegram. Lord knows you've read it over and over until it's black with fingerprints but it's not a signed contract. The month's nearly up and there's no sign of Mr and Mrs flaming Flintock. I'd better start packing up our things, after all."

"No, don't do that, Mum. Cassandra will turn up. We've got to trust her."

Katy bit her nails. They were sore from constant nibbling. She listened to pop of the pea pods snapping open in her mother's busy hands, followed by gentle thunder as the little bullets thudded into her colander. The leaves of the apple tree above her head played with the sunlight dappling the grass around her hot feet. She kicked off her shoes and remembered how she used to clamber barefoot up the tree. Why couldn't life remain that simple?

She turned to topping and tailing the mound of blackcurrants queuing up for attention in a big bowl between the deckchairs. Katy lifted the china dish onto her lap and started pulling the stalks from the dark purple berries. They immediately spurted sugary juice onto her fingers. She pushed her hair off her forehead with a sticky hand, and ignored the ache in her belly. For once, she relished the pain of her monthly cramps, as blood flushed out the fear that Fred might have impregnated her, and took her biggest worry away with the welcome pain. Perhaps now, she might be able to get closer to Jem, as he deserved, but she still shivered at the thought of intimacy. Damn that Stavely man to hell. She'd put a stave right through his chest, if she ever saw the sod again.

Another man cleared his throat, as he lifted the latch on the garden gate.

"Afternoon, Mrs Beagle," Mr Hayes said, lifting his straw hat to her mother. "Don't get up, please."

"Nonsense, I've got to put these peas in the kitchen. Care for a lemonade, Mr Hayes?"

"Not this time, Mrs Beagle. I've come on estate business. I have an unpleasant duty to perform."

Agnes dropped her colander and peas cascaded around her feet, their spheres lost in the matching green of the lawn.

"Oh, dear, Mrs Beagle, you've lost all your lovely peas," Mr Hayes looked quite crestfallen.

"That's not all I'm about to lose, is it, Mr Hayes?" Agnes said, pale despite the heat.

"No, I'm sorry to say. Is Mr Beagle about?"

"He's up at Home Farm, helping with the wheat harvest," Katy said.

"Of course, of course, how stupid of me. It's so early this year with the dry weather. Would you like me to return when he's home, Mrs Beagle, err, Agnes?

Agnes shook her head.

"I'm afraid, now it's getting near the end of the

month, I have to issue you with this eviction order. I've managed to secure you another month, so you'll have to be out by the first of September. I said your husband couldn't be spared while we're harvesting."

"Another month, well, I suppose that's something," Agnes said, looking dazed.

"Thank you, Mr Hayes. That was kind," Katy said.

"It's a bad business, Mrs Phipps," Mr Hayes said, not meeting her eye.

Katy had heard all the rumours about her. No smoke without fire, they said; same old story as with Charles Smythe. No wonder Lady Amelia was angry and never wanted to see her again. And there had been something funny going on with that vicar who left so suddenly, during the war. Oh, yes, she'd heard it all and didn't doubt Mr Hayes had too.

Katy didn't answer him. She wasn't going to provide fuel for Mrs Threadwell and Mrs Hoskins to spread about. She hoped her silence looked dignified. Another cramp rippled across her stomach and she managed to smile through it.

"Thank you, Mr Hayes, I'll take the notice and give it to my father," she said, holding out her hand.

Mr Hayes said, still avoiding her gaze, "I'm sorry, Mrs Phipps, but I have to put it in the hands of the tenant."

Agnes extended her hand and opened her fist. She took hold of the paper and held it like a firework that might explode at any minute.

"Right, I'll leave it with you. Good-day to you, ladies," and Mr Hayes doffed his straw hat again and left the way he had come.

CHAPTER THIRTY

Cassandra had never been so glad to leave a place in her life. Boston was now a dirty smudge on the horizon. She turned away and looked out over the windswept, wet desert of the Atlantic, without all the ugly structures people built on land. The boat lurched, worsening her nausea. She must tell Douglas about the child soon, but the time had never seemed right after their wedding and all the fracas that had ensued. She shuddered as she remembered the Flintocks' reaction to their marriage.

The strange sense of anti-climax that had attended the ceremony persisted when they'd announced their new status over dinner that night. The atmosphere had remained charged with tension since their last meal together, and being served by a black-eyed and martyred Gallagher really hadn't helped to lift it.

Douglas had tried to make light of it. That hadn't gone down well with his pious father.

He'd said, "Mother, we'll need to make some different domestic arrangements. My wife and I will be sharing a bedroom from now on."

Mrs Flintock's fork had remained suspended in mid-air but her husband's had clattered on to his plate.

"Am I to take it that you and Cassandra are *married*?" his father had thundered.

"That's right, Father. Cassandra and I tied the knot this afternoon," Douglas had said, cutting his tough meat through and through without ever conveying it to his mouth.

Cassandra hadn't even attempted eating.

"But where?" Rose had said. "How could you marry without going to church?"

"Hole in the corner job at the registry office, was it?" Cheryl had said, her voice caustic with scorn.

"Douglas, how could you?" Mrs Flintock had whispered.

252

Douglas had pressed his foot against Cassandra's under the tablecloth and smiled at his mother.

"We didn't want a fuss, you see, Mother dear, and quite frankly, neither of us are believers anymore, so going to church seemed irrelevant. Blame the war, if you like. I doubt any of you'll understand, but then, none of you ever witnessed the fighting, as we did. Changes a person, you know," Douglas had said, and gave up all attempts at dissecting Maureen's gristly beef stew.

"Oh, Douglas, how you've changed," Mrs Flintock had said, her pale eyes fixed on her son's face.

Cassandra had been sorry for the sadness in those liquid blue orbs. "I'm sorry if it's upset you, Mrs Flintock, um, Selina, but Douglas and I are so committed to each other, we just wanted to seal the knot without further upset or bother to anyone."

Cheryl had stared at her through narrowed, speculative eyes that fell to Cassandra's stomach.

"Are you feeling quite well, Cassandra? Only, you are very pale, for a bride," Cheryl had said.

"I've never felt better, thank you, Cheryl," Cassandra had said, looking straight at her, while hating her acute perception and medical eye.

She had breathed in and drawn her stomach inwards, and squared her shoulders, ready for the next wave of outrage.

"You have disappointed me many times, Douglas, but never more than now. I cannot condone the exclusion of your entire family at this important event. Your mother is very grieved, I'm sure, and I no less so. A marriage is a solemn occasion, one that most people share and celebrate with those dearest to them. I am shocked at this announcement but, I suppose, we must all wish you well," Mr Flintock had said, looking as if he wished them anything but.

"What makes you assume that the ceremony was conducted without due solemnity, Father? Cassandra and I took our vows as seriously as anyone could wish, but, after the recent display of intolerance towards our friend, Kate, I chose not to include any of you in our private commitment to each other," Douglas had said.

Rose had jumped up then, clutching her glass in an unsteady hand.

"Father's right! We must wish them well! I give you Cassandra and Douglas! I hope you will be very happy, my dears," Rose had said, and drunk her glass straight down.

When no-one joined in except Douglas and Cassandra, Rose had sat down, deflated into silence. Only her pleading eyes, directed at her father's stern face, had expressed her generous spirit.

Cassandra blinked the memory away and looked out at the wavy horizon. Dear Rose, what a genuinely kind person she'd turned out to be, these last few weeks. Especially later that night when Mrs Flintock had drunk herself into a stupor, only to be found by her upright husband, sprawled and giggling on their bedroom floor, unable to put herself to bed. Rose had come to the rescue again, until Cheryl had shoved her out of the way with ruthless, cruel efficiency and got Maureen to help undress her mistress, so that Mrs Flintock's shame was publicly discussed throughout the district, via her cook's unguarded tongue.

At least, while they were on this ship, they were between families and being away from either set of parents meant they could simply be themselves.

Mr and Mrs Douglas Flintock.

Her new title would take some getting used to but Cassandra didn't feel comfortable giving her entire identity away. She preferred the name Mrs Flintock-Smythe and hoped Douglas wouldn't object to her suggesting it. It would provide continuity at Cheadle Manor. The Smythes had occupied it for centuries. She didn't want the family name to die out now. Oh, damn it! she'd think about all of that when they got nearer to England. For now, it was enough to be able to breathe more easily and concentrate on her new husband.

She found him propping up the bar in the first class lounge.

"Martini, darling?" Douglas asked, hopping down from his bar stool to greet her.

"Err, no thanks, just soda water," Cassandra said.

"Oh dear, that's not like you, Cass? Honey, don't tell me you're seasick?"

"No, well, maybe a little. These bigger boats do roll so. It's a little early for me anyway," Cassandra was relieved to see that Douglas accepted this explanation without question. They took their drinks out on to the open deck, where Cassandra was delighted to see that Boston had rolled right off the horizon and all she could see was clear blue water in every direction.

"This is the life," Douglas said, "Hey, Mrs Flintock?"

"You bet," Cassandra said, sipping her drink and laying back against the deck chair. She closed her eyes against the sunshine and acknowledged her fatigue. Was this the moment? No time like the present.

"Douglas?"

"Hmm, what is it, honey?"

"I have something to tell you," Cassandra said.

She sat up and watched his face. Douglas seemed to sense her mood, put his drink down on the wooden deck and turned to face her.

"Until Fred ruined it, I had a wonderful time on the coast with you. I think of it now as our honeymoon and I will treasure it all my life, especially as something rather special has resulted it from it."

"Oh?" Douglas said, his eyebrows raised.

"We're going to have a child, Douglas," Cassandra said.

"Oh, my! Really? So soon?"

Cassandra could only nod until she could read his expression. Relief flooded through her when his eyebrows lowered and his face broke into the widest smile she'd ever seen.

"Cassandra! By all that's wonderful! A baby, wow! Hey, it's a good job we're legal."

Douglas reached over and kissed her, on the mouth, in front of the other passengers. Some smiled but others moved away. Cassandra didn't give a hoot.

"Are you sure you're happy about it?"

"Happy? I'm the happiest man on this boat!"

Cassandra thought he might have said in the whole world, after all, that *was* traditional, but it was a big ship. She'd settle for that.

The voyage passed in a blur of renewed intimacy, once she had reassured Douglas that her pregnancy only made her want him more. Cassandra was only too aware that this was the only time they would have to themselves and begrudged each sunset, however spectacular, signalling the end of another love-filled day.

But, five short days later, they were docking in Liverpool. There was a fair bit of baggage to negotiate with the porters but it was delightful to tell them to strap it on to Douglas's roadster, which had made the crossing underneath them in the hold, and had now been hoisted onto the dockside. Driving home would be so much easier than struggling on to train platforms with a queasy stomach. Odd that she was nauseous now, when she was such a good sailor.

They decided to stop overnight at the Smythe's London house and had telegrammed ahead to inform the butler, Hewitt. Cassandra loved introducing Douglas as her husband and inviting him into her bedroom without any need for subterfuge in front of the servants.

She woke the next morning and turned her head on the pillow. And there he was; his dark hair and lashes laying quietly against his smooth skin. She stroked his arm and he woke instantly and smiled at her. Cassandra rolled into his body, knowing hers would fit perfectly.

"Welcome to England, husband mine," she said, kissing his eyelids awake.

"Best welcome, I've ever had," came the sleepy, eager reply.

"Let's go home today, shall we?" Cassandra said.

"Not just yet," Douglas said, "I want to give you a welcome of my own."

Hewitt's voice floated up the stairs when Cassandra walked down them, much later.

"I must say, being married does suit Mrs Flintock, as we've got to call her now. I've never seen her looking so well."

"And if you'd heard them earlier, you'd know why," giggled the housemaid.

Cassandra cleared her throat, loudly.

Hewitt joined her in the hall, his face pink with embarrassment.

"Can I help you, ma'am?" he said.

Ma'am. She'd never be 'Miss' again. Cassandra dismissed the thought, and focussed on the many compensations.

"Yes, Hewitt. I need to telephone the manor and let them know we're on our way."

"Of course, ma'am. The telephone has been installed in the drawing room and the number is right next to it, on the little notepad I've placed there for the purpose. Or would you prefer me to dial it for you?"

"I'm sure I can manage, thank you."

She didn't speak to her mother but left a message with Andrews, the butler at Cheadle Manor. She was confident that Lady Amelia would have plenty to say once they'd arrived. Let the battle lines be drawn.

Driving down to Wiltshire, with Douglas by her side, just the way she'd imagined it months ago in the drear, lonely winter, turned out to be a treat. They had the top down and the English summer obliged them with a rare good day. Thunderously hot, in fact.

They stopped at a pub for lunch.

"Mother would say this was dreadfully common," Cassandra said, thoroughly enjoying her draught beer and ploughman's cheese and bread.

"What, eating lunch in a public house?" Douglas said, screwing his face up in distaste after his first sip of beer. "Ugh! This beer is warm."

"That's the way Englishmen like it. It's not usually such hot weather. Should bring in a good harvest."

"Here's to prosperity then, and warm beer," Douglas said.

As they neared Cheadle, the sky became dull with cloud and Cassandra's earlier relaxed mood faded away with the sunshine. She rehearsed her speech to her parents over and over in her head. She had deliberately not written to tell them she was married. After reading Lady Amelia's spirited account about her eviction of the Beagle family, she needed to keep her trump card well hidden. Or would news of an imminent grandchild soften her mother's vengeful temper more?

She would know soon enough.

"I'm enjoying driving along your country roads," Douglas said. "Much more challenging than our straight American ones. All these bends and dips makes you use the gears more. No wonder you're such a good driver, Cass, darling, if you learned to drive here."

Cassandra smiled at him. Much as she loved to drive, she enjoyed Douglas being at the wheel and, although he drove much faster than she liked to, she never felt in danger. He had a way of accelerating through a bend that made the little roadster stick to the tarmac like glue. And it was lovely to be back in English countryside again. The summer dog roses hung languid in the hedges and honeysuckle sweetened the warm breeze. She took off her little cloche hat and let the wind ruffle her hair. It would be a mess when they got there but she'd simply replace her hat and tuck it all away again. She couldn't let Mother rule everything.

The sky was so overcast when they turned into the gates of Cheadle Manor, Cassandra wondered if a rainstorm threatened, but the still air remained very warm and dry.

"We'd better stop here and let Kate know we're home," Cassandra said.

"Okay, honey," Douglas said and stilled the engine, which hiccupped to a standstill. "Seems the motor's had enough for one day, anyway," he added.

They knocked on the front door. Jem answered. His smile cracked his face as if it was no longer used to his mouth stretching across it.

"Hello, Jem," Cassandra said. "It's good to see you."

She kissed him on both cheeks.

"Miss Cassandra, Mr Flintock - welcome home and, um, congratulations. I'll tell Katy you're here. She's in the garden."

He disappeared. Cassandra quailed at his muted welcome. The sooner she spoke to her mother, the better.

Katy looked washed out. "Cass! Doug! How lovely to see you! Won't you come in?"

"No, darling, we won't stop," Cassandra said, after a quick hug. "Just wanted to say we're home and ask what's happening?"

"We've had the eviction notice. We have to be out by the first of September, after the harvest."

"We'll soon see about that!" Cassandra said. "Tell your parents not to worry. I'm determined to set things to rights with Mater. I'll be back tomorrow with, hopefully, some good news."

Jem and Katy's drawn faces lit up. Cassandra felt nervous at the enormity of her task when she saw them exchange a desperate look of hope. Her mother had much to answer for.

"Come on, Doug. Let's get up to the house and get things straightened out. See you tomorrow, Kate. Give my regards to your parents and tell them I'll do all I can, won't you?"

Katy nodded and waved them off.

A bright spark of anger ignited Cassandra as they

drove up the long driveway. "That wretched mother of mine! She rules her little empire like a despot. She's always had it in for Kate."

"Don't you think it might be grief for her son that's coming out all wrong?" Douglas said.

"Douglas, I think you might have hit the nail on the head. Thank you for that insight. I know just what to do now," Cassandra said, kissing his cheek and making him swerve onto the lawn.

"Better put the car in the barn," Cassandra said. "None of the servants except Jem and Kate can drive."

Little Jack Beagle came running in when he heard the engine.

"Hello, Miss Cassandra!" he said, looking at the roadster, not at her.

"Hello, Jack. Could you run in and tell Andrews we're home, there's a good lad?"

"Yes, miss," and Jack skipped off.

Despite the heat, Cassandra drew on a pair of light gloves, which hid her new wedding ring. She and Douglas walked round to the front of the house, by which time a few of the staff had gathered on the wide steps in welcome. Her mother loitered in the hall, out of the daylight.

The maids bobbed curtsies and Mr and Mrs Andrews bowed to them as they entered. Cassandra avoided meeting Douglas's eyes, knowing how ludicrous he would find their formality, and afraid she might laugh with him.

"Welcome back to Cheadle Manor, Douglas," Lady Amelia said, extending her hand.

Douglas kissed the fat, ringed fingers with gallant enthusiasm. Cassandra's mouth twitched at her mother's rapid withdrawal of her hand.

"It's good to have you home, again, Cassandra," Lady Amelia said. "We'll take tea in the drawing room, Andrews."

"Very good, my lady," Andrews said and shooed

the staff away.

The blinds were down in the drawing room, making the room stuffy, despite its size, rather than cool. Cassandra instantly returned to the feeling of suffocation that usually afflicted her when confined indoors with her mother. They sat on the sofas around the unlit fire and discussed the journey.

"Where is Father?" Cassandra asked, after Andrews had silently delivered a laden tea tray and her mother was pouring out from the silver pot.

"He went to see Hayes about something. He'll be back shortly. He must have heard that noisy vehicle of yours from the stables," Lady Amelia said.

"I hope it didn't disturb you, Lady Amelia," Douglas said, falling into the trap.

"Cars always disturb me, Douglas. I can't abide them. I think they're vulgar and I'm very sensitive to the fumes they spew out. It makes me despair about the future. You can't go to Woodbury now without having one overtake the carriage and upsetting the horses."

Cassandra changed the subject. "What time is dinner?"

"You should know that, Cassandra. Dinner will be served at seven o'clock, as it always has been. At least in this, we can preserve tradition."

"Right, well, I'll go up and change then. I need to refresh myself after our long drive," Cassandra said, accepting her dish of tea.

"I suppose you do, I must say, you are looking rather, shall we say, bedraggled?" Lady Amelia sipped her tea, keeping her little finger raised at a ludicrous angle.

"We had the top down on Douglas's sports car, Mother. You should try it sometime, it's very exhilarating."

"I? Travel in a sports car? I don't think so, young lady. Now, you are in your usual bedroom and I've had Andrews make up the blue bedroom for Douglas, where he stayed before."

"That won't be necessary, Lady Amelia," Douglas began.

"Thank you, Mother. That sounds lovely," Cassandra said, drowning out her husband's words.

"But?" Douglas said.

"Come on, Douglas, let's get our things sorted, shall we?"

Cassandra didn't want to disclose her marital status without her father being there. She got up, leaving her tea-cup half full, and took Douglas's hand. Lady Amelia screwed up her eyes at this intimate gesture but Cassandra pulled Douglas from his comfy seat and tugged him towards the door to the hall.

"Just follow my lead on this one," she said to Douglas, as they mounted the stairs.

"But, darling, I don't want us to sleep apart! And I don't need a separate room," Douglas said.

"No, but I want to tell them over dinner, in my own time, when Father is present," Cassandra said. "So keep your voice down until then, darling Douglas. Trust me?"

Douglas didn't reply but looked mulish as he trudged off to his allocated room at the far corner of the corridor, well away from Cassandra's bedroom, which no doubt was part of her mother's plan.

Cassandra needed some time to think, without the tempting distraction of Douglas's kisses. Her cases had already been delivered to her spacious bedroom. She wished Katy was here to organise them. Maisie, the housemaid, popped her head around the door and offered to help but, although she knew Maisie to be a sweet girl, she also knew she was all fingers and thumbs and had none of Katy's quiet efficiency.

"Don't worry, Maisie. I'll sort it all out tomorrow, but thank you."

She found an outfit and shook it out on a hanger. She dressed with care, but without ostentation. She wanted to please her parents tonight, not frighten them with the short, fashionable dresses she'd bought in America. She chose the coffee and cream coloured outfit she had worn the first evening she had met the Flintocks, and pinned her hair up the way her mother liked it, neat and clamped down.

When the gong sounded from the hall, she was ready, and knocked on Douglas's door. He hadn't unpacked a thing but had slung on a dinner suit and brushed his hair. He looked militant and uncooperative.

"Douglas, darling. This is temporary. By the time dinner is over, you'll be coming to bed with me. I must tackle Mother about the Beagles' situation, so I need to ease into telling her we're married. Please support me in this, for Kate's sake, if not my own."

"I can see all that, but I sure hope you succeed. This is the gloomiest bedroom I have ever seen."

"Oh, don't sulk, darling. By midnight, you'll be in my arms again."

They kissed, lingering until the second gong rang out.

"Now you're wearing my lipstick instead of me," Cassandra said, dabbing at Douglas's mouth with her handkerchief. "Come on. Into battle."

Sir Robert greeted them with all the warmth his wife lacked and enfolded his daughter in a boozy embrace.

"Welcome back, Cassandra, my girl. Good to see you, Douglas!"

Sir Robert gave Douglas a hearty handshake and a walloping slap on the back.

She'd better get the talking in early, before her father had more wine.

"I thought we'd have champagne with the first course, to celebrate your return," Sir Robert said.

"What a marvellous idea, Father," Cassandra said.

Andrews popped the cork and came round with the tray.

"Not for me, Andrews," Lady Amelia said, "I'll

have my usual sherry."

When Andrews had departed, and they were faced with quail's eggs in a rich Hollandaise sauce, Cassandra judged the time to be right to begin her revelations.

"Good health!" Sir Robert said, glugging his champagne down so the slender flute was instantly half empty. Andrews had left the ice bucket by his master's side and Sir Robert refilled his glass, offering the bottle around, but no-one else had taken more than a sip.

Cassandra started to toy with the tiny quail's eggs. "Douglas and I have an important announcement to make," she said.

"Jolly good," said Sir Robert, "Give us all the news, my dear."

Cassandra pulled her long evening glove from her left hand and held it out to her mother. "Douglas and I decided to get married in Boston, a few weeks ago."

"By Jove! You didn't waste much time, Douglas!" Sir Robert said.

"You did *what*?" Lady Amelia said, laying down her cutlery and grabbing her daughter's left hand. "But what about having the wedding here? In Cheadle? I've made plans! How could you not consult us about *our* wishes?"

"We thought we'd save you all the expense," Cassandra said. "What with the war and everything, it didn't seem appropriate to have a grand wedding, when so many are bereaved, don't you agree, Mother? After all, people, the Ponsonby's for example, might think it a tad vulgar, and I think we should avoid *that* at all costs, don't you?"

Lady Amelia's mouth dropped open and stayed that way, for at least thirty seconds, without any words issuing from its usually busy orifice.

Douglas rose to the occasion and Cassandra longed to kiss him when he said, "We thought about it very carefully, Lady Amelia, and we wanted to handle it as diplomatically as possible, bearing in mind your own loss of a son. I hope you find it a nice surprise. To be honest, Sir Robert, I couldn't wait any longer to marry your beautiful daughter."

"I say! Good show! Have some more champagne, Douglas. Very well said. Congratulations are in order. What do you say, my dear?" Sir Robert looked pointedly at his spouse, something he avoided in the general way of things.

"Well, I, I..." Lady Amelia still seemed lost for words. Cassandra counted that as a goal for her side.

"A toast!" Sir Robert rose to his feet. "To Mr and Mrs Flintock!"

More champagne slipped down their throats. Cassandra found it rather acid but it was deliciously cool. Her mother didn't sip her sherry at all but sat staring at them, her mouth slightly open, but remaining miraculously silent.

Cassandra filled the breach, grabbing the opportunity to drive home her objective. "I knew you didn't want to travel to America, Mother, especially while you are in mourning."

Still Lady Amelia sat mute.

Cassandra hurried on, "Actually, I was thinking of combining our names and calling myself Mrs Flintock-Smythe, if you don't mind, Doug?"

Douglas shook his head, his eyes dancing with amusement.

Cassandra continued, "You see, I thought it would be better for the manor to keep the family name going. What do you think, Mother?"

Lady Amelia blinked rapidly and cleared her throat. Finally, she sipped her drink, and said, her usual strident tones sounding reedy and weak, "Flintock-Smythe does have a certain ring to it, I suppose, but I'm truly shocked that you married with such indecent haste. Though I do take your point about unseemly celebrations so soon after the bereavements so many of us have suffered. I suppose life must begin again, without those we have lost, but I deeply regret your unilateral decision to legalise your union in this surreptitious manner. It is all most irregular and underhand. To think that I have seen neither of my children's weddings! Yours because you have chosen to exclude me and Charles because he will never have one."

Lady Amelia wiped her eyes with her serviette instead of her handkerchief, and said "You have been most deceitful about yours, Cassandra. Why, it's almost as bad as an elopement."

Lady Amelia sniffed and swallowed some more sherry. Cassandra waited for a cue that the tide might have turned in her favour, before venturing any further remarks.

Her mother continued, in a stronger voice, "We shall have to have some sort of gathering to announce the event, of course. And, I do approve of your keeping the Smythe name for posterity. After all, Flintock is hardly local - I doubt if anyone's heard of it in the county. And it is so important for the lower orders to have some sense of history preserved, but it will all take a great deal of getting used to. I do not like surprises," Lady Amelia said, picking up her fork again.

Cassandra saw this as a very positive sign.

"Oh, I'm so pleased you like my new name. Continuity is such a good thing, I feel. It's reassuring for the whole community and let's face it, they've all been through enough lately."

Andrews entered at this point to clear away the first course, as yet largely uneaten. He went to withdraw again, when he saw how slow they'd been, but Lady Amelia raised an imperious finger.

"No, wait, Andrews. You might as well hear the news straight away. Mr Flintock is now married to my daughter, apparently. They had the ceremony in Boston. You may tell the rest of the staff this evening and, of course, make any adjustments to the domestic arrangements as necessary."

"Yes, my lady. May I offer my congratulations to the happy couple?"

"Indeed, you may, Andrews!" Cassandra said, beaming at him.

"Very best wishes to you both, I'm sure," Andrews said, and an incongruous smile made a rare appearance on his long face.

"Shall I clear away, now?"

"Yes, please do, Andrews, or the main course will be spoiled," Lady Amelia said.

Cassandra decided to keep the news about the baby for another occasion. Lady Amelia could too easily calculate that there had not been a decent interval for conception to be established *after* the wedding. It wouldn't harm to keep that card up her sleeve, ready for the next battle about Katy and Jem, which would also have to wait for another day.

Judging by her mother's reaction to the news of her marriage, she didn't dare broach the thorny subject this time and risk alienating Douglas with another row.

CHAPTER THIRTY ONE

Katy was at a loose end the next day. Cassandra hadn't showed up with a magic wand and the disappointment hit her like a lead bullet.

Jem had gone off to ask Mr Stubbs if he could help with the harvest at Home Farm. He'd insisted on going on his own, when she'd suggested coming with him. Katy guessed he didn't want her to witness his humiliation, if he was refused the work because of his arm. Her mother was busy catching up with cleaning the lodge house, and wanted the place to herself, even though Katy had offered to help.

Agnes had said, "No, I've got my methods, thanks. I know this place inside and out and I want to sort it out in my own way - the way I've always done. This house is like an old friend to me, Katy. I do love it so. It will break my heart to leave but I shall make sure it's left spotless. I can let things sink in when I'm polishing and scrubbing and I need a bit of time to myself, if you don't mind, love."

Her father was up at the manor, setting the stables to rights for the same reason, and Jack was helping him. Daisy was up there too, assisting Mrs Biggs in the kitchen, as there were two more to feed in the big house, and the school summer holidays weren't over yet.

So Katy took herself off for a walk, with no particular direction in mind, feeling more redundant than ever. She meandered out on to the main road next to West Lodge. Despite not sleeping well, she felt restless with unspent energy. As usual, she was racking her tired brains about the future but she was clueless as to what to do with it. Only one thing comforted her - that she and Jem would face it together.

She wished they were together in every sense, but, what with the lack of privacy and the way her skin crawled when she touched anyone else's, there was fat chance of them renewing any intimacy. It made her feel pent up and crotchety and she knew Jem felt the same. She hoped he would get some harvesting work. Not only did they need the money, but he needed some physical outlet for his frustration.

Privacy would be the least of their worries soon and they couldn't stay at the lodge anyway, once Agnes and Bert had been evicted. Agnes had asked her old aunt in Woodbury if they could stay with her in exchange for taking care of her. Agnes visited her once a week to do her chores and shopping and the old girl had reluctantly agreed to the invasion rather than see the family split up in the workhouse. Anything would be better than the fate that everyone dreaded. Aunt Maggie's house was even smaller than the lodge. How they would all fit in was occupying Agnes's mind for much of the time. Just thinking about the confinement of winter filled Katy with foreboding. No, there just wouldn't be room for her and Jem too. She, they, must get work and find a home, and soon, but where? what? how?

A bee buzzed next to her, and sank its proboscis deep into the umbel of a purple foxglove in the hedgerow. She envied its sense of purpose. What was hers? Well, she knew she was good with machines. Maybe, if they did move to the city, she'd find work in a factory. She pictured Jem in a mean little terraced house amongst rows of others. He'd be a fish out of water and what job would *he* do? She'd read about the men begging in the streets of London in the newspaper. It was nothing short of a scandal, the article said, and someone had started up a scheme called 'Homes for Heroes' for the war wounded in the capital, but nobody round here seemed to care about the broken soldiers left on the scrapheap. Apparently, Lady Amelia was getting up a fund for a war memorial for the two Cheadles. Huh, that wouldn't give you dry shelter in the rain. Typical of the old bat, too. All show and no compassion. Some things never bloody changed.

The sun rose higher, making Katy overheat. She took off her straw hat and fanned her face. She'd walked quite a way along the main road and was nearing the bridge that spanned the river Cheadle. She could do with a drink. When she reached the stone hump-backed bridge, she left the road and went down the embankment to the river. She knelt down, scooped up a handful of the clear water and drank it greedily down, splashing some on her face. Ah, that felt better! She sat down on the riverbank and looked over the countryside bedecked in all its summer glory. Cow parsley fluffed along the edge of the field and meadowsweet wafted its vanilla scent across the flowing water.

Never mind about Jem, she didn't want to leave here either, and wondered why she'd ever wanted to before. Talk about the grass being greener on the other side. Katy sighed at the aptness of her thought and looked across to the opposite embankment. There were some round roofs peeping above the tree-line about two fields away. She didn't remember them being there before the war. They must be Nissen huts, by the looks of them. Curious, she got up, and returning to the road, crossed the bridge to have a look.

Sure enough, behind a confusion of brambles, elders and nettles, a short, wide path, rutted with dried mud from tyre-tracks, lead to a gate off the road. There was a notice pinned to the gate. Katy read,

"KEEP OFF!
TRESPASSERS WILL BE PROSECUTED
BY THE AUTHORITY OF
HER MAJESTY'S BRITISH ARMY"

Tough! The war was over now and anyway, hadn't she been a member of that army? Katy climbed over the padlocked gate and jumped down on the other side into a make-shift yard, to find it contained two Nissen huts and a jumble of old crates and tyres.

The huts stood in line with each other, about fifty yards apart, just like at Étaples, where the British

Expeditionary Force had had their base and she had worked for two long war-torn years. She went up to the first hut and peered through the dirty window. There wasn't much inside, just old sacks of flour that the rats had ripped open. A few of the dirty critters scuttled away, when she tapped on the glass.

She wandered across to the other hut. These windows were even filthier and she rubbed them clean with a tuft of grass. A little spike of excitement shot through her stomach, when she looked inside. A motorbike, painted in army green, stood in the centre of the hut, with one tyre-less wheel cranked up on its stand, just as if someone had been changing the tyre and had stopped halfway.

Katy's pulse quickened. Why stop in the middle of such an easy job? She went to the front of the building and rattled the door but the padlock looked heavy and reluctant to yield. She walked all around the hut, swishing the overgrown nettles away with a stick she pulled off a dead branch. One of the small window panes at the back was broken. Katy jabbed at it with her stick and cleared it of the remaining fragments of glass. If she reached in, she might, just might be able to grab the window clasp.

Blood sprang from her arm as she stretched to her full capacity and scraped it against the jagged window's edge but still her fingers only just touched the tip of the handle. Damn! It was just too far. She withdrew her arm, sucked the blood away from the ragged cut, spat it out and wiped it with a dock leaf, the way her mother had taught her. Then she remembered the crates tossed about in untidy heaps in the yard at the front. She held the dock leaf on her cut to staunch the wound and jogged impatiently to where the crates were. Discarding the leaf, and checking that the trickle of blood had been arrested, Katy picked up one of the crates and tested it would take her weight, before returning to the broken window and jamming it against the wall underneath.

Now then - this should do it! She hopped onto the

crate, leaned in and grasped the window catch. It was stiff and caked in dust. She applied more pressure and suddenly it gave way, wobbling her off the crate. She landed on a patch of nettles that stung her arm around the wound.

"Ouch," she said, and searched around for more dock leaves. Rubbing all along her arm soothed the sting enough for her to right the tumbled crate and climb back on to it. If she was very careful, she could just, yes, only just, climb through the window. She was in! It was a long drop on the other side, but she landed safely on bent knees and grinned her satisfaction.

Ignoring her stinging arm, Katy adjusted her eyes to the gloom of the interior. Some rough shelves, obviously erected in haste, lined one wall. Katy inspected them, seeing the tools of her trade with a welcome thud of recognition. Spanners, hammers, wrenches and cans of oil covered in dirty fingerprints; rows of spark plugs, bits of wire and a soldering iron; old cocoa tins containing screws, nails and rivets - such useful things - and all abandoned. A sharpening stone was clamped to the edge of a solid-looking bench at the far end. Katy turned the handle and the stone circle whirred around, grating slightly where it's metal arm had rusted. Instinctively she rubbed it clean with a piece of sandpaper lying next to it, reflecting that the bench was sited well, below the biggest window. On the other side of the motorbike were some oil drums. Surely, they hadn't left petrol in them? She went across and rattled them. No, all empty. If they hadn't been, no doubt this place would have been burgled long since. It was surprising no-one had trespassed before her, in the six months since the Armistice.

She supposed people had been too preoccupied fighting the 'flu last winter and adjusting to peace without their lost boys and men. The hut smelt of mice, musty and damp.

Why had the bike been abandoned? It was in a sorry state. Perhaps the Army didn't think it worthwhile to renovate, once the fighting had stopped. She sat astride the bike's seat, with her feet braced on the floor, and ran her hands along the handle bars. It was a Triumph 550cc one cylinder bike, just like the hundreds she'd worked on in the war. All the despatch riders had used them and it had been affectionately known as 'Trusty', due to its reliability. She'd fixed them up ready for action loads of times.

Katy's eyes misted up and she said, out loud, "You poor old thing. They've worked you to death and left you to moulder here on your own."

She brought her feet up to the pedals, tempted to try and start the motor and see if it would fire but reluctantly decided against it, until she could find out if the fuel lines were clear of blockages.

She gave the engine a cursory inspection. As far as she could see, without stripping it down properly, it didn't look too bad. At least no parts appeared to be missing. Perhaps all it needed was a good clean up. She unscrewed the cap on the fuel tank to check on its level. It had plenty of petrol.

Katy folded her arms across her chest, as her heart had started to thump and she needed to keep a lid on it. She looked around the Nissen hut and breathed in the mixture of dust and damp, motor-oil and diesel.

The best perfume in the world.

Her kind.

CHAPTER THIRTY TWO

"So, how did you get on today?" Katy asked Jem, later that day. They were sitting out in the lodge garden, enjoying the cool of the evening, after supper. Jem's face gave his answer for him. He'd caught the sun and looked whacked.

"Alright, thanks," Jem said, stifling a yawn.

"I'm glad they took you on, love," Katy said.

"Yes, old Stubbs is a good bloke. Didn't turn a hair when he saw my arm. And, once I'd worked out a technique, like, it wasn't too bad. Couldn't use a pitchfork of course, but they got me stacking the stooks, as they come off the trailer. Hard work, but I'll have a bit of cash once the harvest is in," and Jem yawned again.

"What time do you have to start tomorrow, Jem?" Katy asked, trying not to scratch her itchy arm where it had been stung. She had been careful to change into long sleeves to hide the cut when she got home. She was none too sure that any of her family would approve of harbouring a burglar.

"Not long after dawn breaks. Old Stubbs says we've got to catch this weather while it lasts. It'll be a long day, so I think I'll go on up, if you don't mind." Jem stood up and said, "Coming?"

Katy shook her head, "No, think I'll sit here for a bit. It's so peaceful."

And she had so much to think about.

She watched her husband go through the open back door and nod goodnight to Agnes and Bert, who were sitting around the kitchen table. Agnes, never idle for long, was bunching herbs to dry and Bert was sucking on his last pipe of the day. He looked shattered too. Harvest was always exhausting and Bert had to work the shire horses as they pulled the haywains from the fields.

Her parents were sitting in their cottage, as they had always done and as she'd expected they always would do, contented and secure - as much as anybody could be in this crazy world - and now, thanks to her, their little world was upside down. Why should they suffer like this? Wasn't losing a son enough? So much waste.

Like that Triumph motorbike gathering dust. Katy turned her head back and studied the trunk of the apple tree. Its bark morphed into pistons and gears, transporting her back into the Nissen hut. She recalled that profound sense of home-coming that she'd experienced in the scrubby old place. She'd found where she belonged alright, but how could she make use of it? She couldn't take on the whole ruddy army. There must be a way she could prove she could make engines work and she'd relish the challenge of getting that old bike back on the road. If she could get someone, anyone, to take her on as a mechanic, that hut would be the perfect workshop. The tools were there, it was right on the road and Katy knew she could make a go of it. It wasn't as if the army needed it anymore. That motorbike was going to rust away to nothing, if left there. The whole place had felt neglected and abandoned. You could hardly even see it from the road, it was so overgrown with elders and nettles.

So... if no-one could see her... what was to stop her mending the bike - get it running again? Then she could ride it to the local barracks and show the top brass what she was made of. Maybe they'd give her a job? Yes, and maybe they'd chuck her in jail for trespass too.

"You coming to bed, Katy?" Bert called from the house. "Only, I want to lock up for the night."

"Coming, Dad," Katy said and stood up. All the heat of the summer's day had gathered inside. It was like walking into an oven.

Jem was asleep already when she got to their little room, having tiptoed past her brother and sister's beds and round the dividing curtain. She slipped under the covers. Jem's hot body made hers warmer than ever. She let her leg hang out of the bed and pushed the covers off. When this long dry spell gave up the ghost, they'd be in for one hell of a storm.

Her mind refused to let go of her mad idea all night. She'd only just fallen asleep, when Jem got out of bed at a very early hour the next morning, and woke her up.

"Sorry!" he said, smiling under his mop of tousled hair, "didn't mean to wake you. Got to get over to Home Farm."

He leaned over and kissed her tenderly. He looked tired but a lot happier than she'd seen him for weeks. It meant so much to him to be able to provide for her. Bloody war. She watched him go with affection. Thank God he'd survived, but there was more to him than being a farm labourer and that thought took her straight back to the Nissen hut. She'd go there again today. It was completely irresistible.

She ate a good breakfast and tucked some bread, cheese and an apple into a napkin for her lunch, behind her mother's back. Agnes was busy with Emily, who was playing up. The hot weather had aggravated her and she hadn't slept well. Katy felt for her mother, who looked like she rarely slept these days.

Katy hoped her little sister wasn't brewing up for anything serious, like poor Florence. She never visited her daughter's grave in Lower Cheadle anymore. She'd seen too many, and however personally painful the death of her only child remained, Florence's short life now seemed lost in the sea of genocide she'd witnessed. Katy shook her head, shaking it free of the grim images that always lurked there, ready to crowd out her thoughts.

It was time to look ahead. Time to have another look at that bike.

She marched straight down the main road, thinking how strange it was, that if she kept right on walking, she'd end up in London. The London to Bristol road. What better site could there be for a garage? She stopped stock still in the road as this radical new idea hit her tired brain. What if the army agreed to give her a job in the Nissen hut workshop and she made enough money to buy it off them somehow, through a mortgage or something, and set up her own garage? She could service cars like Dr Benson's old T Ford and Douglas's roadster and, surely, in time, there would be more? However much her Dad resisted the idea, tractors would take over from the plough, of that she was quite certain. Trade could only increase. She could get a petrol pump like that one she had seen in Boston! That would bring in some steady money.

Soon she was over the bridge and climbing the gate into the yard. She had walked quickly and covered the couple of miles in much less time than yesterday.

Katy stood and looked at the two huts. The round tin roofs and concrete block walls weren't exactly beautiful but she knew from her war days they were strongly made and weatherproof. If they had one as a garage, perhaps they could live in the other? Even share it with the rest of the family? She didn't care how rough it was inside - she'd lived in a tent for two years - and it couldn't be worse than that. She wondered if the army owned the land, or just the huts that stood on it. How on earth could she find out?

She couldn't solve that problem now, so she went around the back, impatient to get started on the Triumph.

The crate was still there and she hopped up on to it and slithered through the window like a practised thief. First thing she had to do, was to put on her dungarees. She'd borrowed Jem's army rucksack and stuffed them inside with her picnic and a bottle of her Mum's lemonade. She looked out of the front window. No-one was about; in fact, she could barely see the road from here through the bushes. She slipped off her dress and pulled on her old army dungarees.

My, did that feel good! She tied up her hair in a scarf and rubbed her hands with glee. She'd start with that tyre. She cleaned up the beaded edge around the rim of the wheel and checked for dimples. Once satisfied with the soundness of the wheel, Katy climbed back out of the window to look at the heap of tyres gathered outside. She found a match for the Triumph and trundled it back. It wasn't too heavy but it would be tricky to lift such an awkward, round object in through the window. Katy searched in the undergrowth, and surprised a grass snake basking on a long plank in the sun.

"Sorry, mate," she said, "but I need this plank."

The snake slid off and disappeared into the abundant greenery. Katy lifted up the wooden board and tapped off any other unwelcome visitors, before hefting it onto her shoulder and offering it up to the window. The plank was long, so it wasn't too acute an angle for her to roll the tyre up its broad platform and push it through the window, but she was sweating by the time it landed inside with a crash against an empty oil drum. Katy jumped and looked around guiltily to see if anyone else heard the noise, but all she could hear were the birds, chirruping her on with enthusiasm, as she followed the tyre inside.

Katy hummed a tune as she replaced the tyre, easing it on to the wheel rim with some tyre levers and thoroughly enjoying the return to her favourite work. The tyre need inflating in an ideal world and she hunted high and low for a pump, eventually finding one under the workbench, next to an enormous spider. She hooked the pump away from the malevolent beast with the toe of her boot and tapped it against the concrete floor to make sure there were no other creepy hostages. Pumping up the tyre with the foot-pump was exhausting but she was rewarded by the tyre inflating slowly, with no sign of a puncture. Having squeezed it to test the pressure, she let the stand down as slowly as she could. The bike settled back to the floor with a pleasing bounce.

She sat on an empty oil drum and munched her bread and cheese and contemplated her achievement. Next, she'd tackle the engine but first she'd have to strip the parts. Katy found some rags and a can of oil, still joyfully a quarter full, and started cleaning the engine. She removed the spark plugs and wiped them with the oil and then their cylinders before replacing them. Then she did the same with the valves so they wouldn't stick against the piston. By the time she had broken every fingernail, the engine was starting to look like a goer again. Katy found the repetitive nature of the work soothing rather than boring. She carried on all afternoon until the light started to fade. It was only when she was tidying up that she realised she hadn't thought about Fred Stavely once.

Her hands were filthy, black with soot and oil. She found a jar of paraffin and dipped her hands in and rubbed them vigorously. There was no disguising its whiff and she despaired of fooling her mother with that stink on her hands.

Katy looked out of the back window and saw the sun slipping down behind the tangle of trees surrounding the huts. She had no watch to tell the time but it must be later than she thought. She grabbed her things and tumbled out through the window, shoving it shut by pressing a brick against the broken pane. Still in her dungarees, she climbed over the gate, gave a quick look up and down the road and trotted to the river, where she washed the paraffin off her soiled hands as best she could, then wriggled her dress back on behind a bush. She half walked, half ran along the road back home, feeling like a criminal about to be caught in the act. It was almost dark when she reached the lodge.

"And what time do you call this to be home? Jem's been back an hour since, fretting about where you were, but he's gone out again," Agnes said.

Katy remembered her mother had been up half the night with young Emily and tried not to be cross. She was feeling so pleased with her clandestine day's work, she hadn't the heart to retaliate. She could remember, all too well, how distressing a sick child could be.

"How's Emily?" Katy said.

Agnes's lined face softened immediately. "Tucked up in bed, she is, and feeling much better, I'm glad to say."

"That's good then," Katy said, and went to the scullery to wash her blackened hands before her mother spotted them.

"Where's Jem?" she asked, on her return.

"Gone up to East Lodge, to see his parents and, no doubt, hoping to find you somewhere along the way," Agnes said. "Do you want supper, or have you had some?"

"Yes, please, Mum, I'm starving!" Katy said, sitting at the table.

"Right you are then," Agnes said, putting the remains of a cheese and onion flan on the table, with a plate of lettuce studded with red radishes.

"So, what have you been up to?" Agnes said, watching Katy eat. "You been out all day."

"Just walking mostly, Mum," Katy said, through a mouthful of food.

"What? All day? Time you found something better to do with yourself," Agnes said, as she sliced runner beans for the salting jars. "I know I wanted the place to myself yesterday but I didn't mean for you to feel like a refugee without a home. There's so much to harvest from the garden, we're not short of chores to do and God knows we'll need to take all the preserves we can to Aunt Maggie's. There'll be nothing else to eat."

Katy's ebullient mood began to slip away. She wanted to spend every waking minute at the hut, until she got that bike ticking over again. Only then, when it was purring like a kitten, would she show Jem her handiwork. She knew he'd need some convincing about her mad idea and she was determined to do it right. She mustn't be impatient but pick the exact right moment, if she had any chance of persuading him.

She murmured something non-committal and was relieved when Bert and Jack walked in through the open back door.

"I've shut the chickens up for the night," Bert said to his wife, "and I'm taking Jack up to bed. I've promised him a story and he won't take no for an answer."

Jack kissed his mother and nicked one of Katy's radishes.

"Oi! They're mine, you little thief!" said Katy, thinking how like Albert he was getting. None of them had got used to Albert's absence. He'd always been up to tricks, keeping things lively and messing up Agnes's clean house and Jack had just that same cheeky way with him. It was as endearing as it was annoying. How would Jack feel shut up in a tiny townhouse when he'd been used to the free run of the manor's stables and fields?

"Alright, Bert," Agnes said, "Goodnight, Jack, love, sleep tight."

The others departed upstairs. Agnes said, "Right, I'll take these beans out to the scullery and bottle them up."

Katy was left alone, glad to have got away without an inquisition. She'd make sure she was up bright and early tomorrow morning, just after Jem left for the harvest and before her eagle-eyed mother was about.

CHAPTER THIRTY THREE

Jem hadn't felt so tired since his army days, but at least this time, he had something to show for it. Not like those everlasting months in the prisoner-of-war camp in Germany, after he'd had the influenza. That had been true exhaustion. He'd never forget it, or that he was lucky to have survived it with the mean rations they had subsisted on. So many of his fellow prisoners had never made it home.

His muscles screamed their protest at the demands the harvest made of them. He could put up with that. For the first time since he'd come home at Christmas, he could sleep through the night. He woke up refreshed, despite the aches and pains all over his body. He was pleased with his wooden arm too. He'd whittled away at the imitation hand, so it worked really well now, with the two metal claws curved up so he could grasp things - sort of.

It was good of old Stubbs to take him on and he worked harder than anyone, until the farmer took him to one side and said, "You don't have anything to prove, lad. Take it easy, you're doing fine."

Jem doubted Mr Stubbs would ever know how much his kindness meant to him. He saw respect in the old man's weather-beaten face and took pleasure in the sweaty, honest work. After a few days, he could feel his muscles strengthen their tone and get accustomed to their daily battering. He walked back to the lodge house feeling really well at the end of the week, his pocket jangling with coins from his labour. Only fifteen shillings, not a patch on the wages he'd got from Hayes for driving that old Sunbeam, but still, it was ready cash.

Another week and the harvest would be in, if the weather held. He couldn't wait to see Katy and share his good mood. He was coming in so late, they'd hardly exchanged two words together lately, but it would be worth it when he got paid in full after the harvest was over.

The others had already eaten, so he gobbled down the leftover shepherd's pie in splendid isolation. Agnes and Bert had taken the children over to see Aunt Maggie about the move to Woodbury, a note on the table said, and he had the house to himself. Had Katy gone with them? If only she were here, while the place was deserted. Maybe he could persuade her to get close again. He knew she was frightened and he understood why, but he missed their private moments together more than he could ever say. He wondered - a lot - if she missed them too or was glad to have the excuse to keep herself to herself.

Come to think of it, she'd not been in one evening this week. He'd been so knackered every night, he'd hardly noticed. What was she up to? And with whom?

A horrible, unbidden thought crept into his head. What if she *had* encouraged that American bastard? And Charles Smythe before that? She was so beautiful - after all, that vicar had admired her too - what man wouldn't fancy her? But he'd never seen her flirting with any of them. No, that wasn't true, was it? She was all for Charlie-boy when she was a nipper. The old worry about not being good enough for her stole into his mind. Katy had always wanted more out of life than Jem could give her.

That damn Fred Stavely was rich too, like his friend, Douglas Flintock. Had she had her head turned over there? He only had her word for it, didn't he? And she wouldn't let him near her now. Night after bloody night, they lay next to each other like strangers. God knows it was hard not to hold her; not to show her how much he loved her, even with Daisy's sniggers to put him off.

Where was she now? She should be here, waiting for him to come home from work. Why couldn't she be more like her mother? Agnes might have a tongue as sharp as a scythe but he'd never met anyone more loyal. No flightiness there - not like her daughter.

Jem sluiced his dirty plate in the scullery sink

with too much force and broke it. He was clearing up the mess, when he heard the latch of the garden gate click open and shut. Katy was walking up the path between the flower beds. She looked tired, but happy. What had she been up to all day? And with whom? She obviously hadn't gone to pay her respects to old Aunt Maggie.

"Hello, Jem, love," Katy said, when she entered the house. "Had a good day?"

Jem looked at her hands. They looked rough and sore, with blackened fingernails, much like his own. At least his wooden one didn't have any blisters.

"Hello, Katy," Jem said.

"Is there any grub about?" Katy said, taking over from him at the scullery sink.

Jem watched the water staining the white ceramic a dirty grey as she washed her hands in it. What had his wife been up to?

"Shepherd's pie's keeping warm in the oven," Jem said, following Katy into the kitchen.

"Oh, good, I'm famished," Katy said, and helped herself to what was left, straight out of the serving dish.

"Don't you want a plate?" Jem asked.

"Can't be bothered," Katy said. "Mum's not in, is she?"

Jem watched her wolfing it down as fast as he had done, only half an hour before.

"Well, you've certainly got your appetite back, Katy," he said.

Katy looked up and smiled, then carried on eating like a woman starved. Jem found it annoying that she was too hungry to chat. Silly, when he'd been worrying how thin she was since the war, no before that, since she had that dratted pneumonia and nearly died. His heart lurched with love for her. Why was he doubting her now, but then, how could he not?

"So, Katy, where have you been this evening? It's late to be coming home. Why were your hands so dirty and what's that cut on your arm?" he said.

Katy pushed her empty plate away and wiped her mouth with the back of her hand. Jem had never seen her do that before, she was usually so pernickety about table manners. What had got into the woman?

"Were they? Oh, well, I've been out blackberrying, you see, and scratched my arm on a thorn," Katy said, looking decidedly shifty.

"Sorry about your arm, but it's nice you've picked some. I love blackberries, they're my favourite," Jem said.

"I know, that's why I picked them," Katy said.

"Wouldn't mind some now, actually," Jem said. "Where have you put them?"

Katy got up from the table and turned away from him, "Um, I've left them in the shed, to keep cool overnight. I'll make some jam tomorrow, if Mum's got enough sugar."

"Won't they spoil in this hot weather, if you leave them all night?"

"Shouldn't do, no," Katy said.

Just then the rest of the family came pouring in, looking as miserable as he felt, limp like lettuces left out in the sun. Although they had his sympathy, he'd never been less happy to see them. By the time the children had been settled down for the night, Katy was asleep.

And he was none the wiser.

Nor had he eaten one blackberry.

CHAPTER THIRTY FOUR

"It's all very well walking back home, Doug, but I wish we'd brought the roadster. A spin through the countryside before lunch would have been very welcome," Cassandra said, glad of his arm, as they walked back up the steep hill to Upper Cheadle. They'd been to Lower Cheadle to ask the vicar about a blessing ceremony for their marriage. He'd been delighted to officiate and a date for two weeks' time was amicably agreed.

"We'll go out afterwards," Douglas said, stopping to sniff at a wild mint flower that had strayed from its hedged boundary. "Hmm, heavenly. Are the summers in Wiltshire always this beautiful?"

"You must be joking," answered Cassandra. "More often we have weeks of rain and a ruined harvest."

"It's going well this year, didn't you say?"

"Yes, look there's some stooks standing to dry over there in that field," Cassandra said, stopping for a rest on a tree stump.

"Are you feeling tired, darling?" Douglas said, budging her up so he could share her wooden perch.

"Just a little, it's so warm." Cassandra chewed the stalk of a long piece of grass.

"Do you think you should chew that, honey? Think of the baby - what if someone's pissed on it?"

Cassandra pushed her husband off his improvised seat and he went sprawling into the hedgerow.

"Don't be disgusting!" she laughed and spat out the grass.

Douglas got up, dusted down his trousers and pulled her to her feet. "I think we'd better get you fed, Mrs Flintock-Smythe, you're getting too frisky for a mother-to-be."

They linked arms and walked home in comfortable silence. Life was so much more relaxing, once you had a soul-mate to share it with, reflected

Cassandra. They wandered into the cool hall, to be greeted by Andrews, just as the clock chimed noon. The peace lily on the hall table had flowered in the heat; its single petal stood white and feminine against the dark foliage but the shape of its stamen looked decidedly phallic. Cassandra thought it peculiarly unsuitable as a greeting for visitors and wondered if her mother would understand why.

"Would you care for some lemonade on the lawn, ma'am?"

"Andrews, that would be divine," Cassandra said.

"You can add a shot of gin to mine," Douglas said.

"Very good, sir," Andrews replied and bowed, before going off towards the kitchen.

"I must say, Cass, your lifestyle might be a little claustrophobic at times, but it sure has some good points," Douglas said, as he stretched out his long legs, his hands behind his head, smiling.

"We are so lucky, Doug, aren't we?" Cassandra agreed and carried on, "but not everyone is so fortunate. I've been thinking about Kate. Now that Mother has got used to our married status, it's high time I tackled her about finding somewhere for Jem and Kate to live or some employment for them. We can't live in the lap of luxury with them homeless. And I feel quite dreadful about Kate's parents. They don't deserve such punishment, any more than Kate does. Mother's overstepped the mark completely. I'm going to say something over lunch. Will you back me up?"

Douglas winked his assent, as Andrews soft-shoed his way across the lawn to beckon them into the dining room.

Lady Amelia was unusually quiet through lunch, after Cassandra told her the news about the blessing ceremony, but Sir Robert chatted away to Douglas about the harvest, and how everyone was hoping that the dry, hot spell would last until it was over. Cassandra took her cue from her mother and ate in silence, absorbed in her thoughts, while studiously ignoring the heavy sighs from her mother's end of the long table.

As a concession to the thundery weather, Mrs Biggs, the cook, had made a salad for the main course. A radical but welcome change to her usual heavy concoctions. Cassandra actually enjoyed the little new potatoes and salty Wiltshire ham. It gave her the energy she needed for her next assault. The strange morphology of the peace lily in the hall had prompted unwelcome memories of Katy's plight. She could put off the confrontation no longer, and cleared her throat to signal the commencement of hostilities.

"There's something I wanted to discuss with you both. It's about the Beagles' eviction. I understand that Douglas's sister, Cheryl, wrote to you about a distressing incident that occurred when we were staying out at Cape Cod?"

"Must we discuss this at the dinner table? Such a sordid affair," Lady Amelia stopped her rigorous chewing and took a sip of sherry.

Douglas immediately chipped in and Cassandra marvelled at her husband's tact.

"Lady Amelia, Sir Robert - I feel *I* must take the blame for what happened to Mrs Phipps," Douglas began, his face serious and earnest.

"Fred Stavely is my oldest friend, though I no longer call him one. I've known him all my life and I knew he had a temper but I never imagined he would vent it on a defenceless woman. We should never have left Mrs Phipps alone with him, but I had no idea that he was not a gentleman. Neither had we realised how keen he was on Kate, Mrs Phipps, that is. I can assure you both, though, that Mrs Phipps did not give Fred any encouragement at all. She was the victim of his dreadful behaviour and, I must insist, entirely innocent."

"But," Lady Amelia said, "This young woman, and you may not know this Douglas, has misled a young

288

man before! Our own dearest Charles, in fact. Before the war, before he left us never to return, she was carrying on with him and going out on jaunts, without a chaperone, even into Woodbury! Don't you think there's a common denominator at play here?"

"Mother, that was a long time ago. I've worked with Kate Phipps on the ambulances since then. She's as sound as a church bell. Charles simply turned her head when she was too young to know better. But in this instance, she has done no wrong. I will not allow you to punish her entire family when, what we should be doing, is helping her to get over this terrible ordeal," Cassandra said.

"*You will not allow*? Who do you think is master here, Cassandra? Your father isn't dead yet!" Lady Amelia dabbed at the corners of her mouth with little stabs of her serviette.

"I am present, you know," Sir Robert said, suddenly sober.

"And can I ask you what *you* think, sir?" Douglas said.

Cassandra wondered at this master stroke, grateful to have such a strong partner on her team.

"These things happen, of course," answered Sir Robert.

Cassandra caught the look Lady Amelia shot at her husband and was shocked at the malevolence in her mother's eyes. What had her father been up to over the years?

Sir Robert, seemingly unaware, continued, "They always have, of course, but I must say, my dear," Sir Robert looked directly at his wife, whose eyes still sparkled with anger, "I don't wish to part with our head coachman. Bert Beagle has always kept the horses and the stables in very good heart. What would I do without him during the hunting season?"

"Exactly, Father," Cassandra said, and pressed her advantage home. "You see, Mother, it was all a giant mistake. Cheryl wrote that letter in anger. She was sweet on Fred and felt jilted. We can't throw the Beagles out of West Lodge. It's their home and they've given us years of faithful service."

"No fury like a woman scorned," Douglas ventured.

Lady Amelia certainly looked furious, especially with Douglas. "It seems I am outnumbered," she said. "Mark my words, if you don't discipline the staff, they will always take advantage and I'm not convinced of that young woman's innocence."

Lady Amelia laid down her cutlery and continued, "Very well, Mr and Mrs Beagle may remain in the lodge, but I will not extend the reprieve to their eldest daughter and her husband. I stand by my decision that I do not want either of them to remain on Cheadle Manor land where I might see them. I will not employ, or suffer anyone else to employ, Katherine Phipps anywhere on the estate. And that is my final word."

CHAPTER THIRTY FIVE

"A Nissen hut?" Jem said, as they tramped along the road under a leaden sky.

Katy nodded and couldn't help smiling at his baffled face. She'd waited until the harvest was fully gathered in and Jem had got paid, making quite sure she was never late home again all that week, and had bottled several jars of blackberry jam too. She'd kept quiet through an interminable Sunday, while he'd rested on his laurels in a withdrawn and morose mood. Now it was Monday, everyone else was busy, and Katy could wait no longer to show her husband what she'd been up to.

Jem had been unusually grumpy when she'd suggested going out for a walk, mumbling about likely downpours, and breaking their handclasp as she tugged him along the road. "What's the rush, Katy? I'm still knackered from the harvest! Can't you slow down?"

"No, I bloody can't, Jem," Katy said, and had tried not to break into an impatient run, before adding, "Oh, what the hell, I can see you're not going to go the distance until I tell you," and had told him where they were going.

Now, Jem repeated his words, "You want us to look at a ruddy Nissen hut? What on earth for?"

Katy nodded, too disappointed in his reaction to trust speech.

"I had enough of those in that blasted prisoner-of-war camp, thank you very much!" Jem said, coming to an abrupt standstill in the road.

"I'll tell you why when we get there," Katy said.

She marched on, mute with anger at his response and Jem followed after a moment's hesitation. They covered the two miles from the lodge in record time, with no easy chatter to slow them down.

The weather mirrored their antagonism. The fine spell, that had lasted so miraculously through the harvest, threatened to break any minute. Purple clouds, not much paler than the blackberries she had hastily gathered, lowered the sky until Katy felt she could touch it. She hurried on, afraid they would be caught in the storm. A few fat drops, weirdly warm to the touch, splatted on to the bridge as they mounted it.

"There," Katy said, breaking the dead silence.

They stood in front of the gate, now almost completely hidden by the overgrowth of a long, hot summer.

Jem said, "But it says, trespassers will be prosecuted, Katy! We can't go in there, can we?"

"Just watch me," Katy said and climbed over the gate with practised ease. "Come on! What are you waiting for?" She didn't wait to see if he followed, but walked swiftly round to the back of hut, smiling when she heard the thud of his footfall behind her.

Katy showed Jem the broken window and pushed him through it. She wriggled in behind him, just as an almighty clap of thunder broke nearby. Rain pattered on the tin roof, as she and Jem stood inside the workshop.

"See this bike? It only had one tyre when I first saw it, and I've already stripped the engine down," Katy said, patting the seat with pride, but Jem didn't smile.

He was just standing and staring around.

"I still don't understand why we're here, Katy," he said, eventually.

Katy paused. She must give him time. She sat down on the bike's seat, and watched Jem wander around, just as she had done, touching the tools, running his hand through the dust on the workbench and peering into tins of this and that.

He stopped when he reached the gleaming bike and stared at her.

"What are you playing at, Katy? How did you find this place? You can hardly see it from the road. Who told you about it? Who else has been here?"

"No-one!"

"Someone must have let you in. I can't see how you'd have managed on your own," Jem said, his face still grim.

"No! Honestly, no-one knows about it, but me. I discovered it all by myself," Katy said, as the reason for his mood suddenly dawned on her.

"Oh, yes? Very clever of you, I'm sure," Jem said, twirling his finger in some sawdust on the workbench.

"Jem, do you think I've been here with another man?" Katy started to shake.

His faith in her innocence over Fred's attack had been the one thing that had kept her going through these ghastly few weeks.

Jem couldn't meet her eye and said to the floor, "I knew you were out a lot but I didn't know who with. How was I to know you'd been breaking and entering an old army depot?"

"How could you think I was seeing someone else? Don't you know what I've been through? Working on this Triumph has made me feel whole again, Jem. Made me remember who I really am. I've felt such peace here in this hut, all on my own. Don't you trust me?" Katy couldn't stop trembling and gripped the motorbike's handlebars to steady herself, while her eyes never left her husband's face.

Jem looked up from the bench and back at her. He shook his head, "I'm sorry, Katy, I didn't mean to doubt you, but we've been apart so much, what with the war and everything. We never seem to have anytime to ourselves, and I couldn't help worrying that you might have found someone better than me; someone whole."

"Oh, you daft man!" Katy said, not needing to cling to the bike anymore, now her shaking had stopped. "When are you going to realise that I don't want anybody but you and I never have! All I want is for us to be together."

She got off the bike to go to him, then checked herself, and perched on a petrol drum instead, and looked at her husband. She wanted to run to him and reassure him but she still didn't know how he was going to react to her schemes.

"I'm very glad to hear that Katy, truly I am, but what's this army hut got to do with it?" Jem said, brushing his hand against his corduroys to rid it of the sawdust.

"Because it's where we're together now and, we always could be," Katy said.

"What do you mean?" Jem said, his face still serious, listening.

"I found it by accident, just over a week ago. I couldn't believe my eyes when I saw the bike and the workshop. I couldn't resist having a look inside either, so I broke the window and climbed in. I know it was wrong but I couldn't stop myself. It took me right back to my old job, which I loved, Jem, I really did. So, I thought I'd have a go at fixing the Triumph. It was in a right old state, I can tell you, but I've got the tyre back on and the engine's running as sweet as a nut now - I'll show you in a minute. I know I was trespassing but I thought, if I could get it working again, maybe the army would take me back on as a mechanic," Katy said, taking her time and choosing her words carefully.

Jem remained silent. She had his whole attention now.

Katy continued, "If they did take me on, I was thinking to ask them if I could work in this workshop. And then, and I know this is a crazy idea, but I thought, maybe, we could start a garage business here, of our own, as well. It's on the main road and would get a lot of trade from passing traffic. Cars aren't going to go away. It would be a real chance for us to turn our lives around."

Katy waited, breath held, for his reaction, knowing their future depended on it.

Jem never rushed things and he took his time now. Katy watched his beloved face frowning in concentration. The rain drummed on the tin roof, drowning out all other sound.

"A garage? How could we ever afford to buy a place like this - who owns it, for a start?"

"I don't know how it could work out, Jem, maybe we could rent it or something, but can't you see what a wonderful opportunity it would be?"

Jem looked about him again, slowly taking in the details of the workshop before he nodded his head and turned back to his wife.

"You might be on to something, Katy, you just might, but it's a long shot alright," and he laughed and ran his hands through his mop of hair. "So, 'Mrs-Mechanic-the-sky's-the-limit', you reckon you got the motorbike working again, then, do you?" Jem said, with a grin.

Katy's held breath was released in a laugh. "Let me show you what I've done with the bike and then you'll see why I'm reaching for the skies. You just listen to this, Jem!" and she whirred the pedals round and round until the engine responded with a gentle growl and a little puff of blue smoke.

Jem laughed with her. "Katy! That's marvellous! Can I have a go?"

Katy got off, leaving the engine running and showed him the accelerator on the handle bar, leaving it out of gear so the bike stayed immobile on its stand.

Jem revved it up with glee. "Shall we take it out then? Take a ride into this glorious future?" he asked.

"Oh, I'm not sure about that," Katy said. "Someone might see us."

"We could just go round the yard, couldn't we?"

"There's no way we could get it out of the hut, without forcing the door," Katy said.

"How are you going to ride it up to the barracks, then?" Jem said.

Instead of an answer, Katy slid on to the bike seat in front of him and rejoiced as his mis-matched arms slipped around her waist. He nuzzled her neck and she leaned back into him, twisting her body around to find his mouth. Their lips met and parted in welcome. Katy's blood soared in her veins with a rush of familiar sensations she thought she'd forgotten. Jem's arms

295

tightened around her and the Triumph wobbled ominously.

"Oh, Katy, Katy, how I've missed you, my love, my little grease monkey," Jem said and pulled off her headscarf to release her hair. He ran his hand through it and kissed her again, hungry for more.

At first, they didn't hear the key in the padlock against the drum of the rain on the tin roof. It was only when the front door was shoved open on rusty hinges that Katy and Jem became aware of their audience. Above the din of the storm they heard someone shout and broke apart to stare at the intruder.

"Oi! What the hell are you doing in here?"

A soldier, dressed in khaki uniform, stood in the open doorway. Rain glistened on his cap as he reached for his gun and raised it at them. Katy stared at the barrel, too stunned to answer.

Jem pushed her away from him and got off the bike. He walked up to the soldier who still stood in the doorway, looking a bit scared, as the rain sheeted behind him. He looked no more than sixteen - too young to have served in the war.

Jem appeared completely at ease and spoke to him in a calm voice. Katy watched in awe as the young soldier's gun wavered, before Jem lowered it with his hand.

"Don't go pointing that thing at me, son," Jem said. "They have a habit of going off and causing no end of damage."

The young soldier stared at the space where Jem's arm used to be.

"Yes, lad, I lost it in the war, so I know what I'm talking about."

The young man flushed brick red but he lowered his gun and said, "Have you got permission to be in here?"

Katy got off the bike and joined them in the doorway. "No, we haven't but I was fixing this discarded motorbike. I was going to take it up the barracks and return it."

"Then that's trespass, isn't it?" said the soldier, looking doubtful. "I'll have to report it to my senior officer." He shouted over his shoulder, "Sergeant Trimble, sir! Intruders!"

A large middle aged soldier, who looked like he'd never take no for an answer, barged past his young colleague and surveyed the scene.

"What the..." he said.

"I can explain," began Jem.

"You'll explain alright, my lad. I'm taking you straight to the barracks. Come on! This is army property, I'll have you know. Didn't you see the sign? It clearly states trespassers will be prosecuted. I think a little trip in my lorry is in order. Sheldon!"

The younger soldier saluted and said, "Yes, Sir!"

"Escort these people to the vehicle and keep guard. I shall collect the supplies we came for and lock up the premises."

"Yes, sir!"

Jem and Katy were hustled out of the door and into the rear of a waiting army truck. Ramrods of rain hammered onto its tarpaulin roof and splattered through its open sides.

"Oh, Jem! I never meant for this to happen!" Katy said, squatting down amongst the packets of blankets jammed against the sides of the truck.

"Looks like you're going to get a chance to ask for that job sooner than you planned, my love," Jem said, with a smile that didn't reach his eyes.

The sergeant returned swiftly and, after giving them a cursory glance, jumped in the front of the truck, behind the wheel. "Sheldon!"

"Yes, Sergeant Trimble!"

"Get in the back with the prisoners, lad. Can't have them jumping out, now, can we?"

"No sir!" said the young recruit, and put one leg

on the lowered tail-gate of the lorry.

"Not yet, you idiot," barked the sergeant. "Shut the bloody gate first!"

"Right, sergeant."

The young lad fumbled with the padlock, while the sergeant showed his impatience at his ineptitude by revving the engine. Fumes from the exhaust floated up, making Jem and Katy cough. Eventually Private Sheldon extracted the key from the padlock and clambered in the back of the truck with them, panting slightly. He pulled up the tail-gate and rammed the bolt home.

The truck lurched forward making all three of them fall over. Katy rubbed a bruised elbow, glad it was bundles of blankets and cardboard boxes they were squashed up against and not sharp bits of ammunition or guns.

"Seems the twenty mile per hour rule doesn't apply to the army," Jem said, in a low voice.

Katy nodded and tried to smile.

The army barracks was only a couple of miles away, on the northern fringe of Woodbury but Jem and Katy were both stiff when they climbed out of the truck, under the nervous eyes of Private Sheldon. The rain had eased off by the time they got there, leaving puddles in its wake.

Sergeant Trimble stood before them on the parade ground, puffing out his cheeks with self importance, as other soldiers stared openly at his two captives.

This was not the triumphant arrival by motorbike that Katy had fondly imagined and a resentful ember of anger began to glow in her belly.

Sergeant Trimble bellowed to two other soldiers, who were standing to attention at an inner archway. "Ford! Petworth!"

"Yes, sir," they replied in unison, with smart salutes.

"Follow us to the colonel's office with these two prisoners."

"Yes, sir!" they chorused and brought up the rear, as Sergeant Trimble and his nervous young colleague marched in front into an inner courtyard, through the arch.

Katy felt so conspicuous as they traversed the expanse of gravel under armed guard. The injustice of the situation, when she'd just been trying to help the blasted army, washed over her in a hot wave. Fred's attack on her kept on rippling into her life, and tearing it apart. The unfairness of it all fuelled the ember growling in her stomach and it had flamed into a torch of righteous wrath by the time Sergeant Trimble rapped on the door marked "Headquarters" and ushered them in with a wave of his rifle.

Katy was ashamed to find her body trembling as she stood in front of the Colonel but couldn't decide if it was from rage or nerves.

"Well, well, what have we here, Sergeant Trimble?" the Colonel said. His voice was deep and should have been soothing but Katy could only hear the poshness of his accent and dreaded his reaction. She had a history of upsetting her betters that she wished she could forget at this moment.

"Intruders, Colonel Musgrove." She could hear the satisfaction in her captor's voice and hated the sound of his too.

"Intruders? Where did you find them?"

"In the workshop depot on the main road, sir, near Cheadle. There's those two Nissen huts we've been using there, and they were in one of them, sir, fiddling with an army motor bike," Sergeant Trimble said.

"Stealing were you? Fancied your own means of transport, courtesy of Her Majesty's Army? Well, speak up!" barked the colonel.

Katy's anger boiled over and said, "'I'm no thief! That bike is in perfect working order now, thanks to me! I've been working on it all week and it had been abandoned anyway. Just like all the soldiers who fought in the war, like my Jem here! And I'll have you know that my husband is completely innocent and it's entirely my fault. I was exploring round the huts and found the bike, and..."

"Exploring?" roared the colonel. "Did you think you were on ruddy safari? Are you able to read, miss?"

Jem cut in at this point, "My wife is a very able reader, sir."

"Oh, is she now? Then why couldn't she understand the large sign on the gate that says trespassers will be prosecuted? Do you think it doesn't apply to you Mrs...?"

"Phipps, sir. My name is Katherine Phipps."

"Well, Mr and Mrs Phipps, unless you can come up with some extraordinary explanation, you'll have to face charges."

Katy swallowed hard. There was nothing to lose. She'd blown all chances of a job with her outburst. She spread her hands wide in supplication and said in what she hoped was a more humble tone, "I know what it looks like, sir, but Jem and I - that is, my husband here - we've no employment since the war, even though we both served our country. You see, I was a mechanic in the WAAC at Étaples and worked on ambulances and bikes, just like that Triumph. I know I shouldn't have been poking about around the huts, but when I saw the bike through the window in disrepair, I thought I could fix it and my intention was to bring it up here to the barracks and return it to the army."

"And you expect me to believe that? Don't tell me you weren't planning to keep the bike for yourself, young woman!" The colonel's bushy eyebrows were almost touching his grey hair-line.

"No, sir, honest I wasn't! I told you - I'm not a thief! I thought, if I could show you the bike in good order, you might take me on as a mechanic for the army again."

The colonel sat down behind his desk with a guffaw. "Even if I do believe this noble ambition, Mrs

Phipps and you are telling the truth, the army has no need of women, now the war is over. You may have worked in France, for all I know - and believe me, I shall check the records. In fact, we'll do that now. Sergeant?"

"Sir!"

"Go to Central Office and telephone WAAC HQ. Ask if Mrs Katherine Phipps served at - where was it? Ah, yes, Étaples, - the BEF HQ during the war. Let's see if we can verify this woman's story."

"Yes, sir," Sergeant Trimble shouted and left, slamming the door behind him.

Katy sensed that the colonel relaxed in his sergeant's absence.

"Please, sit down, Mr and Mrs Phipps," Colonel Musgrove said, and tapped out a pipe that he took from his desk drawer.

He plugged it with fresh, fragrant tobacco and looked up at Jem as he struck a match and lit it. Through the blue smoke, he asked, "Can I ask how you lost your arm, Mr Phipps?"

Katy felt proud of her husband, as he answered with solemn gravity and no hint of nerves, "In the war, sir."

"Fought for long, did you?"

"Over two years, sir."

"Where were you stationed?"

"Arras and then The Somme, sir. The last few months were spent in a prisoner-of-war camp, in Germany."

"That couldn't have been a picnic."

"No, sir, food wasn't abundant," Jem said, with a flicker of a smile.

The Colonel's lined face broke into an answering smile. Katy's heart lifted a fraction.

"I see," Colonel Musgrove said, and puffed on his pipe.

There was a rap on the door and Sergeant Trimble entered, looking a little subdued.

"Permission to speak, sir," the sergeant said.

"Go ahead, Trimble," answered his senior officer.

"WAAC HQ have confirmed Mrs Phipps' service record, sir," Sergeant Trimble's voice was pitched at a much lower volume than Katy had heard him use before. She knew a moment of intense satisfaction.

"Right, thank you, Trimble. Dismissed."

Sergeant Trimble saluted smartly and left.

"This world is a sorry place and good intentions rare to find. I'm inclined to believe you, Mrs Phipps." The colonel lifted his hand to stop Katy's gratitude. "There is no way I can give you a job though. The British Army has no need of female mechanics any longer - or trespassers. You'll have to return to your husband's fireside and mend his slippers again. And after all, he's a war veteran. Doesn't he deserve a bit of looking after?"

"But sir," protested Katy. "That's just it! We have no home of our own and my parents will shortly be losing theirs. We're desperate for work and you're right, Jem does deserve looking after, but instead he's just thrown on the scrapheap, like all the other disabled men!"

Katy wished she'd cut her tongue out when she saw the hurt on Jem's face. She'd never called him disabled before and winced as she saw Jem's body stiffen.

The colonel laid his pipe down and looked from one to the other. "I'm sorry, I can't help you, Mr and Mrs Phipps. Neither can I change the way the world works. Frankly, you're lucky I'm not going to press charges. I suggest you take yourselves off and forget all about the army and the war and sort out a future away from all that. Good day to you." And he stood up and extended his hand.

Katy turned away and couldn't shake it, but Jem took the Colonel's hand in his own, shook it firmly and thanked him for their reprieve. Katy opened the door, looked back at the Colonel, who stood, his hands leaning on his desk and a pained expression on his face. She tutted her annoyance and walked out into the courtyard with Jem following her.

Katy strode quickly across the barracks parade ground, not looking to either side, fuelled by the anger that still burned within her, aware of Jem walking beside her, equally silent. Every hope was dashed. The British Army had taken everything, even the ruddy bike.

CHAPTER THIRTY SIX

On Sunday morning, while it was still cool, Jem was busy fixing one of Agnes's chicken arks at the back of West Lodge. Agnes had told him not to bother, as they'd be gone before the autumn weather struck, but he had to do something or he'd start behaving like those poor devils who had suffered shell shock. He'd perfected holding the nail with his claw while hammering with his good hand. There was a knack to it, of course, but he was getting the hang of it.

"Hello, there!" Cassandra appeared from the direction of the woods.

She must have come cross-country from the manor house. Jem stood up and waved.

"Another warm day, Jem!" Cassandra said, smiling.

She did look well. Marriage obviously suited her. Jem wished Katy looked half as happy.

"Good to see you with a hammer in your hand," Cassandra said. "You always were resourceful, Jem."

"Thank you, Mrs Flintock," Jem said.

"I'm calling myself Mrs Flintock-Smythe, actually, Jem. Got to keep the old name alive, you know. But please, call me Cassandra. Kate and I are such friends now, that old formality doesn't sit right anymore."

"If you insist, Cassandra," Jem said, attempting a smile back.

"I do. Now, where is everybody? I've got something to tell you all. I know it's early, but I wanted to catch everyone before you all get off to church."

"I think Agnes and Katy are in the kitchen, preparing lunch, and Bert's probably in the garden, picking vegetables," Jem said, laying his hammer down.

"Well, let's round them up then!" Cassandra laughed. "I'll see the women in the kitchen and you fetch Bert in. I think they'll want to hear what I have to say."

Jem wondered at Cassandra's jovial mood,

wishing he could match it. He'd been back to Farmer Stubbs and asked if he could stay on, after the harvest. He'd told him he'd do anything, however menial, but the kind old man had shaken his head, saying he couldn't afford another permanent worker. Jem shook his head free of the memory and strode quickly to the vegetable patch and, sure enough, found Bert picking runner beans for his dinner.

He explained about Cassandra's visit while they walked into the house. All three women were gathered around the kitchen table, looking tense and expectant.

"Wash your hands first, Bert," Agnes said.

"Don't fuss, woman," he said, but Bert gave them a quick sluice in the sink.

When they were all sitting down, Cassandra spoke with the brisk assurance that characterised her.

"I wanted you all here because I spoke to my mother last night. I managed to convince her of Kate's innocence and that Cheryl Flintock is a silly, jilted girl who wrote a vindictive and incorrect letter. Enough of that. The upshot is that you, Agnes and Bert, are to keep this house for as long as you need it, and Bert is reinstated as head coachman at the manor stables, with all his duties and responsibilities unchanged."

Agnes betrayed the strain she'd been under with a sob she stopped by clamping her hand over her mouth.

Bert found his voice first. "Oh, Miss Cassandra! By all that's marvellous!"

Cassandra held her hand up for silence, reminding Jem of Lady Amelia. "It's not all good news, I'm afraid. My mother, in her infinite wisdom, didn't extend the truce to Kate and Jem. Oh, she believes, as we all know, that Kate did nothing wrong, but she still doesn't want her around the place. I'm so sorry about that, and it may change over time, but at the moment, there's no shifting her. So we can't employ either of you at Cheadle Manor. Jem, I know I sent instructions for you to be installed as chauffeur while we were away. Did that become official?"

Jem nodded. He had known all along it had been too good to be true and told her he'd already handed back his uniform. "At least I've learned to drive, Cassandra, but Hayes told me I can't ever work in the gardens again, so if I can't be chauffeur either, I reckon that's it."

"Well, quite frankly, with Douglas and I arguing over who's going to drive, as we both love it so much, we won't be needing one anyway and with all the taxes we've got to pay, we're going to have to draw in our horns for a while. But I'm sure something will turn up and at least, Kate, your parents' livelihood and home are safe."

Jem felt proud of his wife, when Katy immediately said, despite the despair she'd shared with him earlier that morning, "That's the most important thing, Cassandra. Thank you from the bottom of my heart. Don't worry about me and Jem. We'll sort something out. We were thinking of moving to London, or maybe Bristol, to find some work."

"Were you? Is that what you really want to do?" Cassandra looked surprised.

"Needs must," Jem said.

"But you love it here, don't you, Jem?" Cassandra said.

"Got to go where the work is," Jem said.

"It'll be a fresh start," Katy added, and smiled at him.

Leaving Cheadle was the last thing Jem had ever wanted to do, but he kept quiet.

"Hmm, can't say I'm convinced, but we'll see. I wish you good luck, whatever you do and wherever you go, and Bert, I'm so glad you'll be staying. I have a hunch motors might take over from the shire horses on the farm, but Father will always need a good hunter," Cassandra said, and shook Bert's hand.

"Thank you, Miss Cassandra. I'm much obliged to you, I'm sure," Bert said.

"Nonsense. Just restoring the status quo. You should never have had this upset in the first place and I feel completely responsible for the strain you've been put under. It's *I* who is in *your* debt. Right, I must be off to get presentable for church. Oh, Kate, you've no idea how much I'm missing you helping me to tidy myself up. Just look at my hair! Walk me to the gate, would you?"

They all stood up to see her off, and watched her stroll out into the morning sunshine, with Katy's arm tucked in hers.

"Well, I don't know if I'm coming or going!" Agnes said, with a wavering smile.

"You's coming home, girl, that's what!" Bert said, and wrapped his wife up in a bear hug.

"Congratulations, Bert, Agnes," Jem said.

"But what about you two?" Agnes said.

"We'll be a lot happier knowing you're still here and we'll work something out, don't you worry," Jem said, and got back to his hammering out the back. He was really pleased for his in-laws; couldn't be more so, but the thought of wrenching himself away from this place again put a dampener on his relief. Neither Katy nor Jem had told them about the motorbike fiasco. There had been enough bitter disappointments already, without adding another.

Katy found him half an hour later. If he hadn't been holding nails in his mouth, he would have kissed her. She looked happier than at any time since she'd come home.

"Isn't that wonderful news, Jem? I can't tell you how relieved and happy I am for Mum and Dad. I feel as if a weight's been lifted off me, I really do! And Cassandra told me something else, and all. She's expecting already. I can't say I'm surprised, the way they've been carrying on, and it'll shut Lady Amelia up, once she hears about it. No-one but me and Doug know yet, as it's so soon after the wedding, so keep it under your hat. She must have caught at the house at Cape Cod, straightaway."

Jem took the last nail out of his mouth and tapped

it in. "Is she pleased about it?"

"Oh, yes," Katy laughed, a welcome sound Jem hadn't heard in ages. "She said she might as well get on with re-building the dynasty."

"That's good, then. Things are getting sorted at last," Jem said, standing back to look at his handiwork.

It wasn't bad. Only rough work, but serviceable. Perhaps he could get work as a carpenter somewhere. Somewhere they didn't need too much skill.

"I'm really pleased for your parents, Katy. In fact, I couldn't be more so, but what about us? I'm not a chauffeur or a gardener anymore and you're not a housemaid - or a mechanic for the British Army. What the hell are *we* going to do now?"

Katy put her arms around his neck and pulled his face down for a kiss. She hadn't done that once, since she'd reached for him in the Nissen hut before they'd got arrested for trespass. Jem's lips sprang into a response but Katy quickly withdrew. Little steps, he reminded himself, don't rush her. If only their intimate moment hadn't been interrupted in the Nissen hut. He'd tasted passion again then, but never since. Katy ran her hand through her short hair. He wished she'd left it long. He'd loved to see it falling onto their shared pillow and running his hands through its warm brown waves.

"I don't know, Jem. Let's just be pleased for Mum and Dad today."

Agnes insisted that Katy and Jem attend church with them. She wanted everyone to know that she and Bert weren't going anywhere, and that Katy had nothing to be ashamed of.

"I know you're right, Mum," Katy said. "In fact, Cassandra said the same thing, but I can't say I'm keen to go."

"You'll go, my girl," Agnes said, with some of her old vigour and a wagging finger, "for shame's sake. I want our family's name and reputation scrubbed clean again. I've barely been able to hold my head up this last month or so. I want people to see you've nothing to hide, or be blamed for. You'll come to church on your father's arm and I'll take Jem's."

"Alright, Mum," Katy said. "It's good to have you bossing me around again."

"Go and get ready then, and make sure you look smart, mind!"

Agnes bustled off to find her Sunday hat and Katy and Jem went to get changed. There wasn't a hair out of place when the whole Beagle family settled into their pew at church in Lower Cheadle. Cassandra turned around from the front row and gave them a sneaky wink. Jem's mother sat, next to his father and siblings, in the pew alongside. Both his parents looked worn out. It was easy to forget that they'd felt threatened with eviction too. All this being beholden to the Smythes and particularly Lady Amelia's spite, made Jem feel distinctly trapped. Maybe it would be good to get away from here.

The new vicar preached about the virtues of forgiveness in his short, solemn sermon.

Jem smiled as he listened. Cassandra *had* been busy.

After the service, the villagers seemed inclined to linger in the sunny churchyard. Jem found it hard not to be angry, as stares and whispers attended Katy wherever she went, but when Katy spoke to her mother-in-law and told her the good news, Jem could feel the malevolent mood change. This was compounded by Cassandra and Douglas, who circulated through the throng, giving the glad tidings of their marriage. Jem could hear Katy's name mentioned more than once by her former employer and sent them silent blessings.

When even his mother acknowledged Katy publicly, imitating the new Flintock-Smythes, Jem's heart swelled with love for both of them. He kissed his mother on both her tired cheeks.

"Thanks, Mum, my goodness, that new vicar's sermon has had quite an effect!" he said.

"T'isn't that, Jem, love. Miss Cassandra's put the record straight. I'm sorry I didn't believe you, Katy, really I am," Mary said, nodding her Sunday hat in apology but not quite managing to add a smile.

Katy just squeezed her arm in gratitude.

Cassandra came up then and said loudly, "Kate, dear. I need to go on a shopping trip on market day. Will you come with me?"

"I'd be delighted, Cassandra," Katy said.

"Good, I'll drive you both," Douglas said, and shook Jem's hand. "You don't mind if we borrow your good lady, do you, Jem?"

"Not at all," Jem said.

Lady Amelia came up to them.

"It's time to go, Cassandra," she said, looking straight through Katy and Jem, as if they weren't there.

"I'm not ready yet, Mother," Cassandra said. "I'm talking to Mr and Mrs Phipps here."

Lady Amelia still didn't acknowledge Jem or Katy, but started walking away, saying, "Then I'll see you back at the house."

Sir Robert gave Jem a brief nod and a guarded look of sympathy, before following his stately wife up the lane to Upper Cheadle. Jem reckoned Sir Robert was the one who needed sympathy.

Cassandra smiled at Katy and Jem. "Take no notice," she said in a low voice. "I'll bring her round. Just give me time."

She embraced Katy, while Douglas and Jem shook hands. Cassandra made quite a performance of it, and Jem looked around at the little crowd hovering around the church porch. Every single eye was watching them. He treated each to a forced smile, until they had the grace to look away and carry on gossiping amongst themselves.

CHAPTER THIRTY SEVEN

A few days later, Cassandra wandered into the stables and went up to Blackie's stall. Dr Benson had forbidden her to ride whilst she was pregnant, when she'd seen him in a private consultation to confirm her condition. She was finding it hard not to escape from her mother's all pervading presence while keeping her secret. A good gallop along the chalky downs would have lifted her mood more than anything.

Blackie whinnied a welcome and she raised her hand to her horse's velvet nose and stroked it.

"Hello, old friend," she said, "how are you today? Missing freedom as much as I am?"

Blackie nuzzled her hand for the apple slices she always brought her. Cassandra fed her the pieces, one by one, and her mare crunched them happily. If only she could appease Douglas so easily. Her husband had become morose under the roof of Cheadle Manor and she couldn't honestly blame him.

If only he was a keen rider, then he could go out with her father, who spent most of his day astride his big bay horse, as far away from his wife's tongue as he could get. Douglas had complained, in the privacy of their bedroom, of boredom. Hayes was managing the estate well now, and needed little direction while he followed the plan that she had formulated in the spring, before her trip to Boston.

Douglas had taken to going out on long drives to explore the countryside and, worryingly, didn't always want her company. Was he seeking someone else's?

Cassandra reflected on the speed of their romance and how little she really knew about him. With a shudder, she recalled how Fred Stavely had turned nasty so quickly - quite out of the blue.

Did Douglas have another side to him too? Could he be unfaithful to her? That he loved her, adored her, she had no doubt, but she felt unattractive and fat, even though her pregnancy hardly showed and her constant nausea had put her right off lovemaking. Douglas couldn't understand why she still hadn't got around to telling her parents about their impending grandparenthood, but the prospect of her mother's fussing had been too awful to contemplate and she kept putting it off until her changing shape made it unavoidable.

She ran out of apple slices and Blackie nudged her for more with a rough shove of her dark head.

"Ow, take care, you!" Cassandra said, and buried her face in her horse's mane, willing herself not to cry into it, as she had as a child.

Through the coarse hair of Blackie's mane, Cassandra heard male voices in the stable-yard. She lifted her head and recognised them as belonging to her father and his old hunting friend, Colonel Musgrove. She didn't feel like socialising with anyone and hoped they wouldn't come into the stables.

Bert Beagle appeared instead, to fetch Sir Robert's mount, Rufus, who had started to kick at his stable-door at the sound of his master's voice.

"Hello, Ma'am," Bert said with a curt nod.

Cassandra looked up at his sharp tone and was startled to see Bert's face, usually so placid, livid with anger. Rufus picked up on his handler's mood when released from his stall and, even though Bert had a bridle on him, reared up.

Cassandra went to help. "What's up with Rufus this morning, Bert? He's not usually so jumpy?"

"There's nothing wrong with the horse but my eldest daughter is a sore trial," Bert said, almost under his breath, so Cassandra could hardly catch his words.

"Do you mean Kate?" she said.

Bert threw her a fierce look. "I don't know where I went wrong with that girl, Miss Cassandra. Sometimes I wish I'd used my strap on her and knocked some sense into her."

"Goodness! Whatever has happened?" Cassandra

let his reversion to calling her Miss go, in the face of his grave mood.

"Only stealing and trespass, that's all! And on army land, would you believe! I just heard it from the Colonel, hisself," Bert tugged too hard on Rufus's bridle and the big bay tried to rear again. Remembering himself, Bert soothed the horse with the skill born of many years experience.

Cassandra was alarmed by what he'd said but glad to see he was collecting himself again.

"Let me hold Rufus a moment, while you fetch his saddle, Bert," she said.

Bert grunted and turned to lift the heavy saddle from its holding bar along the wall. He calmly patted Rufus before he gently laid the saddle on his strong back. The big horse snorted in appreciation and submitted gracefully.

Cassandra said, "Please tell me what you mean about Katy, Bert. Is she in trouble?"

"She'll be in trouble with me when I gets home, I can tell you, Miss! But no, Colonel Musgrove there, he's let her off the hook, though I don't think he should have, like."

Cassandra gritted her teeth with impatience. "But what has she done?"

"She took it upon herself to break into them Nissen huts on the London Road and mend some damn motorbike, belonging to the army, what was there. She says, apparently, that she were going to take it up to the barracks, once it was mended, but she got caught and brought up in front of Colonel Musgrove. Jem was with her and, in view of their war records, he let them off."

"When was this?"

"That's just it! It were over a week ago and they never said a word to me or Agnes about it! And they's both living under our roof! Well, not any more they're not!" And Bert led Rufus out into the yard.

Cassandra followed him, deep in thought. Colonel

Musgrove was still there, astride his horse, while her father mounted Rufus. They were laughing.

"Morning, Cassandra!" her father said, mounting Rufus and leaning down to adjust his stirrups.

"Good morning, Father. Good morning Colonel Musgrove," Cassandra said, squinting up at them through the sunlight.

"How are you today, Cassandra? You're looking very bonny, if I may say so," Colonel Musgrove said, touching his riding hat with his crop in salute.

Cassandra supposed he thought she looked fat too. Spurred on by this irritation, she said, "What's all this I hear about Katy Phipps breaking and entering, Colonel?"

The colonel gave a hearty laugh. "Ah yes, Mr and Mrs Phipps. They've got some spirit, what? Caught them red-handed on army property. Let them off with a caution. They'd seen enough action in the war, I thought. Poor chap had lost an arm. Didn't need a criminal record to go with it. Never get a job."

"I'm glad you let them off, Colonel. They are good people and you're right, jobs are scarce. What were they doing?"

"Well, it was remarkable really. Mrs Phipps was a trained mechanic in the WAAC and was mending a Triumph motorbike. She said she was planning to bring it back to the barracks, but I have my doubts about that. Good-looking sort of woman. Pity."

"Where is this hut, Colonel?" asked Cassandra.

"On the London Road - on your land which we requisitioned for the war, as it happens. In fact, I was meaning to speak to your Estate Manager about them - there are two you know - and we've no use for them now the war is over. Nuisance to have to maintain the place. Sir Robert - would you like to have the land returned to the estate? We might as well pull the huts down. They're only a fire hazard."

"Well, if they're no use to you, Musgrove. What do you say, Cassandra?" said her father.

"Do the buildings have any monetary value, Colonel?" Cassandra asked.

"What? No, I suppose not, really. Like I say, they're more of a liability than anything. I should be glad to be shot of them," Colonel Musgrove said, stroking the neck of his horse, who was beginning to fidget at the delay.

"What about the motorbike?" Cassandra said.

"Oh, I've had that removed. It's in good working order, now. I must say, Mrs Phipps did a splendid job but we've no use for women in the army now, saving your presence, my dear. I know you did your bit," Colonel Musgrove added hastily.

Cassandra supposed her annoyance must have shown, but she wasn't going to worry about that, not when her mind was whirring at a hundred miles an hour.

"Then, I think we should reclaim the land, Father," she said. "But don't pull down the huts, Colonel. I think we might have a use for them - storage, you know."

"Just as you like, my dear. Now Sir Robert, shall we be off? Your Rufus is straining at the bit to have his head," and Colonel Musgrove nudged his booted heels into his horse's flanks.

The two men rode off, quickly breaking into a canter. Bert had already retreated into the tack room. Cassandra watched the two middle-aged riders, both so upright in the saddle, disappear down the drive.

She was thinking so hard, it took her a moment to register they had vanished into the woods. She turned around and headed for Haye's estate office, all her worries about Douglas effaced by her grand idea.

By the time Douglas returned, just before dinner, Cassandra's idea had had all day to crystallise and she'd had a very satisfactory meeting with Hayes. When she saw the roadster zooming up the drive, far too fast, she skipped down the manor steps and went to meet Douglas in the barn, where the car was housed.

Douglas silenced the engine and turned to her

with a weary smile. "Hello, darling, how are you feeling today?"

"Sick as a dog and twice as tired," Cassandra said.

"You'd never know it to look at you," Douglas said, opening the car door, "I've never seen you look more beautiful."

"Thank you, Douglas," Cassandra said, reassured by this and emboldened to add, "I'm very excited about an idea I've had," Cassandra said, kissing his cheek as he got out of the car.

"What's cooking, honey?" he said, kissing her back.

"If you mean dinner, something drenched in cream that was recently grazing on Salisbury Plain, I should think," Cassandra said, feeling queasy at the image.

"No, I didn't mean dinner!" Douglas smiled. "What's your idea?"

"It's about Kate," Cassandra said, and told him about Katy's escapade.

Douglas roared with laughter at the tale. "You've got to hand it to her, she's a trier!"

"Exactly! And she's in a mess because of us - you know, our neglect of her at Cape Cod," Cassandra said, tucking her hand under his elbow. "I feel responsible for the hole they're in, with no jobs and no home to go to. We should have handled things differently in Boston. I'm afraid I blurred the boundaries, making Kate my travelling companion."

"You're an angel, honey, but it's me that's to blame. I should have put Fred straight, right from the outset. I was too busy falling back in love with you to think about anyone else," Douglas said.

"I'm no angel, Doug, but I do feel we've got to make amends," and she explained her idea of Jem and Katy living in one of the Nissen huts, on the reclaimed army plot. Pleased he was listening so attentively, she chided herself for doubting his love earlier and pushed her

316

curiosity about where he'd been to the back of her mind.

"It's the perfect solution, Doug," Cassandra said. "The plot the huts are on has already been fenced by the army and it's a nice parcel of land to get Jem and Kate off to a new start."

"So, you think you could mortgage the land to them and they could live in the Nissen hut?"

"Yes, the land belongs to the estate and it's not worth much - Hayes thought about £300 - or I could rent it to them as tenants for a peppercorn rent," Cassandra spoke with an enthusiasm she hoped would rub off on Douglas.

He certainly looked interested. "They are mighty proud, those two, though. You Brits seem to be blighted with an excess of that virtue, do you think they'd accept your charitable gesture?" Douglas said, as they turned out of the barn and started walking up the drive to the house.

"Yes, you're right, I'd have to handle it very carefully. It would make a good smallholding though, Hayes thinks there's around three acres there," Cassandra said, "More, if you take in a strip of woodland at the side."

"You could grow a lot of turnips on that," Douglas said.

"Yes, you could," Cassandra said, thoughtfully. "You know, Jem could create a market garden there. He's so good with his false hand now, he might be able to do it."

"It's hard to dig fresh ground one-handed, Cass," Douglas said, shaking his head.

"We could help," Cassandra said.

"You couldn't. You're carrying the next generation, don't forget, but I could. I'd enjoy having something to do. Gin slings on the lawn are all very well, but even they pall after a while."

Again, Cassandra felt that little worm of doubt about Douglas's absences. Was he giving her all these compliments to cover up for something he shouldn't be doing with someone else? She shivered as they mounted the steps to her home.

Lunch was indeed heavy. A rib of roast beef crowned the meal. Standing up to carve it, a tradition Sir Robert insisted upon despite his wife's censure, Cassandra's father seemed in an ebullient mood and Colonel Musgrove, who had joined them, looked invigorated by their ride too.

"Have you heard the latest about that fiery daughter of Beagle's?" Sir Robert said, plunging his carving knife into the bloody centre of the joint.

Before Cassandra could stop him, he continued, his voice hearty and loud, "Go on, Musgrove. Tell my wife about your recent fracas with the locals."

Colonel Musgrove obliged with enthusiasm and told them about Katy's arrest with far more embellishment than he had relayed to Cassandra earlier that morning.

"That young woman's behaviour is scandalous! Colonel, I don't think you should have let her go with no more than a caution!" Lady Amelia said, poised to pounce on the carrots Andrews held out for her. "Katherine Beagle, or Phipps, or whatever she's called, is never anything but trouble wherever she goes. I won't have her on the estate, you know."

"That seems a little drastic, Lady Amelia, if you don't mind me saying so," Colonel Musgrove said, looking blissfully unaware of the storm he was unleashing.

Cassandra's nausea resurfaced. She looked at the red juices oozing from the meat and pressed her serviette to her mouth, trying not to retch.

"It seems you can't control the working classes too much to me. Give them freedom and people like Mrs Phipps simply abuse their privileges. Look what happened when she went to America, for instance," Lady Amelia said.

Cassandra let her serviette drop to her lap. "Mother! We do not need to discuss that incident in front of Colonel Musgrove."

"Am I to be censored at my own dinner table?" Lady Amelia said.

"Kate Phipps is my friend, Mother, and as such, I would prefer it if you could respect her, if only for my sake," Cassandra said, swallowing the bile that threatened to fill her mouth.

Douglas, sitting opposite, looked across at her, his eyes loving and sympathetic.

"And she's my friend too," he said. "So is her husband. I'm happy to count them among my equals."

"Equals! Douglas, as a foreigner, you understand nothing of our ways. I suppose that's understandable, considering your background, but I can assure you, it is essential to preserve the boundaries between servants and their betters," Lady Amelia said, and attacked her laden plate.

"And who is to say that we, because we own land and property, are better than the likes of Jeremy and Kate Phipps, who are both resourceful and honourable war veterans?" Douglas said.

"My dear boy, Lady Amelia has a point, you know," Colonel Musgrove said. "It's the same in the army. There has to be some order or the whole thing would fall apart. Nothing wrong with hierarchy. Someone has to take charge. You can't expect raw recruits to make important decisions."

"Colonel, I must protest," Douglas said, sipping his claret instead of eating his beef. "What was so admirable about some of the decisions made by the highest authorities in the war? I saw raw recruits and able men, like Jem Phipps, cut down like the wheat harvest here on the estate, and for what? No territory was won for years. There was a complete stalemate in Flanders at the cost of thousands and thousands of troops."

Cassandra felt a wave of love for her husband through the different wave of nausea that now threatened to engulf her. She dare not speak in case she was sick across the damask tablecloth, though she longed to support his brave words.

"And anyway, Douglas," Lady Amelia said, her own appetite unchecked, "as you do not own either land or property, you have no experience or knowledge of these local matters."

"Now that is a situation I am about to redress, Lady Amelia," Douglas said, surprising even Cassandra. "I shall be buying the land that the army requisitioned for the war from the estate."

Lady Amelia was momentarily silenced.

Sir Robert filled the breach. "What are you planning to do with it, Douglas?"

"I intend to either rent or sell it to the Phipps. They can use the Nissen hut for a home, until they can afford something better. Haven't you heard of the 'Homes for Heroes' scheme? Quite frankly, I think you should be ashamed of your attitude and reward these people who have sacrificed so much for your country."

"How dare you speak to me in this manner, Douglas!" Lady Amelia said. "I will not allow this sale to go ahead. It's outrageous!"

Colonel Musgrove looked as if he fully understood the situation now, and chose not to comment. Cassandra dared not open her mouth, in case something other than words escaped, despite Douglas's desperate, pleading look.

It was Sir Robert who had the final word. "I can't think of a better use for that little scrap of land than to enable these young people to make a fresh start. I fully condone your action, Douglas, and I applaud your enterprise. You have my wholehearted support to go ahead."

"How dare you countermand my wishes, Robert!" said his spouse, who threw down her cutlery across her half eaten dinner and splattered gravy all over the tablecloth.

Cassandra could contain her sensations no longer.

320

She opened her mouth and spewed across the table. Her vomit met her mother's gravy stains and pooled there on the white linen.

Wiping her mouth with her serviette, Cassandra smiled at the appalled faces around her. "I'm so sorry, I couldn't help it. Please, Mother, don't be upset. Let Douglas do this thing for Jem and Kate. It's right and proper that we help them on their way.

"And anyway, we have much to be thankful for; you see, I'm expecting a baby."

CHAPTER THIRTY EIGHT

Katy was beating carpets on the washing line in her mother's garden. Her throat was choked with dust particles and she sneezed. She'd been whacking the rug with all her might and wishing it was Fred Stavely. It was a relief to see Douglas and Cassandra wandering down the drive towards the lodge so she left the dust clouds to settle and went to join them.

"Hi, Kate, how are you doing on this beautiful evening?" called Douglas, with a wave.

Katy waved back and walked up to meet them.

"Is Jem about?" Cassandra said. She looked pale, but happy. Katy supposed her pregnancy was to blame.

"Yes, he's mending the picket fence at the back of the garden," Katy said. "How are you, Cassandra? You look a bit washed out. Do you want to sit down?"

"I've just been sick all over the dinner table," Cassandra said, with a smile that Katy thought looked oddly triumphant.

"Congratulations," she said, with a laugh.

Cassandra laughed with her. "Yes, it was one way to announce the impending new arrival. Mother was torn between shock and jubilation. I haven't seen anything so funny for ages!"

They were all still laughing when they found Jem, hammering away with sober intensity at the broken fence that separated the lodge garden from the extensive parkland.

"What's the joke?" he said, straightening up and flexing his back.

Cassandra repeated her embarrassing moment with glee.

"So now the whole county will be issued a daily bulletin of my progress," Cassandra said. "We had to get out of the house for a stroll. Mother's high spirits can be as oppressive as her rages."

Katy smiled in sympathy but her heart remained untouched by Cassandra's obvious joy. She was glad for her friend, but Cassandra had so much, when she and Jem had so little. Less than ever since the row with her father. He'd made it very clear that she and Jem were no longer welcome in the lodge, which was why they were spending every evening in the garden on chores. The atmosphere inside the house had become unbearable. She was at her wit's end as to where they could live instead. Jem's proposal of moving in with his parents had struck her as a horrible idea. She could no more share a house with her mother-in-law than fly to the moon and she was quite sure that Mary Phipps would feel the same way, so she had forbidden Jem to ask her. Which meant they were stumped for a place nearby and had no alternative but to move to a large city - the fate they both dreaded.

She tried to forget her worries and concentrate on the conversation at hand by dragging her gaze away from the distant woods and back to the present. Cassandra was saying something about the Nissen huts. Katy would rather forget they existed. She still hadn't got over her disappointment at losing her one chance to right all the wrongs that had beset her since she'd come home from the war.

"Did you follow what I was saying, Katy?" Cassandra said, frowning at her.

"I'm sorry, I was miles away," Katy said, running her hand across her tired eyes.

"Look, let's sit down somewhere, shall we?" Douglas said.

Katy led them to the orchard, where the apple trees cast long evening shadows across the daisy-studded grass. There was an old knarled table in the sunniest corner, with benches around it. Katy made her way towards her favourite spot, and wondered when she would sit there again.

"Do you want a drink or anything?" she asked, when she remembered her manners.

"No, nothing, thank you," Cassandra said. "I think it might be better not to risk it!"

Katy smiled, but she still felt sad inside. Would *she* ever be settled enough to think about starting a family again?

Douglas looked across at Cassandra with raised eyebrows and, after his wife had nodded at him, cleared his throat as if he was about to make a speech.

"This isn't really a social call, Jem and Kate," he began.

Katy tried to concentrate.

"I have a proposal to put to you," Douglas continued. "I've just made an investment. My first in England. Makes me feel damn good, I can tell you."

"That's nice," Katy said, mystified.

"Yes, I bought some estate land, actually, but I'm not sure what to do with it," Douglas said, smiling.

"I'm pleased for you, Douglas, but I'm not sure that it's any of our business. We're not exactly experts on estate management," Jem said, looking politely interested.

"No, but you're pretty good at working the land, Jem," Douglas said.

"Used to be," Jem said, looking across at the sunset beginning to gild the tree-line beyond the park boundary.

"And could be again, wouldn't you say?" Douglas said, his eyes focussed on Jem.

"Don't see how," Jem said, pulling his eyes away from the distant view and looking at Douglas with a face devoid of hope.

"Well, this is my proposal. I've bought a few acres - the ones with those Nissen huts on the main road. I have no use for them. I'm no good at growing things, but you are and you need somewhere to live. I know it's not much but you'd be doing me a favour if you would turn it into something useful - what do you say?" Douglas looked from Katy to Jem.

"What do you mean, Doug?" Katy said.

"I need a stake in the estate and I'd like you to take the place off my hands and see what you could do with it. You could buy it with a mortgage, which I would provide, with the land as equity, or pay me rent, whichever you prefer," Douglas said.

"Really? We could live there?" Katy was galvanised now. Could her dream be coming true after all?

"It would be the ideal solution, dear Kate and Jem," Cassandra chipped in. "I couldn't bear to lose you by your having to move away, not with the baby coming. How would I cope without you to confide in when Mother's on the warpath? And we owe you, after what happened out at Cape Cod. We both feel we should have looked after you better. Please, Kate, say you'll take it and salve my conscience?"

"I don't know, we don't want handouts," Jem said.

"It wouldn't be charity at all - you'd be helping me to belong here," Douglas said.

"Oh, Jem, we've got a second chance! Do say yes, please, say yes?" Katy said.

"As long as we pay for it properly like, I suppose it would be alright and if it would really be helping you, Douglas?" Jem said, slowly and deliberately, as if he was thinking out loud.

"You bet it would," Douglas said.

"And we'd definitely pay for it ourselves somehow?" A slow smile spread across Jem's face.

Katy felt strange and shaky.

She watched as amazement mixed with wonder dawned in Jem, as he said, his voice vibrant with hope, "My own land - I never thought to see the day! It's the answer to a prayer, Douglas, it really is. Thank you, thank you, from the bottom of my heart."

He looked at Katy, whose own heart was threatening to choke her, and said, "Alright then, we'll do it."

Douglas immediately shot out his hand and

grabbed Jem's, shaking it until Katy thought Jem in danger of losing his one good arm.

She got up and hugged Cassandra."Thank you, oh, thank you!" she said, squeezing her friend.

"Not so tight, Kate," Cassandra gasped, "or I'll be puking all down your back!"

They all laughed and then Katy summoned up all her courage and said, "You have made my dream come true because, when I was working on the motorbike, I had another idea about that place."

"What is it, Kate?" Douglas and Cassandra said in unison.

"To open a garage!" Katy said, enjoying the astonishment on their faces.

She nodded at them and Jem clutched her hand, as she continued, "You see, it's on the London Road so there will be passing traffic. I'll sell petrol - get a pump like we saw in Boston - and sort the workshop out so it'll be a proper tool shed to service cars. I had it all planned out, but then thought I'd blown my chances but - aren't we forgetting something? What about the army? Don't they own the huts?"

"Already sorted out," Cassandra said and told them about the arrangement with Colonel Musgrove and that they would have nothing to pay for the buildings, just the land.

"I guess you'd have to buy the tools from the regiment," Douglas said. He looked thoughtful and then grinned. "You know, Kate, I think you've hit on the perfect role for that place. I don't know why I hadn't thought of it myself. I'm looking for a project to invest in. I've been travelling all over the county, searching for a business to work away at and I've seen nothing as exciting as your plan."

"So that's what you've been up to!" Cassandra said, and Katy watched the colour return to her friend's lovely face.

"Sure I have, honey, what did you think I was

doing?" Douglas said, looking surprised. Then he turned back to Jem and Katy. "Would you object if I was a partner in your enterprise? Oh, I wouldn't cramp your style, I promise, but I could give you the financial backing you're going to need to buy equipment and set yourselves up. Why, it would be really exciting to be part of it!"

Katy felt her heart soar. She looked at Jem, sitting next to her. His eyes were shining. He nodded at her with brimming eyes, full of love. She hugged him, in front of Cassandra and Douglas, who were sensitive enough to get up and walk to the fence and look back at the house, now bathed in gold by the setting sun.

Jem and Katy clung to each other for a long moment. Katy couldn't speak but just held on to Jem for dear life, overwhelmed by her emotions.

Jem released her and addressed Douglas, "Douglas, we'd be proud to have you as part of the business and Cassandra too."

Cassandra nodded her head at being included, and walked, smiling, back to the table.

Douglas shook Jem's hand again. "That's settled then. I look forward to working with you both. We'll get Hayes to draw up the papers tomorrow. Do you want to visit the place?"

"Yes, please, Douglas, and thank you so much," Katy said.

"Don't thank me, Kate, until you find what it's like working alongside me!"

"Douglas, darling," Cassandra said. "This has all been wonderfully exciting but I'm feeling rather tired. It's been a long day. I think we should leave these two entrepreneurs in peace to discuss their plans and head back up to the house."

"Sure thing, Cass," Douglas said. "So long, partners! I'll see you tomorrow and we'll get the keys and go visit your new place."

Katy and Jem stayed talking about the reversal of their fortunes in a state between disbelief and wonderment until the sun completely disappeared, then went inside to tell Agnes and Bert the good news.

"You mean to say, they're giving you this land?" Bert said, his mouth a perfect 'o' of surprise.

"No, we're going to buy it," Jem said.

"But how?" Agnes said.

"Douglas is going to lend us the money, and we'll pay him back," Jem said.

"It'll take years, maybe all our lives, but it'll be ours by the end," Katy said.

"By all that's wonderful!" Bert said. "Well, I s'pose you'd better stay on here a bit longer, till you move in, then."

Katy hugged her father and then Agnes. "Thank you, Dad! We won't be in your way, I promise. We'll be spending all our time up at the huts. And, I just want to say, how sorry I am for all this upset you've had. I wouldn't have had it happen for all the world."

Agnes and Bert hugged them back with bemused smiles and then shuffled off to bed, shaking their heads at the news.

***

It wasn't until the following afternoon, after he'd got the keys from Colonel Musgrove, that Douglas drove them down to the huts and parked alongside them with a flourish.

Katy and Jem leapt out of the car and went to the gate. Jem tore off the 'Do not trespass' notice and threw it in the hedgerow. Cassandra and Douglas elected not to come in and watched them from the car.

"I don't fancy wading through all those nettles, thanks very much," Cassandra said.

"We'll come back another day, when you've had a chance to clear the path," Douglas said. "It's your place now. I think you should have time to get to know it on your own."

Douglas brandished a set of keys and threw them to Jem, who caught them easily with one hand. "Congratulations, Mr Phipps, on joining the landed gentry. Welcome to your new home, both. Kate - I wish you well, partner. Come on, Cass, let's get you home."

He revved the engine and the sports car stuttered and backfired.

"Looks like you're opening a garage in the nick of time. This car can be your first job. I'll come by tomorrow and you can have a look at her," and Douglas let in the clutch and roared off, with Cassandra waving and smiling through the window. Jem and Katy waved back until they could no longer see them.

Jem turned to Katy and gave his wife the bunch of keys. "This was your idea, Katy. I think you should open up the place, now it's legal, and we needn't fear getting arrested by her majesty's army."

Katy could hardly contain her excitement. She inserted a key into the padlock and it fitted perfectly first time. She had to wrench open the door of the workshop against the weeds that had grown up against it.

Katy said, "I'll do everything I can to make it work, I promise you, Jem. I'll move heaven and earth, if I have to. I thought I had to travel the world to find excitement and adventure but it's all here, Jem. *You* are here, and I'm going to put every ounce of my energy into making a go of this business. This is our *home*, Jem. Our ticket to independence. Your home for the hero you are."

Jem surprised her then. He came over and put his arm around her shoulders, kissed her cheek and whispered, "I love you," in her ear.

A shiver of exquisite pleasure rippled through Katy's whole body. It had been so long since she had been able to welcome his touch, she took a moment to recognise the joy of it.

Jem stepped inside the hut and Katy followed. The workshop looked the same as when they had left it under escort. They wandered about amongst the dust and grease, taking in the momentous knowledge that it was now legally theirs and breaking into grins every time their eyes met.

"Let's look outside," Jem said. "Just how much land is there?"

Katy took him by the hand, her cheek still tingling from his kiss. Her body was waking up in ways she'd forgotten about; sensations she had suppressed ever since Fred had brutally assaulted her, except for that one time, here in the hut when the army had rudely interrupted them. Neither of them had had the heart to try again.

As they walked out of the door and around the side of the hut, the skies opened and a torrential downpour soaked them within minutes.

"Will it rain every time we come here?" laughed Jem.

Katy's earlier footprints showed the way, along the path of trampled nettles. Her focus had been on the garage alone, so she hadn't bothered to look at the plot before, but Jem swished away at the undergrowth with his wooden arm, until he reached the fenced boundary. The huts were built on a high vantage point and they stood together looking out across the valley stretching below them, shrouded in the thundery rain. The river Cheadle meandered in a silvery strand through the shorn wheat-fields, as a sparrow-hawk dived for a stranded field-mouse.

"I could get used to that view, alright," said Jem. "How wide is this plot?"

"This way," Katy said, laughing, and brushing the rain out of her eyes, as she ran towards the copse of trees to the east.

Jem swished his arm through the rosebay willow-herb that ran along the barbed wire fence until they struck a right angle."There's more land here than I could ever hope for! Look over there! We could manage that bit of woodland for our fuel and we could have chickens, even some pigs, and I could grow vegetables to feed us. We could sell them from the road, too!"

"Yes, Jem, we could do all of that," Katy said. "I don't care what it looks like or if it's uncomfortable. Only that it would be truly ours, when we paid the debt off. "

"To think that one day," Jem's voice grated with emotion at this point, before he continued, "we might be able to call this patch of land ours."

"Yes, Jem, our own land. And a garage for our livelihood. And a home of our own!" Katy knew she was still grinning; she could feel her face stretch so wide it hurt, but she couldn't stop.

"Shall we look at the other hut?" Jem said, rain bouncing off his shoulders in spurts.

Katy nodded and rummaged in her pocket for the keys. Her dress was clamped to her body, it was so soaked. She ran to the door and fiddled with the padlock with wet, slippery hands. It broke free and Jem pulled the door open and bundled her inside.

The hut was emptier than the other one and had obviously been used as a store. The rain drummed a tattoo on the corrugated tin roof. It was coming down harder than ever and drowned out any chance of conversation, but Katy didn't want to talk anyway.

That tight band around her chest, the vicious one she'd had since leaving Cape Cod, had lifted off at last, and a warm glow expanded in its place. It flooded her whole body and then reached out to include Jem, who stood before her, raindrops dripping quietly in a pool at his feet.

She stepped towards him and he opened his unequal arms. Inside them, she felt her whole body relax at last and lifted up her face to be kissed. Jem looked back at her with his brown eyes full of love and rainwater.

Then Katy shut hers, as his mouth touched her lips in the gentlest kiss he had ever given her. His tenderness undid her. Her lips opened in welcome and Katy kissed him back with all the unspent passion in her bruised heart.

"Love me now, Jem, you wonderful man," Katy said, "love me here, in our new home.

THE END

I hope you have enjoyed this sequel to Daffodils in The Katherine Wheel series. Peace Lily is a stand-alone book but you can find out more about Katy and Jem's lives before and during World War One in Daffodils, if you haven't yet read it.

Here is the blurb for **Daffodils**:
"Katy dreams of a better life than just being a domestic servant at Cheadle Manor. Her one attempt to escape is thwarted when her flirtation with the manor's heir results in a scandal that shocks the local community.
Jem Beagle has always loved Katy. His offer of marriage rescues her but personal tragedy divides them. Jem leaves his beloved Wiltshire to become a reluctant soldier on the battlefields of World War One. Katy is left behind, restless and alone.
Lionel White, just returned from being a missionary in India, brings a dash of colour to the small village, and offers Katy a window on the wider world.
Katy decides she has to play her part in the global struggle and joins the war effort as a WAAC girl. She finally breaks free from the stifling Edwardian hierarchies that bind her but the brutality of global war brings home the price she has paid for her search."

And here's the link to the book on www.amazon.co.uk: http://amzn.to/141yEIG
And on www.amazon.com:
http://amzn.to/19iDLtI

Alex Martin's first book, based on her grape-picking adventure in France in the 1980's, is more of a mystery/ thriller than historical fiction but makes for great holiday reading with all the sensuous joys of that beautiful country.

It's called **The Twisted Vine** and here's a brief description of the story: "Every journey is an adventure. Especially one into the unknown"The Twisted Vine is set in the heart of France and is a deeply romantic but suspenseful tale. Roxanne Rudge escapes her cheating boyfriend by going grape-picking in France. She feels vulnerable and alone in such a big country where she can't speak the language and is befriended by Armand le Clair, a handsome Frenchman. Armand is not all he seems, however, and she discovers a darker side to him before uncovering a dreadful secret. She is aided and abetted by three new friends she has made, charming posh Peter, a gifted linguist, the beautiful and vivacious Italian, Yvane, and clever Henry of the deep brown eyes with the voice to match. Together they unravel a mystery centred around a beautiful chateau and play a part in its future. Join Roxanne on her journey of self discovery, love and tragedy in rural France. Taste the wine, feel the sun, drive through the Provencal mountains with her, as her courage and resourcefulness are tested to the limit."

and the links for The Twisted Vine are:
www.amazon.co.uk: http://amzn.to/1ngDBcs
www.amazon.com: http://amzn.to/1mY080T

Alex Martin writes about her work on her blog at:

www.alexxx8586@blogspot.com

where she welcomes feedback and comments.

Constructive reviews oil a writer's wheel like
nothing else and are very much appreciated on Amazon,
or Goodreads or anywhere else!

You can contact Alex Martin via her blog or
email her on alexxx8586@talktalk.net

CPSIA information can be obtained at www.ICGtesting.com
Printed in the USA
LVOW10s1916300615

444456LV00001B/25/P

9 781502 748850